MARIAN HALCOMBE

OTHER BOOKS IN THE MARIAN HALCOMBE SERIES

The King of the Book
The Jaguar Queen of Copal
The Earl in the Shadows
The True Prince of Vaurantania
The River Horse Tsar
The Nautilus Knight
The Compass of Truth
The Pirate Princess
The Single Musketeer
The Cobra Marked King

MARIAN HALCOMBE

BRENDA W. CLOUGH

Book View Café

MARIAN HALCOMBE

Copyright © 2021 Brenda W. Clough
Cover illustration © 2020 by depositphotos.com

ISBN: 978-1-63632-022-9

An earlier version of Marian Halcombe was originally published as *A Most Dangerous Woman* at Serial Box in 2018.

Production Team:
Cover Design: Thomas Nackid
Proofreader: Chaz Brenchley
Interior design: Marissa Doyle

This is a work of fiction. Any references to historical events, real people, or real locales are used fictitiously. Other names, characters, places, and incidents are the product of the author's imagination, and any resemblance to actual events or locales or persons, living or dead, is entirely coincidental.

Book View Café
304 S. Jones Blvd., Suite 2906
Las Vegas, NV 89107

www.bookviewcafe.com

BOOK 1

❧ Marian Halcombe's journal ✣

Yule Day, 1856
I start this new volume of my diary rather early! All orderly minds would agree it would be more proper to begin next week, on the first of January. But what is to be done? My dearest sister Laura's gift to me was this most wonderfully handsome blank journal. It is far more grand and expensive than my usual run of black cloth-bound Letts volumes. This book's luscious blue Morocco leather cover smells divine, simply begging to be opened, and the sleek cream-coloured paper implores the pen's ministrations. So, I must begin.

Let me start this new volume as is proper for the New Year, with a report on all our household.

Baby Walter – Wally – is now quite the young man! Almost five years old, my darling nephew is teethed, breeched and walking and climbing like a young monkey. His mother has been teaching him to pick out simple tunes upon the piano while I undertake the sterner task of introducing him to his letters. Alas, too often our alphabet blocks are requisitioned to become fortresses for his toy soldiers. But he grows in intelligence every day, the light of the household.

His sire, my brother-in-law Walter Hartright the elder, has devoted his energies to mending fences with all our neighbours. During the residence of Laura's uncle the late Mr. Frederick

Fairlie social martyrdom reigned. Relations with all the county were at best suffered to fall away to nothing. When Mr. Fairlie had the energy, or folk were so foolish as to actually call, he did not hesitate to offer direct insult. But now under Walter's head we have rejoined the community. We occupy the family pew in Limmeridge church; call and are called upon, dine and are dined with. Though he is an incomer to the district, and not born to the gentry, he has been so well received that there is talk of Walter standing for Parliament when the current incumbent Sir Cedric Gratham retires year after next. But when this is suggested he brushes it aside with a laugh, saying that his old friend Professor Pesca foresaw it, and therefore it cannot be.

But my happiest news is of my darling Laura. My sister could not thrive, all the years we lived in humble circumstances in London. Transplanted back to her native northern soil, surrounded by love and kindliness, Walter and I hoped she would gradually bloom again. How foolish we were, and how little we knew of her greatness of soul!

For what dear Laura needed was to serve others. Poor and ill, she could come to no one's aid. How well I remember her desire, even though she was barely restored to health, to assist in earning our daily crust!

Now, chatelaine of Limmeridge, she is come at last into her own. She is the fond patroness of the village school, as our mother was before her. Mr. Frederick Fairlie had an abiding horror of children, but now he is gone we have revived the parish fête, giving over the garden and shrubberies once a year to the great benefit of the church.

And, thus nourished, Laura's energies and spirits have grown wonderfully. She is indefatigable in visiting the poor. If there is a lying-in or a sick child within twenty miles, young Mrs. Hartright is there on the instant with calf's-foot jelly, or some arrowroot, or a basket of baby linens. Already she is the acknowledged mercy angel of the district; I doubt not that before she dies she will be elevated to the rank of saint.

To see my dearest sister, the person I love most in all the world, flourishing like this fills me with joy. And, with another one on the way she, and I, look to be happy and busy for years to come. So when she gave me this volume – oh, I must write it plainly and in order! Let me go back a little.

We were a merry party for Christmas. Walter's elderly mother and his sister Sarah had come up from town, escorted by his old friend Professor Pesca, the Italian tutor. Little Wally had received a stick horse for Christmas and was galloping and shouting up and down the halls.

Little Professor Pesca wore a silver basin on his head, a veritable Quixote, and waved a napkin for a banner. He pelted along behind on his short legs, singing some Italian patriotic anthem at the top of his lungs. Walter himself, between paroxysms of laughter, bestrode a dustmop liberated from a startled housemaid, bringing up the rear. Was it the battle of Waterloo, or the charge of the Light Brigade? In any case the noise was immense.

"At least your floors are becoming cleaner," Sarah noted. We were observing from the safety of the stair. Old Mrs. Hartright sat on the landing and wiped tears of laughter away and Luna, Laura's pet miniature greyhound, trembled and cowered against her skirts at the tumult.

Laura smiled fondly down at husband and son. "I assure you, Sarah, that is the last thought in any of their minds. But, dear Marian, I almost forgot. I have a gift for you."

"What, in addition to Mrs. Yonge? We will begin reading *The Daisy Chain* aloud in the new year."

"Yes, yes. But come through into my sitting room. Wally's voice is so carrying."

We went into her little room, the same chamber that has been the scene of so many important conversations in our lives. We sat on the sofa by the window, which looked out over the wintry garden. In the watery sunshine Laura looked more happy and healthy than I have ever seen her. All the grace and affection of her character from girlhood were blended now with the mature and intelligent gentleness of a woman. She has fulfilled and grown into all her promise; the beauteous rosebud, darling of the garden, is in full fragrant blow. "Love and happiness is good for you," I burst out. "I have not seen such bloom in your cheeks since we were girls."

"And that is what I wanted to say to you, my dear Marian. You will remember, always and forever, that I love you, won't you? And that your happiness is essential to my own?"

I was startled. How could there be any doubt of it, after all we have been through? It is family policy to never speak of the past. "Laura, is something wrong?"

"No indeed, Marian. It is because all is so right, that I give you this." She put the Morocco volume, this very journal, into my hands. When I had finished exclaiming over it and thanking her she went on, "Marian, you are so wonderful and capable. Your life should be more than that of a spinster aunt. You could be so much more."

"Oh Laura, you know that is not a possibility." I did not need to glance at the square mirror propped on the mantel. From the moment of birth the two of us have been the most amusingly ill-assorted sisters: she fair and blessed as springtime, and I the impoverished harsh winter, with my dark hair and unharmonious features. All my life I have been compared to Laura, and am content to be forever second. "If your blessings of face and fortune are no guarantee of happiness, how can a person with neither hope for it?"

"But that is precisely my point, Marian. I am happy, after much storm and peril." She smiled, a smile of such bliss! "Once, in a moment of great distress – do you remember? I made a foolish and unkind demand of you. I asked you to never marry and never to leave me."

"You did?"

"I'm sure you noted it in your journal. When you have leisure, go back and look. And today, now that we can both see how much Walter's love has done for me… Marian, I know that I was wrong. I had no right to make such a selfish demand even of the meanest servant. Love does not lay such requests upon the beloved. You are no slave in chains, but the dearest person in my heart. Surely only the overwhelming press of circumstance kept you from scolding me roundly on the spot for my childish unreasonableness. You pronounced no promise at that time. But if you made it silently, in the corridors of your heart, it was a noble sacrifice to my need. My dearest, dearest sister, now and for always: I absolve you of it. You are no prisoner. You are free. And this journal is the token of that. Let it be the next chapter in your life, Marian. Let it record a wider heart, a life fully lived."

"Laura! Walter spoke of this once. Are you –" I could not go on, my eyes filling with weak tears.

Quickly she put her own slender white hands over mine, which numbly clutched her gift. "Never, not for an instant. Your home shall always be with us if you wish it, and our lives shall always be entwined. Why, little Wally would never tolerate less! But ... consider seeking more, Marian. Yes, it is a risk to change. To reach out, to grow. But you are not nervous, like me. You are a mighty oak. You do not have to linger always in a little clay flower-pot like Limmeridge. You are an eagle. If you spread your wings and fly, that is right and proper. And we, Walter and I, will watch you soar with shouts of joy."

From the open door, below in the hall, came those exact shouts of joy. "Oh, Laura," I choked. "How have I ever deserved a love so pure, so noble as yours?"

"Marian! When you have done so much for me? How can you say that? You deserve all good things, every joy in the world. And because I love you, I want them all for you."

Overwhelmed, I retired to my own room, and when I was more composed I sat at my writing desk and wrote all this down so that I may read it over again, and reflect upon Laura's words. She has not spoken words of rejection. She does not close a door on me. These are words of opening, of liberation. She wants the best for me, as I want it for her. What shall I do, my darling girl, if you become wise as well as good and happy?

27 December

It is all very well to recognise a need for change. Now that dear Laura articulated it, I too feel it. The young tree she spoke of perhaps felt this, a need for a larger space, for new earth and water. A new year is coming, and as she advised I will meet it boldly.

But how? I remembered there was a novel, a popular fiction from several years ago about a young woman in this exact same quandary. Mrs. Ramer, the rector's wife, has spoken disparagingly of the heroine's unladylike example and rebellious, unregenerate spirit. If anything this is a recommendation! Down in the library I found it: *Jane Eyre*. Alas, Miss Charlotte Brontë is notably unhelpful. Advertise for a position, indeed – it does not quite sound respectable. Certainly impossible for Miss Marian Halcombe of Limmeridge House. So I tabled the matter and went down to play with Wally.

The plan was for our guests to stay to see in the New Year. However, this very day – the day after Boxing Day – there was a nut-cake for tea. An innocuous and even cheery occurrence, one might say. But, biting down on a forkful, old Mrs. Hartright cried out in pain. "Oh, oh! My tooth!"

"Mama, was it a bit of shell?" Sarah cried.

Mrs. Hartright spat her mouthful out into a napkin. A white shard of tooth gleamed in the detritus. "You have shattered it," Walter declared. "Mother, will you let me have a peep?"

But this she refused to do. The poor old woman moaned in pain, clutching the side of her jaw. Tears poured down her face. "The nerve must be laid bare," I said.

Laura was already gone in a whisk of long skirts to fetch the medicine box. By the time she returned we had Mrs. Hartright laid out on the sofa. Pesca helpfully fetched a chunk of ice from outdoors, broken off an icicle. Wrapped in a napkin and held to her cheek, this did not calm the pain as we hoped. The unlucky woman was writhing in agony.

Laura unlocked the box and took out the laudanum. "Will she permit me to drop it on the tooth?"

"I don't think so," I said. "Perhaps in water, instead. If she can sleep through the night, day may bring relief. And if not, we have time to send for a dentist."

Laura prepared the dose while Walter and Sarah propped their mother up and then persuaded her to sip it. The powerful opiate soon had its effect, and she fell into the mercy of slumber. She weighs no more than a bird, poor thing. Walter carefully hoisted her in his arms and carried her up to her bed. We three ladies committed little Wally to Pesca's care and followed. When the old lady was comfortably tucked up Sarah undertook to sit with her, while we discussed the next steps.

"We must send to London and have Mr. Stalke come," Laura said. "He is her preferred dentist."

"And in the time it takes to send, and for him to come, we could more quickly just take Mother to him," Walter said. "Her pain is so great that the utmost speed is called for."

"But you cannot go, Laura," I put in.

She had to assent. "Not in the depths of winter, and in my condition."

"And little Wally needs you here," Walter said. "But I do not like leaving you for any length of time. And Sarah is ..." He stopped, and we did not pick up his discourse for him. His sister is not precisely simple, certainly not mentally afflicted as a doctor would define the term. But she is not a female who deals with abstractions. One might trust her to select a pair of slippers, but not to manage the transportation of a fragile and elderly patient.

"Why, we make too much difficulty of it," I said. "Are there not three of us? I shall go. You may trust me to take the tenderest care of your mother, Walter, and to see that she is attended by her preferred practitioner in London and nursed carefully back to full health however long it takes."

"That would be marvelously kind of you, Marian," Walter exclaimed. "Both Pesca and I shall escort you on the express, so that the journey may be swift and easy as possible, and I will then immediately return to Limmeridge. My dear, you can manage for a day or so without me?"

"The new one is not due to appear until April," Laura said, smiling. "And your arm will be needed to help your mother in and out of the rail carriage. Pesca is the soul of kindness, but he is a very small man. I'll be safe here at Limmeridge."

Our plans made, we immediately set about our preparations. I have packed my trunk for a stay of possibly a fortnight or more. It is impossible to predict how long Mrs. Hartright at her age may need to recover from an extraction. I must conclude this entry and go to bed. We depart at first light tomorrow.

Hampstead Cottage, 3 January 1857

A brief entry to note that everything proceeded as we had laid out. Walter and Pesca whisked us to town on the fastest train. Mrs. Hartright slept on my shoulder for the entire trip. I am installed now in the tiny guest bedroom of the comfortable cottage that is the longtime home of Mrs. Hartright and Sarah. It is on a lane bordering Hampstead Heath, a quiet and respectable district north of London. Mr. Stalke, a most excellent dental surgeon, waited upon Mrs. Hartright the very next morning. She bore up under the extraction well. She felt an immediate relief, the pain of a tooth-pulling being far less that the agony of the broken tooth. Walter departed for the north again that very day, leaving myself and Sarah to supervise Mrs. Hartright's recovery. This has been slow, not a surprise in view of her advanced years, and we take it in turns to nurse her. Tedious, but I have my journal and my knitting. I propose to knit a lace gown for the coming nephew or niece.

8 January

A disturbing occurrence took place this evening, which I hasten to note down before I should forget the particulars.

Sarah having a long-standing engagement with the Ladies' Working Society at St. John-at-Hampstead, I sat with Mrs. Hartright all this evening. This is no great trial. She is now able to sit up in bed and take soft food and tea, although she has not yet come downstairs. Her jaw is still mightily swollen on that side, and she is not confident on her feet. At her age a fall could be calamitous. I spent an hour reading aloud to her from the newspapers. Whatever her bodily ailments her mind is active and sharp, and she keeps up with all the latest intelligence both at home – especially the doings of the Royal Family – and abroad. "Is there news of the female anarchist, Daisy Darnell?" she demanded. "Early in the week they had captured her, but yesterday the story was all of her escape."

I turned the pages. "Yes, a short report. Let me read it to you: 'An international hunt continues for the infamous villainess Daisy Darnell. She was last seen in Croatia, where her anarchist lover was at last brought to book and hanged from the snow-white ramparts of the medieval citadel at Dubrovnik. Ludovic Bradamante, once a count of the Austro-Hungarian nobility, was convicted of murder, arson, and bomb-throwing after a heinous attempt upon the life of King Aleksandar Karađorđević of Serbia. His common-law wife Darnell was deeply implicated herself in the plot. But she eluded capture on Tuesday by a ruse at the train station, cloaking her extraordinary beauty under the veil and wimple of a nun of the Little Sisters of St. Anselm…'" It was good full-blooded stuff, very typical of the Balkan nations. I struggled with the difficult foreign cognomens and was grateful that we live where everyone has a pronounceable name. Mrs. Hartright evidently thrilled to the same contrast, paying close attention to every twist in the female anarchist's daring escape.

Then, having settled her down cozily for the night, I went downstairs. Sarah was not yet returned, and the parlour was close and oppressive. I had been indoors all day. Also I had miscounted my pattern and now faced the unraveling of a good inch of complicated knitted lace, a task it was a pleasure to postpone.

I opened the front door and stepped out. Though it was January we were in the midst of a welcome warm spell. There was no snow nor even frost, and a mild moisture hung in the air, the harbinger of spring. The cottage is divided from the lane by a hornbeam hedge. The bright moonlight lured me down the path to the gate.

I leaned on it and took a deep breath. The pasture and woodland of the Heath were black against a glowing golden haze: the gaslights of London. Warm white mist gathered in the low spots of the landscape, and above in a clement sky the moon was nearly full, modestly veiled in pale ravelings. All was still, not a rustle of leaf or twitter of any bird. It was a calm silent night of the full moon just like this, when Walter encountered Anne Catherick on his walk home, not so far from this very spot. What a fateful encounter that had been for all of us! How many lives and deaths had turned upon that one chance meeting! Surely the finger of God was upon Walter that day –

My rather melodramatic reminiscences were abruptly broken off. There was something stirring, moving purposefully in the mist cupped down the slope. For a moment I wanted to retreat into the cottage and bolt the door. But then I schooled myself to wait and watch. What boggart or villain could there be, here in this quiet suburb? It might only be Sarah, returning from the sewing meeting. How silly I should feel, if she had to knock on her own door to be let in.

So I watched as the mist thickened and then thinned again, and suddenly I could clearly discern two small figures, hand in hand. Could they be children, out alone at this late hour? They wandered nearer, up the lane. I could see they were a fair boy and a quite little girl, perhaps seven and five years old, clad in coats over their nightshirts. Innocent of socks or stockings, their little feet were crammed into untidily laced boots. Were not the night so mild they would have caught cold instantly. But no woman, no decent human being, could watch such tiny creatures wandering alone in the night without intervening. As they approached the gate I leaned over it. "Dear children, where are you parents?"

"We're looking for a mother," the little girl replied readily.

"Hush, Lottie," the boy said crossly. "You mustn't blab our affairs all over."

"It's very dark," I observed. "You must have walked a long way. I am Miss Halcombe, and I live in this cottage. Would you care to come in and have some refreshment? I can offer you some warm milk. It's a favorite of mine. And perhaps some seed cake."

"My name is Micah Camlet," the boy said with dignity. "No, thank you."

"Oh, but Mickey, I love seed cake," Lottie cried. "And there's a blister coming on my heel. I wish I had put on stockings, but you were in such a hurry."

"Your legs must be cold. I must make up the fire to boil the kettle anyway. You are very welcome to come and sit by it. And I could look at your blister." I unlatched the gate and held it invitingly ajar. "What is your name, little one?"

Trustingly she stepped in. "I'm Lottie. Pleased to meet you."

Her brother, wiser as males must be even at his age, said, "We must not impose upon you, Miss."

"How is it that your mother let you slip away without her, my dear?" The child put a thumb into her mouth but then, clearly remembering a nurse's injunction, pulled it out again. Very gently I took the child's free hand.

"We haven't a mother," Micah interposed.

"And we want one," the little girl added. "Father Christmas was supposed to bring her, but he must have forgot."

I drew them both onto the garden path, and was just making to latch the gate when there was a commotion farther down the road. There was a clatter of hooves, and suddenly a tall black horse loomed up out of the mist. Its rider was hatless, his long coat unfastened and billowing behind with the speed of his progress. Quite an heroical picture, spoilt only by the glint of steel-rimmed glasses on his face. "Madam, have you seen – great

God. Micah! Lottie!"

"Is that your father?"

"Yes, and he shall be so cross," Lottie said, with composure.

"He read to us about Father Christmas," Micah objected, "so I don't see his complaint."

By this time the rider had pulled up at the gate and flung himself off his steed. "Children, are you hurt? How dare you give the slip to Nurse like that! It's very naughty of you!"

He was, quite naturally, entirely beside himself with anxiety. In the role of peacemaker I said, "Mr. Camlet, I presume. And this is your son and your daughter? They do not seem to have suffered much from their adventure. A blister, I am informed, is all the souvenir –"

"How dare you meddle with my family affairs, woman? It cannot be quite respectable that you lurk in a dark garden like this."

If he had been a big dangerous-looking fellow I might have spoken more softly, but all of this man's height had been lent by his horse. Afoot he was not intimidating, certainly not with spectacles. "It is my own garden, sir, or rather the property of my hostess. If anything I am the aggrieved party. I did not invite you or your family to call. But I see that you cannot be reasoned with, and it is too late for conversation. Good night, Miss Lottie and Master Micah."

"Pleased to make your acquaintance," Micah said politely.

Lottie clung to my hand. "But we were going to have seed cake!"

Gently I extracted my fingers from hers and retreated into the house, firmly shutting the door. Peeping through the parlour curtain I saw the Camlet family in silhouette having it out with itself in the intermittent moonlight. My fear was that the father might be so intemperate and choleric as to beat his children. As their parent he had full right to chastise them as he would, but the sight would be lacerating.

But against that there was the children's placid demeanor when they spoke of him. They had not been afraid in the least. Finally the taller figure lifted the smallest to the saddle and climbed up himself before giving the boy a hand up to the saddlebow. Thus burdened the horse turned slowly, walking back the way it had come. The thick hedge prevented me from seeing more. Sarah came through the gate half an hour later, full of chatter about hemming infant linens. I said nothing to her of my evening, and we went straight up to bed, I pausing only to scribble down this account. Of all the pointless encounters!

9 January

This day for the first time Mrs. Hartright expressed a desire to dress and come down. Sarah and I hastened to wrap her warmly for breakfast. "How well you have kept house, my dears," she said. "Although Milly has neglected the hallway sadly – the slates are gritty. And what is this? Is not porridge reserved for Sundays?"

"It's for you, Mama," Sarah said. "You cannot wish for toast? Would you prefer a lightly boiled egg?"

"Not I," she returned. "This is well enough. You're quite right, I must chew delicately for yet some days."

After breakfast the old lady was delighted to take her favorite chair by the fire in the parlour, declaring herself entirely recovered for any activity not involving mastication. I read aloud to them both, and in the afternoon she settled down to holding my skein of wool while Sarah wound it up into a ball. I meanwhile availed myself of the bright afternoon light to unravel my lace knitting errors of the previous day, anxious and fussy work that took up my full attention.

When the doorbell gave a great clang we all jumped. "Who could it be?" Mrs. Hartright exclaimed. "Is my cap straight, Sarah?"

"Milly is still washing up." I set down my work. The parlour was at the front of the house and I quickly opened the door. If something was wrong at Limmeridge and Laura had sent us a wire –

To my astonishment an enormous bunch of greenhouse blossoms seemed to fill the doorway, lilies, arum and narcissi, all the pale and scentless flowers nursed under glass into bloom in the winter months. "Miss Halcombe?"

It was a servant. But over the shoulder of the menial was a head of light-brown hair brushed straight back, and anxious hazel eyes behind familiar steel spectacles. From behind me Sarah cried, "Mr. Camlet, how kind of you to call! I recognised your brougham at the gate. Please come through. Mother is just come downstairs this day."

"I – Ahem. That is, I –" Clearly the intemperate horseman of last night had not actually intended an afternoon call. But there was no help for him. Sociable Mrs. Hartright added her voice to her daughter's and I stood back to let him pass. Mr. Camlet was haled into the parlour and installed on the other side of the fire, and his coachman set the armload of flowers on the table.

"How very kind of you," Mrs. Hartright exclaimed. "You must have stripped your greenhouse, Mr. Camlet. Flowers are a treasure in January, the rarest of the rare. You are too considerate of an old woman and her ailments." She sniffed a lily deeply, untroubled by its lack of perfume.

"Perhaps I could fetch a vase and put them in water for you," I suggested.

"Will you present me?" Mr. Camlet said, faintly. Clearly our encounter of the last evening was to be passed over.

"Forgive me, sir," Mrs. Hartright said. "Miss Halcombe, this is Theophilus Camlet, our neighbour. He lives in Sandett House, half a mile up the lane – you will have seen it, the big pink-brick house, as our hansom came in. Mr. Camlet, Miss Halcombe is the sister of my dear son Walter's wife Laura. A most excellent family in Cumberland, and Laura's home Limmeridge House has been in the family for seventy years..."

Leaving the ladies to entertain their caller, I fetched the large Wedgwood vase from the sideboard. When I peeped through the curtain I could see the brougham waiting in the lane, gleaming black with wheels picked out in yellow. Two sleek bay horses stood in the shafts. Our visitor must be prosperous, to maintain not only his own carriage but three horses in town.

Thanks to Laura's lush rose gardens I am quite skilled at arranging flowers, but even the Wedgwood vase was insufficient to contain this floral bounty. A pair of smaller vases had to be pressed into service as well. Set on either windowsill in the parlour away from the heat of the fire they looked very fine, and the large Wedgwood vase took pride of place in the centre of the table. Sarah agreed with her mother that fresh flowers gave quite an air to the entire cottage. Between admiration of their beauty, praise of his generosity and exclamations of his kindness in calling, Mr. Camlet scarcely got a word in edgewise. But many men are awkward at calls, from leaving their wives to pay the social arrears.

Within the canonical fifteen minutes he took his leave. All this time I had busied myself counting and recounting my lace stitches, making mere commonplace assents to Mrs. Hartright's remarks. I had dropped a yarn loop somewhere and thrown the whole pattern off, very provoking. Only when I ushered him into the hall did Mr. Camlet say, "Miss Halcombe, in fact I came to call upon you."

"Me?"

For the first time I actually looked at him. He must have been a year or two older than myself. Not a tall man – a little more than my height, though I am reckoned tall for a woman. He was not fat, but merely well-fleshed. His light-brown hair, over a high pale forehead, foretold what his fair children would grow up to be. Side whiskers swooped down and then up to join on his upper lip in a moustache, lending squareness to an otherwise ordinarily pleasant countenance. His features were regular, and the hazel eyes behind the round lenses were gentle. How foolish I had been, dreading he would strike children or horse. If anything this man would be too kind.

And he affirmed my judgment immediately. "To apologise for my hasty words of last night. My terror for the children's safety was so great that I spoke my fears, and not with observation. Of your great goodness, please forgive me, and allow me to thank you for your kindness to them."

"Why, think nothing of it, Mr. Camlet. Only a heart of stone could have turned the little creatures away in the cold and dark."

"And your heart is plainly a golden one. I hope you will think of these flowers as your own, a small token of my contrition."

"They will give so much pleasure to my hostess, I shall never tell her of your intent." But he looked so crushed at my sally that I impulsively held my hand out to him. He took it for only an instant and then with a bow was out the door and down the path to where his carriage waited at the gate.

"Was it not thoughtful of him," Mrs. Hartright marveled.

"Such beautiful blooms!"

"He must be a good neighbour and a close friend," I suggested.

"Well of course we are acquainted any time these past ten years, living so near to each other," Sarah said. "But he has never paid an afternoon call before."

"Nor with flowers," Mrs. Hartright said. "Perhaps he is clearing out his greenhouse. And since there is no lady at Sandett House we do not call."

"There is no Mrs. Camlet?" I said, startled. "How is that? There are children, are there not?"

"Oh my dear, that's the tragedy of it," Mrs. Hartright cried. "A boy and a girl, running wild now all the day long. It was the most dreadful thing, quite the nine days' wonder, and the poor man was nearly prostrate with shame." With very little encouragement the ladies poured the story into my receptive ear, for of course it was common knowledge in the neighbourhood and Mrs. Hartright is something of a gossip.

It was the old tale: Mrs. Margaret Camlet became enamored of another. After the birth of her youngest she fled with this person to the Continent, abandoning children and husband. She died in Salerno, and the widower had been struggling to raise his family ever since.

"It was months before he dared to go out even a little into society," Mrs. Hartright said. "Though of course he was not to blame, he felt the ignominy as much as any man could. Only with the report of the wife's death could he hold his head up again, although he did wear black gloves for the full mourning period. The neighbourhood has expected for years that he will remarry, lest the children grow up to be savages."

"They must need a mother sadly," I said. When Lottie and Micah spoke of seeking their mother, had they been looking for Margaret Camlet? Perhaps all the sordid details had been kept from them, and they did not know she was dead.

"He's well able to afford it," Sarah said. "As the proprietor of Covenant Pamphlets and Printed Materials. You will have seen them, at missions and in pew racks."

"The tracts and leaflets, of course."

"And instructional advice. Should you feel the need for a

pamphlet instructing you on how to evangelise a slave in Alabama, or take tea with a Hindoo, Covenant will have such a thing. A most upright and godly man," Mrs. Hartright concluded, with a nod of approval. "And visiting the sick is explicitly recommended in Scripture."

"You are scarcely to be numbered among the sick any more. Shall we have a little brown soup for supper, do you think?" This evening I must write to Laura. Mrs. Hartright progresses so well, I should be able to return home next week.

10 January

The kindness of our visitor did not slacken. A note arrived early today, offering Mrs. Hartright, and us of course, a lift to St. John-at-Hampstead. The old lady had been too much pulled down to attend services, and accepted the offer with joy. She enjoys the sermons of the Reverend Angier, and I confess to a desire to hear his preaching as well. He administers the Female Preventative and Reformatory League, a group dedicated to the reclamation of wayward females who are weary of sin. The offer was the more welcome since the weather had turned, with a cold sleety rain that made going outdoors a punishment.

This morning therefore Sarah and I wrapped her mother and ourselves up well in coats, muffs, shawls, scarves, gloves and bonnets, and we all wore our stoutest boots. The coachman came to our door with a large umbrella, and the carriage was made welcoming with hot bricks.

"Six of us, but the children do not take up much space," our benefactor greeted us. "If you ladies are too crowded on that side, we may exchange Miss Sarah for Micah."

"Our wraps are so bulky, perhaps it would be as well," I said. "Micah, shall you sit between Mrs. Hartright and myself?"

The exchange was quickly made and we were off. The children had evidently been abjured with sternness not to pester their elders with demands for seed cake. But Lottie, looking like a cherub in a swansdown tippet, put her thumb in her mouth and stared across hopefully at me. I had had the foresight to load my muff with peppermints, and their father reluctantly agreed to one each.

"Not in the pews, mind," he added. "It's holy service, not a box at the theatre."

"Be quiet and good, and we shall have another on the way home," I promised.

He smiled faintly at his offspring's enthusiasm for comfits. "Is bribery, Miss Halcombe, the way to inculcate good behavior in the young?"

"Since they are not yet at the age of reason, the only tools to hand are bribery or duress," I said. "Between pleasure and pain, the first choice is obvious."

"I am very reasonable." Micah licked his fingers. In the daylight I saw that the boy's eyes were a bright deep blue, almost sapphire. His sister had her father's hazel eyes and curls the colour of a golden guinea. What a pretty pair!

"Yes, I see you are." I passed him a handkerchief. "You're quite old enough to understand why it's important to listen to the sermon with reverence."

"Why?" Lottie asked.

"Because the congregation has gathered to listen to it," Mr. Camlet said. "And it would be impolite to disturb them."

"The appeal to social custom," I said. "Would not a higher and better reason be the reverence owed to the Deity?"

"Blessed are they that do not see and yet believe," Mr. Camlet quoted. "In my business we have learnt that Christian understanding must grow, as from a seed. It does not spring fully formed from the young mind."

"Any more that the multiplication tables would, I agree," I said. "Let them be polite now, and they may grow to be reverent later."

Sarah, several conversational steps behind, said, "I should have thought to bring some pastilles myself."

"I would give you a peppermint, but I fear to break my promise to the children." Though Sarah herself did not realise I was teasing her, Mr. Camlet took off his glasses and polished them, to hide his smile.

Due to the rain the church was not overly crowded. It's an affluent congregation and the arches of the high ceiling are most impressive. The Rev. Angier, a portly and dignified figure with a red face above bushy grey side whiskers, preached on Colossians with fluency and learning for a full two hours without referring to a note, taking more than a sip of water, or faltering – a most notable feat.

I sat with the Hartright ladies towards the middle of the nave. Mr. Camlet's family pew was further toward the front and on the other side. The high wooden pew backs made it impossible for us to see them, but I heard no childish disturbances and after the service was prompt to distribute more peppermints. "You have been so very good," Mrs. Hartright said to them in the brougham on our way back. "Are you grown up enough to come to tea?"

"Seed cake," Lottie said with hope, before her father could hush her.

"I'm departing for the north on Wednesday," I said, "so let it be on Tuesday. I'll bake a cake tomorrow."

"Departing, indeed!" Mr. Camlet said.

"I am sadly missing my own darling nephew, little Wally. My task is to teach him his letters. I've been away so long I fear he will start to forget."

Mrs. Hartright averred that her only grandson would never be so bird-witted, and so the date was fixed. Immediately we returned to the cottage I sat down to write this, and to draw up a shopping list for Monday's marketing.

13 January

This afternoon was our tea party. Mr. Camlet arrived at four on the dot. The children were beautifully dressed, Micah in a sailor suit and Lottie in dark blue velvet, her pinafore trimmed with eyelet lace. Their hair had been dampened into place, and all in all they were as uncomfortable as cats in a puddle. Mrs. Hartright poured and Sarah handed seed cake. I sat between the two young ones. "We are to be on our very best behavior," Lottie confided. "So that you ladies will not be disgusted with children."

"I live in the same house as my nephew, so I know children," I said. "He is just your age, and we have had some fine romps."

Micah set his cup carefully down in its saucer. "What games do you play?"

I assessed young Micah, who was too old for blocks or a stick horse. "I know how to make a kite out of lath and newspapers."

"Can you? Would you show me?"

"Indeed I shall. Do you have a pen-knife? Never mind, it is of no consequence. I have one, and when you come to make your own kite perhaps your papa shall lend you his."

The cake devoured, I fetched some lath from the woodshed and a few sheets of newspaper from the tinder box, and with the help of a paste pot soon assembled a simple kite on the hall floor. Some crochet cotton did for the string and harness.

"What a gift you have with the little ones, Marian," Mrs. Hartright said, when we proudly displayed our work.

It is a man's world we live in, and thus the wise woman always allots some credit to any male handy. "Dear Walter taught me the way of it. He's made many a kite for little Wally. Now mind, lad, get a reel of stout kite string for this. Sewing thread will snap instantly."

All this while Lottie had been exceptionally ladylike and demure, sitting on a footstool and sipping her tea as her brother and I cut paper and tied string. Now she tugged her father's sleeve. "This is the one, Papa."

Mr. Camlet hastily flicked a crumb from the front of her pinafore. "Hush, Lottie, you are too bold."

"I want to fly it now!" Micah exclaimed. Unfortunately it was still raining, fatal for toys of a paper construction, but his father promised to help him when weather conditions permitted.

"Miss Halcombe, I'm sorry to hear you shall be leaving Hampstead. Is it a long journey, to your home?" Having neglected our adult guest all this time, I took a seat on the sofa. His manner, intelligent and yet mild, was attractive, although I could see that in age he would be stoop-shouldered as many bookish men tend to be. We chatted of trains and connections for some little time.

Then Mr. Camlet suddenly turned the subject. "Miss Halcombe, your kindness to Micah and Lottie is so great, might I make some small return? My firm is undertaking an English edition of the works of John Calvin. If you will entrust me with your direction in Cumberland I would be pleased to send you a spiritual book or two, suitable for feminine perusal. You will not wish to lade your baggage with heavy tomes."

If anything this sounded quite lowering. "I am not much for Protestant theology, sir," I said tactfully. "My woman's intellect is easily sated with novels and such feeble secular entertainments."

His glance at me through the spectacles seemed to weigh me to the ounce. "This is false modesty, Miss Halcombe. You are visibly more intelligent than three quarters of the men in London." At this I had to laugh, and he smiled too. "I have a happier thought. You spoke of your nephew, Mrs. Hartright's grandson. Perhaps the boy would enjoy one of our most popular works, *Noah and His Animals*. It is profusely illustrated and intended to be read aloud to the very young."

"That indeed I would be charmed to see," I said. "You have little ones, so you know that the nurturance of their growth of mind is an ongoing duty. All contributions to that end are welcome." I gave him my direction, and he noted it carefully in his pocket memorandum book.

An experienced father, Mr. Camlet clearly knew not to try the deportment of little ones for too long. When a second slice of cake had been devoured he rose to take his leave. The children thanked each of us in formal and well-rehearsed terms. Mrs. Hartright and Sarah helped with small coats and mittens.

I was about to give Mr. Camlet my usual brisk and mannish handshake – I am too plain for feminine airs. But he startled me by taking my hand and clasping it in both his own. "Will you write back to me, and tell me how little Wally enjoys the book?"

"Ah, I understand at last. You are a wicked publisher. My poor nephew is an experimental animal, and you hope to try different mental diets upon him and see the results."

Below the moustache his mouth actually dropped open in alarm. "My dear lady – oh, you're funning me."

"I'm a dreadful, whimsical creature," I assured him.

His smile was almost a grin. "You delight me, and I hope for a regular correspondence." Micah broke in with a demand for the umbrella to be opened lest his kite become damp, and they were off to their carriage.

I went up to pack for my journey thoughtfully. A correspondence? He could not seriously want reports on how little Wally responded to Christian literature for the very young. By the time my linens were folded I had the right of it. The man was scouring his acquaintance for some pliable female to mother his two children. "I have little Wally, and Laura is expecting another," I told my trunk firmly. "I already have two children to care for."

❧ Selected correspondence in the possession of Marian Halcombe ☙

(on the letterhead of Covenant Pamphlets and Printed Materials, Founded 1819)

London, 23rd January 1857

Madam,
With reference to our conversation of the 16th inst., please see the enclosed volume *Noah And His Animals*.

I remain,

> Your obt. Servant,
> Theophilus H. W. Camlet

Limmeridge House, 26 January 1857

My dear Sir,
I received yours of the 20th. Young Master Hartright is most grateful for your gift, and begs me to give you his thanks, being too young to handle a pen.

> Yours respectfully,
> M. Halcombe

(on heavy white letter paper in black ink)

Hampstead, 28 January 1857

My dear Miss Halcombe –
My own folly rebukes me! I beg you, disregard that

previous missive. I had handed your direction to my clerk, instructing him to dispatch the volume in question. He, thinking it nothing but one of the day's many transactions, inscribed the standard business letter that is usually enclosed in such parcels. Please forgive my carelessness!

I had meant to write an enclosure in my own hand, as I do now and shall in future if you will permit the correspondence. In my line of business it is an article of faith that the written word is the window to the soul. And further that much may be deduced from the form of the handwriting, the colour and density of the ink, the selection of paper, and so forth.

I trust that you pause here to examine and admire the paper upon which this is written. And I anxiously await your reply.

Yours always and most faithfully,
Theo. Camlet

Limmeridge House, 1 February 1857

My dear Mr. Camlet,
Indeed I can find nothing to deplore in your penmanship, nor your selection of paper. And I wrote truly before, that young Wally does enjoy *Noah* very much. Not only does he insist on a re-reading at least once a day, he has formed the intention of exploring Africa and seeing an elephant for himself. We are all most grateful for your kind gift.

The written word supplies many clues, I agree. But it cannot be a sure compass, still less handwriting and letter paper. Consider that a mere glass of brandy would completely alter your very handsome copperplate hand, and that poverty affects the choice of writing paper. An augury that is so easily swayed cannot be a good guide. To discern the truth is a difficult thing.

Are you familiar with the novels of Anthony Trollope? Do you feel the letters in *The Warden* supply an instructive insight into the characters?

Yours faithfully,
Marian Halcombe

Hampstead, 2 April 1857

My dear Miss Halcombe,
I am delighted that you approve of *The Tenant of Wildfell Hall*. It is a novel fallen into some obscurity now, eclipsed by the repute of the late writer's more famous sister. Miss Charlotte Brontë's premature decease last year was a great loss to English letters. [Two closely written pages of Brontë critique omitted here]

I beg you to write again very soon. I long to hear your thoughts upon Carlyle's masterpiece, which I hope arrived safely. [Five paragraphs' analysis of *The French Revolution* omitted here]

Faithfully yours always,
T.H.W.C.

Limmeridge, 30 April

Dear Mr. Camlet,
You are too generous; your book carriers cannot easily transport such a large box to the north country for anything like a reasonable rate. And three volumes of

Forster's sermons – surely your press can market these as aids to slumber! [A page of argument maintaining that the Old Testament is a more entertaining source for sermons than the New omitted here]

But I confess that after your last letter I am on tenterhooks, waiting to receive *Uncle Tom's Cabin*. My only excuse for missing such a successful novel is overwhelming personal concerns at the period when it first appeared, and I am anxious to amend my omission. Mrs. Stowe must be more than an ornament to our sex. She must be a mighty Christian soldier. [Three paragraphs' discussion of the influence of women on the movement to abolish slavery omitted here]

You will be glad to hear that my sister Laura has been safely delivered of another fine son. The infant is to be christened Fairlie Philip Hartright, so that the family name may not utterly die out. So we are very busy and happy here, I with young Wally and Laura with the new one, and I do not contemplate a return to town at any foreseeable point. However, should your business concerns bring you north some year, I would enjoy meeting you again.

With sincere regards,
Marian Halcombe

Limmeridge, May 28 1857

Dear Mr. Camlet,
Learning from my sister Marian that your business affairs bring you to Carlisle next month, I write to invite you to visit us at Limmeridge House. She has told me so much about you, and of course you are long acquainted with my dear husband Walter Hartright and his family. His mother Mrs. Caroline Hartright

speaks often of your great kindness to her.

If this is agreeable to you, let me know by which train you will arrive, and the pony-chaise shall meet you at the station.

Yours faithfully,
Mrs. Laura Hartright

London 10 June

My dear Miss Halcombe,
I can scarcely compose myself to pen these lines to you. They shall go into the evening's post, and by the time they are in your hand I should be close behind, arriving in the north.

Before all my fine words are swept away by meeting you again, Miss Halcombe, permit me to confide that I have high hopes of this visit. It cannot have escaped your attention that we share many interests. As my old nurse would say, we deal well together. I would like more, and I hope you feel the same.

When I come, I hope to discuss these matters with you more seriously.

Ever believe me, my dear Miss Halcombe,

Yours affectionately,
T.H.W.C.

❧ Marian Halcombe's journal ☙

12 June 1857

Why, oh why did I not go out more in society? I should have been a Helen, a Guinevere! Why did I not harvest men's hearts like wheat, and toss them to one side and the other like chaff? Not that my face could ever allure them close enough to be tossed. Instead I am the Lady of Shalott, cracking mirrors and spoiling my needlework. A gentleman with intentions comes to call and in my inexperience I can neither sit, nor lie down, nor attend to my sewing, nor walk quietly with little Wally in the garden. The only good service I am fit for is to pace the floors holding little Fairlie over my shoulder, because he has the colic.

Although I must present the most comical sight, neither Walter nor Laura are so unkind as to even smile. Walter soberly recommended that I eschew tea, which is said to exacerbate the nerve endings, and instead take a less stimulating beverage like barley-water. Laura, who only recently emerged from her lying-in, sat on the shady terrace in a basket chair with her little greyhound at her feet, and spoke soft words of sense every time I flew by, comet-like, with her baby on my shoulder.

"I know I do not need to urge you to seek true affection, Marian," she said, on one of my orbits. "You will not accept less."

"And that is a point we must settle," I said. "I should draw up a list. If he seeks merely an unpaid nursemaid I must decline the honor."

"But you've corresponded for months," she said, when I next passed by.

"We've exchanged letters at least twice a week."

"Every day," she corrected me. "Sometimes twice a day. And the extracts you occasionally read aloud to me were very diverting."

"He is intelligent, well-read, and right-thinking on all points."

On my next flight she said, "Marian. Could you love him?"

"I cannot tell, Laura. Truly, I do not know!"

"Perhaps you'll know when you see him."

"If only I had conquered dozens of men, then I should know what I was about with this one."

"We haven't met dozens of men," Laura reasoned. "It's idle to yearn for what is not there. And many of the gentlemen we encountered have been the very exemplar of unsuitable."

I shuddered at the memories. "And that's another thing, Laura. You and I know. Even the most pleasant and convincing of exteriors can be a façade for horrors. Suppose Mr. Camlet is, is…" My maiden imagination failed me.

"Walter and his family have been acquainted with him for years," Laura noted. "He's shown no signs of turpitude. And from your report he is an exemplary father to his children."

Little Fairlie began to grizzle again, and I patted his tiny back and paced back and forth so that the great bell of my skirt swayed. I had reacted in the only possible way a woman can to this plight – I sewed a new summer dress. At least the garment was a great success: a creamy tarlatan sprigged in red and with a pretty red openwork stripe, adorned with rows of red soutache braid at bodice, sleeve and hem. It was in the very latest mode, twelve yards in the skirt that was held out to a wide circle with a spring-steel crinoline.

This overleaping ambition had possibly been a tactical error. There is no call for fashionable furbelows in our quiet country life, and I am not perfectly expert in managing the tremendous circumference. Every stitch was calculated not to allure – do men even notice what we wear? – but to bolster a tremulous confidence. Now I was tormented by the idea that a malign gust of wind would suddenly invert the buoyant cage and flip up the skirt. "But what of his wife? She left him for another before she died. Why? How can I possibly ask him if he drove her away?"

"At least this question need not vex you, Marian," Laura said. "We have a man in the family whose duty it is to ask suitors these questions. A man may not be comfortable explaining the failure of his marriage to a young woman, but to another man he may be forthcoming. And if Walter is not satisfied, he shall tell us."

Though Walter is not of gentle birth, nor born to wealth, he has what is far more valuable: a sterling character forged in the fires of adversity, and the soundest judgment of any man I know. But still I could not be easy.

"I should never have suggested he come," I groaned. "He has insinuated himself into my life. We should have simply exchanged letters all our lives on safe literary subjects. The novels of Mr. Thackeray alone would have taken up a decade. Suppose he pares his fingernails in the dining room? Or endlessly resorts to a smelling bottle, like Mr. Fairlie? Or gambles on horse races, or is a slave to gin, or honks like a goose when he laughs?"

"At any moment if he disgusts you, you may send him away," Laura soothed me. "Testing and careful consideration is proper at this period."

"Oh heavens. And he is carefully considering and testing me! What if he cannot bear the click of knitting needles? Or dislikes openwork stripes in dress goods? I should never have acquired these hoops, I must have been mad. Is there time for me to go up and change?"

"Then he would have no socks," Laura said. "Your new dress is very becoming, Marian. Perhaps you should give me Baby now. I hear the carriage in the drive."

I handed little Fairlie over and helped Laura rise to her feet. We stood together waiting for our guest to be shown through, and my sensations were like those of a prisoner waiting for the firing squad. I heard Walter's voice inside, raised in hearty words of welcome. Steps clattered on the marble paving of the hall, and then suddenly he was there.

I believe I said very foolish things indeed. But I cannot recall them, nor can I remember what he said in greeting, even though it was but a few hours ago. I do remember that he bent to let Luna the little greyhound sniff his hand. This at least was auspicious. Luna is snappish with strangers, but she allowed him to stroke her ears.

Then they all three conversed knowledgeably about baby colic and the relative merits of mint boiled in water compared to warm compresses applied to the belly. Suddenly Laura was speaking of putting the baby down for his nap, and they basely deserted me – with him!

I was about to sink into Laura's basket chair, but the thought of my crinoline made me start back to my feet. If my hoops stuck in the chair's sides I might drag it behind me when I rose again, like a cat with a pan tied to her tail. Instead I hastily moved to the armless chair, carefully spreading my skirts so that the steel hoops would stay flat around my knees where they belonged.

Mr. Camlet took the basket chair instead. "Miss Halcombe, you have said little. Have we left you out of the conversation?"

"Do you know what is particularly unfair? It is that all of you, without exception, have experience of this, while I do not."

"I, experienced?" He had been smiling under the

moustache, but suddenly he looked grave. "If you're unwilling to receive my attentions –"

"No! At least, not precisely. I must become accustomed to you, that's all."

"Ah. I understand." Only when the colour returned to his cheek again did I realise he had gone pale.

I scowled, not at him but at the flower urn on the baluster. "You know nothing of it."

"I'm sorry to contradict you, Miss Halcombe, but that is not so. I do know." He leaned back, fixing his bespectacled gaze upon the birds wheeling in the summer sky over the lawn and terrace, and I knew that this was to give me the chance to look at him without shyness. He presented a quite ordinary appearance, a plain man as bread is plain. Under the well-cut grey tweed traveling suit there was strength in his shoulders, and the warmth of the sun brought the colour up into his fair skin. The fawn-brown hair and side whiskers joining in the moustache showed no grey and were painfully well-groomed, and he had taken great care with his green cravat.

"You are very near the sea," he noted. "See how many gulls there are. All my life I've spent at least a part of every day outdoors." He slipped two fingers into his waistcoat pocket, and brought out the last thing I would have looked for, a twist of newspaper. Untwisted, it held an ounce of birdseed. "Do you see that little grey and brown bird over there? *Passer domesticus*, the English sparrow, one of the most common avians of our northern hemisphere. Now, I must ask you to sit perfectly still."

He flicked a seed towards the bird, which was at the far end of the terrace. It was as if he had the power of St. Francis over dumb creatures. Another seed, and another, and in ten minutes the bird was so near I could have brushed it with my toe. It cocked its head to look at us with a bright black eye.

Very slowly and gently Mr. Camlet bent, leaning one arm on his knees and resting the other hand palm up on the slates. On the tip of his forefinger he held out a single seed. For long moments his guest hesitated, and I held my breath. The little bird hopped closer and considered him carefully yet again, a-tremble with desire. With a sudden flurry it dashed in and seized the treat. Then it was gone into the trees again in a flirt of brown wings.

"A pity," he said, straightening. "I should have liked to get the creature to stand on my palm. Perhaps tomorrow." He shot a smiling glance at me. "When it is accustomed."

I breathed again. "You are a magician."

That made him laugh, a pleasant laugh, not irritating or goose-like at all. "No, I'm nothing but patient. I am willing to give others time. Do you remember my horse? The black one – his name is Boreas, after the north wind. Strong and fleet, but when I first bought him a little nervous in the hand. I was run away with more than once, and my coachman advised a barbed bit and the whip. But gentle handling has tamed him better, and he has learned my voice and touch. Little Micah can safely give him sugar now, and he comes at my call."

"You know how to bring the wild things near." I know of only one other man who held a similar dominion over creatures, and he had been one of the greatest villains who ever lived. Now I looked at my guest and felt almost frightened. What had I invited into my safe and sunny existence? The impulse almost overcame me, to jump up and retreat into the house.

If he had moved abruptly, if he had even glanced full at me, I would have done so and never looked back. But the breeze from the ocean had picked up. If my crinoline turned traitor on me, revealing an indecorous glimpse of drawers or petticoat, I would perish of embarrassment. And his gaze was fixed on the summer sky, following the circling of the gulls.

When he spoke, his tone was mild. "I have no luck with the untamable, but a little skittishness is not rare." He opened a hand with quiet confidence. "You are that bird, my dearest Miss Halcombe. Bold yet shy. Take all the time you like. Hop close, and consider the seed from all angles. I hold it out, and wait upon your will."

Only then did he look at me, with a glint of a smile behind the round lenses. Could anything be more comfortable for a woman never wooed? He did not compel, or hypnotise like Count Fosco; his birds were not caged but flew free, to come to him at their own will. He was comfortable enough in himself to sit still and wait. The decision was mine!

All my nervousness was soothed. By the time tea was brought out we were chatting like the friends we were, and I had undertaken to show him our favorite rustic summerhouse and the bower in Laura's rose garden after the meal. These were on the lee side of the house, and my sartorial anxieties abated.

We took little Wally with us, so that the house should be quiet for the baby's nap. He's a handsome romping lad, and he ran ahead to throw sticks into the stream that murmured at the bottom of the garden on its way to the sea. All around us was the scent of roses warmed in the sun, and the sky was broad and blue, heaped high with clouds as only the wide sky of the north country can be.

Mr. Camlet said, "I see now how you know so much of children."

"I had looked to spend all my life taking care of Laura's."

"You did not look for marriage."

"I'm dark, and ugly, and odd, and poor, sir. At least Jane Eyre had youth! Whereas I shall be thirty soon, well past my last prayers."

He smiled at the literary turn. "I have wed wealth and youth and beauty. They were ashes. You are lovely in my eyes. And surely your reading has revealed to you, Miss Halcombe, that all valiant young princesses find their prince in the end. I'm but a poor prince, but I have hopes that you will honor me with your hand."

His voice trembled with quiet vehemence, so that I had to reply lightly. "All you seek is a mother for your little ones."

"As Shakespeare advised, I seek a marriage of true minds." He paused, not for thought, but in reticence. He had told me the truth – he did know. "The companionship and intimacy of genuine marriage, body and mind and heart. I've never had it." After a further pause he added softly, "That joy to which all hearts do yearn."

My own heart felt very strange, an unfamiliar organ in my chest. "I am not of a loving nature," I warned him. "My affections are narrow and deep-rooted – Laura, Walter, the little ones." As if my hands were determined to prove my contrary words wrong, they broke off a small rosebud just about to bloom, a deep yellow one, and began to strip off the thorns.

"And I am no fire-eater. Mr. Hartright is more a hero. How I envy him his expedition to the Honduras."

"Will you consult him? I am guided by his advice, his mind being clearer than my own at this juncture."

Mr. Camlet laughed with genuine delight. "That I have befuddled your razor-sharp wits thrills me more than I can say. Do you love me, my dearest? For you have my heart in your keeping."

Still in open insurrection against my words, my mutinous fingers inserted the thornless rose into his lapel buttonhole. "I suppose I do," I said, ungraciously. "See, what a failure I am at the romantical! Here in an English rose garden a declaration is laid at my feet, and I return your affections the way I would return a borrowed shovel."

Again unspoken emotion made him pale and then flushed. "As long as they are returned I make no complaint." With deliberation he lifted my hand from his lapel and raised it to his lips. His clasp was warm and steady but light, so that I could draw my hand away if I liked.

I did not pull away. Somehow my entire awareness, every nerve in my body, had migrated into those fingers, exquisitely alive, and I could no more pull away than I could tug my own head off. The prickle of moustache and the warmth of his breath brought to mind the snuffle of a friendly horse, but suddenly my knees were weak. I sat hastily down on the garden seat under the bower, perforce dragging him down with me since I did not release his hand.

"I have brought you a ring. Would you like to see?"

"No woman will decline a glimpse of jewelry," I said, feebly. I had difficulty breathing properly.

From a pocket he drew a small box that held a ring of antique style, white gold with a shimmering white opal set between two brilliants. "It was my grandmother's."

This gave me pause. Was this the ring that the first Mrs. Camlet had worn? I remembered Laura's wise counsel. "It is lovely. But before I accept it, and you, may I beg you to speak with Walter? I am guided by him in all things, and would not dare to make such a major decision without his approval and consent."

His eyes twinkled behind the glasses. "Say rather that you feel a need for delay and reflection. And that your brother-in-law makes a convenient and unassailable stalking horse for this intention. For if your will were set, Miss Halcombe, I do not doubt that poor Mr. Hartright's wishes and imprimatur would be over the side with a resounding splash."

"As you say, it is unassailable," I countered. "And you promised me all the time I should wish."

"I shall never hasten you against your judgment. But, if you will permit the liberty, there is one additional experiment that is out of reason informative..."

I could not think what he meant, but then he leaned slowly over and kissed me, very gently, on the lips. Of course – he was a widower, with years of experience in married life, and I had never been touched by a man except on the hand. Again the prickle of masculine moustache and the warm sweet breath, but they were less strange now, and I did not shrink. In fact my impression is that I goggled like a stuck frog. Suddenly what Laura had told me the day she gave me this very journal came surging into my mind. My sister had this, and she wanted it for me.

"It is not only the minds that truly marry," Mr. Camlet said softly. He watched me attentively, the hazel eyes solemn. "You feel no reluctance? No physical drawing back?"

My blood thundered in my ears. "You expect that a respectable and delicately-nurtured female should recoil. But perhaps you wish for blunt and downright language, rather than delicate vaporing."

"Indeed I do, and always will."

How rare that was, a man who wanted truth, rather than missishness. I have always boasted of my blunt speech, knowing that it was not valued and therefore the perfect mask. But now when I spoke truth he would believe it. He would take me seriously. I could grow, and become – what? Perhaps what I truly am.

I looked down at his hand in mine. My hands are large and competent, not very feminine, but his were visibly more heavily boned, the wrist and sturdy fingers of a man. Clasped in his, my hand is delicate, a lady's. I traced the calluses of rein and pen, not visible but perceptible to the exploring touch. If he held my fingers lightly it was by intent, for this was a hand strong to grasp if its master willed it.

"I think ... as you wrote in your letter. That we shall deal well together. Do you remember in the April number of *Household Words*, the article about Brittany?"

He blew out a sigh of what I realised was relief. "The traveller who was comically quizzed by the rural French bumpkins, yes."

Of course a man knew desire, but he wanted me to know it, too! An utterly novel idea, but suddenly not impossible, not when I held his hand like this. "The proverb of the peasantry there was that a kiss without a moustache is like soup without salt."

Under his own moustache he smiled. "Of course the Bretons could be sadly mistaken."

Solemnly I agreed. "It would be only proper to put it to the test."

Little Wally returned five minutes later with an earthworm clutched in his fist, but that was enough time for us to prove that Brittany is not a sinkhole of ignorance. I am a convert to moustaches! I sent my suitor up to the house to Walter, and persuaded little Wally to let the earthworm go find its dinner. When we returned home, hot and grubby, to wash and change, the gentlemen were still closeted in the study, and I hastened upstairs to note all these events down.

That evening

The evening meal was somewhat tense. My appetite was poor even though Laura, in a gesture of great kindliness, had ordered all Mr. Camlet's favorite dishes alternating with mine. More of a relief to me was Walter's readiness to talk politics with him. For a man who declines to stand for office, Walter is well-informed. They agreed that the Young Irelander movement had been mistakenly confused in the public mind with the more reasonable desire of the workers to join unions, and that the justifiable pleas of the poor could not be heard over the flinging of anarchist bombs at crowned heads of state.

As Walter always prefers at home, the gentlemen did not stay for their port, but joined us in the drawing room straight away. When the tea was poured Mr. Camlet spoke. "I am to understand that a most reasonable concern has been felt about my unhappy first union. Mr. Hartright was willing to hear my tale, but upon reflection I thought that it would be better to tell you all.

Then I need not repeat the sorry account to Miss Halcombe, as I fully intend to do, and the questions of her family may help her cogitations."

"It must be a sad story," Laura said in her soft voice. "The more public facts are, alas, common talk."

"Yes, the notoriety of my personal life is a heavy cross to bear. To begin: the union between myself and Margaret Brickley was not of my doing. My grandfather was the founder and proprietor of Holy Rood Publications, a small business that printed religious books of an evangelical bent. Her uncle, Samuel Brickley, was owner of a competing firm. The two old gentlemen conceived the notion of amalgamating the two smaller businesses to form a larger and more profitable concern. To seal the bargain the heirs, Margaret and myself, were wed. At the time I was not yet twenty-three, still up at Cambridge. She was twenty-five."

Walter observed, "Not an unbridgeable gap of years."

"It was folly. We were frantically ill-suited, and we both knew it. I begged my grandfather to call it off, but the business merger had already progressed too far. He assured me that when the children began to come all would be well. She was older than her years, and I regret to report that I was behind in mine. And … well! I too was at fault. In summary, she was hot where I was cool, swift where I was slow, angry where I was calm. She was of an activist spirit, passionately interested in current events and the rights of the oppressed, while I was smaller in vision, weighted with responsibility. The passing of my grandfather made it necessary for me to work almost every waking moment. She was bored with a mate who was always too slow and too deliberate for her passionate nature. I could not even converse with her. There was no good will between us. And she had no interest whatever in the children, in Micah and Lottie. My grandfather was quite incorrect about their ability to heal a union. Their welfare was left entirely to me."

I asked the first foolish question that would come to a woman's mind. "Was she pretty?"

"She was as glorious as the rising sun." His dispassionate assessment reminded me that to him her beauty was ashes. "Micah has her eyes, that gemlike blue, and Lottie her hair. With the mellowing passage of years we might have settled into the marriage. But patience is always my first recourse. It was always her last. She wanted more, sooner. I mentioned that I can tame the skittish. But after years of futile effort I had to face reality. The untamable is beyond me, and she was one of those."

"It is ever a mistake to betroth young people too early," Walter said.

"Our estrangement became complete, and she involved herself with political meetings and the suffragette movement," Mr. Camlet said quietly. "It was there that she met the foreigner with whom she eventually left England. I do not know his name, and have taken care to never learn it."

"Did she hide this connection?"

"No indeed, quite the reverse. In fact – after the example of the arrangements of George Lewes, the companion of the noted authoress Mary Ann Evans – she suggested that we have an open marriage, and that I allow her to go and live with her new paramour."

I felt an actual pang, at his humiliation and pain. Walter coughed in embarrassment, and Laura's clear blue eyes were round with horror. "Can such things be?"

"You are comfortably remote from literary London," Mr. Camlet said courteously. "Lewes's situation is common knowledge if even I, a small fish in the ocean of letters, have heard the talk. They've been living together outside the bonds of matrimony for some years now."

"How tremendously … modern," Laura said. "Your wife must have shocked you greatly."

"I could not countenance it," Mr. Camlet said. "A noted philosopher, Lewes moves in London's most advanced circles. But my living is made more modestly, by publishing pamphlets and religious books. Even if conscience permitted me to connive at her adultery, the reputation of the business would immediately shatter beyond repair. I said so, and so she left me. After Lottie was born she removed with her lover to the Continent, and there died eighteen months later."

"Thus setting you free," Walter said. "I do not doubt your story, but it is my duty to enquire. What was the cause of her demise?"

"There may be some such thing as a death certificate in

Salerno, where she passed away, but I know nothing of Italian procedure. I do have this." From an inner pocket he drew two sheets of paper folded and pinned together: a letter in a cramped foreign hand, and a more legible document in English. "This is the letter from the Catholic priest of the parish she died in. It is of course in Italian, and he sent it to the British Consulate in Rome. There it was translated into English, and letter and translation were forwarded on to me."

Walter is not fluent but he can read Italian. "A quinsy, a common ailment that could happen to anyone."

"It was some years before I mustered the courage to get back into the saddle," Mr. Camlet said, ruefully. "It weighed on me, that I had been rigid, so intransigent that she was driven to seek another, driven to her death. And then ... when I saw you, Miss Halcombe - you were leading the children through Mrs. Hartright's gate. In your pale gown you looked like something not of this earth, and the hedge was like dark wings at your back. A terror seized me, that you lured them into some dangerous scrape. But even though I intemperately shouted at you, you replied with confidence and composure. You were completely mistress of the situation. And I knew then you were something not in the common way."

"My acquaintance with you dates to before your son's birth," Walter said. "You've ever been an upright and honest fellow, Camlet. And your story, though sad, casts no shadow upon yourself. You are a victim, not a perpetrator. I can have no objection to your proposal."

My state was such that I was not sure whether this was pleasing or not. "You give your consent, Walter?"

Almost, but not quite, Walter rolled his eyes - just a brief glance heavenwards. "Insofar as I ever can, Marian. The issue must rest with you yourself."

On occasion Walter really can be infuriating. What is the point of men lording it over us, ruling with an iron rod over a woman's every decision if, when one really wants guidance and assurance, their dominion collapses like a clothes horse? Mr. Camlet's gentle words were like a cooling touch. "I've promised Miss Halcombe as much time as she likes, to make a considered decision."

I took my courage in both hands. Laura had urged me to reach for happiness. And now I saw it before me. "I have thought carefully," I said. "For several entire hours, plenty of time. Mr. Camlet, I give you fair warning. This is now your last chance to draw back. If you truly wish to marry me, I would be honored to accept your offer."

The poor man! His mouth dropped open in astonishment again. My changeable ways shall grey him fast. But he quickly recovered and leaped to his feet. "I feared I would have to wait for years. Dearest Marian –"

He halted, flushing right up to his ears, but I rose too, saying, "You may indeed call me so now – Theo."

It was the first time his Christian name had ever passed my lips, and I almost stuttered over it. An inconsequential advance in intimacy, but the first of many to come: the initial tiny tidal trickle of what would be an enormous ocean wave, a salty surge that would surround me, tumble me off my feet, and soak me to the skin. The thought made me blush painfully scarlet too. What had I done? Suddenly it all felt far too physical, too real!

But he took my hands in both his own and all at once it seemed not only possible, but tardy. How can a thing be too fast and yet too slow to arrive, all at the same time? We had of course changed for dinner, and I saw now that he had transferred the yellow rosebud from his tweed buttonhole to his black dress coat. "You told me you were a patient man," I whispered to this accommodating blossom.

"That I can wait," he said softly, "doesn't mean I wish to." And this was so true – exactly the sensation fluttering in my breast! – that I gave way to impulse and kissed him.

Possibly this was an error. To be clasped by strong arms to a male starched shirt front that smelled faintly of cologne was the natural sequel, and who knows what would have happened after that?

Thank heaven for Walter and Laura! I remembered their presence and blushed again, retreating immediately to the distance of his handclasp. Three hours ago this had been almost too exquisitely close, and now it was not near enough. Both distance and time were doing queer things this day.

He produced the ring and tried it on, where it stuck on my

rather large finger. "I shall have it resized immediately. May we name the day, or is it too soon?"

"Too soon," I exclaimed, as time wriggled like a salmon under my feet yet again. "Let us consult the calendars."

"You must be married from here," Laura said. "Oh Marian, I'm so happy for you!"

"I wish you all joy, Camlet," Walter said, shaking his hand. "She's a woman in ten thousand. And Marian, shall you want me to give you away?"

"I will accept nothing less," I said. "And the little ones shall attend me – yours, Theo, and little Wally, if he can be persuaded to carry a basket of flowers."

Theo shook his head, smiling. "That is a dangerous idea, my dearest, but I can deny you nothing. Let it be so, and you shall learn why children should not assist at weddings."

≈ Selected correspondence and papers in the possession of Marian Halcombe ≈

The Carlisle Patriot 15 October 1857

On Friday morning a wedding of considerable interest to the Cumberland region was solemnised at Limmeridge Church, near Allonby, between Miss Marian Halcombe, daughter of the late Mr. Jonathan L. Halcombe and his wife Celeste, and Mr. Theophilus H.W. Camlet, owner of Covenant Pamphlets and Printed Materials, a publishing house in London. Miss Halcombe's late mother became the wife of Mr. Philip Fairlie, of Limmeridge House. The bride was given away by her brother-in-law, Mr. Walter Hartright, of Limmeridge House, and was attended by his wife, Mrs. Laura Fairlie Hartright. The officiating clergyman was the Rev. Wriothsley Ramer of Limmeridge Church, assisted by the Rev. Nicholas Twinforth. The newlyweds plan to reside in Hampstead, near London.

(A postcard, depicting Notre Dame de Paris)

My dear Lottie and Micah,
Your new mother and I have ascended to the top of this church tower! The view of Paris up and down the River Seine is very fine, and the pigeons peck corn just like the ones in London. We shall be back by the Sunday after you receive this. Miss Marian sends you all her love. Mind your nurse and behave yourselves until the return of

Your own loving
Papa

❧ From the correspondence of Laura Fairlie Hartright ❧

29 October 1857, Paris

My dearest Laura,
Just a few lines to tell you of my great happiness in the married state. You were entirely right! Theo is the best husband a woman could wish for. Paris is a delightful city. I have bought presents for everyone, and made the journey to Versailles, where I left cards on Aunt Eleanor. Her maid said she was indisposed, but now we may say the proprieties are satisfied.

Theo has urged me to take an interest in the business, and perhaps even lend a hand with some of the work. I flatter myself that I can manage punctuation and spelling as well as any, and he assures me that such skills are forever needed in all areas of publishing but ten times ten, in the religious sector.

We shall be back in Hampstead by week's end, and look forward to seeing you and Walter and the boys at Christmas.

All my best love,
Marian

BOOK 2

❧ Loose sheets inserted into the journal of Marian Halcombe ❧

5 February 1858

I almost do not recognise the words of my pen. My spirits are so overset that my mind seems to be mazed. I see as through a glass, darkly, and I am sick to my stomach. Mrs. Hartright urges me to write this so that others may know what I saw, and judge more rightly than I.

She advises me to begin at the beginning. I think it began when Theo and I went out to a lecture yesterday evening. It was most enjoyable, about British shorebirds and illustrated with magic lantern slides. On the way back to Sandett House it was just beginning to snow, and we discussed going to Whitby come summer for the little ones' first seaside visit.

We went in, and were met by little Lottie weeping in the front hall. "You are our mother, Miss Marian, aren't you? She's telling a fib!"

"Of course she's your mother, Lottie." Laughing, Theo swung the child up into his arms and carried her through into the drawing room. "Procured at great expense from our suppliers in –" He stopped dead, and seemed to reel as he stood.

Following, I saw standing at the window a dazzling woman I have never seen before. She was golden-haired and tall, and had opened the Wardian case in the bay window. Several ferns lay forlorn on the marble tabletop, and earth was scattered on the carpet.

"Hallo, Theophilus, you look well." When she carelessly glanced up from her work I saw her eyes were the deepest and most brilliant blue. "Though a tartan waistcoat does not become you in the least. Who is this person? Oh you sly hound, Theo, and after all your moralizing, too. And you've neglected these ferns. How is it you haven't divided them? They're sadly crowded in here."

"Margaret?" Theo gasped as if he were drowning.

She dusted earth off her long white fingers and swept past him in a swish of practical grey woolen skirts. "You must excuse us, my good woman," she said briskly to me. "There are family affairs I must discuss with my husband."

Lottie's wails echoed in my ears, so that if Theo protested I could not hear. I was so stunned with surprise that I made no objection as Margaret Camlet ushered me back into the hall and out the front door. It shut with a firm final click behind me.

For an unknowable time I simply stood in the wintry darkness, my hands at my sides and my mouth open. I could not believe my ears. I did not believe my eyes. I could not grasp what was happening.

Only the whisper of driving snow suddenly brought me to myself. I had shed my coat and hat as we went indoors. My shoes were thin, never meant for rough use, and my gown was of primrose silk. But to turn and knock for entrance again? Reason revolted; it was impossible.

Instead I fell back upon habit. I plunged forward. I shuffled through the snow to the lane. In no time the house, the home Theo had carried me over the threshold of, was invisible in the thick whirl of flakes and fog. But it was only half a mile down the lane to the cottage of Mrs. Hartright and Sarah. Shelter was not far away.

I set myself to walk it. Little Lottie and Micah had had no difficulty, a mere year ago, but the weather then had been mild. Now my delicate shoes were soon wet and broken, and my fingers and toes went numb. My hoops fought the wind. The wet snow soaked my silken skirts so that they dragged around my legs, and the ice of my breath seemed to clog my lungs. The darkness and fog confused me, and when I accidentally stepped off the path I tumbled into the hedge, which caught at my clothing.

After I ripped the wide bell of my skirt free I kept an eye on the hedgerows and trees to the right. If I wandered off to the left, across the open heath, I might never find shelter. And surely Theo would follow me and find me? He would gallop up on black Boreas as he had searched for Lottie and Micah. I was his wife, shut out of my own house. He had to come.

He did not. When I stumbled up to it, old Mrs. Hartright's gate was shut, and my frozen fingers could scarcely lift the latch. I hammered on their door, voiceless, and when Sarah suddenly pulled it open I fell in onto the mat.

I tried to explain to them what had happened, but I was so chilled and overwrought that they put me to bed. This morning I wrote the previous pages down for Mrs. Hartright, so that my understanding of the events might be preserved. She had Sarah copy it over fair. My hand was barely legible, and my tears had blotted the ink. Then she read it to herself, peering through her spectacles and tipping the page to the light.

"Surely it's a mere misunderstanding, Marian. You misheard, or misunderstood, some quite ordinary event. Why, they had a memorial service for Margaret Camlet down at the church. With hymns! She cannot be returned from the grave, it is simply not heard of in respectable circles. Sarah shall wrap up well and walk up the lane. Surely, surely there is some simple explanation."

This Sarah was very willing to do. It had stopped snowing, but the wind was still keen, and she could not make fast progress. My dress and shoes of yesterday were still too wet to wear, and I sat in the window in a borrowed nightgown and several shawls, watching for her return. When I saw her approach I ran downstairs to hear her account.

Sarah began to speak as she stepped in the door. "Mama, it is she," she cried. Bits of ice tinkled down as she unwound her frosty muffler. "I remember Margaret Camlet perfectly well. It is no other. She has moved back into Theo's house, and says that she was away but now is back, and plans to stay."

"Great heavens," Mrs. Hartright said faintly. "But that's impossible."

"What did Theo say?" I cried.

"I didn't see him," Sarah replied. "And I didn't know how to mention you, Marian. To ask Mrs. Camlet, about a second Mrs. Camlet? So I said I was merely hoping to borrow a cup of sugar from their cook. Here it is." From inside her shawl she drew out a tin cup with sugar in it.

Both ladies looked uneasily at me, disheveled in my bare feet and borrowed nightwear. There could be no second Mrs. Camlet, not if the first one was still alive. Suddenly I was Marian Halcombe again.

My voice quavered shamefully. "I must go home," I said, shivering. "To Limmeridge, to Laura."

"Well, my dear," Mrs. Hartright fluttered. "That is well thought of. Yes indeed! Your own family will help you. You are not unprotected. Walter is so capable. But we must find you some clothes, yes. You are too tall to fit into any garment in this house. Your dress, it must be dried and brushed…"

The delicate silk fabric of my dress was irretrievably stained by the damp, but the garment could at least be worn. Milly toiled for hours waving it over the kitchen fire, and when it was dry Mrs. Hartright cobbled together the great rent near the hem where I had torn it on the hedge. My ruined shoes could not be saved, but Sarah lent me a pair of boots that fit well enough.

I was frantic to depart. What was happening? Perhaps Laura and Walter could help me grasp it. I had no other luggage. "I can walk until I find a cab to take me to the station," I said.

"In this weather?" Sarah cried. "Marian, it's coming to sleet again."

"And you are not well, my dear," Mrs. Hartright said. "You are quaking all over, and no wonder. Gladly will I lend you my thickest Shetland shawl, but it will not serve you to walk any great distance."

I felt this was true. My knees trembled under me, my head was giddy, and my stomach roiled. Perhaps these were the symptoms of a broken heart? My dearest Theo had flung me aside without so much as a glance! "Please help me," I said with a sob. "I must go home. I'll walk, every step of the way if need be."

"Don't weep, Marian," Sarah said, tears in her eyes. "Surely this is the worst calamity that can befall a woman."

"Wait," Mrs. Hartright cried. She was peeping through the curtains of the parlour. "There's the Reverend Angier's dog-cart, just coming down the lane. Quick, Sarah – your shoes are stout. Hurry out, and beg him to step in."

This the faithful girl did, drawing her shawl over her head and dashing out into the cold. I sat miserably in the parlour while the great man was brought in and the entire story poured out to him piecemeal, Mrs. Hartright waving my written account and Sarah displaying the cup of sugar.

In spite of his grand connections and good work reclaiming lost women, the reverend's understanding was not swift, and the ladies' discourse was not of the clearest. But after what seemed like hours of discussion it was agreed that it would be best for me to return to Limmeridge. Walter, as the man of the family, had the standing to do what a mere woman however wronged could not.

My good friends debated my fate over my bowed head as if I were a child, for I was too overcome to participate. "He has not even called, not even sought for her," Mrs. Hartright said, her thin bosom heaving with indignation. "Pushed out of the door at night in this winter weather! The kitchen cat is treated better."

"She could have died on the heath in the storm," Sarah said. "I fear we've been sadly mistaken in Mr. Camlet's character."

"We shall take her to the station and see her safely on the train north," the vicar said. His broad dignified face was red with outrage between the bushy grey side whiskers. "I shall send a wire, apprising her people of her arrival, so that she may be met when she arrives. And then, fear not, Miss Halcombe. I shall call upon Mr. Camlet, and interview both him and his, ah, this female. You are not friendless. You have protectors, not the least among whom I count myself. The Female Preventative and Reformatory League has heard sad stories such as yours before, ah! Far too often. Such barefaced amorality cannot go unchallenged. Is this not a Christian nation? The integrity of marriage is the foundation of the English character. Women of decency cannot be despoiled at will. Every man and woman throughout the land must deplore Mr. Camlet's behavior. It is more than ruination. Why, it's bigamy."

This fearful word, once said, lay between us like a loaded weapon. Mrs. Hartright consulted the watch pinned to her dress.

"You had better depart, sir, or you shall miss your tea."

"Quite, quite. There is not room in the dog-cart for four. Madam, let you stay warm here at home. Miss Sarah, perhaps you could come with me and lend a womanly hand of help. Miss Halcombe is clearly overset and ill, and must not be tried any more."

All was in a haze around me as I was loaded into the dog-cart and taken to the station. In my borrowed shawls and tatterdemalion gown blotched with water-stains I must have looked like a madwoman. Sarah and the good reverend saw me into my compartment and watched anxiously as the train pulled away. Kind Mrs. Hartright's final gift to me was a stack of handkerchiefs, for my tears had not ceased to fall.

Not until the train pulled into Carlisle did my mind clear a little so that I saw who was impatiently waiting for me on the platform. "Oh, my Laura," I cried. "At least your love does not fail!" And I fell into her embrace.

Limmeridge, 18 February

Oh, the joy of opening my own dear journal volume again! I had never thought to see it more. It was lost along with so many greater things. But at bottom we are all children. The heavens may fall and the world whirl to its end, but if the girl may clutch her rag doll she holds a moiety of comfort.

The crumpled and tear-stained loose pages I have inserted before this point I have reclaimed from Walter. When Laura met me at the station I was incoherent, but the written account gave my dear ones the outline of what had happened. A hot bath, a toddy, and bed were my destiny, and to my bed I kept for more than a week.

At first I was really ill, but I did not rise even after my weary frame was restored. If I were the heroine of a lending-library novel I could look to die outright. At least I could spend the rest of my days propped up on pillows in a lassitude of despair, sustained on nothing but spoonfuls of bread jelly and cups of tea. Besides, I had not a scrap of clothing in the house but the stained and torn primrose silk gown I had arrived in.

Alas! It was true what I had told him. My affections are narrow and deep-rooted. Once planted, my love cannot be plucked out without violence to body and soul. That Theo had believed in his wife's demise was clear. He had been astonished to see her standing in our drawing room. But that she had so instantly supplanted my place in his heart was a terrible wound.

I cast my recollection back to that one glimpse of Margaret Camlet. Memory conjured up the bright-gold hair waving in a riot of curls around the perfect oval of her face, and the dark-blue eyes. The resemblance to Micah and Lottie was undeniable. She had been tall, taller than Theo or myself, and proportioned like Artemis. How could Theo not fall to his knees and adore this goddess? I remembered how he had described her: like the rising sun. That was no fond exaggeration but a plain and exact description. She was in every way the opposite of my swarthy and ill-featured self.

I wanted with all my soul to believe in him, to believe he had not wiped me utterly from his regard. And it was impossible. There was no evidence for it. Perhaps it is my fate to be forever undesired, unloved. To reconcile the conflict was so Sisyphean that I turned for relief to books.

Most of the volumes he had sent me were in Hampstead, but there were a few of the old Limmeridge books on my bedside shelf. I opened *Jane Eyre* and read it again with aching envy. Fortunate, fortunate young Jane! She had been lucky enough to escape with her virtue. She was not a ruined female, forever barred from decent company. She had hope, prospects. And, oh blessed and happy beyond measure! She had eventually been united with her beloved.

My hopes are gone, all gone. A woman who cohabits with a man for months outside the bond of marriage is lost. We all knew it. I reached for the golden prize, for happiness, and not only had I missed my grasp. I had fallen forever from virtue into ruination.

For the first time in my life I heard words of venom on my gentle Laura's lips. To forgive her own oppressors had been the work of a moment, but on my behalf her fury blazed hot.

"How dare he," she almost hissed to Walter. "That vile, iniquitous scum. He has broken the heart and smirched the honor of the best woman in the world. Something must be done, Walter. This outrage cannot stand. He has done her irreparable harm, and he must pay for it."

"My dear, he should be flogged at the cart's tail, I agree," Walter said. "But let us not damage our case with ill-considered haste. We have Marian safe here, and her account of the events in hand. I have written to the Reverend Angier and expect his return letter any day. Once these testimonies are gathered, they will open the door to legal action. Thank God, past experiences may now guide our hands."

A week after my return the letter from the reverend arrived. I copy it here:

12 February 1858

My dear Mr. Hartright:
In reply to yours of the 6th inst. I write with an account of my pastoral call upon the Camlet ménage at Sandett House. It is all too true. The woman in residence there is indubitably the first Mrs. Camlet, Margaret, returned from the dead. I knew her in earlier days, when I attempted (with small success) to reconcile the young couple, and there can be no possibility of mistake.

I spoke first to her. Mrs. Camlet expressed a very proper surprise that her lawfully wedded husband had, entirely without her knowledge, contracted actual matrimony with another female. However, she takes no great offence at his bigamous state, saying that Theophilus might maintain her in a separate ménage with her good will if he insisted upon cohabiting with another wife. I omit here a great deal of highly deplorable political philosophy about the role of marriage in society which I do not feel I can summarise with justice. But she holds that however he has wronged her, he is her husband, and she is Mrs. Theophilus Camlet. This last at least is sound Christian doctrine, and I could not but agree, although her other ideas fill me with dismay. She offered no explanation for the report of her death that we all relied upon, and attributed it to the carelessness of foreigners.

When I consulted Mr. Camlet himself, he expressed a horror of his situation which may or may not be sincere. Mr. Camlet avers that he will petition for a divorce *a mensa et thoro* – a judicial separation. I could not countenance this. To put aside one's wedded wife is plainly contrary to church teaching. I warned him of his Christian duty to at least attempt to reconcile with Mrs. Camlet. Insurmountable incompatibility, personal distress, even pain and suffering can in no way excuse a man and his wife from living together under one roof. Divorce is not to be thought of.

I thank Providence that the issue will be determined in the courts, and that I therefore need not judge. I have consulted with your worthy mother Mrs. Caroline Hartright, and we are united in the resolution to lay a complaint before the proper authorities. To live in sin is of course deplorable. But barefaced bigamy is an open desecration of an ancient Christian sacrament, and erodes the very national morality of England. I am assured by her that you will be in agreement with this course of action. Unless I hear from you by return I propose to render the case unto Caesar on Monday. Thanks to my leadership of the Female Preventative and Reformatory League I am certain of a hearing, and I trust that a swift prosecution will soon follow.

I am fully aware of the fearful situation of your sister-in-law, now Miss Marian Halcombe. She is purely a victim in this. But her character is ruined beyond any recovery for all time. She has now but little recourse, but a suit may be brought to at least ensure she wrings some monetary recompense from her despoiler. I counsel you to secure legal assistance with all speed, to ensure that her interests are represented. A lawyer may advise you upon the timing of her case. If it is filed after Mr. Camlet's bigamy conviction I believe it will be unassailable.

I remain,

> Your ob't servant,
> Rev. Thomas Wilfrid Angier

N.B. Mrs. Hartright asks me to add that she has prevailed upon the Camlets to pack Miss Halcombe's belongings up. She had the trunk conveyed to the station yesterday and it should arrive shortly after this letter.

Laura brought this letter up to my room the very afternoon it arrived. I read it sitting up in bed while she dandled the baby. "Bigamy?"

"He is surely guilty of that crime," Laura said with an almost feline satisfaction. "Walter says that the maximum sentence is seven years' penal servitude. I think that's just, do not you?"

"No, I do not! At least …"

"Marian. Can you still love him?"

"It seems dreadfully poor-spirited, I know," I said, with tears in my eyes. "Like a spaniel, cringing back to be kicked again. But he was astonished at the sight of Margaret Camlet. He had indeed thought her dead."

Laura had read my written account, and now she frowned, remembering. "He could just as well have been astonished that she had returned so suddenly from Europe."

"I don't know what to think or believe, Laura." I wiped my eyes. "I might have misjudged his character, swayed by affection. But you and Walter, you could not. If only he would speak to me, or write."

"That he has made not the least effort to do so tells us everything we need to know," Laura said. "Walter has gone to Carlisle to consult some legal men, and he'll stop at the station to see if your trunk is come. And see now, you must give over weeping. Here's little Fairlie, to make his dear aunt smile again!"

The daylight is short at this season, and it was already dusk when Walter returned, and my tin trunk with him. The servants carried it up to my room and I undid the cording. All my clothing was bundled in higgledy-piggledy by careless hands. The luxurious veneered traveling dressing case with its gold and crystal fittings, my wedding gift from Laura, was crammed at the side. But when I lifted out the last crumpled petticoat at the bottom, there lay this journal!

I leafed through its smooth pages, shedding an occasional tear over the record of happier days in the past. But stuck in at the back was a note, in a hand not my own. From Theo! It was a single loose sheet of scratch paper, nearly illegible, not his usual careful copperplate. I held the sheet close to the candle and breathlessly read:

My dearest girl,
I am so very, very sorry. I have destroyed you for ever, and myself as well. Believe that I love you and shall always and eternally be,

Your own,
THWC

And all at once I was myself again. The roots of my life were firmly in place. I brushed and pinned up my hair, donned some of my newly-arrived garments and went down to dinner. He still loved me! I needed no more.

Neither Walter nor Laura was so untactful as to comment upon my sudden revival. There was no moment for conversation until the children were put to bed, but then we retired to the drawing room. Laura sat down at the piano and practiced her scales with the soft pedal down. It is rare that she has time for music these days, with the new baby.

Meanwhile Walter spoke of the lawyer he had chosen to represent me. "Mr. Binyon is well regarded in family law, and has practiced both in London and the north," he said. "He warned me that you have little recourse, Marian. If the villain lied to you from the outset about his married state –"

"No, Walter," I said quietly. "That I do not believe. I believe he wed me in good faith, truly believing himself to be a widower."

"Mr. Binyon gives it no credence. It is unheard of."

"Mr. Binyon does not know him. And, Walter, to what purpose? Why enact a fraud? I'm no heiress, as Laura was. I'm plain, poor, and no longer young. There is no gain that can accrue to any man by marrying me."

"Your purity of mind does you credit, Marian." Walter's gaze, fixed upon the fire in the grate, was dark. "There's always something a man may gain by marriage." I blushed hotly when I realised what he referred to, but could not gainsay him. "If you're no longer confined to your chamber, I'll send Mr. Binyon word. He wished to call and interview you as soon as you were well enough to receive him."

I agreed this should be done. At least, if Walter files suit against him, Theo shall have to talk to me. How foolish I had been, to just walk away from my wedded husband and the home we shared. Perhaps Theo believed I had stormed off in a rage, seeing myself betrayed. I should have immediately gone back into the house and confronted Margaret Camlet. Never again, I vowed, would I fail to fight for my happiness – for what was mine.

19 February

He is come! Oh, I am so happy, I am almost dizzy with joy. But let me record it from the beginning.

This morning I was not entirely recovered from my malaise, but little Wally would have none of it. Having heard that I was down to supper the night before, he begged for all the old tiring games that we used to play. The poor little man, now that he shares his parents with an infant brother he misses his Aunt Marian sadly. We romped all the morning, so that after the midday meal I yearned for a respite. I said, "I dare swear you have forgot all your ABCs, Wally. Let your Aunt Marian sit here by the nursery fire and hear you say them."

Immediately he went and fetched his alphabet book, and climbed into my lap. He had of course not forgotten a jot, the dear clever lad. "A is for apple," he said, with his finger under the bright pictures. "And ape. And B, it is for bear."

"And what else?" I prompted.

He looked trustingly up at me with those big blue eyes. "Baby. Will you have a baby, Aunty?"

I gaped at him, at a loss to reply. The nursemaid saved me by bursting in and crying, "Miss Marian, 'tis Mr. Camlet in the drive!"

With a gasp I leaped to my feet and thrust little Wally into her arms. As I ran down around the corner of the main staircase I saw him just come through the doorway. The butler was taking his hat, and the housemaid had not even shut the door. The mere sight of the top of his head made me weak. Oh, my poor darling man! In this brief time his formerly neat whiskers and moustache had gone untrimmed and blurred into a short dense beard. His spectacles were fogged from the cold, so that he did not see me.

Overcome, I sat down on the top step of the landing as he wiped them, just as Laura came out of the parlour. "Theophilus Camlet," she cried.

"Laura?" He put his spectacles back on again and hesitantly held his hand out to her.

She brushed it aside. Never, never have I seen Laura be discourteous! "You scoundrel," she said in low passionate tones. "You dare to come here? I had wanted to greet you with a blow across the face, but I find I cannot do it. Thank God, there is one here who can. Walter!"

To my complete horror Walter followed close behind her – with a riding crop in his hand. "I promised Laura that you should pay, Camlet," he declared. "For daring to believe that the ladies in this house have no protector."

I jumped to my feet. "Walter! No, stop!" I flew down the stair and skimmed right under Walter's raised hand into Theo's arms.

When he kissed me our tears mingled. We were both babbling at once, words like forgive and sorry, when suddenly the door flew open again, tearing out of Phoebe's grasp. Micah and Lottie pushed in, calling my name. The noise redoubled, filling Limmeridge's grand front hall with clamour. The February wind buffeted through the open door. I hugged them, Theo hugged me, and Laura said, "Walter, can it be that he truly loves her?"

"I do," Theo said over the cries of his children. "Hartright, Laura – I would sooner cut my own throat than hurt Marian. My calamity is overwhelming, but far, far the worst of it is the damage and pain I have caused her."

I intervened to master the chaos. "Now why are we standing here in this chilly hall? Phoebe, close the door. Laura, let us adjourn to the parlour, where there's a good fire. Louis, see that tea is brought in directly. Lottie, there's no need to cry any more. Has no one combed your hair through this past week? Nanny shall see to it directly you have some refreshment. Micah, you remember from the wedding, the way to the nursery. Here is your cousin Wally to lead the way. Wally, I rely upon you to be hospitable to your cousins, and to share your toys."

Nanny and the nursery maid took charge of the little ones, while I drew Theo through into the parlour and installed him in the armchair nearest the fire. Walter followed behind me, protesting. "Marian, we're filing suit against Camlet. Mr. Binyon will wait upon you on Monday to hear your account. You cannot set a legal opponent by the fire and give him tea."

Paying no heed to this, Theo pulled a hassock up for me. "A wise man once observed that any tragedy could be converted into comedy by having the principals sit down."

With an irritable gesture Walter flung the whip into the corner. "Is levity suitable in your straits, Camlet?"

"If it would give you relief, Hartright, to accuse me of hiding behind the skirts of women and children," Theo said mildly, "do indulge yourself. Only humor keeps me from despair." When he looked at me he did not seem able to keep from smiling. The sight filled me with joy, and I sat on the hassock to enjoy it better. How could I ever have doubted him, even for an instant?

He held my hands in both his own. "I thought you had left me. I ran to the door, and you were gone into the storm. Only when Mrs. Hartright called for your trunk did I learn where you had taken refuge. I thought that in your disgust you had washed your hands of me and mine forever. I came here to fling myself upon your mercy. And I find your forgiveness poured out unasked into my lap, like a river of gold."

"I thought you had lost your love for me. That you wanted me gone."

"Never!"

Walter broke in on our avowals. "Camlet, I believe we all see the truth of it, but I will ask you to state it now, for all to hear. You did not intend bigamy. You did not plan this crime. You had no intention to ruin Marian."

"By my hope of salvation, Hartright." The light in his eyes as he gazed at me warmed me better than the coal fire. I had not recognised the lump of ice that was lodged in my heart, until it was melted.

Laura, bless her, instantly repented of her harshness. "Oh, thank heaven. Theo, I refused to take your hand just now. I should have been guided by Marian's heart, ever a reliable compass. Forgive me my uncharity in your time of trouble, and count me your friend henceforward."

"Thank you, Laura." He looked away from me, into the fire. "But … my lawyers inform me my intent counts for nothing in the eyes of the law. I shall be taken up for the crime of bigamy soon. The police have stayed their hand only so that I may settle my most urgent affairs. I do not see how I can escape conviction. I am indeed guilty of this heinous crime, and the maximum sentence is seven years' imprisonment."

I could feel his hands in mine grow cold. "This speedy prosecution is my mother's work," Walter said.

"Say rather the Rev. Angier. Above all things he abhors immorality. To have so blatant an offender in his flock is intolerable to him. And he has influence."

"God have mercy on you, Camlet," Walter said.

"And … I cannot look to survive it."

"No, how can that be?" Laura cried. "Prisons are better than they were in our parents' day."

"Only in the sense that the rack and thumbscrew are now out of fashion." Theo took a deep quiet breath. "Do you remember *You Visited Me*, my dearest? The collected sermons of a prison chaplain. I sent the book to you last spring. Much of the harsher material in the Rev. Esterforth's manuscript had to be cut for the sake of the readers' sensibilities, but I handled the original text. I will not harrow you with the details, but I know what is before me. I am neither tall nor vigorous. I do not do well in closed spaces, without air and light, and I have no influential acquaintance to plead for better treatment. Even among felons there is an hierarchy. I will be among the lowest of the low, one of those convicted of concupiscently preying upon women or children. The hardest bed, the scantiest food, and the harshest toil shall be my lot. My mind, or my body, or my soul – one or another of these will assuredly crack."

His voice held steady, but in spite of the good fire he was

shivering. I was close enough to see it. For my own weak self I had wept copiously, but for him I held strong. He would need my strength in this trial. "What can we do, Theo? Walter, surely there is something that can be done."

Theo said, "There is. Here, my love. Take this." From his breast pocket he drew a packet of papers, and put them into my hands. "Marian, in preparation for this great legal storm that is to break over my head, I have made over all I own to you. Every shilling I possess. All is now yours."

My mouth dropped open in astonishment. "This is too much, Theo."

"It is all I can do, my dearest love. The business itself and the house are tied to Margaret, the co-heir. She may have them. As a business Covenant is withering fast. Not a one of my customers cares to purchase religious books from a man accused of bigamy, and she thinks of turning it into a political publisher. I want you to know that this is already fixed, and all the legal matters relating to the deeds of gift are accomplished, before I make my final request of you."

Unable to speak, I turned the packet of papers, still warm from his pocket, over in my hands. But Walter spoke for me. "And what is that?"

"It is that Marian, and Hartright, you and your wife as well, raise up my children. Of your Christian charity I beg you to take them in."

"And if we do not?"

"I cannot permit their mother to take them. An adulteress is not fit to raise such innocents. Rather than permit her pernicious influence to blight their young lives, I have instructed my lawyers to place them in a respectable orphanage. They will have nothing, since all my substance is now Marian's."

No lamps were lit, and the day was fading fast. In the firelight Walter's brow was lowering. "It's a species of blackmail. Forcing your money upon her so that she has no choice but to do your will."

Theo bent his head under this onslaught. "Hartright, I can only fling myself upon her mercy, and yours. You see before you a man stripped of everything – good name, character, love, family and career. I've made what recompense I can to the woman I love.

It is these complex legal matters that have delayed my journey north. Whatever my children's fate, it cannot be worse than my own. Marian is free to do as she wills. In token of that I've stripped myself of every farthing in her favor, without precondition or even her knowledge. She now has in her power not only the maintenance of the children, but my own legal defense, for I cannot now even pay my solicitors. If she wishes to leave me to my fate, then so let it be."

He held out the seed, but would not confine the bird! The protest burst from my lips: "No, Theo, no! How can you even ask? Of course I'll take them, and love them as my own."

Laura said, "Can you contravene the natural rights of the mother who gave them birth like this?"

"I can," Theo said. "English law still protects the father's rights to a far greater extent than the mother's. No judge will give custody to a confessed adulteress. With my written instruction I can allocate the children as I wish, even to the workhouse. But their best and happiest destiny must be with you, Marian."

"And – here? Walter, what is your will in this?"

Laura cried, "Marian's home is here, Walter. And whatever else, the children are surely innocent."

Walter heaved a sigh. "I must concur. Yes, yes, it shall be so, Marian. Have mercy, and don't weep. You shall all live here at Limmeridge House. And now for all love let's go in to dinner. I see Louis ready to call us to table, and Camlet, you look to be a man in need of sustenance. You will of course stay the night."

Laura had ordered roast lamb, a heartening meal. With good food and wine came new strength and hope. "Surely, Theo," she said, "they cannot condemn you to certain death. You are no criminal."

Walter said. "I agree, Camlet. It may not come to penal servitude. Surely your lawyers mount a defense."

"What defense is there? I stood before God's altar with two women who yet live. There are two parish registries with my signature upon the marriage lines."

"But you did not mean to do this," I said. "It was a mistake."

"Yes, I was misled. By..."

"By the letter that the priest wrote you," Walter said thoughtfully. "From Salerno, announcing the first Mrs. Camlet's death. How did that letter come to be written, Camlet? There's something extraordinarily fishy there."

"She was, manifestly, not dead," Laura said. "Surely a man of the cloth would not lie. He must have been deceived in some way."

Walter said, "Do you still have it? You showed us the original, in Italian, and the translation."

"My solicitors have both documents," Theo said, "but copies shall be made."

"If it can be proved you were merely deceived and not malevolent, then English justice may save you," I said. "They cannot imprison you for a crime you had not intended."

"We may hope for justice to be done," Walter said. "But as we have seen, one cannot depend solely upon the courts. When you return to town to give yourself up, Camlet, I shall go with you. There are things that may be done to aid you."

"No man could be a better help," I said, heartened. Family history has shown that Walter can accomplish anything.

"Thank you, Hartright," Theo said, with real gratitude. "You're true as steel."

"And there are other possible avenues. How valid, for instance, was your marriage to Mrs. Camlet? Who officiated over it?"

"Her grandfather," Theo said, "a canon at the cathedral at Winchester. Not promising."

"History does not perfectly repeat itself, dear," Laura said to Walter, fondly.

Assured of Theo's love, I could be generous. "What does she make of your peril, my dearest? Could Margaret Camlet cast some light upon this erroneous report of her death?"

Theo stared down at his laden plate as if appetite failed. "You recall that we have almost nothing in common. She has told me nothing of these intervening years. She is writing a book, a memoir I believe of the sights and people she saw while on the Continent. She says I may read of her travels then. It is to be the first publication of the reconstituted press. She spends all day at this, shut up in her room. She refused to come down and meet my lawyers, and when I carried the letter and its translation up to her, asking for an explanation, she had no suggestions. In Campania they will say and do anything, she says."

"She seems scarcely interested in your peril."

"Perhaps I describe her character badly. Her mind is very different from mine."

When the meal was over we took tea in the parlour. The children were ready for bed, and came in to say goodnight. When kisses and hugs had been liberally dispensed and they were safely gone with their nurse, I at last nerved myself to speak. "Before we adjourn, my dear ones," I said, "I too have a secret. Which I must tell, here and now."

Laura stared. "You, Marian?"

Such announcements should be joyful. I sat looking at my own hands clenched in my lap. They were ringless, for I had put off the antique opal. I was no longer married, and now the most excruciating of all confessions had to be made. I've always been bold, but it took all my courage to speak forthrightly now. "Theo, I'm expecting a token of your affection. I calculate the baby should arrive in September."

I looked up and watched with despair as my dear man slowly bowed his head under this fearsome new burden. He hid his face in his hands. Only one sob escaped him, a horrible harsh noise that seemed to tear at his chest.

Laura, ever faithful, instantly exclaimed, "Marian, don't be afraid. I'll be with you. Childbed is a trial, but endurable."

"Shall you, Laura?" Theo raised his head to look not at her, but at Walter. Behind the eyeglasses his gaze was grim. "To take in a fallen woman, your sister ruined by a despicable bigamist, is one thing. To allow an unwed mother to give birth to a bastard under your roof, and raise the fatherless thing beside your own children? They shall be tarred with the same brush. Their prospects will be blighted, the family name clouded. Your neighbours and friends will fall away if you condone this. It's beyond the pale of propriety."

"Then so it must be," Laura said. "I will not desert Marian."

But we both glanced at Walter. As the man of the house he had the final word. He leaned forward, elbows on knees, so that none could see his thought. After a long pause Theo drew a deep breath. "It's too sore a trial, Hartright. A straw may break the camel's back. You need not draw your entire household into the morass of my downfall. Marian is now a woman of some substance. She may make her home anywhere, and the child – all the children – with her."

Laura leaped to her feet. "I beg you, Walter. Do not force me to choose between the two people I love most in all the world! Please, at least let Marian stay here until her confinement. Then after, if you will, drive her out."

"My darling, I absolutely forbid you to kneel before me." Walter smiled thinly at her, slowly straightening up. "Limmeridge is famously home to eccentrics. Shall I banish my own nephew or niece? No. Let the child be the equivalent of the late Mr. Fairlie's bibelots and portfolios and smelling bottles, my personal oddity. Camlet, Marian and the babe shall always have a home here. I shall raise him or her as my own. And if the county looks down its nose and shuns us, the devil fly away with them."

Walter is never profane, so we knew what this cost him. Both of us burst into tears, and Theo jumped up to wring Walter's hand.

"I must return to town," Theo said. "I look to be arrested and charged at any moment. Now that the children and Marian are safe, I can face my fate with courage."

"And I go with you," Walter said. "We'll take the first train tomorrow morning."

20 February

Last night before bed I was in my chamber, writing the above in this journal by the light of my bedroom candle. I heard nothing, no tap at the door or step in the hall. The entire house was silent and asleep, and the only sound was the far-off mutter and tumble of the wind-lashed surf. A late-winter storm was blowing in from the Atlantic.

But I could feel a presence, and I hastened to open my door. Theo stood there bundled in his brown brocade dressing gown, not knocking nor even touching the door, but simply drooping unhappily. He stood hunched with his hands tucked in his armpits against the chill, so still that no light flashed from his spectacles.

"Oh my dear," I whispered, and drew him in.

I shut the door softly behind him and held him close. When he pressed his lips to mine it was for comfort and not desire, I knew. Misery and guilt seemed to flow out from his very skin, and he murmured the words into my ear as if he could not bear to watch me hear them. "It's hard to admit my weakness. But I'm afraid, Marian. Afraid of the trial, afraid of imprisonment. To be closed in, in the dark... And, oh heavens. You expect my child. And you must bear it alone. My fearless bird, I lured you near, and now you're ensnared in my ruin. And our child also. To be illegitimate – oh God, have mercy upon the poor little thing. It shall bear the stigma all its life."

I hugged him close. "I know, my dearest."

"How can you forgive me like this? I've utterly failed you, and the child."

"It's not your fault."

"But this..." He kissed me again. Suddenly I was very aware of the texture of his dressing gown, the slight scratchiness of the brocade. And every inch of what was beneath it, warming under my palms. "This shall be my fault. What I do now, I know to be wrong. I'm married to another."

"No, it is I, my dearest. Let all the blame be laid upon the weakness of woman." His hands slid down my back, and even through the layers of dressing gown, bedjacket and flannel nightgown I was shatteringly alive to his touch. "Did she...?" There seemed no good way to ask this.

"No, we have not been ... close. In many years."

"But you confided your feelings to her. Your fears, your hopes."

His smile in the beard was without humor. "She assured me that she's been in prison herself, and it's not such a much."

"Then I am your wife, and you my husband. For better or for worse, for richer, for poorer, in sickness and in health."

"And I love you more than words can express." My hair hung down braided ready for sleep, and he lifted the long black length of it and put it around his own neck, binding us together.

"How I've longed to do this." When I brushed the over-long strands back from his brow I noticed that my hand was trembling. "Anyway, I can hardly become more *enceinte*." Almost he laughed, and my heart lifted as I blew out the candle.

That night was a sweet core in much bitterness, taken in the knowledge of bitter draughts yet to come. I made him welcome in every way I knew, so that he should have this little joy to warm his heart later. He dreaded the darkness of his narrow cell, but I feared the loneliness. Isolation is by intent one of the chief pangs of prison. They even hood the prisoners in the exercise yard, lest they glimpse another human face. I kissed his eyes, his brow, with terror and grief in my heart. No one would kiss him, perhaps even touch him again, for years. Men are driven mad by such cruel treatment.

"You are my true mate," he murmured in the dark. "Never forget that, never let them take that from you. Promise me."

"I promise," I whispered. "And you are mine. Forever."

"Until death do us part."

My room is the one I have always slept in, next to Laura's, so we had to be very quiet. Our brief happiness was so great, we fell asleep in each other's arms. I woke with a start to hammering on my door. Voices I did not know were calling Theo's name. Hastily I dragged my dressing gown back on over my bare body. "My dearest, wake!"

Before I could open it my door was flung open. "Here he is, sir," the uniformed policeman shouted. "Red-handed, as it were."

"Sirs, your noise disturbs the ladies," Walter said, at his heels.

"No ladies here," the policeman said, ogling me up and down.

I clutched my dressing gown around me, gasping. The shock was like being dashed with a bucket of cold water. Walter and Laura's love had been so encompassing, this was the first stinging taste of my fallen state.

Theo had pulled on his dressing gown. His pale cheeks flushed scarlet at this impudence, and I saw again the furious paladin on his black horse. "You dare speak your sauce, sir?"

With a supreme effort I put a restraining hand on his arm. "It's nothing, dearest."

Walter said, "Speak respectfully to all of my household, sergeant, or I report you to your superior officer."

A second policeman pushed into the room. "No offense, sir, no offense. You, there. You are Theophilus Henton William Camlet?"

Theo put on his glasses. "Yes, I am."

"We have a warrant for your arrest. Please come with us."

"May I dress for the journey?"

There was some reluctance about this. "You cannot let the man travel in his night garments," Walter interposed. "It's winter. It would be indecent. Women and children may be on the train. And his clothing and baggage are just here, down the hall."

It was agreed that the proprieties had to be observed, and Theo was allowed to put on his suit and cram his possessions back into his carpet bag. Meanwhile Laura darted into my room and helped me dress. "They may let you say goodbye," she said. "Quickly, my love, quickly!"

We were waiting downstairs in the hall when they took him out. My poor Theo! He was ghastly pale, but calm. He was able to choke out, "Hartright. Laura. Thank you for all your great charity." But when he came to me he could not speak, and nor could I. I made to embrace him, just one last time. They thrust me back, and I fell wailing into Laura's arms.

☙ Walter Hartright's narrative ❧

I arrived in London late today, and took a room at the Mahlstick. Though I'm no longer a professional, I maintain my club membership specifically for trips to town. The day of Camlet's arrest had been full of distress. Marian very naturally was overcome, and the Camlet children could not understand what had happened to their father. The facts of his situation are beyond juvenile comprehension. They had been told only that they were to stay with their new mother Miss Marian for a period while their father was away.

Our nanny wisely kept them from going downstairs to see Camlet being dragged away by the police. But then we were faced with explaining his vanishment without even saying goodbye. A responsible father who knew well the needs of his motherless children, Camlet's habit had been always to bid them farewell, every time he left them. Now only Laura's loving persuasion reconciled them to staying at Limmeridge House in his absence, and she was forced to promise that they would be reunited soon. God grant that she not be forsworn.

In this turmoil we had all forgotten that Mr. Binyon the solicitor was scheduled to call. On Monday I was just loading my carpetbag onto the pony-chaise when his carriage came rattling up the drive. "How are you, Mr. Hartright," he cried jovially, lowering the window and leaning a plump elbow out. "Glad to see you looking so well, sir. Is the lady ready to be interviewed? I hope you aren't going to slope off and leave me. It never fails. The ladies always resort to tears, and I abhor a weeping woman."

"Mr. Binyon, I regret you've had your journey for nothing. I no longer contemplate legal action against my brother-in-law, and I apologise."

"Not at all, not at all. If you call him your brother-in-law then clearly you no longer consider him a mortal legal adversary! But it's chilly work so early in the morning, and in February, too. You'll invite me in and give me tea, eh? Or small beer. Never prudent to discuss these things out in the drive, never."

This was true enough, and Mr. Binyon's opinion would be helpful. I brought him in to the study, where we could talk in private. This dark paneled room is no artist's workroom or studio – its natural light is inadequate. It has always been the administrative centre of the estate. It was stacked with files and papers, the deeds and contracts in their boxes on the shelves. The only item in it not of the strictest practicality was a split nautilus shell the size of my head, which hovered on its stand pale and glimmering on the mantelpiece.

Over refreshments I laid out the entire sorry business. Mr. Binyon heard the tale with interest. "Ah, what would the legal profession do without the ladies? Marriages are a great source of good business. Although not bigamy! That's a little more rare, sir. Most men, if they feel the need to stray, they simply do it. Like dogs, the animal nature sweeping them away without fuss or feathers. They feel no need to actually walk into a church with the new woman."

"Camlet has convinced Marian, and all of us, that he had never intended a crime or deception. He genuinely believed his first wife to be dead."

"Always view the body," Mr. Binyon said. "That's my advice to you, Mr. Hartright, should you ever be in this situation. Too late for that now, eh? And now the unlucky fellow's encumbered with two wives."

"They've arrested him on the charge of bigamy."

"Quick work they do in London, they do indeed. And may I hope that your sister-in-law will move to sue for recompense of her honor and good name?"

"He already made over all his property to her, without condition. There's nothing left to sue for."

This made Mr. Binyon laugh heartily. "How shall poor lawyers put bread in their mouths, if their clients are so brimful of the milk of human kindness?"

"If he can be acquitted somehow, Camlet vows he will divorce his first wife for her longstanding adultery, and marry, or remarry, Miss Halcombe."

"Remarry, that's very good. Wise to be sure all the tees are crossed and the i's dotted. Quick and quiet is what I recommend. An archbishop's licence, not banns. Scandal enough as it is." He cocked his head over the teacup at me, like a plump and intelligent grey parrot over its cuttlebone. "But allow me to point out to me some legal wrinkles that you possibly do not know of."

"I would be grateful for your expertise."

"In the ordinary run of events – if such things can ever be termed ordinary! Well, sir, until this year even the blatant adultery of a wife did not allow the husband to divorce her."

"What?"

"Indeed, Mr. Hartright, indeed. The cuckold had an undoubted legal right to divorce. Not vice versa, I should tell you, by the bye. When the gentleman strays the lady can whistle for it. What is sauce for the goose is not in this case sauce for the gander. But the divorce could only be secured at great cost. An Act of Parliament. Thousands of pounds, putting it out of the reach of all but the most wealthy. You have heard the jibe, that both rich and poor are entirely at liberty to sleep under bridges?"

I smiled at this even though it was not very amusing. Mr. Binyon went on. "The most a husband of moderate means could do was to file for a legal separation. But just last year one of the major renovations to British jurisprudence was passed into law, the Matrimonial Causes Act. Supervision of these issues has been moved from the ecclesiastical side to the civil side. This very year, a new Court of Divorce and Matrimonial Causes opened, to hear cases and, ultimately, dissolve marriages. Mr. Camlet may now lodge a petition for divorce *a vinculo matrimonii*. If this is granted it is more than a legal separation. He would be entirely freed from the bonds of his first marriage, as free as any man to marry again."

"Great heavens. Then my sister-in-law is saved. Camlet's case is unassailable. Mrs. Camlet was openly adulterous, and eloped to the Continent with her lover."

"Ah! It may well be that Miss Halcombe has the best timing in Britain, and we should make our fortunes by forming a syndicate to invest in her wagers on horse races and prize fights. Alternatively, she may be an unfortunate lady indeed. The first thing which the Court will look to when a charge of adultery is preferred is the dates. The date of the charge, the date of the criminal fact charged, and the date of its becoming known by the party alleging it. To put it more simply, sir. Under English law the privilege of petitioning for divorce is withdrawn if the husband is not prompt."

"Prompt? To divorce her, you mean?"

"Indeed that is what I mean. If the husband is too patiently long-suffering – if he allows the situation to stand while a considerable time passes – it may be deemed that he has consented to his wife's unfaithfulness. That he has condoned her adultery, do you understand me, Mr. Hartright? And in this eventuality he has no further recourse. No divorce is possible."

"Great heavens. What would be the point of such a law? It sounds like madness."

"One of those little wrinkles of our fine English legal system that make steady employment for lawyers, sir. If common sense sufficed in such cases, what need for barristers and solicitors? Are you familiar with *Scenes of Clerical Life*?"

"Is it a novel?"

"You do not take *Blackwood's Magazine*, I see. The stories that comprise that volume were published there last year. The author, one George Eliot, is actually a woman behind a *nom de plume*. Her real name is Evans, a Miss Mary Ann Evans. And she, sir, is the example that we lawyers point to when we are discussing this little legal wrinkle."

"I believe I have heard of her," I cried, enlightened. "Camlet was speaking of her marital entanglements. She's not married, but lives in sin with a paramour."

"Indeed, their situation is common talk in intellectual circles.

Her longtime companion, George Lewes, has a wife, Agnes. The foolish fellow allowed Agnes to stray for many years, even to present him with children sired by another man, his best friend, if you please. Some high-flown nonsense about free love. But you and I recognise it for what it was. Laziness! Always eschew it, Mr. Hartright, it never leads to good. In recent years Lewes made the acquaintance of a more prepossessing female, this Miss Evans. Then and only then did he discover a wish to divorce Agnes, and make an honest woman of his new love. And it was too late. He's trapped, sir. For the rest of his life."

"This must be a calamity for Miss Evans."

"She does not regard it in the slightest, sir. She's living with Lewes outside the bonds of matrimony, merry as a mouse in a Stilton, and writes her stories without the least trouble. A bright literary future is before her, and I look forward to her novels. But you see now the light their case may cast upon the Camlet marital situation."

"I do," I said slowly. "Camlet did not move to divorce his wife. At the outset because she had flown to the Continent, and then because he thought her dead. And now six years have passed."

"Exactly, you are most astute. He may find that he cannot now divorce her at all."

"Then the key point, it seems to me, is the passage of years," I said. "How many years are deemed to be too many?"

But this Mr. Binyon could not tell me, nor whether the law would apply to Camlet's situation at all. He took his departure shortly after this, still regretting the loss of Marian's promising lawsuit, and by that time I had missed the last train.

Because of the uncertainty, I resolved not to tell Marian or Laura the possible trouble that Mr. Binyon outlined to me. If Camlet is convicted of bigamy and sent to prison the issue will be moot until his release. The first and most vital task was to secure his exoneration, All other hurdles might be ignored until this was done.

I arrived in London on Tuesday. I began the work that very evening, late though it was, by sending a note to my good friend Professor Pesca, inviting him to dinner on the following day.

I would be remiss in my duty as a son and a brother if I were in London and did not call upon my mother and sister. I admit that when I went to their Hampstead cottage first thing Wednesday morning I had additional ends in view. It was a fine sunny day, quite clement for February. I had my cabman drop me at Sandett House half a mile up the lane.

The house was a handsome pale-red brick structure in the Georgian style, set well back from the lane. A short drive lined with winter-weary boxwood curved up to the graceful columned half-moon portico that sheltered the front door, and the metal jigsaw-work on the roof of a greenhouse could be glimpsed in the side garden. I rang the bell and gave my card. "The missus sees no male callers," the housemaid said.

I was dressed as a gentleman, the prosperous master of Limmeridge House, so I dared to ask, "Does she go out?"

"Not at all, sir. Given her circumstances."

Baulked, I turned away, very thoughtful. This was the gentle delicacy that one sees in the highly-bred lady in time of trouble: discreetly veiling herself from vulgar gaze and commentary, holding aloof from even the most distant taint of scandal, secluding herself in the sanctity and purity of her home. It was how my dearest Laura would behave – perhaps not Marian, who though a true gentlewoman is bolder and inclines towards action. A woman who deserted husband and children to elope with a Continental lover would be long past such exquisite care of her good name. It came to me that all I knew of Mrs. Camlet was what her estranged husband had told me. I still believed that Camlet was no deceiver. But could he be genuinely mistaken? He had admitted to us that he did not understand her. When man and wife are at odds, the truth becomes hard to discern.

Thus reflecting, I walked on to my mother's cottage. Here I was welcomed with the usual joy and a Bakewell tart fresh out of the oven. My mother prefers these delicacies made in small dishes rather than in a large tart pan, and when I saw half a dozen lined up to cool on the kitchen table I had an idea. "Mother, how would it be if you took a few of these over to Mrs. Camlet? I am told she does not go out."

"What a neighbourly thought, Walter," my kindly mother said.

"I'd be happy to help you carry the basket." While she

changed into a visiting dress I considered tactics. Mrs. Camlet knew that her husband had been arrested. And she had met Marian, and probably knew her maiden name. But Marian and Laura are but half-sisters. The name Hartright might be nothing to Mrs. Camlet but the surname of the pleasant neighbours down the lane. If Camlet had not told her their children had taken refuge under my roof, perhaps it would behoove me to hold my tongue on that point. And if that were so, then I should not tell my artless and sociable mother of our recent doings at Limmeridge, for she would infallibly confide all.

So it was I walked back up the lane again around three in the afternoon, this time with a fresh-baked excuse for a call in hand and my mother to pave the way for me. And sure enough, a call from an elderly neighbour of her former acquaintance was more acceptable to Mrs. Camlet. We were shown straight into the drawing room.

This was a handsome and modern chamber at the front of the house, with all the trappings of prosperity – fashionable ferns in pots on stands, damask draperies layered over the windows, a large mirror and Chinese cloisonné vases on the mantel shelf, and a grand piano shawled and crowded with bibelots. In the north window on its own marble-topped table a large Wardian case stood overflowing with lush green fronds. Marian had not spoken of redecorating, so these must be the furnishings from before their marriage. Yet it did not seem a very suitable background for Camlet either. He's notably a modest and unpretentious man.

Then the lady came in, and all was made clear. This was my first introduction to Mrs. Camlet. Marian had mentioned fair curls and blue eyes. She had utterly failed to do her rival justice. Margaret Camlet was taller than I and robust, with the figure of a queen. Her face was the perfect oval that Raphael favored in painting his angels, and the arch of her brow as finely cut as a cameo. Suddenly my fingers itched to pick up my watercolour brushes; such beauty calls for art. Marian's coal-black hair, swarthy complexion and unharmonious features could not possibly compare.

The grace of face and form would have been attractive, except for the intelligence that glinted in those brilliant blue eyes.

On occasion Marian claims a manlike spirit. Long acquaintance with her assures me that this is a mere smokescreen flung up to placate or distract foolish men when she intends something they will complain of. At core her nature is purely feminine.

Now I saw the true thing, a man's heart and brain and strength in female form. It was terrifying. No, watercolour was inappropriate, too delicate. The lady should be painted in oil, as Boadicea in her war chariot, the blonde curls streaming out from under a bronzen helmet and her fierce sapphire gaze fixed upon her defeated and cringing foe.

My mother presented me. "Mrs. Camlet, my dear son Walter." I pressed my hostess's hand dumbly. Her attire – bloomers! Black cloth rationals, as they were termed at that period, were sometimes seen on women at athletic exercise. Tennis, perhaps. To see a female dressed thus, even in the seclusion of her own home, rendered me speechless. Clearly she was no gentle lady; I hardly knew where to look.

It was sunny enough that one of the windows stood open, and Mrs. Camlet sat with my mother on the sofa near it while I perched uneasily on a slippery horsehair armchair. My mother was too gracious to make any untoward comment, and made easy conversation about the difficulty of obtaining the almonds that go into Bakewells. "But I understand that almonds are grown in warmer climates," she said. "Did you ever see them growing in your travels?"

"If I did, I did not recognise them," Mrs. Camlet replied. "If a tree has not visible apples or oranges on it, it's unknown to me. But I believe almonds are grown all around the Mediterranean."

"And is that an Ottoman style you are wearing, my dear?" my mother continued. "It becomes you wonderfully."

"It shows that the Turk and the Mahometan have some things they could teach the English," Mrs. Camlet said. "Consider how much lighter and more comfortable I am dressed like this. They are named 'rationals' for a reason. Mrs. Hartright, you should try the fashion some day."

The idea almost made me laugh, but my mother said serenely, "I fear they would not suit my figure. And truth to tell, modern fashions do not look well on a woman of my years."

"Your petticoats, stays and gown must weigh a good thirty

pounds," Mrs. Camlet said. "When next you don them, gather all the garments together in your arms and judge the weight. Mr. Hartright, you are married? You may try the same experiment, when your wife dresses for the day. Would you hang a thirty pound weight around her neck every day? How do you think such a weight, carried every day for years, affects the back and knees? Men are ignorant of how burdensome and heavy the clothing mandated for women can be. Whereas my bloomers weigh ounces, merely."

"They look it," I said, and lest this sound rudely critical added, "And much safer."

"You are quite right," Mrs. Camlet said. "How many women fall down the stairs, their feet caught up in their layers of petticoats, or set their garments alight, standing too close to the fire?"

"And do the ladies of Constantinople truly wear these garments?" my mother asked. "Where else have you been?" Hastily I busied myself with my teacup, so that our hostess might be inclined to answer the question.

"I've never been so far east as Constantinople," Mrs. Camlet said. "But I've traveled in Germany, Austria and Italy."

"How far south in Italy did you go?" I said. Would she be so foolhardy as to mention Salerno?

"I went to Naples, and toured the ancient city buried at Pompeii," Mrs. Camlet said. "I did some sketches, and brought back a plate, a copy of a Corinthian antique. Would you like to see?"

Mother expressed interest, and when Mrs. Camlet brought out a red-figure plate depicting a Minotaur the talk was diverted into the Grand Tour. Meanwhile I took the sketchbook, having a professional interest in such things. It was of cheap German manufacture, with a red paper cover. A schoolboy might have carried it. The pages at the front were small studies in charcoal of Roman sites and antiquities, indifferently and hastily executed with poor handling of perspective. Mrs. Camlet had plainly never been instructed in landscape or architectural rendering. Even Marian, who claims to be devoid of talent, was a better artist, and Laura left Mrs. Camlet quite at the post.

But I happened to let the volume slip from my knees, and as

I caught it back again I glimpsed a great black scorch mark on the last pages. Turning the book over and paging from back to front I saw that three pages had been charred, almost completely destroyed by fire. Whatever images they had held were lost beyond recall. Beyond the ruined pages were more drawings of a very different sort.

These were expertly executed in fine hard pencil, and seemed to be diagrams for the assembly of a device or machine. There was no scale indicated, so it was hard to say how large the final construction would be. Unless the small outline in blue pencil of an outspread hand in one corner was an indication – this would make the device roughly the size of a pony. I know nothing of machines, and so did not understand what I was looking at. But I do have an eye for draughtsmanship. These were drawn by a different hand, for a deliberate purpose. These were diagrams, meant to convey information. There was an initial in the corner of each page, a W. Was this part of Theophilus Camlet's monogram?

"Oh," Mrs. Camlet exclaimed. "Don't look at those, they're dull. Those were left from the original owner of the sketchbook. It was given to me by Louis." She took the book from me and turned it right-side up again before passing it to my mother.

"And who was Louis?" I asked, as carelessly as I could.

"My lover," Mrs. Camlet replied readily.

My poor mother! Her thin cheeks flushed pink with embarrassment. I said, "You are a proponent of more modern relationships between the sexes, then."

"You are familiar with the subject?"

I knew she was taking in my impeccably respectable attire, the genteel kid gloves and gleaming top hat. "I am an artist," I said, not entirely untruthfully, "and have heard the discussions in advanced circles."

"It's plain to any observer that the institution of marriage is oppressive," Mrs. Camlet said.

My mother gave a squeak of shock. Remembering what Mr. Binyon had told me I had to admit, "The laws, certainly, could do with some reform. But marriage itself is ordained by God."

"'The Sabbath was made for man, not man for the Sabbath,'" she quoted. "That so many are unhappy in it shows that there's some deep foundational flaw."

My mother caught my eye, plainly ready to leave. But before Mother could gather up her gloves Mrs. Camlet glanced out into the side garden. Without rising she reached and lifted an oddly-made pistol up from where it had lain concealed on the windowsill behind the sofa back. Without even seeming to aim, she fired out the open window. There was no loud explosion but only a pop, and neither smoke nor the smell of powder could be discerned. I realized it must be an air pistol. She wielded it with the utmost casualness, the way I would pick up a match.

At the report my mother started, jerking a great splash of tea onto the carpet. "Oh my goodness," she said weakly. "I see that you are keeping up your shooting, my dear."

"I beg your pardon," Mrs. Camlet said easily. "Theo's plantings attract rabbits, which I simply cannot resist harvesting for the pot. Let me just ring." When the maid came in she said, "Ellen, tell Davey that there is another bunny out near the boxwoods. With the two from yesterday there should be enough for a nice hasenpfeffer."

The housemaid's face was absolutely wooden. "Yes, madam," she said, and withdrew.

I could not help demanding, "You're certain you killed it?"

"Have a look," she invited, and I rose to peer out the window. A small brown rabbit lay on the lawn, perhaps fifteen yards away. Its head had been entirely blown off, the brains and blood spattering the boxwoods. "A .46 caliber ball," Mrs. Camlet told me. "A head shot is the only possibility, otherwise there's nothing edible left."

"Stewed hare, such a delicious dish," my mother fluttered, with unfaltering politeness. "It's good housekeeping, I do not doubt, to dine upon the garden pests. Your butcher's bill must be so much less."

"I shall send you a couple," Mrs. Camlet offered, "if the rabbits continue to assail the new boxwood shoots."

"So kind of you. Oh, look at the time. Sarah will wonder where we are, Walter. Mrs. Camlet, such a pleasure. I hope you enjoy the pastry..."

And so we made our departure. As we walked back down the lane Mother chattered to me of the appalling notions Margaret Camlet had acquired, and marveled at her accurate shooting.

"She must have had much practice," she said. "Did you observe? She didn't even aim."

"Has she always known how to shoot?"

"Oh yes, she's handled firearms since girlhood. Her father taught her, I'm informed."

So the air pistol had been in her trousseau? How had the household rubbed along, with the master calling birds down from the sky into his hand on the one side while the mistress blew them to eternal glory on the other? The two made a strange pair, the leopard mated to a faithful hound. That was the gulf that yawned between the two Mrs. Camlets. I could understand why Marian loved Camlet. After our previous adventures any member of the gentry would fill her with unease. He was a mere business owner, a man of hearth and desk and pew – domesticated, safe and solid. His wife was quite the opposite.

That evening I met Pesca at Simpson's-in-the-Strand. We sat at a secluded table in the main dining room and dined on roast saddle of mutton and potatoes à la Lyonnaise. He heard of Marian's woes with extravagant sympathy and a truly Italian sentiment. "Woe is me, the poor Mrs. Marian!" he cried. "It is like the opera! The beauteous returned wife, the forsaken lover cast out into the snow, the pistol in the garden, the man in the dungeon chains, the fatherless baby in swaddling clothes."

"Not quite yet," I said. "At least, no swaddling clothes and no chains. But you see, Pesca, where I need your expert assistance."

The little man nodded. "This letter. You fear it is not translated well, and so has ensnared the unlucky Theophilus. Pesca shall come to the rescue."

"You may see it," I said. "Camlet's lawyers had accurate copies made of both the original letter and the translation for me." Although I can pick my way through an Italian text, I do not have the fluency of a native. In this crucial situation I wanted an expert eye. I drew the papers from my pocket book and handed them to my intelligent friend.

Pesca read the letter with care, muttering rapidly in his own tongue, and then comparing it line by line with the British Consulate's translation. "Ah, bah. It is well enough. Not felicitous. All the grace, the panache, of the beautiful language original is squeezed out. It is dry! But the understanding, she is there. Alas, my good Walter, no help can I offer you here."

"Not here, perhaps," I returned. "But there is more, Pesca. If you will consent to aid me in it."

"Ask, Walter, ask. You saved my life – it is yours to command!"

Carefully I did not pursue this opening. Reminiscence of how in the early days of our friendship I had lifted Pesca from the terrifying depths of four feet of sea water still tended to move him to tears. Instead I tapped the letter again. "See here the signature. Father Camillo Ercole is the inscription, of Saint Donatus church in Salerno. This is the man who attested to the death of Margaret Camlet. He witnessed it, gave the last rites to the dying woman, signed the burial certificate and presided over her funeral."

"And he was mistaken! Or bribed, hah! A liar, a villain, to be unmasked. By me!" Pesca seized his coffee cup and drained it, as if to fortify himself for the coming conflict.

"By you, Pesca, if you will undertake it. You're unquestionably the man for the job, Italian and fluent in the language. I have here fifty guineas." I set a heavy leather purse on the tablecloth. "It's Marian's money, made over to her by Camlet. On her behalf, I send you to Salerno. Find this Father Ercole, and learn the truth of the matter. If at all possible – if his account will save Camlet – bring him to London, to testify at the trial. Failing the presence of the actual man, take his testimony in an ironclad form that will stand up in court. Get him to the British Consulate. Have him make a sworn and notarised statement, and have the British officials witness it and put their seal to it. And bring this document back to me."

"A mighty sum, my Walter. This letter to the unlucky Theophilus, it is dated 1853, more than four years ago. Suppose the priest, he has died? Or will not speak? Mrs. Marian's money will be wasted."

"We must take that risk. It's Camlet's only hope. He is indeed a bigamist. He certainly married two women. His only chance is if we can prove beyond any doubt that he was acting in good faith, that any ordinary man would believe the truth of this letter. Only then may he claim that he made a reasonable error and sway the jury. They cannot call the case before the Easter term, which begins this year on April 6th. You have therefore five weeks to go and come back. Is that time enough? Will you go?"

"Money makes the way smooth and speedy, my Walter. And, to return to Italy! To my own country, and the rich English lady with the bag of gold to pay. How can Pesca say you nay?"

"Very good. And your pupils?"

He bounced to his feet. "I will write to them all tonight, that their devoted Pesca goes to the eternal Rome to refresh his Italian tongue at the Apennine fountains of his birth. And that I will return. Refreshed, renewed, ready to lead them through the dark woods of Dante and Petrarch once again!"

"Write or wire to me at Limmeridge if I may assist you," I said, wringing his hand. "And Godspeed, my friend."

My final errand in town was one of mercy. Marian had been swift to avail herself of the letters of credit Camlet had given her, so that moneys could be quickly put behind his defense. But the other essential was to buy him some comforts in prison, lest the rigours of Newgate kill him before he was released on bail.

The morning after my supper with Pesca I therefore turned my steps towards the Old Bailey and the grim gate of Newgate Prison. The place was like a great cliff of stone, without a single window and pierced by only one small iron-studded door. At that period the gallows still stood outside. The regulations for convicts were stringent, but persons remanded for trial loitered in a more anomalous state. There were plans afoot to improve and modernize the cell blocks, but these had not yet been begun, and conditions were harsh.

The turnkeys were very willing to take my money and move Camlet to the wing reserved for the most respectable prisoners. A larger cell, better food, all these luxuries were purchased. For a fee I could bring him parcels, even books. Then I demanded to see my man, and even this was achievable for a price.

I was shown down many narrow flagged corridors and through many a locked and barred gate, each unlocked and then carefully locked behind me again by a turnkey, into what they termed the visitor's box: a tiny cell, a mere doorless cubbyhole, with a further barred doorway opening beyond. On the other side of these bars was a gap of more than six feet, and beyond that was another barred doorway.

Into the tiny room beyond that, eventually, Camlet appeared. "Great heavens, man," I could not help exclaiming. "You have suffered."

I had not realised that so many of the rigors of imprisonment were applied even to those awaiting bail. The spruce and respectable businessman I knew was entirely gone. Persons held in Newgate for trial were not compelled to wear the prison uniform. But our good Saviour Himself would look like criminal scum in that setting. Poor Camlet now presented an entirely fallacious air of villainy in his crumpled grey suit – the same garments he had worn at his arrest – untrimmed whiskers and overall grubbiness. "They haven't let me shave or bathe," Camlet said meekly. "Well, worse things happen at sea."

"I've just ensured you better quarters and treatment. And I undertake to lie to Marian, so that she shall not swoop down and pummel your jailors."

"That would be very kind of you. Ordinarily I would never deceive her, but she cannot help me now."

"It's only for a short time, and then you shall be acquitted and free." The gap between us was barred so that no item could be handed across. It gave me the sensation of calling across some dreadful divide, from freedom to captivity, from life to death. The things that I ought not to say, ought not to burden a prisoner with, weighed on my tongue.

At last he spoke. "How are the children?"

"They miss you sadly," I said, grateful for the change of subject. "And resented your failure to bid them farewell. But Laura is teaching them to sing, and Marian has promised Micah that if he's still in Cumberland in the autumn he shall start at the village school."

"If ... if I'm not free by then, then that would be the best course. I hope the other children will not torment him, a lad with a felon for a father."

"Laura will not permit it."

"And the one to come. Oh, Hartright, that I have fathered a bastard is intolerable. More unbearable even than being closed in like this. All my life I've worked to provide the best for my children. Now this poor infant shall bear the awful stigma until his or her dying day. Its terrible prospects haunt my slumbers. I would do anything, Hartright, anything! to avert this. What shall I do? What can I do?"

"The stain does not inevitably lead to bad," I said. "Illegitimacy is not the mark of Cain, dooming a child for all time."

In the gloom, behind the bars across the gap, his eyes were invisible behind his spectacles. "It's good of you to say so, but I wonder that you believe it."

I could make no reply. "At least your conditions will now be better," I said at last.

"And my solicitor called. They hope to have me out on bail by week's end. In the meantime, Mr. Erbistock is sending to Sandett House, to fetch me clothing and books."

"Excellent." Although, what was Mrs. Camlet about? Marian would not have waited for a hired lawyer to perform these simple errands of help. She would have been here that very day, with food and clothing and every comfort for her spouse her energetic imagination could contrive. Did the breach between man and wife preclude even human decency? I thought back to the bright golden goddess I had met yesterday deftly killing rabbits. They say that the pagan deities are antipathetic, unable to feel the pangs of mere mortals. "I've put a ferret down a hole or two," I said. "And I shall return to town for the trial. What else can I do for you, my friend, before my departure?"

"You've done everything a man can do, by taking in my children. I wish I could shake your hand."

"The day will come. Be of good cheer, Camlet. You have the staunchest of friends, for you have Marian's heart. And she's never yet deserted anyone she loves."

❧ Marian Halcombe's journal ❧

Limmeridge, 6 March 1858

Laura came in to breakfast this morning, her lovely complexion flushed with annoyance. "That foolish woman. Do you know what Mary's mother has done? Mrs. Dwight has insisted that Mary give notice."

"How odd," I said. "It's not that easy to get a place in this district. And she was in service here herself before marrying, was she not?"

"Yes, in the kitchen. But now Mrs. Dwight refuses to have

Mary work here any more."

I opened my mouth to ask why, and left it open. Suddenly I knew why a careful and respectable mother might not want her pretty housemaid daughter to serve at Limmeridge now. Waiting upon a fallen woman might taint the girl's prospects.

Seeing my face Laura quickly said, "And much good may it do her, the silly old creature. The girl was weeping with frustration."

Last week, after all its upsetting events, neither Laura nor I felt well enough to go to divine service at Limmeridge church. Tomorrow, however, I think we must. It is high time the ruined woman of the family shows her disgraced countenance in public.

7 March

I was a little ill again this morning, so that Laura and I arrived somewhat late to church. We slipped into the family pew, dedicated to the Fairlies since time immemorial. The service was just as usual – the Rev. Ramer has only a few dozen favorite texts – but afterwards? I had steeled myself inwardly for rejection, even open insult. A woman fallen from purity may look for no justice. That my state was no fault of mine would make no difference whatever to the tabbies of the parish. However, I hoped for better, that because I had known my friends and neighbours so long, they would have sympathy instead of contempt for my predicament.

And now ... I am in doubt. Not an unkind word was so much as breathed, to Laura or myself, as we emerged from the little stone church into the graveyard that surrounds it. Even behind my back, I felt no whispers or sharp glances at my ringless left hand, or the set of my skirt. My interesting condition, if the news is not already being chattered over breakfast tables, will soon be known. Such things cannot be hidden for long. The servants all gossip, those girls who are doing my laundry and washing my sheets. Already they bring me sugarless tea and rusks to help settle my stomach of a morning. In a few months when I'm forced to put aside my stays it will be visible to all.

But though nothing unkind was said, there were – how can I phrase it? Little drops of sugary acid. Nothing that I could take open offense at, but just a tiny pinprick, here and there. After the service, for instance, Mrs. Ramer said, "I see you have put off your ring, Miss Halcombe. I've always felt it is a mere superstition, that opals are unlucky."

I pushed my left hand deep into my sable muff. "They're more fragile than other stones, it is said."

"Perhaps that would account for it." She didn't smile, the old trout. The Ramers came in during the reign of Mr. Frederick Fairlie, who gave absolutely no thought to the selection of a vicar. But there was just a flicker of spite in her eye. If I openly broke with her however, the Rev. Ramer might act on her behalf. He's a good man but weak, and after all he has to live with Mrs. Ramer. And I would find myself cut off from the church and all the social functions centreed around it.

And were there an unusual number of congregants gathered to look at the notice for the diocesan sewing project? Layettes for unwed mothers were to be collected from the district next month. No one said a word to me, but there was some chat among the ladies about their projects, and someone murmured, "But what do you expect, from someone in trade?" Was I being excessively sensitive?

We walked home along the path we had walked ever since we could both remember, that runs between the fields and the sea. Above us the sky was grey and thick with cloud, and across the firth it was probably snowing on the Scottish hills. But the hedgerows were just putting out the first hint of spring green, and the trees were beginning to leaf out. Soon the view across the water would be hidden by their boughs. I put the question to Laura, and she immediately slipped her hand through my arm. "If anyone's unkind to you, Marian, tell me," she said. "I shall not tolerate it."

Once I had fought for her, and now she defended me. "I do not believe anything will be said to my face," I replied. "Anything overt, I could reply to. I could fight! But for the first time now I fully understand Mrs. Catherick."

The sudden mention of this name from the past made Laura start. But she said, bravely enough, "Her case was quite different, Marian. She had no family, no home, and a poor little afflicted daughter. And so she had to make her way alone."

"Whereas I have you. And Walter."

"No matter what happens, Marian."

I squeezed her hand. If my darling man was convicted, if he went to prison, I would live here at Limmeridge until his release. It was a depressing prospect. There was something attractive in the idea of emulating Mrs. Catherick, or Mrs. Graham in *The Tenant of Wildfell Hall*. To go where nobody would know of my disgrace. I could pass myself off as a widow. And then there would be none of these invisible and not-quite-perceptible pin-pricks. Was it a relief, to consider that Laura would never permit this? I too am in a prison, though the bars are loving. My course is fixed here until Theo's return, even if it's years from now.

14 March

Walter has been home this past week, there being nothing he can do for Theo now. He returns for the trial in a month. "Would Theo be encouraged to see me in the audience?"

"By no means, Marian." Walter's face went stiff with horror. "Consider Mrs. Camlet. Even with her advanced notions she's careful to keep herself secluded. Did you see in Mother's letter the other day? Mrs. Camlet never goes out except in a heavy veil. The case is already notorious, and poor Camlet's name bandied from every lip. The penny press would like nothing better than to have a sketch of one or the other of you. I saw the most appalling headline in *Reynolds' Weekly News* before I left town – "Between Two Wives!" And you're the less secure female, the one in peril. You would be pointed at, possibly jeered or even set upon. Consider how it would lacerate Camlet's feelings, if you were abused and he unable to help."

"But you'll be there, Walter," I argued. "You can defend me."

"Think of your condition, Marian," Laura pleaded. "No lady should even go out of doors in your state, except possibly to church. And travel? A rough train journey may possibly ending-er you. A woman must take the greatest care of her health at this delicate time."

"It is not to be thought of," Walter said with decision.

Nonsense. Of course I can think about it! My morning sickness is gone, and I'm quite fit and vigorous. The woman's old trick, of hitching the top hoop a little higher, will hide all visible signs of my condition for a good while yet. I too could wear a veil, and sit unrecognised at the trial as Margaret Camlet doubtless intends to. The irritations of living under a cloud here could be left behind, and I could see Theo, if only from across a courtroom. I have a full month to talk Walter around. I shall begin immediately.

En route to London, 1 April

See the smudges my fingers leave on this fair page! It is the ink of many newspapers. As we got on our train in Carlisle, Walter stopped at the news agent and bought a copy of every news sheet they had in stock. It was a great huge bundle, taking up an entire seat in our compartment, but luckily the train was not crowded.

"Do you intend to read all these papers?" I asked, as the train picked up speed.

"No indeed. I am in search of one particular news article, and if you like, Marian, you may assist." He took out his penknife and began to slit open the folded pages. "You recall that I sent Professor Pesca to Italy more than a month ago."

"And you received a wire, saying that he had arrived safely in Rome."

"Yes. But since then, there has been no word, for good or for ill. And Camlet's trial is three days from now."

"It must be that a message has gone astray. You cannot fear he has absconded with the money."

"No, that I would never believe. Pesca is an honest fellow. But ... he is mortal. What I dread now is misadventure. If there is a shipwreck, a train derailment, some other calamity in these papers, we could inquire if he was among the passengers."

He handed me a stack of newspapers and I began paging through them, skimming the headlines. The international reports were full of foreboding, especially from Italy. An Italian nationalist had tried to assassinate Napoleon III, and had been guillotined only a fortnight ago. A period of nothing but the rustle of paper and the rattle and sway of the rail car, punctuated by the occasional sound of pages being slit, and then I ventured, "Misadventure can be un-newsworthy, but no less fatal. If he were run over by a wagon in the street in Rome it would not appear in the British press."

"No. But I can think of nothing else to do." His tone, more than his words, told me how worried he was.

"Oh, Walter, how awful if he is lost. One of your oldest friends. And on my errand! Sometimes I feel that I am infectious. That I carry a deathly aura around me that dooms everyone near me to unhappiness and disaster."

"Now that is simply not so, Marian. You will do yourself an injury, if you allow your imagination to run away with you in such unhealthy directions."

Walter has such common sense, it's a great comfort. "You are right. I beg your pardon. My condition makes me fanciful."

For another good half-hour we systematically leafed through publications in quiet, without result. Presently, however, I spoke again. "Walter, when you spoke to Mr. Binyon. Did he mention how long a divorce suit takes?"

"No, the subject didn't come up."

I was watching his honest face. After all these years I can read it like print. "There's something else, I can see it. But I know it, Walter."

"You do?"

"Yes. That it is impossible for us to be legally wed before my confinement. Even if Theo had filed to divorce Margaret the moment she returned to Sandett House and all went perfectly, six months must pass before the decree is absolute. Bastardy is a permanent and indelible stain that even our marriage later cannot remove."

I fell silent, and he said nothing. We were both remembering those we had known for whom birth outside of wedlock had been a terrible doom. But, remembering his advice to avoid morbid imaginings, I spoke with resolute cheer. "If Theo begins proceedings when he is at liberty, we may hope to be properly married before the child's first birthday."

"I most sincerely hope so, Marian," Walter said gently.

Too gently – there was yet something more. "Oh Walter. Tell me, please."

He shook his head. "Sufficient to the day is the evil thereof, Marian. If Camlet goes to prison you'll have larger and nearer troubles."

Weak tears rose to my eyes, but I swallowed them. If Theo is jailed I shall need all my strength and self-control. I folded the last newssheet up neatly, and took up this journal. And writing here has composed my spirits a little, as it always does.

That evening
What a blessed relief to arrive in London. The one thing I had not considered about traveling in my condition is the demands of one's body. Water closets suitable for women are already few and far between in the metropolis. Walter has selected a respectable small hotel on a quiet street just beyond the centre of the city, securing me a bedroom and sitting room on the second floor. He himself is staying at his club, the Mahlstick, but two blocks away. From here it is a short cab ride to Newgate Prison and the Old Bailey. But our first call tomorrow will be at the offices of Plockton, Smithee & Erbistock, Theo's solicitors. Since I am paying their bill, I look for their full attention.

London, 2 April
Walter and I went to Lincoln's Inn this morning. Mr. Erbistock, the youngest partner of the firm, was tall, while Mr. Smithee was portly and afflicted with curly hair that seemed possessed of an urge to grow into a point at the top of his scalp. They both had a trying habit of addressing themselves to Walter, rather than myself. And every time Mr. Erbistock spoke of me, his 'Miss Halcombe' had an unpleasant undertone to it, while Mr. Smithee was excessively gallant, exquisitely aware of my condition. However, since the firm is renowned in the area of family law, I could tolerate much.

Mr. Erbistock was of a decided opinion about the tactics of the case. "On no account should Miss, ah, Halcombe be called to testify. Our argument will be vastly bolstered by interrogating Mrs. Camlet instead. Judicious questioning will lay bare her unwifely ways and unseemly actions. This will firmly fix the jury's sympathy with the husband. Miss, er, her appearance would not enhance this, and only hurt the cause."

"A lady in her delicate circumstances should not have troubled to come all the way to town," Mr. Smithee said. "Mr. Plockton must never hear of her presence. Her health must be the most paramount consideration."

This was almost exactly what Laura had said, barring the worries about Mr. Plockton. And the words were frequently on my own lips as well. So perhaps it was unreasonable for me to be offended, but I was. "It is Mr. Camlet's acquittal which is of the first consideration, and all others must go to the wall," I said tartly. "Will it be possible to secure his release without the testimony of the Italian priest who wrote the notice of Mrs. Camlet's death and officiated at her funeral?"

"An English judge and jury would scarcely give the time of day to a foreigner anyway, Miss, ah, Miss," Mr. Ebistock said. "Although it was enterprising, quite forward-looking of you, Mr. Hartright, to think of sending for him."

"It is as well," Walter said, "since I have had no word from him."

"Unsteady, these Continentals," Mr. Smithee said. "I strongly advise you, Mr. Hartright, to come alone to the Old Bailey tomorrow. Quite a scrum there will be, I foresee. Most of these bigamy cases involve labourers and the working-class. The more sensational papers are forever hot on the scent of lurid crimes, and a respectable and devout man in the dock will draw something of an audience. They may be rowdy, which would lacerate the feelings of any delicately-constituted female."

"My condition may be delicate, but I am not delicately constituted," I declared. "My sensibilities are such that I could not tolerate not witnessing the trial."

Walter merely sighed, but Mr. Erbistock said, "Miss, ah, Halcombe, surely you would be more comfortable –"

"In fact…" I pulled out my fan. "Dear me. I wonder if I am quite well."

"Oh heavens," Mr. Smithee gulped. "Oh my heavens."

Mr. Erbistock's tall frame seemed to crumple slightly. "Miss! Miss, ah, would you care to perhaps lie down? There's a sofa in my office."

I fanned myself with a steady hand, grateful that Walter refrained from rolling his eyes. "Just a passing twinge, I think."

"I will have the clerk fetch you a lemonade," Mr. Smithee said. "Or water, yes, water. Barnaby, fetch a glass of water, on the instant!"

"I think that as long as I may attend the trial, I will do," I said firmly. "I will be heavily veiled, but I will be there."

5 April

I dressed carefully for Theo's trial. In a decent black bombazine and a respectable bonnet, I was utterly unexceptionable. A long thick veil ensured that no one would recognise me. Black lace mitts, a bag, a voluminous shawl and a parasol completed my going-to-court ensemble.

But as Mr. Erbistock had warned, the rowdiness and disorder of the Central Criminal Court at the Old Bailey was repugnant. It was a small shabby room, darkly paneled and ill-lit. Crowds of people filled the seats. Some of the men were Theo's friends and associates – I recognised faces from our brief married life. But of course I could not dare to obtrude myself upon their notice, not now. I was a pariah, a strayed and soiled female. Most of the audience was there in hopes of entertainment, as if it were a show. I even saw people cracking nuts and passing ginger beer, and one man had brought a meat-pudding in a deep tin basin.

Bewigged barristers in black robes wandered in and out like straying chickens, and the judge on the bench seemed to be dozing, his triple chins resting upon his scarlet chest. There were twenty cases to be heard today, and it was some while before Theo's was called. Considering the seriousness of the crimes, and the severity of the sentences, everything seemed to be unduly hugger-mugger, and conducted with indecent speed.

But suddenly it was time. And there was my dear man, being conducted into the dock by the warders. He looked very small and insignificant between those tall big fellows, but he was dressed like a gentleman, in a snuff-coloured coat, a cravat and collar. I feared that the horrors of legal peril would alter him. We were seated behind the dock and too far back to see him well. Were his eyes confused, vicious? Oh, surely he was not changed! Behind my veil I was unrecognizable, but beside me Walter was tall, his brown wavy hair easy to spot in the press as Theo turned to survey it. And – I knew it, I felt it! He saw me. I lifted my hand as if to adjust a hatpin, and he raised his bearded chin, heartened.

The clerk read the charge out in a carrying nasal tone: "The charge of bigamy, against Theophilus Henton William Camlet, age 32. Feloniously marrying Marian Celeste Halcombe, his wife being alive."

I shivered, grateful for the shelter of my thick veil. I had not realised they would name me in the charge. It was both comforting and annoying to see that the case excited far more interest than the ones before. There was a rustle of anticipation from the audience, a settling-down like a theatre audience preparing to enjoy the star turn.

The barrister for the Crown was a Mr. Gleeson, who in his dirty white wig looked like a pug dog who had got into the curds in the dairy. He rose to present the case for the Crown.

The first witness he called to the stand was Police Sergeant Roger Gregham. His testimony ran: "I arrested the prisoner on the 22nd of February this year at Limmeridge in Cumberland. I said, 'I am going to take you into custody for feloniously marrying Marian Halcombe, your first wife Margaret Brickley Camlet being alive. In reply to the charge he said, 'I did not know she was alive.' I produce these certificates which I have examined with the originals; they are correct."

The documents were displayed to the jury. One was the certificate of marriage of Theophilus H.W. Camlet and Margaret Harriet Brickley at St. Swithun-upon-Kingsgate, Winchester on 9th June, 1847, and the other that of Theophilus Camlet and Marian Halcombe, at Limmeridge Church, Cumberland, on 10th October, 1856. These were the documents Theo had feared would fully suffice to damn him.

Then it was our barrister's turn. Mr. Todwarden was an imposing well-fed man, very pink in the face under his wig. In his black robe he loomed impressively wide. He rose to present the Italian priest's letter and the translation. "A document clearly proving the honest belief of the defendant on reasonable grounds that his first wife Margaret Camlet was dead," he said, with portentous confidence.

I expected that the case would then be turned over to the jury for its decision. The previous cases had taken no more than fifteen minutes all told. But the pug-like Mr. Gleeson suddenly went off on quite a different tack. "Is this convenient letter genuine?" he demanded. "That the accused is the joint heir with Mrs. Camlet of a considerable inheritance makes it oddly opportune that she is discovered to be deceased. I suggest that this peculiar letter was a fraud from the outset."

Beside me Walter muttered, "Oh God, that my gallant Pesca were come!"

I was watching Theo, and even from this distance I could see him sway with the shock. Prisoners in the dock are not allowed to sit but must stand. Under the veil my mouth was open in horror as well. Mr. Gleeson went on with the most repellent cheer. "The defendant must have had an associate write a letter, purporting to be from some priest, saying that his wife is deceased. But this letter was written and mailed to the British Consulate in Rome, from Switzerland. And I produce here an affidavit testifying to this incontrovertible fact."

The affidavit was read aloud by the clerk. It was from an assistant consulate secretary at the British Consulate in Rome, saying that he received the letter and had it translated from Italian and then sent to Camlet. But he remembered it as odd, because the stamps were Swiss, not Italian. He collected stamps and noticed particularly because the 'standing Helvetia' image was one he had already acquired for his collection.

The gallant Mr. Todwarden was on his feet in an instant. "And where on earth would an ordinary Englishman get a Swiss to forge letters for him?"

Mr. Gleeson retorted, "Camlet had considerable business connections in Basel, from which Covenant Pamphets and Printed Materials was organizing a new translation of, let me see here now, John Calvin's *Institutes of the Christian Religion*."

But, oh thank heaven! There was a bustle and a turmoil at the doorway. Pushing through the crowd and the bailiffs came a dear and familiar little figure, Professor Pesca himself. His suit was travel-stained and the gaiters he invariably wore were muddy. In one small hand he carried his umbrella, and with the other he towed by the sleeve a ridiculously tall and thin man, clad in long black clerical robes and a rusty black cloak that fluttered down to his heels. This priest was further adorned with a broad-brimmed and shallow-crowned black hat. A more foreign-looking and bedraggled pair could scarcely be imagined, and the bailiffs were very reluctant to let them approach the bench.

In a shrill tone Pesca cried, "Walter, I have come. Good

Theophilus, fear not!"

Poor Theo, who has never met Prof. Pesca in his life, looked on with dismay, but pressing forward Pesca cried, "Lord Parwich, Lord Parwich!"

"Eh?" The dozing judge in the red ermine-trimmed robe started awake with a snort. He blinked rheumy eyes and gazed up and around before espying Pesca below him. "Eh? Eh, what's this?"

"Lord Parwich, you remember the good Prof. Pesca, who instructed your daughters in the beautiful Italian language. How are Misses Venetia and Augusta?"

"Eh, well." Lord Parwich shook out a handkerchief and blew his nose into it. "Miss Venetia is now Lady Bexley, and Miss Augusta is at Bath. Well, well. I do remember you, Prof. Pesca. Bless my soul. And what is this? Why are you in court, eh? Should you not call at the house? Miss Maria could be old enough to start in on Dante, eh?"

A flood of passionate and complicated explanation followed, and Walter rose and went down into the well to help. Through the gap he left on the bench I was able to see below and over. And, oh heavens – the man sitting at the end two rows down was Charles Dickens! I recognised the shiny bald head fringed at the side with wiry curls and the thin chin whiskers and moustache, from the portrait engravings in the frontispiece of his novels. The famed Inimitable was small and slender in build, and sat with friends. He scrawled rapidly in a stenographer's notebook on his knee, apparently not needing to look at the page. The great man is known to be interested in the more notorious trials at the Old Bailey, and even paid ten guineas to attend the execution of the Mannings in 1849. His energetic research has wonderfully informed some of his works. My poor Theo! Now I had even better reason to pray for an acquittal. If convicted, my poor man's appearance in sensational fiction and drama was certain, and to spare him the mortification I would have to cease sending novels to him in prison.

Many minutes passed and there was a great deal of scurrying of lawyers and white woolly wigs bending together to mutter, but finally the black rail of a priest was put into the witness box, Prof. Pesca translating.

"Of course Prof. Pesca can translate," Lord Parwich rumbled. "Known him for years. Dante, very important for young ladies of accomplishment. He's entirely fluent."

Questioned, the priest affirmed that he was indeed Father Camillo Ercole, of St. Donatus church in Salerno, Italy. When presented with the Italian letter he identified his handwriting and signature as his own.

Prof. Pesca rattled the English out at top speed, but scarcely kept up with the floods of Italian. And the gestures! The priest's hands were nearly as fluid and eloquent as his tongue. "Oh yes, the English woman. She died at the Pension Salzburg, and I was called in to administer last rites and see to the burial. Not a good Catholic, no. But her traveling companions wanted her interred decently. They paid handsomely for the service, yes. Where were they from? Where were they going? Why do you ask me, eh? I cannot recall, they do not tell me. But they were not Italian. All these foreigners, they look alike. You, you all look alike to me, all of you English persons. I wrote the letter, they took it away. No, I know nothing of Switzerland. They did not say where they were going."

Mr. Todwarden, looking very pink and smug, said, "With the court's permission, I should like to confront the good Father here with Mrs. Margaret Camlet, your honors."

This was agreed to, and a tall heavily-veiled woman was called up. I recognised the sensible grey gown, the queenly figure and the proud carriage of the head, but under the black veiling no details could be seen. There was huge excitement in the crowd when Mr. Todwarden asked her to unveil. In an undertone she refused, pleading modesty, and after some more hot argument it was agreed that only Father Ercole would see her face.

The audience growled its disappointment and the nut-eaters flung shells at the bench. Mr. Dickens clapped his hand to his forehead in frustration, but the judge called for order and Mrs. Camlet was allowed to discreetly lift her veil. From his perch in the witness box Father Ercole had to stoop like a black stork to peer in under the brim of her bonnet. Another torrent of energetic Italian, which Pesca translated: "He says, well, this lady was not the lady I buried. Nothing like."

"But her name is the same," Mr. Todwarden said.

Pesca translated, "I cannot help that, sir. The woman who died, she was not so tall, and much rounder, yes, like so." The priest held out a thin hand parallel to the ground, chest high to himself, indicating a quite shorter woman. "And the hair, it was grey, a long braid, yes, like this. Whereas this lady is like the Madonna. I have never seen her before, this fair hair. They told me her name was Margaret, and so I wrote it."

By this point Theo's trial had gone on for more than an hour, far longer than any of the others, and there was a distinct feeling that it was time for an intermission. The prosecution concluded by pointing out the appalling nature of the crime, the shameless and cruel damage done to decent English women. Mr. Todwarden smiled and noted that from beginning to end Theo had acted in the most honorable and honest manner. The jury retired to the back of their box to consult for only a minute, and then returned with their verdict: Not guilty.

Lord Parwich affirmed this, saying, "Where the defendant acts under a mistaken belief of the circumstances they may be afforded the defence of mistake. Where a defendant acts under such a mistake, the mistake prevents them forming the *mens rea* of the crime and thus mistake is not really a defence as such, but relates to the absence of the elements of establishing liability." A bang of the gavel, and my darling man was free!

There was a surge of black-robed barristers back and forth. With another rap of his gavel Lord Parwich adjourned the court for its mid-day meal, adding, "And I look to see you before very many days, Professor. Bless my soul, think of little Maria." Below me his friends jumped to their feet, and Mr. Dickens shut his notebook and made ready to leave. But I watched Theo as Margaret Camlet came up to him. And a thought came to me, seeing them side by side, which sank my heart. All this work and worry, and the outcome was to reunite Theo with his first wife. He was further from me than ever.

BOOK 3

≈ Walter Hartright's narrative ≈

I had worried that Marian's sensibilities would overwhelm her at the verdict, and that she would dash down to embrace Camlet, or even burst into tears and attract unwelcome attention. I was cautiously pleased that her control was perfect, and she waited in quiet up in the seats until I could make my way back through the crowd and escort her out. I waved down a hackney and helped her in, and we went around to the prison gate.

There was a lugubrious delay, but at last I saw the turnkey behind the bars. I got down and was in time to meet Camlet as he came out. "My hearty congratulations," I said, shaking his hand. "Did I not promise that I would clasp your hand in the sunshine one day?"

"I am your debtor forever, Hartright," he said. He was pale and thinner, but the brown beard was split in an enormous grin. "It was your thought that saved me."

"Thank rather the good Professor Pesca, who did all the hard work."

"Nothing would give me more pleasure."

"He's taking Father Ercole to a lodging, since the man speaks no English, but someday soon I shall make you acquainted with him." I drew him to the hackney, where Marian was fretting in a fever of impatience. I held his bag and busied myself giving careful instructions to the driver, while the tearful reunion took place. By the time I climbed into the cab myself the first tempest had passed. They sat close together, holding hands and looking like April and May, and I took the seat opposite.

The carriage jolted into motion. "I'm sure neither of you noticed at the time, but I was profoundly shocked at the time of your arrest, Camlet, that you were in Marian's room."

The scarlet flamed up into Marian's swarthy cheeks. "But we're married!"

"I would not have brought the subject up at all," I returned, "except that Camlet is not your husband. Your marriage to him was invalid. His wife is Margaret Camlet."

"I shall divorce her immediately," Camlet said. "I shall have Mr. Erbistock set it in train the first thing tomorrow morning."

"That is well. But until the decree absolute, you must see that you should continue to live at Sandett House, and Marian must continue to make her home with Laura and myself. Anything else would be grossly improper."

"And it would impact my case," Camlet said. "The authorities are far more reluctant to grant the decree when both parties have strayed. I knew at the time that I was acting wrongly, and I apologise for abusing the hospitality of your home. Only the terror of trial and imprisonment made me fail in rectitude. The fault is entirely mine, and Marian was swept away by my importuning and her own warm and loving affection."

"No, it was I," Marian broke in. "My condition renders me delicate, and I needed his care." Reluctantly she released Camlet's hand.

With an effort I kept my face straight. "It was ill done of you, Camlet, to put her into that condition. She wields it like a brace of pistols, ruthlessly exploiting it at every opportunity." I looked at my watch. "Unfortunately I have an errand now that I can no longer postpone. Laura has expressed a desire for a bonnet from London, and I must visit the milliner."

Marian's mouth dropped open. Camlet would not know this, but I have never taken the slightest interest in ladies' fripperies. Luna the greyhound would have a more informed opinion about hats, and only a blind woman would dispatch me to buy her one. Ignoring Marian's astonishment I shook Camlet's hand warmly, congratulating him once more upon his acquittal, and tapped the roof of the cab. "The cabby has been instructed to take you, Camlet, to Hampstead and then bring Marian back to the hotel."

When the vehicle halted I stepped down. Before I could shut the door after myself Marian caught it and put her head out. "Cabby, in my condition I find that I cannot tolerate a great rate of speed. If you will proceed at a walking pace to our destination, I will double your fare."

I had to grin up at them. "You see, Camlet?"

It was good to see him leaning back and laughing heartily. "Yes, she's incorrigible, I agree. Good day to you, Hartright, and thank you once again. I shall write."

Selected correspondence in the possession of Marian Halcombe

Primrose Hill, 13 April 1858

My dearest girl,
[Two pages of passionate personal material omitted here]

Send me your dear reply by return, at the above address. I have removed from Sandett House and am shifting for myself in furnished lodgings, so that the divorce filing may have substance. Give kisses to Micah and Lottie for me, and keep your beloved self in the tenderest of care.

All my love, your own faithful
Theo

Primrose Hill 19 April 1858

My beloved Marian,
It gives me such joy, to see your handwriting on a letter! Do not fear to bore me, with your detailed accounts of Lottie and Micah's doings. I miss my daily

dealings with them more than I would have thought possible.

[One page personal avowals omitted here]

Mr. Erbistock assures me that the divorce proceedings are well in hand and progress as quickly as may be. Possess yourself in patience, my dearest. Some day these travails will be in the past and we will all be together once more, as a family. How I yearn for that day!

Always, my dear Marian,

All my love,
Theo

London, 11 May 1858

My dearest, most beloved Marian,
I have bad news. The worst that you can conceive. Mr. Erbistock presented my petition to the Court of Divorce and Matrimonial Causes today. And it was rejected. The court cited several grounds. The most serious is that of connivance – that I knew of and permitted Margaret's misconduct for some years. My own adultery (i.e. our marriage) is also an issue. The possibility that I have connived with her to undo the marriage is in itself a bar to divorce. The argument that I thought her dead, and believed myself legally married to you, had no impact. There is no appeal.

Oh my dearest. I feel as if I've been pole-axed. I am stunned, and do not know what to do. I had hoped, beyond reason, that we might somehow be married before the birth. Now it is entirely possible that we may never be together. The thought drives me mad.

Mr. Erbistock advises that you retain your own legal counsel. I concur, in the faint hope that another legal mind may see an avenue that he does not. Also, I beg that you consult Hartright. Show him this note, if you will. He has achieved wonders in the past.

Though my heart towards you shall never change, I am filled with despair.

Still yours,
Theo

❧ Walter Hartright's narrative ❧

Mr. Binyon waited upon us again today at Limmeridge. He would have preferred us to go to his offices in Carlisle, but Marian's condition keeps her – or should keep her! – within doors.

The solicitor eyed her figure knowingly. "A suit for paternal maintenance? No? Alas, hope springs eternal in the legal breast. Well, Miss Halcombe, if you are not to take your seducer to the courts, how may I serve you?"

Our visitor had been installed in the place of honor on the sofa in the drawing room. Laura sat on his right and poured the tea. On his left, Marian held some fine needlework in her lap with what I can only describe as an entirely deceptive meekness. "Oh Mr. Binyon, you are my only hope," she said, dovelike in her helplessness. "If you will be so kind, explain again to my sister and myself this terrible legal dilemma, so opaque to the female mind. I must rely upon wiser heads for advice at every turn."

Obligingly Mr. Binyon weighed in once again with the recent renovations to divorce law, and the complicated history of the philosopher George Lewes and authoress Mary Ann Evans. "So the rightness of a divorce may spoil with time?" Laura asked, with disbelief. "As if it were a dish of cream?" She passed the dish.

"Precisely, Mrs. Hartright. A very good analogy! Thank you, yes, a scone. Yes, an unreasonable delay in presenting the petition is a ground for denial."

Marian helped him to a scone. "It seems pointlessly cruel

and difficult. Why would they do such a thing?"

Mr. Binyon plopped a large spoonful of clotted cream onto his scone. "There you have it, dear lady. Divorce is meant to be difficult, deliberately rare. High barriers were erected of a purpose, so that only the most determined petitioners could achieve the prize. Thus morality is preserved and licentiousness held in check, for the fear is that without this bridle the inborn concupiscence of the nation would rise up rampant and gallop away with all decency. Over in France, they were not so prudent in drawing up their laws, and divorces are as thick as autumn leaves. Hence the adultery of the petitioner being an absolute bar. Mr. Camlet's union with yourself, although not recognised, is yet an impediment."

"It's unjust," Laura said. "Deliberately unfair, especially to the lady."

"Divorce is held to be a reward for the innocent." Mr. Binyon shook his head. "Not a service, like a penny stamp, that any may avail themselves of. You are almost surely not aware that a considerable modernization of British law shall be achieved in our lifetimes. But we are not yet at that happy state."

"I begin to think that marriage laws are not designed for the happiness of the many at all," Laura said.

Unwillingly I quoted Mrs. Camlet: "That so many are unhappy in it shows that there is some deep foundational flaw."

"How very advanced your opinions are, Mr. Hartright. Had not thought it of you." Mr. Binyon eyed Marian consideringly. "Your options, Miss Halcombe, are few. All depends upon what you are willing to dare."

Marian lifted her chin. "I do not lack for courage, Mr. Binyon."

"But would you dare, like Miss Evans, to live with your man out of wedlock?"

"Oh!"

"Aha, a possibility. A distinct possibility. But a dangerous one." He nodded over his scone. "Full of peril. Because Mr. Camlet has already settled money upon you, however, you are in a position of relative strength. You are not destitute and without support. You could live with him in sin. And if, or when, he abandons you or dies, you would still have support. You would not then have to sue him or his heirs to maintain you."

I was pleased and relieved to see that Marian hesitated long in her reply. "I … do not think I could do that," she said.

"Certainly not without due and careful consideration. For you would be estranging yourself from respectable society. You would be a scarlet woman, the malign home-breaker, the ruination of a respectable family, and this odium would follow you your life long. The man in this case is less trammeled. He could move among his friends and associates without too much scandal. But the lady would bear all the burdens."

"That is not fair," Laura repeated. "I begin to think that women must vote, and change these terrible laws."

"Do not the moral considerations weigh with you, Mr. Binyon?" I asked. "If I thought you were truly advising Miss Halcombe to live in sin with Camlet, I would have to throw you out."

"What, and leave these delicious scones uneaten? I do no such thing, Mr. Hartright. That is not her lawyer's job. Miss Halcombe's lawyer has a duty to point out the legal ramifications of any action she decides to undertake." He took a large bite of scone and cream, adding, "A famously amoral breed, we are indeed. 'Tis unreasonable of you to ask it of us, sir."

"I see that is so," I said ruefully.

"And, Mrs. Hartright, know that the man also has burdens he must bear. As long as Mr. Camlet is married to Margaret Camlet, he is obliged to maintain her and their children. If Miss Halcombe lives with him – and, good heavens, if you do not all reside in the same ménage!" Mr. Binyon paused in the act of accepting another scone, transfixed by legal visions. "A fascinating and quite Biblical possibility which we must consider. Abraham, Isaac, King David, all practitioners. And a harem would certainly be a monetary savation. But a moment's thought reveals that this would be especially wearing upon all parties. No, I cannot recommend it to you, Miss Halcombe, although there are precedents more recent than the Old Testament, and if you contemplate this avenue I could seek out the details for you. Ahem! To return. Assuming he does not pursue these more radical possibilities, Mr. Camlet will almost certainly be in the unfortunately costly position of maintaining two households."

Marian met my glance. Sending Pesca to Italy to secure Camlet's acquittal from the bigamy charge had not been cheap, and she was surely bearing the expenses relating to his divorce suit. He had been well-off before, but now? By the time this was all over, Camlet might come to be like the Jarndyces in Dickens, all of his substance devoured by lawyers.

Laura refilled his cup, and thus fortified Mr. Binyon produced one more startling possibility, like a magician pulling a card from his sleeve. "The second avenue open to you, Miss Halcombe, is to simply walk away."

Marian's needle paused in midair. "I beg your pardon?"

"Close out this unhappy chapter of your life, dear lady, and go on without him. Sever your ties with the gentleman. Cease to write, and let your union, already so blighted, perish of its natural causes. Leave Mr. Camlet and his two children to his Margaret, and maintain your own child upon the funds you have so prudently already secured."

I remarked, "I sense, Mr. Binyon, that this is your true recommendation."

"I make no recommendation, Mr. Hartright. But yes, if it were I myself in Miss Halcombe's shoes, this is what I would do, I would indeed. It is what the divorce decision handed down in London already decrees, and it is but prudence, eh? To bow to those great legal minds in London. And, Miss Halcombe, if I may be so bold, I think you would be happier in the end for it."

"I would agree," Marian said, faintly. "But none of us – Theo, Margaret, or myself – wish it to be so. I cannot see why, if all three of the parties involved are agreed upon our course, it cannot be achieved."

"It cannot, Miss Halcombe. In fact, that you all three agree is a bar. The act of desertion must be against the will of a spouse. Divorce cannot be consensual and cannot be justified by estrangement and unhappiness alone, however overwhelming. You have no legal leg to stand upon, if I may put it that way. And therefore the options before you are so few that they may be summarised over two cups of tea." He lifted his cup to her before sipping from it.

All the painful tempests revolving around recent developments had mostly passed, but at this firm word Marian trembled and had to take her handkerchief out. Alarmed, Mr. Binyon set down his cup with a clatter. "Never weep, Miss Halcombe. I find it intolerable. I beg of you! At the very least, no precipitate action is called for on your part. To wait, and see how your heart speaks after the healing passage of time, is simple and easy. I recommend it to you." He hastened to make his departure before the tears should actually begin to fall.

When I came back into the drawing room after seeing Mr. Binyon out Laura had moved to sit close beside Marian, the black head and the fair bent together. " – and the little one to come," she was softly saying. "You shall have all of Fairlie's baby linens, of course. But now is the time to hem some more. This pretty deep blue cannot be for an infant, can it?"

"It's a dress for myself," Marian said, with a sob. "For my second wedding, for I shall not fit into any of my gowns."

"Oh my dearest." Laura hugged her, and I sat on the other side and held her hand.

"Theo's dearest wish is that his child shall be legitimised. And oh, it cannot be now, never."

Laura and I watched with pity, as this courageous woman struggled to reconcile herself to her ugly fate. "I agree with Mr. Binyon," I said quietly, patting her hand. "Let time be the healer and arbiter, Marian. Our path must be clearer after September."

One problem that lingered unresolved was the fate of Micah and Lottie Camlet. The return of Mrs. Camlet had disturbed them, but removed to Limmeridge House they had settled down, playing with little Wally and enjoying the spring in our beautiful district as it slid towards summer. Micah was learning to fish and to ride a pony, and Lottie dug in the garden, erecting a fortress of pebbles and earth for her doll. We had been careful to say nothing of their father's legal tribulations, and in this quiet household we could supervise what was told to them. So their innocent days were untroubled and sunny.

In spite of Mr. Binyon's counsel Marian continued to exchange letters with Camlet almost daily. She assured me these were reports upon the doings of the children. As long as they continued here, there would be no severing the connection. I foresaw the natural terminus of this when the baby was born. Marian's time would then be fully taken up with the infant, and the coming winter would make Limmeridge less attractive for outdoor play. Camlet would come up to see the baby, and take his children away with him. And then? Then, perhaps, the natural death that Mr. Binyon recommended. I could see no happier outcome.

May 23 was a Sunday. On May 24, unusually, no letter arrived from London. Marian did not begin to worry until the following day, but by that evening she was greatly concerned. When the post boy came to the door with a wire she was there on the instant.

Laura was close behind. "Take care, Marian," she cried. "If it is bad news, do not let it overset you. At the least, sit down. You must take the greatest care of your health."

Paying no attention to this good advice Marian tore the envelope open. As she mastered the contents her large dark eyes almost seemed to start from her head. She turned white, and then red again. "Walter," Laura cried. "She swoons! Help me!"

I was in time to support Marian as she tottered. I would have lowered her to the floor but she suddenly sprang to life again, crying, "Laura, Walter! Read this to me, so that I may be sure I understand it!"

With trembling fingers she held the telegram out. Laura took it and read aloud, "Margaret dead. Accident fire. Funeral Saturday. Come. Letters follow. Camlet."

"Mrs. Camlet dead, in an accident?" It took me a moment to fully comprehend this. "I'm astonished. She was in the bloom of vigor and health."

"A fire! That happens too often to ladies," Laura said. "Our sleeves and lace petticoats catch a flame too easily."

"God have mercy upon her, poor woman." Marian pressed both hands to her face. "What an awful way to die."

"We must look to the letter for more details," I said.

More practically, Marian added, "I must finish my dress. Laura, will you help me with the sewing? We have but a day!"

"Perhaps we can get Phoebe to help with the hemming," Laura said. "And Lottie knows how to pick out basting threads."

And they were off and away on their dressmaking. But the

thought I did not voice was, how convenient. Margaret Camlet's death solved all of Camlet's difficulties, and Marian's too.

The promised letters arrived the next day, and I append the one addressed to me here:

Hampstead, 25 May 1858
My dear Hartright,

You will have received my wire. Margaret has perished by misadventure. While passing through the greenhouse she let fall a lamp, accidentally setting her skirts afire, and so perished. It was late on Sunday evening. Passersby saw the flames from the lane, and called for the fire engines. I was notified shortly thereafter. We had our differences but I am sorry she died in such a shockingly sudden way.

The funeral will be on Saturday. May I beg you to attend? And bring down Micah and Lottie, and most importantly Marian? Custom dictates that a widower must wait a year before remarrying, but I think that we must be somewhat more precipitate. I will consult with her when you come.

Yours most faithfully,
T.H.W. Camlet

We arrived in London on the Friday afternoon, and Camlet met us at the station. Laura and Marian's nimble needles had worked wonders. Marian's dress, of blue striped with grey, was loose enough to hide her condition but mysteriously fashionable as well. Under the wide hoops any thickening of her figure was invisible. A white collar and cuffs cunningly drew the eye up and away from what she wanted to conceal. Over all she wore a dove-coloured cloak, a voluminous black lace shawl with a long knotted silk fringe, and a veil trailing from her bonnet down to past her knees. Behind all this voluminous fabric only close observation revealed anything of her state.

The children pressed their faces against the windows and

screamed, "Papa! Papa!" The compartment doors were opened and they tumbled out into his arms. I helped Marian down and then directed the porter about our many bags and cases. When I turned my attention to them again it struck me how much a family they looked, the affectionate bewhiskered paterfamilias, an adoring dove-like mother clinging to his arm, and the two hooting children cavorting around the platform to the great inconvenience of the other passengers.

"How you have grown, in a mere three months," Camlet exclaimed. He was dressed in deep mourning, all in black with crape in his hat. "Has your Aunt Laura been regaling you with country milk and fresh eggs? My dearest, you look marvelously well. That colour looks uncommonly lovely on you. Micah, this is not the place for cartwheels. Lottie, if you tumble onto the rails I shall be seriously displeased."

I hastened to capture Lottie's hand, and Marian seized the slack of Micah's jacket. Camlet's brougham waited outside and with infinite trouble, for the confining yet exciting train journey had made the little ones wild, we got bag and baggage loaded and set off. "You are looking well yourself, Camlet," I observed. "Better."

"Ahem. Thank you." Of course we were all constrained from mentioning serious subjects in front of the children. "I'm residing at Sandett House again. I hope you both will accept my hospitality there."

"I had intended to stay at my mother's," I returned. "But her cottage is so small that I believe I will take you up on your kind offer, Camlet. Marian of course has the first claim on the guest room, and the idea of camping in Mother's little garden is not attractive."

"Ah. Well, that would be very suitable." His disappointment was visible. I was clearly not the guest he hoped to secure. But I was amused and pleased to see him hide it. "I shall be delighted to entertain you, Hartright. You may assist me with these two wild animals, now returned to the nest."

Marian had her hand tucked in his. "It would not be suitable for you to invite me to dinner. You cannot entertain while in mourning. But I will take it on myself to invite all of you, after the obsequies are over, to come to tea every day."

"Seed cake!" Lottie shouted.

"No no," her father reproved. "The guests do not set the bill of fare. You shall eat what is set before you, young miss." Between the side whiskers his smile was like a drunk man's, only the intoxicant was happiness. Everyone was full of simple joy. Why did I not feel it? There was something wrong.

I got out with Marian at my mother's cottage to help her carry her bags in, and undertook to walk up the lane to Sandett House for supper before dark. My mother and Sarah greeted us with great cordiality and gave us tea. And they were well supplied with all the neighbourhood tittle-tattle about the tragedy.

"I've always taught you children to be careful of fire," my mother said. "Candles of course are the worst, and gas is explosive, but lamps – that oil! – are also dangerous. Extraordinarily dangerous, and this proves it. A crinoline fire, so tragically common among women. We are burnt offerings to fashion!"

"She was in the greenhouse," Sarah said. "You remember, Marian, those beautiful lilies and narcissi? I hear tell that since Mr. Camlet moved to his lodgings in Primrose Hill, the grounds and greenhouse are sadly neglected."

"No tell is needed," my mother chimed in. "You can see the state of the greenhouse from the road. But, so fortunate! Because that night, the flames could be seen from the lane. It was Mr. Brewster who saw them, you remember him, Walter. He lives on the other side of the village, but he was walking home from visiting his daughter. And thank goodness he's hale and fleet of foot, to run for the beadle."

"Dropped the lamp, and the burning oil touched off her petticoats," Sarah said.

"A terrible thing. But providentially the house did not go up. Such a tumult the fire engine made. The horses came at a gallop, and all the village boys ran yelling behind."

Marian recalled, "The greenhouse is removed from the main building by a corridor."

"It was the drugget on the floor that caught, though the floor beneath was of slate," Sarah said. "She must have been overcome by the fumes."

"Do you go to the funeral, Mrs. Hartright?"

"It's not at all the thing, in this parish, for women to attend funerals," my mother said. "Surely you, my dear, do not look to attend. In your condition! In fact I wonder that you were so daring as to come to London at all."

Marian bowed her head and modestly made no mention of a second wedding. Until everything was fixed it would be imprudent to tell my mother about it. "I wanted to support Theo in this sad time," she said vaguely. "I hope I may trespass upon your hospitality for a little while."

"Oh, by all means, my dear. Your room is ready, is it not, Sarah?"

Before the last of the daylight was gone I made my departure and walked up the lane to Sandett House. As my mother had reported, the damage was visible from the road. Several of the panes in the roof of the greenhouse were shattered, and the rest were grimy on the inside from smoke. I was shown in, but Camlet was occupied, something about running the bath for Lottie. I took the opportunity to wander through the main level of the house.

Only the Wardian case in the drawing room window seemed to be lush and in good health. The glass lid keeps the moisture in. The other ferns on the window sills or plant stands were dying or dead, clearly unwatered for weeks. The air pistol was tucked behind one of the cloisonné vases on the mantel. Beyond the drawing room was the study, and on the other side of the central hall were a morning room and the dining room. From the study a French door led out into a short, flagged passageway, also glassed in and fitted with plant shelves, that ended in the ruined greenhouse.

Here also neglect and drought reigned. Aspidistra leaves trailed down, yellow and ailing, and palm stems fainted over the rims of their pots. Particularly sad were the hanging pots up near the peak of the glass roof. In the last light of the evening the drooping fuschias seemed to reach down, pleading for help. Camlet was the green thumb of the family, and in his absence no one had thought to tend any of the plants. Dry leaves shed by the potted lemon tree carpeted the flags except for the wide central area of the burning, which showed black. Smuts and soot overlaid everything, tracked over all the unburnt sections of drugget runner by many feet. A raw wind whistled in through the shattered panes of glass.

I stood in the doorway, unwilling to track soot back into the house. And although I had never seen this room before, my heart grew cold and I shuddered as I recognised it. This was no closed vestry, walled in ancient stone, its stout oaken doors banded and studded with iron. This open and airy glass house was the very reverse, and yet no less a place of death. Neither reason nor logic were to hand, but instinct shivered like ice water down my spine. These haunted aspidistras were witnesses to a crime. Someone had died here, a soul cut cruelly off. Margaret Camlet would be as unmourned and quickly forgotten as Sir Percival Glyde, burned to death just as he was. But this had been no accident. She had been murdered.

From behind me Camlet spoke, making me start. "Gloomy, is it not? I came over regularly to exercise Boreas, but did not enter the house. I see now that I should have insisted on it."

"The house has missed your presence," I agreed. "Was that on Mr. Erbistock's advice?"

"Along with my removal to lodgings. Part of the legal effort to demonstrate the complete collapse of our union." He sighed. "I raised that lemon tree from a seed. It was fifteen years old."

I could not hold back my question. "Your late wife seems to have deliberately and intentionally neglected all you value, Camlet. Did she … hate you?"

He touched an orchid on its glass shelf, brown and sere but still clinging to its bark. "Perhaps a better word would be contempt, Hartright. I cannot describe to you, the frustration and misery of being chained to a partner who not only dislikes you but regards you with immoveable disdain. She could not abide me, and she was not one to hide her opinion or soften her expression of it. It was almost a chemical, an atomical repulsion, like magnets forced like pole to like. And I was by no means free of fault … But *nil nisi bonum*. Come, it grows chilly here – you're shivering. Let us step back into the drawing room and have a little sherry before dinner."

I had but little inclination for the wine. My eerie insight in the greenhouse oppressed me; I weighed whether to confide it to my host. Camlet was also subdued, but this was proper for a man just widowed. The children came down in their nightgowns to say goodnight to their father, and when they were gone upstairs he said, "I must thank you again, Hartright, for your excellent care of my children. Your kindness was an enormous comfort to me –"

The doorbell chimed. Strange voices were heard in the hall, and soon an older man was shown in. He had a handsome grey handlebar moustache, and wore a long brown tweed coat. "Inspector Radenton," Camlet greeted him. "I believe it would be incorrect for me to offer you sherry. May I have them bring you tea? This is a family connection, Walter Hartright, down from the north country for the funeral."

The sight of a police official overset me even more. "Never say it was murder, Inspector?" I blurted.

Camlet gaped at me, and Inspector Radenton shouted with laughter. "Oh lord, are you another one of them? If ever I get my hands on that fellow Edgar Poe, I shall thrash him. Do you realise what that silly American magazine story of his has done? If we're unlucky the police shall be cursed with imitators of Arsène Dupin of every stripe: old ladies, minor nobility, oddball students, Oxford dons. Meddling, trying to assist us, searching for clues, deducing! There'll be no end to it."

"I beg your pardon," I said hastily. "I was more disturbed by the sight of the greenhouse than I thought, and spoke at random."

"It's late for a call, Inspector," Camlet said. "Do you bring news?"

"I do, sir. You recall that our first assumption that the late Mrs. Camlet was a victim of a common household accident."

"A crinoline fire," I said, "touched off when she dropped the lamp."

"Simple and plain," Camlet said. "What possible development could be made of this?"

The inspector frowned horribly at me over his moustache. "If you say 'I knew it,' I shall press charges on you, Mr. Hartright. Murder, indeed. The post-mortem results have just come back. Mrs. Camlet was struck on the head, possibly by the very lamp found by her body, and then set alight. She did not die of the fire. The back of her skull was cracked in. Camlet, have you made an inventory of the valuables in this house? Could it be that the lady was slain during the commission of a burglary?"

"Why –" Camlet blinked. "I've had no occasion to do so. But there's little of value here. Come through to the dining room, and we shall see if the silver is still in the sideboard."

We quickly adjourned to the dining room, where the maid was laying the table for dinner. The polished black oak sideboard that took up much of one wall had no great treasure on display – a china bowl, some pewter candelabra, and the usual dessert service. Camlet opened the drawers and we saw the silver spoons and forks, all apparently undisturbed.

"And you keep no large sum of money in the house," Inspector Radenton said, making a note.

"No indeed. Except for the weekly household budget, which is in the care of Mrs. Youngblood, but that can scarcely amount to ten pounds."

"What of the lamp?" I asked. "Which room was it carried from?"

For this we had to consult Mrs. Youngblood the housekeeper, and Ellen the housemaid. Both women agreed that the household inventory of lamps had been fixed for a generation. Gas was laid on for the streetlamps but had not yet been run into the house. It was Ellen's task to clean and fill the lamps every day, and so she knew them well. "It was one of the two big brass lamps in the drawing room," she said. "They were a matching pair, and you can still see its fellow on the table."

"Burglars," the inspector said, with satisfaction. "Knowing there were only women in the house, they broke into the greenhouse, where entry was easiest. When Mrs. Camlet came suddenly upon them, they struck her down and fled."

"How terrible!" Camlet said. "This has always been a safe district. My neighbours will be greatly alarmed. Hartright, your mother and sister also live alone! Inspector, have there been other housebreaking attempts?"

"She was armed," I reminded them. "An air pistol, and she was a crack shot. And would professional thieves seize upon an ordinary metal kerosene lamp, glass chimney and all? I had imagined bravoes of that sort complete with their own dark lanterns, or perhaps a bulls-eye."

Inspector Radenton glared at me. "Be warned, sir, be warned! Leave these thoughts to the professional police, if you please."

"I would be delighted to," I hastened to assure him.

"You will keep me abreast of your discoveries, Inspector," Camlet said. "Do you wish to interview Mrs. Youngblood, or any of my other staff? Possibly Ned Matson, my coachman, could be of help. He sleeps over the stable, and may have seen something."

"I will just step downstairs with a few questions, if you will permit. Do not let me interrupt your meal, sirs."

Leaving the inspector to his duties, we sat down to a simple meal, boiled beef and roast potatoes. At that period Camlet was not possessed of luxurious tastes. His only indulgences, so far as I could tell, were a mild tendency to dandyism, plants, and Marian. After dinner he prevailed upon me to accompany him in walking down to the cottage again, ostensibly to warn the ladies about the possibility of housebreakers in the district. I gave way to him in this, though I knew it would serve no purpose except to alarm.

I sat in Mother's parlour soothing her while she fretted about the sturdiness of the latches on the windows, while Camlet walked in the summer evening garden hand in hand with Marian. Allegedly he was discoursing to her upon how the roses had been pruned, but it would make a cat laugh, the way the pruning was in need of the most thorough inspection in the darkest and most secluded garden nooks. As a result we did not return to Sandett House until very late.

The funeral was to take place in Highgate Cemetery, not far from the Camlet home. I would have attended alone, but Marian insisted on coming too, even though we all assured her that the presence of a second wife at the obsequies of the first was unheard of and not at all necessary. She maintained however that Camlet would appreciate her presence, and promised to stay well at the back and wear her heavy veil. Before she could cite her condition I gave way.

In the event our scruples were utterly unnecessary. Over the years there had been enough notoriety about Camlet and his wife that the crowd of onlookers at the chapel just inside the cemetery gates was immense. All the neighbourhood turned out, every person who had ever been acquainted with Camlet, and many other vulgar onlookers as well, both women and men. In the press

Marian, in her veil and black bombazine, was unremarkable, and nobody paid the least attention to us.

Camlet was nearly the sole mourner. A distant cousin or two were all the connections left of the family. The Reverend Angier had been persuaded to overlook all the deceased's notions and preside over the interment. The service was simple, with no reference at all to any of her lurid history. The grave was in a peaceful spot on the western side near a mossy stone wall. Marian whispered to me, "He intends to plant it with ivy, after the earth settles. And perhaps winter jasmine."

"May she rest in peace, poor woman," I replied.

After the burial we followed the crowd. Under the great bell tower the tall gates of the cemetery stood open. We had walked here, and I had planned to walk back, but Marian said, "Do you mind, Walter? I need to sit down."

"If you look to ride back with Camlet in the carriage –"

"Of course not," she said, serenely untruthful. "My feet in these shoes are giving me some trouble, that's all."

Resigned, I waited as she settled herself upon the low stone coping of the fence. Neither of them had been so improper as to discuss a second wedding yet. It would have been in extraordinarily poor taste, before the funeral. But now plans could be quickly made. For some while the crowd passed out of the gates, dispersing into their carriages or walking away. At last Camlet came into view, walking down the graveled lane in company with some of the cemetery managers. Marian brightened, adjusting her veil and shawl.

As she rose to her feet a knot of men suddenly emerged from between some carriages. "Theophilus Camlet?" I recognised the inspector, with his grey handlebar moustache.

"Yes," Camlet said. "Great heavens, Inspector. What is this?"

"We have some queries that cannot wait, sir," the inspector said. "Will you come with us?"

Camlet said nothing, seemingly struck immobile. Suddenly his face was ghastly, dead white above the short whiskers. In that one glimpse a new and terrible idea came into my head. He was the man. Camlet had murdered his own wife.

"Sir?" Inspector Radenton bent his head to peer under the

brim of Camlet's top hat. "Did you hear what I said?"

"No," Camlet said, with a gasp. "I mean –"

"He's going to swoon," Marian exclaimed.

But instead of collapsing Camlet shocked us all. He turned and took to his heels, surprisingly fleet in his dress boots. There were four or five policemen, not uniformed but recognizable enough. Dodging past them, Camlet ran right back through the cemetery gates, looking neither to right nor left. I doubt he saw Marian or myself.

"Is he gone mad?" I said. "To run from the authorities?"

"He's beside himself," Marian cried.

The policemen were already hot on his heels, calling out to each other so that their voices rang in the great entry courtyard, human hounds baying on the trail. Camlet had run not up the central stairs but up the slope to the right along the graveled lane that led to the gravesites. The ground was open, with few trees planted yet and one could see a long way.

I made to follow but suddenly Inspector Radenton confronted me. "He compels us to arrest him, Mr. Hartright," he declared. "Only a guilty man would flee in fear. And you, his friend. Perhaps you are an accomplice?"

"Since I was in Cumberland on the day of the lady's death, that would be quite a feat," I retorted.

"And your companion? Present me, if you would."

Very reluctantly I did so. "Marian, this is Inspector Radenton, who is investigating the death of Mrs. Camlet. Inspector, my sister-in-law, Miss Marian Halcombe."

Her veil, cloak, and shawls might fool the casual eye but the inspector's glance seemed to skin them all off. "Miss Halcombe? Your name is in our files. The co-respondent in the Camlet bigamy case."

Marian flung the useless veil back. "You cannot accuse Theophilus Camlet of this crime," she said boldly. "It's unthinkable. He is widely respected and is of notably gentle habit."

The furious light in her large dark eyes made me quail, but not knowing his opponent the inspector merely bowed. "I must have a more vigorous imagination than you, Miss Halcombe," he replied. "I could easily envision a bigamist moving on to other, larger, crimes."

"That was an accident, and he was acquitted!"

"Very dubious," Radenton countered. "How does one accidentally commit bigamy? He must be a prey to absentmindedness." He chuckled at his own wit.

"I have had occasion to note before," Marian said hotly, "that the authorities hold their awful powers over the populace with a shocking lack of seriousness!"

Radenton frowned at her. "You have not given up on the gentleman, I see, Miss Halcombe. Perhaps, if Camlet does not surrender, we could invite you to Scotland Yard to aid in our inquiry."

I would have protested this, but Marian's frank and forthright speech could not be stopped. "If you mutton shunters are so desperate as to consult a mere female, and in my condition," she retorted, "I would of course be happy to assist."

There was a yell from some of the policemen within the gates. "Marian," I hissed in her ear while the inspector was distracted. "For God's love, hold your tongue!"

"They cannot take him back to Newgate, Walter! He barely survived last time, even though they awarded him bail. A second detention will kill him."

"Do you think Radenton is inviting you to supper? Marian, you could be in prison yourself!"

But then Camlet himself came into sight, frog-marched along by three policemen back down the hill. He was limping, and leaves and earth clung to his black funeral suit – clearly he had taken a fall. His collar was twisted awry up under one ear, and the coat was torn at the shoulder seam. He was panting, and seemed dazed, unable to grasp what was happening to him. Marian cried out his name, but he didn't look around.

"Marian, you cannot interfere!" She would have run to him but I held her back by main strength. Trembling, she tried to pull away, but I said, "You cannot help him like this. We have a clear duty to go back and take care of the children in his absence."

"The children, oh yes." Tears ran down her face. "Oh Walter, what shall we tell them?"

"We'll think of something." We watched as Radenton and his men manhandled Camlet into a carriage. All the remaining onlookers and neighbours gaped and stared as well. I doubted this time we could hide the truth from the little ones.

When the crush of carriages was less we saw Camlet's own brougham. Recognizing me Matson pulled up. "Your master is gone in another carriage," I said. "Will you take us back?"

"Yes, sir." I helped Marian up. It was only a short drive. She wept, overcome by this new calamity. I sat half-stunned, scarcely regarding her. The thoughts steaming through my own head frightened me. Had Camlet ever really been worthy of trust?

I remembered Marian's account of her first sight of him. Shouting at her over the garden gate was not consonant with the clement and kindly face he had shown since. Could he be a quite different person in reality – as Count Fosco, as Sir Percival Glyde had been? A stranger, deft with blackmail and the coercive power of money, who could play Marian's noble heart the way Laura played her piano? We had both been mildly astonished at how quickly Camlet had wooed and won her. He is plainly no Lothario, and Laura declared it showed the power of true love. Now this deftness took on an ominous aspect.

Camlet had the key to his own house, and knew all the ways of it. He admitted that he came by regularly to exercise his horse. Margaret Camlet had been a crack shot, but he, alone of all men, would find it easy to surprise her on a dark evening, perhaps after one of those horse excursions. Even yesterday evening, a less cunning murderer might have hidden some of the silver, to lend conviction to the idea of burglars. But a bolder man would rely upon his respectability. He would simply say the truth, so that he could never be caught out in a lie.

His nerve had broken just now at the cemetery gate. But why? Was it merely an overwhelming dread of the horrors of yet another incarceration? He had mentioned a dislike of being closed in, which surely had been exacerbated by his stay in Newgate. Or was it something uglier – guilt? Another Fosco, holding tame animals in his palm all the while cloaking the blackest rascality in his heart...

He had said to me himself, that he would do anything to legitimise the child to come. To marry Marian. If he had really murdered Margaret Camlet to achieve this, then he ought to hang. He certainly ought not to wed Marian. However much she loved him and believed in him, to tie herself for all time to a man of violence could only lead to misery. And as we all knew to our cost, once the marriage bond was forged there was no going back.

None of these words could be said as I sat across from her. Marian had never been anything other than an ally, but now for the first time we were at opposing purposes. Instantly I resolved never to openly cross swords with her. Her womanly airs and concealing shawls were merely the white feathers of the Arctic falcon, concealing it against its native snows. In the past Marian was a ferociously formidable opponent. In the defense of those she loved she knew neither pity nor fear. She was the deadliest foe imaginable, those dark eyes the piercing glare of the predator bird.

And if I forced things to that pass, I might lose Laura as well. Put to the ultimate test, my dear wife might well choose her sister over myself. The two are very close, almost the same heart in two bodies. Almost the very first words that Marian had ever said to me were, "You must please both of us, or neither of us." No, my course must be to watch and wait. If Camlet was acquitted yet once more, all the circumstances of the crime would necessarily be made more plain. And if he was hanged in Newgate for the murder? Then these concerns would lie hushed in my breast for all time.

❧ *Marian Halcombe's journal* ❦

Hampstead, 29 May

Micah is nearly eight years old now, and Lottie six. No one is old enough to bear the dreadful burden we had to lay upon them. But they could not be sheltered any longer, not here in London. Not with newsboys crying the news of the bigamist Camlet arrested for murder, and my poor man's name blazoned on scandal sheets at every newsstand. We agreed on the way home that we had to tell the entire household as soon as possible. Thank heaven that Walter is here to help me with this! As the father of two he knows well how to manage the little ones. He was quite pale and distressed, and I could see he was considering how to best phrase the terrible news.

"And perhaps it would be better if you remove back to Sandett House," he suggested. "At least until it's known what Camlet's fate will be. Propriety clearly will no longer be offended if you do, and the children need every consolation."

"That is very well thought of, Walter," I said. In times of trouble his delicacy and right thinking has been always a great support. "I shall certainly do as you say."

When the carriage halted in the drive the children tumbled out to meet it. Lottie peered into the carriage as I descended. "Miss Marian, where is Papa?"

"Let us call the staff together," Walter said, "so I may tell everyone at once. Matson, let the horses stand for a moment."

The entire household was assembled in the drive, half a dozen souls all told and the children. Walter stood on the portico step and said, "I have bad news. Mr. Camlet was taken away this afternoon by the police, in connection with the death of his wife Margaret Camlet."

There was a murmur of horror. "But Miss Marian is his wife," Lottie put in, and I hushed her.

Ellen burst into tears, and Mrs. Youngblood wrung her hands. "But what will happen to him?" Micah cried.

"No one knows," Walter said. "But we, Miss Halcombe and I, are certain that the truth will be uncovered. The guilt will be fixed in the correct quarter. Until that happy day everything here will continue as it always has, and everyone should continue to do their duty."

"So it was a mistake," Lottie said, tears in her eyes.

"Yes, a terrible mistake," I confirmed. "Your uncle is quite right. The truth shall be uncovered. Someone else is responsible for this dreadful crime. And Uncle Walter is just the man to find that person!"

"I?" For some reason Walter looked entirely astonished.

"Of course you, Walter," I cried, hope springing up in my heart. "Oh, thank God you are here. Micah, Lottie, your uncle has no peer, in tracking down the true course of events. He has performed mighty tasks! I shall render you such poor assistance as I can of course, but it is your intelligence and will, Walter, that shall find the true culprit, and exonerate Theo."

"Thank you sir, thank you," Mrs. Youngblood said. "Never was a kinder master, and I'm sure there has been some terrible error."

"God's blessing on the work, sir," Ellen the housemaid said

with a sob. "The master wouldn't hurt a fly, and so I shall tell that inspector if he dares to show his face here again."

"Mr. Hartright and I shall put our shoulders to the task immediately," I said. "To this end I plan to take up residence here at Sandett House again. Davey, when the horses are put away perhaps you will walk down to Mrs. Hartright's cottage and bring up my baggage. I will write you a note to carry to her. Lottie, wipe your nose. Nurse, do you have a handkerchief for her? Mrs. Youngblood, let dinner be served when convenient."

As I bustled everyone off onto their duties Walter followed me indoors. "Marian, you should know that Inspector Radenton has declared a strong dislike of imitators of Mr. Arsène Dupin. He will certainly not abide amateur meddling in his official business."

"Is that a novel? I have not read it," I said. "I doubt I'll have time now. A man of your gifts and power will not let such a minor obstacle deter you. Consider only how you brought both Sir Percival Glyde and Count Fosco to book. And it was your foresight that ensured Theo's acquittal only this season. No, I shall thank God on my knees that you take the matter in hand, Walter. And I know that you will not, you cannot fail!" Tears sprang to my eyes and I clasped his hand in both my own. "For my entire happiness now is in your keeping."

"Marian, I – do not pin your hopes upon my efforts, I implore you," he said. "Mrs. Camlet could have been slain by anyone at all. Very probably it was nothing but a burglary gone awry, the culprit concealed forever among the teeming slums of criminal London. The crime may be impossible of solution."

"We cannot let that be a consideration." I took a deep breath. "You and I, Walter, we must sort it out. Before it's too late."

31 May

The hardships of Newgate were so awful, no wonder my poor man had been unable to face a return. A man accused of murder cannot be freed on bail, and the thought of his fear and misery made me wring my hands. Therefore the first task on Monday morning was for Walter to go to the prison and purchase more comforts for Theo, as he had before. I spent yesterday amassing a basket of items: clothing, bedding, soap, nourishing and compact food.

I would have carried it myself, but Walter absolutely forbade this. "Newgate is the vilest and most notorious prison in England," he declared. "It is no sight for women and children."

"How can that be so," I demanded, "if sensation-seekers may pay to go in every Wednesday?"

I wondered if Walter was going to tear his hair, a gesture he can ill afford since his forehead is making inroads upon his scalp. "I can promise you, Marian, that Camlet himself would beg you to stay well away. No man would wish the mother of his child to be exposed to such a place. Are you aware that such appalling spectacles can actually mar children not yet born?"

Nurse assured me that this was true. Women in the family way are far more sensitive to outside influences. She spoke of harelips caused when a hare crosses a woman's path. So for the sake of the infant to come I reluctantly gave way.

While Walter was gone on his errand of mercy, I therefore set about another necessary task. I would search the house for possible information about Margaret Camlet's death. And I would combine this with spring cleaning. Margaret had apparently never directed Mrs. Youngblood to do this, and Theo living in Primrose Hill had never done it either.

In this housewifely spirit I sallied into the greenhouse. All these dying and dead plants were untidy, shedding their leaves everywhere and lowering to the spirits. Any that could not be revived by watering could be cleared out. That done, the greenhouse could be cleaned and repaired. When Theo came back he would enjoy restocking it.

But before I set this in train I inspected the scene of the tragedy with the most minute care. The greenhouse was a relatively small space, not more than twelve feet by fifteen, built in the fashionable style with an elaborately gabled roof. Theo's loving care usually made it a jungle in miniature. Now nearly everything was dead. All plants that were crisp and brown I set aside for disposal. Only the largest sago palm, a great prickly thing with stiff fronds as long as my arm, seemed partly alive. All the woody outer leaves were dead but the innermost ones were green. I watered it, soaking the pot, and hoped it would survive.

The drugget ran up the centre of the space. Halfway along,

the slate floor beneath showed through the great burnt spot where Margaret Camlet had lain. If she had been kinder and tidier – if she had watered the plants so that all their leaves had not dried out and drifted to the floor in heaps – there would not have been quite so much dry tinder here.

I stepped softly around the place, drawing my skirts close. It was broad daylight, the sun pouring through the glass and warming the room, but I felt a chill. Surely, if the dead haunted the place of their demise, the ghost of the poor woman lingered here.

"We will avenge you," I said boldly aloud, in case the spirit still lingered. "The guilty party shall be discovered." In a quieter tone I could not resist adding, "I know that you shall not object if I love him better than you did." I do not know if anything heard me. But the sun warmed my back like a comforting hand, and a tumbled pot beckoned for me to straighten it.

There was nothing here that should not be here – clay pots, gravel, scattered earth, dry fallen leaves. But I had not really expected it, had I? To find a handy murder weapon that the rescue people and the police had all overlooked? Several of the glass panes had been shattered, either by the heat of the blaze or by the rescuers in dousing the fire. I swept up and poured the sweepings into a box for later examination. When Mrs. Youngblood found me pulling burnt drugget up she cried out in dismay. "Madam, your dress will be spoilt. And consider your condition!"

"I do not want to hear about my condition," I said.

"At least let Payne do it, madam." This was the gardener's day with us, so I consented to this and went indoors to wash. Then I sat on a chair in the back garden and gingerly sifted through the box of sweepings in the bright afternoon light. All the pieces of glass were window-glass, flat sharp shards. Would there be any point in fitting them together? Ah, but here – there was one shard, about the size of three fingers, that was not flat. It was curved. The curve of a lamp chimney? I took it indoors and compared it to the remaining lamp in the drawing room.

The glass of this lamp was clear, not milky or coloured like the glass bases of some lamps. My shard was precisely the right thinness and curvature for the chimney of its mate. I picked up the remaining lamp and hefted it in my hands.

Full of oil, it was heavy. I was not strong enough to do it, but a man might use it as a club or a missile. But it was an awkward weapon, hard to wield quickly. At night when it was lit it would be hot and splashing oil. It would not be difficult to set your own hair alight instead of your victim's. One would not set out with such a lamp intending murder, or lurk in waiting with it. It was a weapon of impulse, the tool at hand when the need suddenly became dire. No expert – no professional burglar, for instance – would choose this as a weapon. And yet someone had slipped into this very drawing room. He had lifted the mate to this lamp high above his head, and stepped softly after her as she walked into the greenhouse. And he had used the massive brass base to crack Margaret Camlet's skull.

Then our housemaid Ellen came into the drawing room. "Miss Halcombe, is something wrong? Do you wish the lamp to be lit?"

"Not until the usual time, thank you." Hastily I set the lamp back down upon its doily. "Come upstairs with me, Ellen, and show me Mrs. Camlet's things."

The mistress of the house had her own chamber, but when I had been his wife I had happily shared a bedroom with Theo, using my bedroom next door only for dressing. His room was the largest bedchamber in the house and dominated by an enormous old-fashioned four-poster bed with crimson curtains. The heavy bureaux and chests were also of the last generation, giving the chamber a solid masculine air. Last night I had moved back into this room again and slept deliciously, surrounded by the male scent of him on pillows and covers. Now I went across to the connecting door. When I had been in residence this door always stood open. "Odd," I said, turning the knob. "It's locked."

"The missus always kept it locked from her side," Ellen volunteered.

"How long have you been in service here, Ellen?"

"I was third housemaid with old Mr. Henton Camlet, his grandfather, Mrs. Youngblood being first housemaid. The old gentleman had a great barrack of a house in Wiltshire. And when Mr. Theo married we both came with him here."

I considered her, a prim woman in her late forties, her fading hair neat under a lace cap. "I find it difficult to believe that Mrs. Camlet was slain by burglars," I said slowly. "And if she was not, then who would kill her, and why? The answer must lie in the family's past. And you, Ellen, must have seen a good deal of it."

"I would do anything to help Mr. Theo," the good woman replied. "Surely to goodness you should lie down a bit, Miss Halcombe. Suppose you put your feet up and I bring you a cup of tea, and then I'll tell you what you like about the missus."

"Bring a cup for yourself, and it's a bargain." And in no time I was comfortably disposed on top of the coverlet and Ellen on a hassock, the tray of tea on the bed between us.

"I don't want you to tell me what would make Mr. Theo uncomfortable," I began. "But I do want to hear about Mrs. Camlet. Did she visit in Wiltshire, before they married?"

"Only once, miss, during the hunting season. We were all struck by her beauty and spirit. She carried her own gun and went out with the old gentlemen, and they brought back six pheasants. Such a lovely lady, with that curly golden hair! He should have been very happy. But for some reason they didn't suit at all."

"From the very beginning?"

"Even before," Ellen said, shaking her head. "Mr. Theo went and begged his grandfather to call it off. Mr. Henton was a great sportsman, and he said that a horse sometimes refused the fence, but eventually got over."

It struck me that the elder Mr. Camlet had had an unpleasantly agricultural view of the whole business. He might have been breeding cattle, selecting a likely looking cow for his bull. "And that did not happen."

"She disliked it as much as he." Ellen tipped her head at the locked connecting door.

I considered this. My poor darling man! "But there were the children."

"Both the old gentlemen looked for an heir, and insisted to him it was his duty." Ellen hesitated. "She blacked his eye."

"What?"

"That was poor Master Micah's beginning," Ellen recalled, "and she never could abide the poor mite."

This was horrifying. That men sometimes beat their wives is sadly not unknown, but the reverse? I remembered how Margaret

Camlet had towered nearly a head taller over me. Younger and smaller, Theo had never had the mastery. And Margaret herself deserved no less sympathy, harried by greedy and selfish relatives into a repugnant union. Alas that she had never lived to meet Laura, for there is much they could have said to each other.

But ... "What of little Lottie?"

"That was all on account of the Rev. Angier."

"Indeed? How does he come into it?"

"Why, it was his pastoral duty, he said, to foster a reconciliation between man and wife. He had them over to St. John's, together and separate, regular-like for months. And in the end they did agree to try again, and all went well. For a week or two."

So in addition to the pressures of family, the church had been called in. All to rivet together a shattered union that should never have been made in the first place. With an aching heart I remembered how careful our courtship had been, how anxious Theo had been that I was not hurried or unwilling or repulsed. Even on our honeymoon – I had put his kindness and consideration down to the instincts of a true gentleman and his respect for the shyness of a new bride. But he had been more the wounded veteran putting his full weight on the scarred leg for the first time. He had learned from his mistakes, but how costly the knowledge had been! He had spoken of how long it had taken him, to try again. And Mrs. Hartright had mentioned the neighbourhood's long-frustrated expectation of his remarriage.

I was surprised now that he had been able to contemplate matrimony again at all. No one should have been surprised if he had taken a vow of celibacy. Such a calamitous first marriage would have embittered a lesser character. But his heart was still affectionate, his nature loving. This amazing courage showed that, like the hero in *Jane Eyre*, he had an irresistible bent towards love and marriage.

"Once Miss Lottie was born," Ellen went on, "the missus washed her hands of the entire boiling. She had her own friends and lived her own life, and paid Mr. Theo and the little ones no mind at all. But you know the very worst?" I found it hard to imagine what could be worse than abandoning your children and striking your husband, but Ellen shook her head portentously over her cup. "She gave up Christianity. Fancy! She said she was no longer a believer, and refused to go to church any more."

I leaned back on the pillows, filled with pity. What a miserable and unhappy pair! Every societal institution that should have been a comfort and a support had failed them utterly: their families, the children, the church. And yet they could not get free, tear at each other as they would. The chain that bound them together was adamant, indissoluble perhaps even to the death, for it was entirely possible that Margaret would drag Theo with her down into her grave.

I was lying on my back, my growing abdomen outlined by my loose gown, for I was not wearing stays. And I felt it – an internal bump. I thought it was my digestion. But no, it was a movement, a quickening. My baby was alive! Wild with excitement I cried, "Feel, Ellen, feel! Right here, can you perceive it?"

"Yes, Miss Halcombe. How lovely, a fine strong baby it is already!"

"I must write and tell Laura, immediately." And so I shall, but first I record all these doings, for Walter's benefit. He needs to know all of this.

❧ *Walter Hartright's narrative* ❧

I was dismayed to learn that Marian assumed that I would be visiting Camlet in Newgate at least twice a week. "His spirits must be kept up," she said. "His terror of the place is already so great. The isolation and loneliness of incarceration can drive men to madness."

The idea filled me with reluctance. I was certain, almost, that Camlet was as guilty as Ananias. But I did not want conversation to bear this out. I felt like the worst sort of swine, a Judas enacting the role of a friend and a brother-in-law. Deceitfully encouraging a desperate and lonely man to implicate himself! It ought not to have felt shameful if he was a murderer, but it did. And Marian would insist that I recount everything her beloved said to me!

But Marian was implacable. "How can you fail in such a small charity, Walter? If you do not go, I certainly shall."

"No, no. Of course I'll go. But not every day. There's too much else to do."

"Oh, that is so. It would be extraordinarily foolish to visit Theo faithfully but thus fail to secure his release, you're quite right. What is our first step?"

Her brilliant dark eyes were full of expectation, pinning me to my seat at the breakfast table. Writhe as I would, I could not escape. "Well, the greenhouse is cleared out. But has anyone examined the lady's personal effects?"

"I was about to do so yesterday, but the chance to plumb Ellen's memory was too good to miss. Let us go up and begin straight away."

We went upstairs and to the bedroom next to Camlet's. Marian had related to me how the connecting door was kept locked in Mrs. Camlet's time. When I have a moment of leisure I resolved to look over her account of her conversation with Ellen. Marian was ever an acute observer and had no peer as a recorder of talk. On this day however she opened the door to Mrs. Camlet's bedroom, and we went in.

The maids had made up the high bed with its blue half-tester, and swept and cleaned in their usual way, so everything was tidy. The fire was laid ready for lighting in the fireplace, and a bowl of potpourri stood on the dressing table, lending its faint fragrance to the close air. The blue velvet curtains were drawn, to save the carpet from the sun. I went across and pulled them aside, raising a sash to let in the fresh summer air. The room was at the front of the house, and from the windows there was a fine view through the leafy trees to Hampstead Heath rolling away green and gold in the distance. It was a handsome chamber, with blue and white medallioned wallpaper, a Chinese carpet to match, and a chaise in front of the fireplace, redecorated in recent years, like the drawing room, for the new mistress of the house.

"You did not sleep in here last night," I said, surveying the pristine space. "But this was your room, when you lived here."

For some reason she blushed, the red coming up under her rather swarthy complexion like wine. "Yes, it was. But Margaret Camlet has been in residence for some months now. I'm sure that Theo has not ordered yet the tidying of all her possessions."

I concurred. Such tasks are properly undertaken after the funeral. "Do you begin on the wardrobe and the bureaux, then. It would be less inappropriate for another female to sort through her clothing. I shall go through the writing table."

"And what are we looking for?"

"Anything of interest, I suppose. Truly, I have no idea."

"We are seeking one, then." Full of confidence, she opened a bureau drawer.

I did not expect Mrs. Camlet's possessions to tell me her full story. The chambers of the past are walled off each one as we leave them, and she had brought little luggage with her from the Continent. But even a man could be surprised that the lady had so little in the way of clothing: some linens, a bodice or two, and the black twill 'rationals' I recognised from my call with my mother. She must have had one other gown, the sensible grey woolen one she had worn in the courtroom, the one she had died in. But otherwise, drawer after drawer rattled open, empty.

"Can she have lived like a nun?" Marian exclaimed. "If this was the usual extent of her wardrobe, then my poor Theo! The bills for my extravagant sartorial demands must have made him faint and ill." This was of course nothing more than Marian's usual raillery.

The only personal item of interest was in a little red velvet bag in the topmost drawer of the dressing table. "A ring." Marian held it up to the light, a heavy gold band elaborately worked and set with three magnificent square-cut sapphires in echelon. "This is a costly bauble."

I examined it closely. "But not hers. See here, the inscription."

Marian read the curly letters aloud. "'L. to D. Love.' A Brickley family heirloom, perhaps her mother or grandmother's? But the style's not terribly antique. My own white opal is older."

"No." I half-closed my eyes to visualise the hues. "Could it be chosen for the wearer? Mrs. Camlet's eyes –"

"Just this colour." Marian nodded in recollection. "It must have looked marvelously striking on her hand. But perhaps blue eyes are a family trait. Little Micah has them."

"And these stones. There's a king's ransom here." The two outer sapphires were large, but the centre stone was enormous, the size of my thumbnail.

"You must ask Theo about it, when next you visit. If he ever glimpsed it he could not fail to remember."

I made a note of it. She was always so full of things to tell Camlet, a running tally had to be kept. I had begun on the mahogany writing desk, which stood between the windows. It was a lady's desk, with a central drawer but only two larger ones to either side, leaving enough space below for the amplitude of skirts and petticoats. There was a clutter of materials, pens, inkpots, penknives, crayons and pencils, penwipers, all crammed into the wide centre drawer. It took some time to sort through.

In no way was anything remarkable. Many of the items were Marian's. This was her sketchbook, with her name inked on its marbled-paper cover – the make I favored and had taught the sisters to use. All these materials must have been swept into the drawer by Mrs. Camlet when she moved in. I had trained Marian and Laura to put tools and materials neatly away. Instinctively now I sorted and put items in order, all the pens together, the pencils sorted by colour and hardness.

"What a tidy man you are, Walter," Marian remarked. She pulled open a side drawer. "You've always been pernickety about drawing implements."

"What is that?" The drawer was solidly filled with one of those pasteboard boxes that reams of foolscap are sold in. The box was tied together with tape.

With some difficulty Marian pried it up and read the words scrawled on the end of the box. "Travel memoir."

"Ah yes. Did not Camlet say that she was writing an account of the sights she had seen on the Continent?"

"Dear me. It sounds dull. And did she travel widely, or see sights of note?"

I remembered the awkward charcoal drawings in the sketchbook. "I fear not. But that reminds me. Where is her own sketchbook? Not this one. Hers had a red paper cover."

Marian wedged the foolscap box back into the drawer and opened the one on the other side. This held an extraordinarily heavy box half-full of .46 caliber shot for the air pistol, and the firearm's traveling case and cleaning kit. The sketchbook was not there. "She showed it to you and your mother down in the drawing room, you said."

"Yes, and I'd like to see it again. Not her sketches of Rome, but the partly-burnt drawings at the back. Those I will swear were not hers."

"Whose, then?"

"Could they not have been Camlet's? They were initialed 'W'."

"It doesn't sound likely," she said. "He's never been to Italy, only Germany and the Low Countries. Protestant theologians worthy of reprint tend to congregate in northern climes. When he abbreviates his name he uses all four letters. You and I have both seen that in his correspondence. And he works with words, not pencils and paint. Perhaps the sketchbook is still downstairs."

There was so little here in the bedroom that we had seen it all. We adjourned downstairs to the drawing room, where I carefully went through the books on the table and even peered under the sofa and shifted the tables. Marian carried dead ferns out into the greenhouse and then dusted the windowsills. "It isn't here," I said. "We must search the entire house. And if it is not to be found, then only three things could have happened to it."

Marian met my gaze, her large dark eyes glittering with intelligence. "Either she sent it away – gave it to someone or posted it through the mails. Or she destroyed it. Or some person took it."

"Precisely."

"She did not go out, you say. So if it was posted, either Ellen or Davey the stable boy took it to the post in the mailbag."

"And if she had a visitor, Ellen would have let that visitor in."

Marian beamed at me. "Do you begin systematically searching the house, since you've seen the sketchbook and can recognise it. I'll go ask Ellen and Mrs. Youngblood."

At least Sandett House is not the size of Limmeridge. It took me an entire exhausting afternoon to comb the place from top to bottom. At the end of that time I could put my hand on my heart and avow that the red sketchbook was not anywhere on the premises. If it was buried in the garden, or flung into the well, or dropped into the cesspit, or burnt in the fireplace, then I would have missed it, but otherwise not.

It was some satisfaction to tell Marian this at dinner. She had spent the afternoon in the kitchen, helping the cook to shell three pounds of peas and then partaking of the servants' tea. I envied it, the high-bred ease that made her welcome at all levels of society. And in her condition Marian could effortlessly exploit the commonality of female nature. It was almost in passing, that she informed me that no packages had been put into the post.

"And I have a list of every caller to the house in the period after your visit with Mrs. Hartright in February. There were very few. Your mother called again in March, with a baking of bread, and in April, with some lettuces. The Rev. Angier called twice, and both times Margaret Camlet was not at home to him."

"Indeed? That seems rather severe."

"Let me make known to you the history of his ministrations to the family – Ellen has been most informative." Over the meal Marian summarised for me all of Ellen's revelations of the day before, and added more gossip garnered today from the cook and Mrs. Youngblood. "...And after she returned in February Margaret Camlet told them she did not approve of service."

"What, the maids and the cook? How did she propose to have meals, or her laundry done?"

"I assume her thinking was not on a practical level. She spoke to Mrs. Youngblood about the necessity of the labourer to be free. The poor woman, she immediately took it to mean that they would all be given their notice."

"Oh, that must have created turmoil."

"It did. The servants' hall was full of the most terrible apprehension, especially when Theo was arrested the first time. They lived in daily dread that Margaret Camlet would take the opportunity to close up most of the house and send them all away."

"Surely she reassured them of her intent? If only to ensure that she got decent dinners."

"When she began potting rabbits it exacerbated their fears even more. She was fortunate they think of Theo as their employer, and not herself. In earlier days Mrs. Youngblood, a devout Methodist, wanted to give notice when Margaret renounced the faith. But Theo dissuaded her. And – you cannot conceive how this has shocked Ellen. I am sparing you much outrage. She fell in with the movement for female enfranchisement."

"Mrs. Camlet wanted to vote?"

"I believe she actually expressed a wish to run for office herself."

This was so far-fetched that I could not even laugh. "Could she have thought of herself as good as any man?"

"I believe she did, Walter."

She spooned soup as I stared at her. "Marian. How often do ladies believe that?"

"I cannot speak for all my sex, Walter," she replied. "But I believe it is not anywhere near as rare as men like to think. Laura's aunt, Madame Fosco, the Countess, once advocated the rights of women. But you recall that she completely altered her thinking after marriage. In the main we are too tactful to upset our males by being frank. Margaret Camlet seems to have been that rare female who said what she thought."

"And enforced it. Though I find the black eye impossible to believe."

"Mrs. Youngblood confirms it," Marian said. "And Cook as well. She prescribed a slice of raw meat to hold over the place, and Mrs. Youngblood carried it up on a plate. And Matson saw it the next day, when he drove Theo into the city. No, I think on that point you have a cloud of witnesses."

I thought about this as I ate. Girls in England are not taught to strike out. Whereas all hardy lads are taught to manage their fists. Ladies like Mrs. Camlet are deliberately schooled to be soft and gentle. Laura has never raised her hand to any living thing. In February she had found it impossible to slap Camlet even though she was enraged at him. The very animals know it. Luna the miniature greyhound has Laura's measure, and encroaches upon her mistress's sweet nature without shame. Marian, who is of sterner stuff, would only fight physically if cornered – I found myself pitying that imaginary opponent. It was inconceivable that Margaret Camlet could have attacked her husband without provocation. And therefore… When I thought of what that provocation must have been I put down my fork, my appetite suddenly taken away.

"What is it, Walter?" Marian asked, ever observant. "You've thought of something."

I gazed across the table at her and realised that I could never tell her. From Laura's hard experiences, Marian must know that women have few rights in a marriage. She might not know, however, that these rights do not even extend to the wife's own person. It is not possible for a husband to rape his wife – there is simply no such crime. He owns her body just as he owns her property.

And the only bar to a man beating his wife is his own decency. Any violence Camlet did to Margaret had been perfectly legal. No court in the land would defend her, even if she had bruises, even wounds to show, or a baby. A man's rights over his wife are nearly as absolute as a god's. Camlet had spoken of how he could eternally separate mother from children with a stroke of the pen. Only outright murder allowed the law to step in.

But I had to speak, to say something before Marian became alarmed. "It comes far too naturally to me, to think the worst of others," I said at last. "I begin to fear it is a flaw in my character."

She stared at me, dark eyes enormous. "Oh my heavens, Walter. I see it too."

"What?" I was seized with alarm. "What?"

"The servants," she said, low. She glanced around, to be sure that Ellen was not coming in with a platter. "Walter, I understand. They had the best possible motive for murdering Margaret Camlet. They believe she threatened to close up the house. Their places would be lost."

"Oh heavens." It was all horribly plausible. Only the servants would find a lamp the easiest weapon. To select a propitious time would give no difficulty. Mysterious burglars could be blamed, and the truth would never be known. And everyone's place would be secure. "But," I remembered, "they were genuinely disturbed, when I announced Camlet's arrest."

"Yes, Ellen began to cry, you recall. She and Mrs. Youngblood have known Theo since he was a boy."

"I'm certain they meant Camlet no harm," I reasoned. "Perhaps they had not realised he would be accused? But we must not impugn innocent people. Without proof, motive is too easy. Anyone could have wished to kill Mrs. Camlet. Even –" I stopped, appalled at where reason was leading me.

"Even I," Marian finished for me.

"I did not say that."

"How fortunate that I was at Limmeridge House all that period of time," She smiled merrily at me, and I saw with relief that she was speaking in fun. "Perhaps you're right, Walter. You have a gift for thinking the worst. But acknowledging a character flaw allows one to keep watch upon it."

"I will endeavor to do so," I promised, still shaken.

The following day I had to go to Newgate again. It was a melancholy errand. The summer heat had made the river Thames unbelievably foul, and the news sheets were calling it the Great Stink. This time Marian laded me with reading material to beguile Camlet's weary hours. A Trollope novel, some sermons in pamphlet edition which he might have a professional interest in, and a dozen magazines were packed into the basket, and an apple tartlet was tucked in on top. Once again I made my way to the grim visitor's box, and in due time Camlet was shown into the cell across the barred gap. There were few visitors on a week day, and by tipping the warder I ensured we would have as long a visit as I liked.

On my first visit three days ago Camlet had been almost unable to speak, stunned with the thunderclap of his return to prison. Today instead of his battered funeral black he wore the fresh clothes I had brought him. But he still looked ravaged. The rigors of prison are notorious, especially for those unused to hardship, and this was his second incarceration in a year. Accused of murder, he had not even the hope of bail to look forward to. He was pale and grubby, the light-brown beard straggling untrimmed, and his limp had not improved. In the single trickle of sunshine from above his eyes looked haunted, with bruised-looking shadows under them, and his fingers clenched upon themselves, too tight. The last time, in the spring, he had been in better heart.

This was a man who, if he could, spent part of every day outdoors. He had spoken of breaking, in body or mind or spirit, and I feared this was what I was seeing. After I assured him of the health of Marian and the children I paused, notebook in hand. "How are they treating you, Camlet? Did they move you to a bigger cell?"

"Yes." He spoke with precision, the control of the speaker who dares not lose control. "It is now four paces by five, instead of two by three. And there's a window. Too high for me to see out of, although I can reach the sill. Unglazed, but fortunately the prevailing wind sets the other way, so that rain does not blow in.

And although the stench from the river is considerable, it's not so cold as it was last time, in February."

"God above."

"I don't know which is worse. To come to prison, not knowing what to expect. Or to know, and dread it with all my soul. Oh God, I hate this. The darkness. The bare boards I try to sleep on. The airlessness. The way I can only read by standing under the window and holding the page to the light." His voice wavered. "Don't let her come, would you, Hartright? If I saw her I fear my courage would crack. Again. And once it's leaked away, I don't think I can piece it together again any more."

"I have absolutely forbidden her to visit you, for all the good that will do. But her condition is that I visit you instead, and report back in minute detail."

"You lie to her."

"Have no doubt of it."

"You have my profound gratitude. I would rather have her think me a coward, than to know the actual horror of my situation." He took a deep breath, forcing himself to speak with calm. "To see another friendly face is an inexpressible comfort. I understand now why visiting the prisoner is enjoined upon the Christian."

Conscience smote me. "I have a confession to make to you, Camlet. My dearest Laura's oppressors gave me too hard a schooling. I find it almost impossible now to give credence to the innocence of any who hurt women."

For an instant he failed to understand me, but then his mouth opened in a silent gasp. "Hartright. If you believe me guilty of this dreadful crime, I am lost."

"I do and I do not, Camlet. My mind's divided and I cannot reconcile the halves. I must say, in this setting, you always look a dreadful villain." I smiled at him across the gap. "Marian has put her finger on the true solution to this: to discover Mrs. Camlet's real murderers. And in this goal she has enlisted me. In my worst moments, I do believe we will wind through the labyrinth and find you at the centre, a Minotaur in steel-rimmed spectacles. But I cannot find it in me, Camlet, to interrogate you, a vulnerable prisoner. It's too reminiscent of kicking a man when he's down. If you raised your hand to your wife, if you murdered her even, I beg that you will not tell me."

"No!" With a tremendous crash Camlet flung himself against the iron bars, reaching. But the bars held firm and the gap was too great. "Oh God, is there no end to this? Hartright, you must believe me. You must! We had fearful quarrels, Margaret and I. I have indeed been the offender many times. But murder is not in me!"

I saw that exactly what I wanted to forestall was happening – that Camlet's terrible straits made him defenseless against me. They say that the danger in victory is that you become your enemy. The late Count Fosco could have been no wilier, tricking his opponent into self-betrayal. I found I was reaching across too, but six inches separated our fingertips. "Hold fast, man," I said. "I – I believe you. You are no murderer. And there are almost no other crimes a man may be indicted for, if only he commits them against his wife. So you are innocent."

He slumped down to sit on the floor of the gloomy stone box, and buried his face in his hands. "I knew I was making a mistake, marrying her. They insisted, to both of us, that all would be well. And then, after, that she would be reconciled. And after that, that children would help…"

Against my will the question rose to my lips. "Did you force her?"

"I? Her?" He raised his head to stare at me, wild-eyed behind the smudged lenses of his spectacles. "You met her. Do you think that was even possible?"

"No," I had to admit. Even putting aside her handiness with firearms, I was taller than Camlet by a good two inches, but Margaret Camlet had been taller than I.

"I persuaded her, once. And she was persuaded by others, on one other occasion. I knew I was doing wrong, I knew even though others assured me it was right. I allowed the voices of those older and supposedly wiser than myself to override the clear voice of my own conscience. After that I swore that never again would I pursue a woman unwilling. If she did not consent, come to me of her own free will – if I felt her slightest recoil – I would retreat. Marian is the rarest of the rare, a woman stouthearted as an oak. I thought I would never find her. And, oh sweet God." He dropped his head into his hands again. "I see now. You dread that I shall abuse her."

"As Laura was used cruelly, by her first husband." I sat on the cold stone floor as well, so that we could be on a level again. "Camlet, I say again, I believe you. You are innocent. Marian has enforced upon me a schedule of visits here, twice a week. Discussing your situation cannot help you endure. But I know what to do. Do you remember the nautilus, the great curved shell on the mantel in the study at Limmeridge House? Though it is deliberately flouting family custom, we shall talk about the past. We will peer into the nautilus's back chambers. I shall tell you how I met Laura, and how I came to marry her. It's a long story and should serve us for many days. And then you'll understand why I respond as I do. In a sense my reactions are as deformed by my travails as yours are. Since you're a member of the family now, it's right you should know the tale. And Marian was a crucial participant."

Camlet stared across at me. "Marian?"

"I've known Marian even longer than I have known Laura. By perhaps several hours – I remember I met her at breakfast, and Laura only after luncheon. It was my first day at Limmeridge."

"Then you –" He caught himself up, and for the first time today he smiled a little. "I must count myself fortunate then, that your heart inclined toward the second sister and not the first."

We gazed at each other, possessed of the exact same thought: how could any man living not instantly prefer my choice? "We are the both of us fortunate," I said at last. "Perhaps you've noticed that both sisters married down. Neither you nor I are of their level. A wariness about any suitor of their own class – it's one of the scars they both bear."

"How old was she, when you first made her acquaintance?"

"It was the August before Laura turned twenty-one, and so Marian must have been twenty-three. I was twenty-eight at the time."

"What was she like, then?"

I might think of myself as the hero of the tale, and Laura the rescued heroine. But evidently in Camlet's mind the main protagonist was different. "Exactly as she is now. Forthright and true as steel. It was Professor Pesca, who suggested me for the post of teaching the sisters drawing…"

❧ *Marian Halcombe's journal* ✍

4 June

I cannot understand what Walter is doing at Newgate. Suddenly he's spending hours at a time there. Although he does report that Theo says he had never seen a sapphire and gold ring in Margaret's possession. But at least Walter no longer has to be prodded into visiting. Surely my dear man finds a familiar face a comfort. If only it could be myself! But Walter is steadfast, insisting it would be injurious for Theo as well as myself. I will contrive it at some point.

To go and call upon lawyers and bankers, however, was entirely allowable, and I did this today. We took the carriage, and Matson let Walter off near the Old Bailey before taking me on to Goslings & Sharp in Fleet Street. The narrow street was crowded with people of all sorts and orders, hurrying on their own errands. The noise was immense. And the city's air was foul this season, adding to the effect: a thick yellowish haze that stank, and cloaked every passerby with menace.

I was glad to step into the hush of the great bank's marble lobby. But it had not occurred to me that I would be the only lady here, possibly in the entire building. Clerks looked up from their counters, accountants from their inky ledgers. A solid banker in a black coat approached me, his eye grey and cold as ice behind gold-rimmed spectacles. "May we help you, young woman? Perhaps you are lost?"

"I am not lost," I said firmly. "I am Miss Marian Halcombe, and I have monies on deposit at this bank."

"I am Mr. Fittleworth, at your service, miss." Cloaked and shawled as I was, the silhouette of my figure surely was concealed. But I did see Mr. Fittleworth glance sharply at my left hand. An unmarried woman, in my condition, could not be respectable.

However, when the ledgers were consulted there was a slight thawing, and I was shown into his office. "Ah, Miss Halcombe. Doubtless you are here to inquire about your holdings. They are still moderate."

"Still?"

Behind the spectacles his gaze was chilly. "Does some man in your family manage your funds, Miss Halcombe?"

"No," I said. "I am reckoned to be competent to manage my own affairs."

"I see." He so carefully did not look at my waistline that I could have slapped him. "You should consider it then, Miss Halcombe. You have, imprudently, dipped into your capital this past season in a way that cannot be sustained."

"And I am going to encroach upon it yet more." From my handbag I produced the latest account statement from Plockton, Smithee & Erbistock. "See that this sum is forwarded to their offices by close of business this week."

"My dear Miss Halcombe! This is a very considerable amount of money."

"They are a firm of solicitors, who are charged with defending my –" Hastily I changed my wording. "Defending a man accused of murder. This money is well spent."

"Your income this year will fall by a quarter," Mr. Fittleworth warned. "You have heard the stories of these lawyers, Miss Halcombe. Vultures are not in it. They can and will suck your bones dry. Be advised by me. Do not impoverish yourself, even in the noblest cause. You will do no one any good if you are destitute."

"I have been poor, Mr. Fittleworth," I replied. "And I do not fear it."

"Then you are unusual, Miss Halcombe. It shall be done as you instruct." He rose, indicating the close of our conversation.

Though it was midday it was as gloomy as evening out in the street. Peer as I would I could not make out Matson and the carriage. Passers-by loomed suddenly out of the haze and jostled me.

Suddenly there was a nudge of more intent, in my side. "Do you eat your greens, miss?"

"Oh!" I turned, drawing a quick breath. "Remove your hand or I'll scream."

"Eh, sorry, miss," the man cheerily replied, entirely unoffended. "Thought you was one of the good-natured company." And he melted away into the fog.

I recoiled and almost overbalanced. If I lost my footing on the narrow walk and fell I would surely be trampled, unseen in the dim street. But a strong hand gripped my elbow, and Matson the coachman said, "Ma'am – you should have waited in the doorway for me. Here now, the carriage is this way." With a sigh of relief, I allowed Matson to hand me up into the vehicle and sank back onto the cushions. Under the shawl and cloak I pressed my hands against the roundness of my abdomen. I reminded myself that I could no longer rely upon my lightness of foot, not for some months.

By the time we arrived in Lincoln's Inn at Plockton, Smithee & Erbistock I was ready for a cup of tea. I was pleased to step into Mr. Plockton's office and take some refreshment. Mr. Plockton was the founder of the firm, old but still hale, a cautious and reserved man with deep creases like parentheses around his narrow mouth further echoed by the curve of woolly white side whiskers. He sat behind a wide wooden desk that took up more than half the small room. It was stacked neatly with briefs in piles, and on the side of it closest to me was a large silver tray with a little kettle on a spirit lamp to keep it hot, and the tea things. Since his specialty was criminal prosecution and defense this was the first time I had met him. It was a good sign, I felt, that he was overseeing Theo's case himself.

"I know that the account Mr. Camlet has to date is very considerable," Mr. Plockton said, sipping from his own teacup. "What a pity that he lost his nerve and ran. He has not helped his case. The authorities are like hounds, always the most eager in pursuit of the fleeing. I understand that you, Miss Halcombe, are bearing the current costs of his legal troubles."

"With funds that he gave to me for that purpose," I replied. "You need not fear, Mr. Plockton. You shall have all the financial backing necessary to win Mr. Camlet's acquittal."

"His second in this year alone," he said. "I am a cautious man, Miss Halcombe. I cannot feel that he would wish you to beggar yourself."

I was surprised, and slightly wary. Surely Mr. Plockton was not suggesting that he did not want to be paid? "His life is worth any money to me."

"Have you considered perhaps that some other arrangement could be made?"

Remembering Mr. Fittleworth's chilly warning, I realised I should not fail to consider every possibility. To bankrupt us both and save Theo's life was all very well. But suppose the money ran out before the acquittal? I did not dare to run our finances too close. I stared at the solicitor across the wide brown ocean of his desk top. "As a going concern Mr. Camlet's publishing business is worth little without him and his skills. In any case I am not empowered to sell it, or borrow upon its value."

"Is that so? Then allow me to make a suggestion which may not have occurred to you." He rose, creaking, to his feet and courteously refilled my cup with his own hands, adding the milk and sugar before I could offer to do it myself. Then he went to the door. I had assumed he was going to call for a document or book, but to my surprise he simply turned the key in the lock. Returning, he sat in the other client chair rather than returning to his side of the desk. "In return for some trifling personal services from you, I would be willing to adjust your accounts with the firm."

The only thought that came to my mind was lace knitting. He wanted to purchase knitted lace, and ... "Sir!" I gasped. "In my condition the last thing on my mind is dalliance!"

"Your condition is precisely what makes you so attractive to the cautious legal mind, Miss Halcombe. So many lawsuits have I seen, for parental maintenance. It would disgust you, dear lady. This would not be an issue with you for many months. You would not need to tell your family or your, ahem, paramour, for there can be no unpleasant mementoes of your – our – experiences."

I jumped to my feet, but to escape I would have to pass close by him. "I most certainly would speak. And shall!"

"And you are aware that I shall simply declare that you made a most improper offer to me in hopes of lessening your legal bills." Mr. Plockton smiled up at me, an elderly crocodile's toothy smile. "A person who has lost her virtue, that inestimable jewel, may hope for very little credence in matters of this sort."

"You would never make such vile suggestions to a married woman!"

"And you are not a married woman, Miss Halcombe. You are a notorious and shameless character, three-quarters of the way to whoredom. Come, come now. A little adventure will make your fallen state no worse, and will be of mutual benefit..."

Boldly I tried to sweep past him. To my complete horror he

seized the blue-and-grey flounce of my gown, bringing me to a halt. He put his other hand on my rounded belly, brushing aside the cloak and shawl. When I leaned in, he chuckled and pressed his whiskery face into my bosom. Over his shoulder I snatched the tea kettle from its stand.

It was not quite at the boil, but when I poured it down the back of his neck the effect was most notable. He shrieked at the top of his lungs. "Aaa! You termagant!" Writhing, he fell out of the chair with a crash.

I dropped the kettle on top of him and, stepping past, turned the key in the lock. His cry had been heard, and the young clerk at the desk in the outer office started to his feet. "Barnaby, Mr. Plockton has had an accident with the tea kettle," I said calmly. "At his age, it may be that a doctor should be called."

I passed out into the corridor just as Mr. Smithee came out of the suite across the way. "Miss Halcombe? Oh, dear God. You, above all, should not have consulted Mr. Plockton alone. He sees only gentleman clients!"

"Say rather, the firm takes care that he sees no ladies." But then I remembered my earlier visit. "You warned me, Mr. Smithee," I gasped, astonished. "You told me that Mr. Plockton should not hear of the case."

"I am so sorry I did not make my, er, hint more plain." Mr. Smithee's curly hair seemed to nearly stand on end with fright. "Let us step this way, if you would." He drew me into his office as the other clerks ran to Mr. Plockton's aid. "Once they have all passed I will conduct you to your carriage. Our senior partner is due to retire at the end of the year. Although his legal work is still very fine he is, is –"

"Eccentric," I offered.

"Yes, very good. Eccentric, you are the soul of tact. I beg that you will in future let Mr. Hartright consult with him."

"That would be my very great pleasure. I only hope he will be sufficiently injured that he hands the case over to you. And I entirely understand that you could not speak frankly about your senior partner."

"Ah, here is our moment. This way, if you please."

Mr. Plockton's screams could still be faintly heard as I was ushered down the hall and out through the deserted reception room to the street. Matson was at the curb with the brougham. Mr. Smithee handed me up. Before he could shut the door I said, "Mr. Smithee, I hope you will not get into hot water yourself, for your gallantry. And do not fear I will forget this. You are a true gentleman, and we will do business again."

Mr. Smithee's plump face went pink, and he bowed as he shut the door. Only when the carriage was in motion did I notice my heart was beating rather fast. I took a deep breath and allowed myself to slump back onto the cushions. Under my hand a reassuring bump came from under my shawl. In comparison to the old lawyer, the cheery man in Fleet Street on the lookout for good-natured company seemed entirely sweet.

Walter Hartright's narrative

Marian had hit upon the most comfortable way to tell the children, that Camlet's arrest was all a terrible mistake. But in decency more detail had to be supplied, couched in terms suitable for the young intellect, and this was cruelly difficult. The children had been told years ago that their mother Margaret was dead. Now she was back for a scant few months, and then dead once again. "She should make up her mind," Lottie said.

"Do you remember anything of her, Lottie?" I asked. "What of you, Micah?"

We were out on Parliament Hill on Hampstead Heath, flying Micah's newest kite. For his birthday his father had given him a pen-knife, and he had built this kite alone, with no help from either Marian or myself. He had painted the newspaper skin with a handsome red eagle, wings outspread. Warm and breezy, the June weather was perfect for kites. I helped him to get it up into the sky, but once it was aloft the lad held the line competently enough, and we sat on the grass and watched it soar. From this height we could see all the woodland and pastures around. London was distant and bright, a necklace laid on the horizon. "I do remember her from then, a little," Micah said. "But not much." He stared up at the kite, tiny with distance against the fleecy clouds.

"Why did she leave us, Uncle Walter?" Lottie asked.

"I don't know," I said with truth. "I wish I did."

"She can't have loved us, the way Miss Marian does."

"She found another husband," Micah said absently.

"Where did you hear that?" I asked, startled.

"Cook was talking to Mrs. Youngblood," Micah said. "And Ellen said she was an atheist."

"What is an atheist?" Lottie asked me.

"I don't know," I lied. I was certain the facts would be beyond her understanding.

"It's something very bad," Micah said. "I shall look it up in the dictionary ... Look at that, the wind is dropping."

"Reel in your line a little. We know almost nothing of what she was doing while she was away. People have made guesses, but nobody really knows."

"As long as we have Papa, and Miss Marian, we don't need her," Lottie pronounced. She held her wide leghorn hat onto her head as she leaned back, gazing at the kite. "Mickey and I found her, you know. We went on a Quest."

"Like Sir John Franklin off to search for the Northwest Passage," Micah said. "But once we found Miss Marian for him, Papa was able to carry on very creditably." I had to smile, at the way the narrative in their minds was completely centreed around their own lives.

"Yes, he was clever," Lottie said, with judicious approval. "He took all the flowers out of the greenhouse and gave them to her. And that made her love him."

"A pony would have been better. Miss Marian would have liked that. She's as good as a man. Or a boy," Micah added, generously.

"If for some reason ..." I wanted to say this, but in a way that would not frighten them. "If your papa is not able to return for a while, I hope you two will continue to live with your cousins and your Aunt Laura and myself, at Limmeridge. Of course Miss Marian will be there too."

Lottie turned to me, stricken. "Papa might not come back?"

"Miss Marian says he will," Micah said.

"No one knows the future," I said. "Not even Miss Marian, clever though she is."

"I believe Miss Marian," Lottie said, her hazel eyes filling. "Papa will come back. Soon."

"We all hope and pray that is so, child," I said. Dear God,

suppose it came to the worst? The children would be orphans. Would Camlet beg for a last sight of them? Would it be wise to allow that, would it be cruel to deny him? Oliver Twist had visited Fagin in Newgate before his execution, a fictional account that was harrowing even in memory. Perhaps the moment Camlet was condemned I should take the children back to Cumberland, where they could be shielded for a few years more from the knowledge that their father had been hanged for murder. Marian would certainly insist on staying to the end, and so Camlet would not be alone in his final days –

Marian. I lay back on the warm sunny grass and stared up at the sky without seeing it. Camlet had sworn that murder was not in him, and I believed it. But he might not have been the motivator and originator. Margaret Camlet's death gave Marian her only chance to become an honest woman, a respectable wife with a baby born in wedlock rather than a discarded mistress encumbered with a bastard. She never spoke of the shame and ignominy of her fallen state, but I knew it was ever before her, a scorching, corroding bitterness that could only be cleansed in one way. At the cemetery Radenton had suggested bringing Marian to Scotland Yard, and I had assumed that was merely a threat. Now I saw that he suspected her of complicity in the crime. And ... so did I.

Marian had enormous power over Camlet. That their mutual affection was true and strong I could acknowledge. But the power of this bond made it a great motivator. And Camlet was more persuadable than most. If there was steel in him it was well hidden. If Marian asked him to do it – and God knew Marian could be powerfully persuasive – he would have knocked Margaret on the head. Would a man so easily coerced into an unhappy marriage not be easily persuaded into a killing? Camlet would do anything for her. Even to the gallows...

I gazed up at the red wings on the tiny kite hovering far up in the blue summer sky, and felt sick. There was no end to the dreadful phantasy my brain could spin. Some solid fact, some proof had to be found, else untrammeled speculation would drive me mad. But surely this particular wild theory would be easy to put to the test. While she was at Limmeridge this spring Marian had not read aloud extracts from Camlet's letters as she had before their marriage. A suspicious point, now that I recalled it. Why had she stopped? Was it because the letters were now full of nothing but endearments, or was there something more? Only the other day I had been recounting to Camlet how Marian kept all her correspondence, every letter she ever received. I had often seen them, neatly sorted and tied in bundles by sender and date. They are a convenient resource, like consulting a younger self, or looking back into time.

And she has faithfully kept a journal for many years. I may think of myself as a nautilus, carrying the past ever with me, but Marian's journals possibly do this more efficiently. Her life is fixed into place, understood through her pen. She is free to forget, because the past is safely written down. Somewhere, if she had urged Margaret's murder, a written record must exist. To rifle her desk for the letters would be easy enough, or quietly abscond for a few hours with that eye-catching blue Morocco leather journal volume. She was taking Lottie and Micah to my mother's cottage for tea on Thursday. That might be the ideal time.

But if she ever learned of my prying, her righteous fury would scorch my ears. She has copied extracts of her journal out for me before, but never have I perused her unfiltered thoughts. It was reminiscent of a mental theft, or – I winced at this – even assault. There was a better, less morally dubious way. Camlet must have her letters to him. They could not be in his cell, where he had nothing but what I carried to him. Nor was it likely that letters from the woman he loved would be filed with the business correspondence of Covenant Pamphlets. I would find them, therefore, in his study at Sandett House.

I sat up, unable to bear my own uneasy thoughts any longer. The afternoon's promise was failing, and weather altered before our eyes. A towering wall of slate-blue clouds slid swiftly in from the south and west, driving cool air and the smell of rain before it. The wind died away and then fitfully blew with greater strength again, so that Micah had to pay constant attention to his line.

Suddenly there came the strongest gust yet, and snap! went the kite string. Lottie cried out in alarm as the kite was whipped away.

We jumped to our feet and stared as it tumbled away to the

north, higher and further until the red wings were lost to sight. Micah sighed. "It's gone so high. Perhaps it will fly all the way to the North Pole before it comes down."

"A brave thought."

"But we'll never see it again," Lottie said. She slipped her hand into mine, and though she did not look up at me I knew that it was not only the kite she thought of.

BOOK 4

≈ Walter Hartright's narrative ≈

Not until the following day, when Marian was gone to do the shopping, did I slip into Camlet's study. I had searched the room last month, but my mind and eye then had been fixed on the red sketchbook, and I had passed over everything else. Now I closed the door and raised the shade to let in the bright morning light. If Marian had urged Camlet to murder Margaret, the proof must be here.

Limmeridge is full of spaces dedicated to male pursuits. Mr. Frederick Fairlie alone had had an entire wing devoted to drawers of collections and cases for his precious things. Sandett House, a town dwelling, was much more modest, but also had its masculine rooms. The study was paneled below and papered above in a rather old-fashioned deep green, and there was a handsome Turkey carpet. Wooden shelves groaned under Camlet's books. But there was not much in the way of papers. Perhaps most of his correspondence was at Covenant. I wondered if it would be necessary, or even possible, to search there as well.

I concentrated my efforts on the massive cherrywood desk beneath the window. The blotter had fresh paper, the inkstand was full, and everything was dusted and tidy, a tribute to Ellen's attentions. Camlet was not like Margaret. His pens and pencils were neatly organized in trays in the drawer, and the cubbyholes of the desk were tidily sorted with household bills and documents. A large ledger looked significant, closely written in his even copperplate hand, but was merely a record of plants and propagation statistics, divided between the outdoors and the greenhouse. Another notebook neatly recorded books read, with the date and subject. It was sad to see the long gaps in this journal in the past year.

The largest bottom drawer seemed heavy and full. I hauled it open. A large tin canister filled it almost completely. Any label or markings were hidden on the sides. Thoughts of opium, or gold, some dangerous or rare substance that would unmask Camlet for the villain he really was, immediately filled my imagination. The tin was too heavy to hoist out, but with some trouble I pried the lid off to inspect the contents.

Then I had to laugh at myself. Birdseed! It was filled to the top with the best-quality birdseed. A practical fellow, Camlet evidently bought in quantity. I took an envelope from a cubbyhole and poured a handful in. Had Camlet not spoken of a windowsill in his tiny cell? Perhaps it would divert him, to work his taming magic there.

I arrived at Newgate the following morning full of good resolutions. Camlet was harmless and unjustly accused, and I would cease trying to prove otherwise. The task of finding the true culprit was far more important, and it was now lost in endless wanderings among motive. Perhaps I was no genius of criminal detection, as Marian insisted. I was not Arsène Dupin. I was merely a bloodhound. With a clue, a clear culprit pointed out to me, I could track the villain to his lair. But to find an unknown perpetrator was impossible. I hared off after every scent without discrimination, dizzied with too many possibilities and driving myself into confusion.

I passed the looming gallows, through the grim gate and across the gloomy courtyard, guarded with iron railings topped with downward-curving spikes, to the visitor's door. The warder there knew me for a generous and frequent caller, and greeted me by name. "Mr. Hartright, how d'ye do? A hot morning we have of it."

"Indeed, they say the thermometer will reach a hundred degrees." From my pocket I produced the customary coins.

"'Twould be taking your money, sir," the warder said. "He

ain't home to visitors today."

"Theophilus Camlet is not in? How can that be?"

"Gaol fever," the warder said with placid cheer. "He was took sick on Sunday, and yesterday they took him to the infirmary." He nodded at the infirmary building across the courtyard, and crooked a hand at his side for a tip.

"Great God!" I passed over a coin and then hurried over to the infirmary. With some searching about I found Camlet at last, in an open ward crowded with a dozen other sufferers. It was a gloomy bare space, the windows uncurtained and the floor bare boards, but at least it was clean. He lay on the iron bedstead in the furthest corner, near the single window. A hot breeze blew in from outdoors, laden with a sewage stench. His thin mattress must be better than the plank beds in the cells, but he was insensible, covered with nothing but a coarse sheet. Hair and beard were over-long, untrimmed and tangled. Between them his face was grey.

When I put my hand on his forehead I could feel the fever. The single doctor in attendance was beset with other cares, subduing a prisoner raving in another ward. There was nothing else here, not so much as a glass of water or a rag.

Camlet had enjoined me to lie to Marian. I could conceal his misery, but not his death. If he perished of fever alone here, and she unknowing, she would never forgive me to her own dying day. I turned on my heel and hurried out.

I returned that afternoon burdened like a mule. Only the fact that it could not fit into the carriage kept her from bringing an entire bedstead along. I carried sheets, blankets, a feather bed, pillows, and two large baskets of provisions. Marian, in her condition, carried nothing but a parasol, a box of medicines, and a bunch of flowers picked by Lottie and Micah for their father. At the sight of Camlet she gave a low cry. "Oh, my dearest!"

Flowers and parasol went flying as she ran to his bedside. He was conscious, though visibly fuddled with illness. He put on his glasses, smudged with his own sweaty fingerprints, and shaded his eyes against the painful light. "Marian?" he whispered. "Here? Hartright, you gave me your word."

"I'm between the devil and the deep blue sea, Camlet." I set down my bundles and straightening my aching back with a groan. "She has promised, with her hand on the holy writ, to keep at arm's length to avoid contagion."

"No no, Walter did exactly right," Marian said, shedding cloak, gloves, shawl and hat. "I will refrain, with difficulty, from hugging you or approaching too near. Now, dearest man, drink this. When did you last have something cool?"

Not trusting the prison well, she had brought water in a large earthenware jug which I had had to carry. While she set things to rights around him I went in search of the doctor. This person seemed very young to be in charge of so many ailing men. He did not even remember seeing or admitting Camlet. But when he examined him he was optimistic. "The patient is well-nourished and was in good health for many years," he pointed out. "Not like most of our inmates. We lose at least one a week to gaol fever."

The doctor was so short-handed that he was well-pleased to have Marian come and help nurse Camlet. Since the prisoner was not yet convicted, and the doctor's brief was not to let patients die before their trial, he had more latitude. She further wormed her way into his good graces by offering to bring in a night nurse. By the time they had discussed the uses of ipecac and exchanged recipes for cooling fever draughts, it was clear that she was master of the situation. I was sent out to hire a reliable night nurse who would be willing to come to the infirmary, not an easy task.

When I returned it was the end of the day. Camlet lay on clean linens and feather pillows, a white counterpane smoothed over his chest. The flowers were set in a jam jar on the windowsill beside his bed. He had been washed, combed, fed and dosed, altogether in much better case than this morning. She had even polished his eyeglasses to a shine. On a wooden box Marian sat as agreed, by the bedside but at arm's length, holding his hand in her lap. No words were exchanged. They seemed content simply to gaze at one another. I came softly up to the bed but his glance did not shift.

I felt like a brute, breaking into this wordless communion, but the evening was drawing in. "Mrs. Harris will watch over him till you come again, Marian," I said quietly. "You must sleep and eat. Your own strength is not inexhaustible."

"One minute more, Walter, please." For a long moment they

were both silent, but then suddenly she cried, "There, did you feel it?"

Camlet's brown beard split in an enormous grin. "I did!"

"Your son or daughter!"

"I have never felt the like. Hartright, did you ever do this?"

"Not in public," I said, slightly scandalised.

"I must seize my opportunity," Camlet said, coughing. "But for now this is enough. Go, my love, and rest."

Obediently Marian rose, only at the last second setting his hand back onto the counterpane. "Sleep, Theo. All will be well."

"You are better than any medicine," he said. "Ah, God, I'm so happy."

"It's my duty to make you happy, and I always will."

A great bundle of sheets and clothing came back with us, to be laundered and hygienically boiled. I insisted this be tied to the roof of the carriage, rather than sharing its contagion with us inside. "And when we are home you must immediately wash thoroughly, and rest," I said. "He needs you to keep your health. For you to take ill would be the final calamity."

"I must agree." She leaned back on the cushions. A single tear slipped down her cheek, now that it was safe to be weak. "Oh Walter. He has suffered so much. How can he bear it? How can I?"

"While there's life, there is hope," I said, an inadequate comfort. "And when do you suppose it was, when last an inmate of that room exclaimed that he was happy? He will win through, Marian. He's not deathly ill, and good nursing shall save him yet."

"Yes, oh yes." She sat up again. "I'll drive in every day until he is well. Walter, this leaves the larger task to you. I begin to think that Margaret must have been slain by burglars. Where does one find a burglar? Is there a King of Thieves in London, whom we could consult?"

"I believe that is a figure in fiction only, Marian. Surely Inspector Radenton will have thought of this."

"I disagree. Having fixed upon Theo as the culprit, he rests upon his laurels and has no interest in any other theory."

"I'm ill-fitted to this work, Marian. To pin the guilt upon a man I know and can identify is one thing. To find some unknown culprits in the teeming mass of London, of England, is beyond me."

"Now it's my turn to hearten you," she replied. "We've searched the house, with no result. Perhaps it's time to broaden the search. The grounds could be combed; the neighbours interviewed. What of that Mr. Brewster, whom your mother named as the man who saw the fire and ran for the engines? His account might be of interest."

Groaning in spirit I said, "I'll set all these queries in train, Marian."

"There is yet time, since Theo will not come to trial until September. Everything must be resolved by then."

"Yes, it must." Carefully I averted my eye from her thickening figure, more ungainly every day. Someday soon she would have to give up going out at all.

❧ Marian Halcombe's journal ᨇ

London, 7 July

I can confide this neither to Walter nor, of course, to Theo. But I am sheltered, a hothouse flower. Newgate Infirmary horrified me. How much worse must the actual prison be? That my dearest spoke of the larger space, and complained of the light. His cell must be scarcely big enough to turn around in, for the infirmary is crammed with beds. And it's gloomy, the room's one window facing onto a brick wall. Theo must be being held in almost complete darkness. The two of them must have agreed to gloss over the truth of Theo's situation. Someday when this is over I shall tax Walter with it. The coarse ugly uniforms, the bars and spikes, the scant meals of oatmeal gruel and bitter bread – not for a moment could one forget that this was a prison, a place of deliberate pain.

And the other patients wrung my heart, men of all ages but equal in illness and misery, their eyes all similarly haunted with the rigors of incarceration. As I feared my darling man's would be! The truly vicious or mad were locked in private rooms, but here in the open ward were those too meek or sick to be a danger.

There are wardens and officials but few visitors, the most regular apart from myself being the chaplain of the prison, who is much occupied sitting by the besides of the dying. For death stalks the halls, a steady churn among the narrow iron bedsteads as patients die, are removed, and then replaced by new sufferers. When I asked Dr. Gillie if this was an epidemic he assured me that the mortality was if anything a little less than usual, since it was summer and the prisoners were not perishing of pneumonia. If there were an epidemic the dead would be stacked in the halls.

All these lost souls, their final moments spent alone, without even a friendly face or a gentle hand to speed them to their Maker! Not a wife, not a brother, not a child came to visit. For some days I was as rare and solitary as the phoenix. Theo's fever waxed and waned but did not begin to improve for more than a week. For many hours at a time he was too ill to be more than intermittently aware, murmuring in fever dreams or lying in stupor. Cook and Mrs. Youngblood cooked nutritious viands for him, almost too much to carry, and when he was too ill to eat I shared the pasties or bread or jellies with other patients. I brought in pen and paper, and wrote a letter or two for sufferers.

But the hardest thing I did was to sit beside a dying man and hold his hand. No one could tell me his name – he himself was too far gone to speak – but in any case he was a foreigner, not an Englishman. Yet if I did not act, no one else was here to do so. He was in the bed beside Theo's, and so I could often look over to my dear man's sleeping face and pray that I would never have to hold his hand as he passed to his reward.

Today when I returned the dead man was gone and a new inmate had already taken his place. More gaol fever – the scorching fever, the cough, and the wincing away from the light were all familiar symptoms to me now. Ellen was filling a flask with febrifuge every day for Theo. There was enough to share, if the fellow would accept it, and once he woke from his sodden slumber. But first Theo's feverish brow had to be bathed, and his other needs seen to.

I came back from carrying slops out, and was astonished to see a woman sitting beside Theo's bed on the box I had adopted for a seat. No, not beside Theo, but his neighbour. When she saw me she jumped up. "Oh! Miss, I 'pologise! I took yer seat."

"Not at all," I said. "It is mine only in that there was no other to use it." We stared at each other, as if across some great gulf. Another proof that I was a sheltered flower, because this female was not. I had never even seen a kept woman before, but here clearly was one. Her lips were painted in a red and slightly-smudged cupid's bow, and her cheeks were unnaturally pink. Underneath the unartful paint was no great beauty, a plain country girl with freckles and big brown eyes. She was a tiny thing, a head shorter than I. Her honey-coloured hair was tied back and topped with a pink bonnet that I could see must have been purchased second or even third-hand. Her gown clashed cruelly with it, a brick-red wool inappropriate for the season and topped with another wrong note, a paisley shawl. Mr. Dickens' description was no fiction, but plain fact: her attire "miserably poor but extremely gaudy, wretchedly cold but extravagantly fine, too plainly bespeaks her station."

Her assessment of me was no less acute. "And you in the family way," she said, pushing the box forward.

"You are very thoughtful," I said, rather glad to sit down. "Is this your, your husband?"

"My Bill," she said simply.

"If he will take it, I brought a fever draught in for my –" I stopped.

She took in my ringless left hand with one quick glance. "My name's Joan Porter, miss."

"And I am Marian Halcombe."

"Pleased, I'm sure. What's your man in for?"

"He – he's going to trial in September. For murder."

Joan did not seem to regard this as shocking. If anything she looked impressed. I remembered Theo telling of the hierarchy that exists among criminals. My poor man, to be more respected for this! "Ah, that's good, that he's not been tried yet. Happen he'll get off."

"And yours?"

"Theft," she said, with simple pride. "And forgery. Four years – he was going to serve it at Wandsworth, but then the fever got hold of him."

With a slight feeling of shock I realised that we were almost speaking as equals. As indeed we were, in spite of my respectable gown and the comforts I could purchase. Mr. Plockton had recognised my status as quickly as I had identified Joan's. Being a shamed and fallen woman might as well come with a red banner flying over our heads. Oh, if only Theo could wed me! Now that I've lost my good name I miss it terribly, and if that shows smallness of soul? Well, I cannot help it. I saw now that a terrible downward path was open to me, that if he died and I became poor and friendless I might become a Joan too.

I sat on the box, quivering on the verge of tears, and Joan showed she was a better Christian than I. "Woman's lot is cruel hard," she said. "'s harder when you're increasing. When's your babby due?"

It developed that Joan was a mother of a daughter, and so had much helpful if blunt information to share with a woman facing her first confinement. And from there it was not difficult to learn all her story. Like so many country folk Joan's parents had removed, in her case from Staffordshire, to London in hopes of bettering themselves. Her mother died of childbed fever and her father fell into the Thames after too much gin, and drowned. Joan fell in love with this Bill Gartle, but they could not afford to wed, and when he was taken up by the police and goaled she became the mistress of a minor government clerk. "But should he not marry you?" I asked, cloaking my dismay.

"I don't want to marry Albert," Joan said. "A snob hanging out for a rich bride, and when he finds her I'll be out on the curbstone. But happen that won't be for some years yet, and by then my Bill will be out."

I glanced involuntarily at the sick man on the bed, a great huge fellow bristling with black wiry hair. He looked like an ailing bear. "And does Bill know of your ... temporary employment?"

Bill's eyes were closed, but he growled, "She's savin', my Joan. We'll be wed when I'm out."

"How prudent of you both," I said, faintly. "But, ah, Bill – since you're awake, perhaps you'll swallow a dose? This febrifuge is a family recipe, and Theo here has been taking it with good effect."

This he was persuaded to do, and Joan sat in quiet on the floor by his bedside until he dozed off again. I returned to my perch beside Theo, also availing myself of the comfort of his hand. I love him as well as I can, but I don't think my affection would allow me to prostitute myself for his benefit. Did Joan's Bill love her less, or did Theo love me more? Fortunately he was deeply asleep and could not be taxed with these moral dilemmas.

16 July

Now the fever's crisis is past Theo recuperates with a most encouraging rapidity. His underlying health stands him in good stead, but I know that what really heals him is my touch and presence. Even prisoners awaiting trial are kept utterly alone for twenty-three hours out of the twenty-four. But in the infirmary the prison authorities gave visitors more leeway, given the high mortality rate and the shorthanded staff, and I took full advantage of it. In this fortnight I had become accustomed to seeing him every day.

It was a horrible shock this morning when I arrived and found his bed stripped and empty. Joan was there, spooning soup into Bill's mouth, and she said, "He was gone when I come, miss. They must've moved him at first light."

I had brought a berry pie, fresh from the oven. Now I set this down on Bill's knees and stormed off to find Dr. Gillie. "He was recovered, Miss Halcombe," the doctor protested. "He had to be returned to his cell."

"Where he became ill in the first place!"

"Miss Halcombe, you seem to labour under the apprehension that prison is intended to be pleasant, even improving. I assure you, that has never been the tradition at Newgate."

It was a waste of breath to protest his innocence, to complain that all the good work of the last three weeks would be undone. Fighting back weak tears I swept out into the grim courtyard. It was a temptation to immediately go and visit my dear man. But now he was no longer deemed ill, my goal had to change. To visit him will do no good if he is wrongly found guilty and hanged. I must now devote my full powers to his acquittal; distracted by his illness we have made little progress in this past month. I hurried out to the carriage and told Matson, "Home, quickly." It was absurd, but what wrung my heart was that I had missed my chance to give him a kiss. Chances were so few!

Today was a hot summer day, and the city was oppressive, its stench hanging visibly in the cloudy and brownish air. It was good to get out to the heights of green Hampstead. We drove at a spanking pace up the lane in a cloud of dust.

When the carriage halted at the portico, I climbed down without waiting for Matson and hurried into the house and through into the garden. The children had climbed a tree there, and were pretending to be Robinson Crusoe marooned on his island.

Below them Walter had taken over the lawn chair Theo favored for bird watching. He sat in the shade, nominally supervising the little ones but with his nose in a book. An ostentatious volume bound in opulent blue Morocco leather – "My journal!" I cried.

At the sight of me Walter startled violently and went white. "Great God. Marian!"

"Walter, how dare you!" In an instant I had snatched the volume out of his unresisting grasp. "I had not thought you were capable of such ungentlemanly behavior."

"Marian, I must apologise!"

"To pry into my private writings, insult my privacy, without my knowledge or permission? Just because I'm dependent upon you, and under your protection, does not mean that you own me body and soul!" I was sputtering with fury, and might have acted in a way that I would later regret – my fingers itched to slap him over the head with the volume in question – when Ellen stepped out onto the terrace.

"Miss Marian, Mr. Hartright? It's Mr. Smithee, come to call about the master."

Poor Walter was actually cringing, and jumped to his feet with a gasp of relief. I followed him rapidly into the house, where Mr. Smithee attended us in the drawing room. "Miss Halcombe, I hope I see you well," he said, shaking my hand. "But no, you are blooming. Mr. Hartright, sir."

"I am pleased to see you in good health," I said, with emphasis. Indeed he looked plump and prosperous, his curly hair well-brushed for once and showing no tendency to stand up. "Please, sit down."

"Yes, I was surprised that you had taken over Camlet's case," Walter said. "What befell Mr. Plockton?"

"An age-related injury," Mr. Smithee said vaguely, not

looking at me.

I clutched the journal on my lap – clearly Walter had not read that far. "You must be much occupied, if your principal partner is laying aside his duties. You would not have come all this way without important news."

"That is so. As you possibly know, Mr. Hartright, the prison authorities have a duty to run a clean and safe institution."

"One would never know it," I said tartly.

"They particularly deplore the apparently ineradicable presence of gaol fever on the premises. Disease has been endemic to Newgate for centuries, I need not remind you. And because Mr. Camlet has fallen prey to the illness – well, the feeling is that his case should be put forward so that, live or die, he may leave Newgate soon."

"They would rather have him perish on someone else's watch," I cried.

"On the other hand, should he be acquitted, he would be free all the sooner," Walter said more soothingly.

"Yes, this is quite possibly a blessing," Mr. Smithee agreed. "You assured me, Mr. Hartright, that you were working to seek out some other culprit. Now is the time to produce your findings, sir, for we must move on them."

"I –" Walter cast an imploring glance at me. "Only today did I discover what I feel may be a real clue. Miss Halcombe keeps a record of important conversations, and ..."

His words were lost in the singing of blood in my ears, as I flushed painfully scarlet. Oh, thank Heaven I was no Mrs. Robinson, whose diary of amatory adventure dominates all the newspapers this month! I, less imaginative, had been unable to find the words to recount our nuptial joys. All the most thunderous and stirring incidents of our honeymoon nights were impressed forever in memory and trembling flesh. I need no written record while I draw breath. My journal instead was full of daytime mundanities, descriptions of meals in *estaminets*, or our tour of the Louvre. But, oh scalding reflection, Walter was a married man. Very possibly he knew all these things too, as did Laura, and could read between my lines!

I reached for my fan. But then Walter's words penetrated. "You wrote it yourself, Marian, and I have noted the salient words. Camlet told you that Mrs. Camlet had been in prison."

"He did?"

"And she told him that it was not such a much."

"I recall nothing of it," I admitted. "But that's the virtue of a journal, to record what otherwise will fade." Then my ears burned yet again, and more than my ears. I was caught in a perilous trend of thought. The occasion surged hotly back into memory: the bedchamber at Limmeridge House, my hands on Theo's woolen dressing gown, the thick weight of my braided hair around both our necks. Oh, he had to be saved, so that we could taste these joys again! And if he were not? Perhaps all the tabbies and moralists were right. No longer pure and yet without a husband – they all say my fall is inevitable, and now I could see the flaming path opening out before my feet.

Not for my daily bread as Joan Porter had fallen, but even more shamefully, out of even baser hungers, as unbridled desire overwhelmed me. A ruined woman, I would never be able to marry again. Only amative frustration or immoral connections were open to me. All the connubial joys I had learned and loved with Theo would turn against me; I would become not a whore but a fornicatress. Some other man would some day put a hand on my body, or enquire if I was good-natured, or make a crude suggestion, and frustrated concupiscent nature would surge up and sweep me away. As it was surging now! Surely even now the other two, both married men, could see how every nerve in my body scorched with unseasonable, undirected arousal. Even my fan provided no relief. Racked with self-consciousness and discomfort, I was blushing as if I was being roasted in a hot oven. I began to rise to my feet. I would have to withdraw until I could command myself better.

"Mrs. Camlet was imprisoned?" Mr. Smithee stared at Walter. "Where? When?"

"Walter." I sat back down with a thump, personal embarrassments abruptly forgotten. "She wrote it down. A travel memoir."

"Yes, in her desk drawer. Allow me to go and fetch it." Walter jumped up and was off, clattering up the stairs two at a time.

Mr. Smithee said, slowly, "If the lady was in jail, if she was convicted of a crime on the Continent and imprisoned for it, then her death may be a consequence of her past history. It may have nothing to do with anyone in England."

I was trembling, with reaction or anticipation, or both. "We shall soon see."

Walter returned with the pasteboard box and set it on the table. It was tied shut with tape, and when this was untied we saw that the box was solidly filled with the paper it had been sold with, loose sheets of foolscap, perhaps a thousand sheets in all. Every sheet was neatly filled with lines in a firm regular hand. "This must have taken her weeks," Walter said, riffling down through the thickness of the stack. "How shall we read and find what we seek? Perhaps we should divide it in thirds, and each read a section?"

"See, they are numbered and set in order," I said. "Possibly to begin in the middle would not serve. I am a speedy reader, and I do not doubt that you, Mr. Smithee, also can skim rapidly. Let me begin with page one, and pass it to you, and when you finish you pass it to Mr. Hartright. We can soon determine if we should instead divide the stack in three."

I took the sheaf of foolscap and began with the first page, expecting to be bored. And I fell into that account as a donkey stumbles and plummets into a well.

Margaret Camlet began her story on the packet from Dover to Calais, and from there it was a rapid journey full of incident. There was not a word about her past, of Theo or her life in Britain. She might have leaped fully grown with shield, spear and air pistol from the forehead of Zeus. She went to Athens, Berlin, Naples, and Moscow. Her beloved, one Louis Bradamante, sprang to life on the page, a swashbuckling and gallant crusader with a big black moustache and a saber. Together they fought government troops in Wallachia, blew up trains in the Crimea, stole secret papers in Venice, and smuggled arms across the Adriatic.

The child within kicked and turned, annoyed at my stillness, and barely paying heed to it I moved to recline on the sofa, the stack of papers still in one hand and my fan in the other. Absolute silence reigned all afternoon, broken only by the rustle of pages passed from my hand to Mr. Smithee's and then Walter's. Ellen must have brought in tea but I do not remember eating or drinking.

Margaret Camelt's actions could not pass without notice and reprisal. But it was not until near the end – when Louis Bradamante was convicted of assassination and hanged from a gallows erected on the white medieval walls of Dubrovnik while his lover stood tearless, vowing vengeance at the bottom of the battlements – that I looked up.

"Walter," I said. "Mr. Smithee. Margaret Camlet was Daisy Darnell. The famous female anarchist. The most dangerous woman in Europe."

"Could it be?" Mr. Smithee said, stunned. "The bomb at the train station in Bratislava – I read that, in the *Daily Telegraph*." He looked down at the foolscap in his hands. "And, oh my God, here."

"I read of her escape from Croatia aloud to Mrs. Hartright –" I seized my journal. "Yes, it was the eighth of January 1857, and I first met Theo that evening."

"We must consult the published accounts," Walter said. "Compare them to this manuscript. Put it to the proof."

By this point it was quite dark, and Ellen came in for what I realised must be the third or fourth time. "Dinner, miss?"

"Oh yes, let us dine. Mr. Smithee, you will join us."

We ate without tasting the food, passing sheets of foolscap around the table. Occasionally one or another of us would murmur, "On top of the train cars, oh!" or "Goodness gracious, with a single shot." The final page in the box ended at the bottom, in mid-sentence: "When I arrived in London it was a thick peasouper, and just coming on to snow. Pudding island, for all thy faults I love thee still. I instantly hailed a cab, and –"

And that was all. Stunned, I looked into the box for more. It was empty; on its pasteboard bottom was written the words 'Gull Mews.' Do gulls mew? I was under the impression they squawked. But I did not need to read what happened next, on that snowy and fog-bound evening last February. She had confronted her supplanter, the second Mrs. Camlet. In this very house, she had met me.

I passed the sheet over to Mr. Smithee and took a final bite of cold potato and congealed chicken. It was nearly nine in the evening. We had been reading for seven or eight hours without stop. When Mr. Smithee looked up at last he passed the sheet on to Walter. "My God. I feel as if I've been tumbling in a barrel over a waterfall."

"Can this account be true, Mr. Smithee?"

"If it is, our triumph is certain. No one would believe such an adventuress would, or even could, be slain by Theophilus Camlet. Not when she escaped in a troika from the tsar's troops in a driving snowstorm, lashing the horses with her umbrella."

"I liked the part about being smuggled across from Brindisi to Serbia in the guise of mourners, with the rifles packed in the coffins and attended by a Greek Orthodox priest in full regalia."

"I wish I had known her."

"I feel as if I do." Never would I have thought to say that, about Margaret Camlet!

Walter set the last sheet down in the box and drew a deep breath. "This is fantastic. Smithee, what shall you do with it?"

"If you will entrust the manuscript to me, I shall set about having it copied tomorrow. We will surely need to show it to the authorities, and it would be well to have one or even two additional copies."

"A thousand pages?"

"Ten clerks, with a hundred pages each, or twenty, copying fifty, or fifty, working at twenty, and it is done, dear lady."

"And Walter and I will compile a time line of Daisy Darnell's activities as they were described in the press," I said.

"With that and this manuscript," Mr. Smithee said, "I can promise you Camlet will be released by week's end."

I clasped my hands together, speechless with joy. "Thank God," Walter said. "We'll do this tomorrow, Mr. Smithee, and bring it to your offices."

"I look forward to it," the solicitor replied, rising. We were all three rather giddy from sitting so long reading breakneck adventure, and our farewells in the hallway were cordial.

When the door was shut Walter immediately turned and took my hand. "Marian, I want to apologise once more. My intrusion into your personal documents was unforgiveable, and I'm ashamed of myself."

"Oh Walter. Do not regard it, I beg you. All my silly personal thoughts sink into unimportance, compared with the task of proving Theo's innocence. If you had to read my journal to get us to lay bare Margaret Camlet's real identity, then I have no cavil whatsoever." I gave him one moment only, to sag with relief. "But if you ever touch my journal again, I shall pound you over the head with it."

"Never! I promise." He paused, and then irrepressibly went on, "Dickens was at the trial, truly?"

"Someday Theo will be thrilled to learn of it," I declared, and we laughed and said goodnight.

17 July

Bright and early in the cool of the morning today we were off. "And where does one go, to see newspaper archives?" I demanded. "Shall we go to the publications' offices?"

"That would be tiresome, since we may need to consult half a dozen or more," Walter said. "No, my thought was, my club. It has a library which takes all the major news sheets. We may spend as long as we like there, copying out what we wish."

"An excellent thought."

Although Walter was a respected illustrator he no longer actively works in the field. He has kept up all his professional associations and acquaintance however, and now this stood us in good stead. His club, the Mahlstick, is in Bloomsbury in a side street off Euston Road. It is not a grand West End club for wealthy men of leisure, but a workaday place dedicated mainly to meeting rooms for the various specialty societies – Walter is a member of both the water colourists and the newspaper artists.

The cramped hallway was tiled in black and white, and the porter by the mailboxes nodded at Walter and eyed me, bulky in my shawl in spite of the heat, with a knowing glance. There was no Ladies' Lounge or dining room. We scaled a steep and rather narrow stair to the library, not quite wide enough for my hoops – I had to tug to get my grey-and-blue striped skirts past. For the first time I found it difficult to climb up without pause.

"I should not have brought you," Walter said, close behind, when I paused to pant. "Your condition –"

"Only I am allowed to complain of my condition, Walter," I said. "Besides, it shall not be difficult, will it? To spend the day paging through newspapers. My presence will halve the task."

The library was stuffy, but it was not helpful to open the windows. It was just as hot outdoors and the Great Stink was in full play. Walter ordered lemonade while I inspected the place – a large room, its long deal table clearly also used for meetings, and in need of dusting. All around the three inner walls, and also under the windows on the fourth wall, were bookshelves. The ones under the window were stacked, rather untidily, with the newspaper collection. The shelves were carelessly labeled with cards stuck on with pushpins, and I saw that the archive ran at least five years into the past. With luck this would be enough.

"I have it in mind," Walter said, "to write and ask Laura to come to town." He eyed me, broodingly. "Before it's too late."

"It's but July, Walter," I said. "I look to be active through August at least."

"Babies have their own calendar, Marian. Recall that we thought little Fairlie was three weeks early, but the midwife said that Laura had probably miscalculated."

"If you think it best, by all means," I said. "Although August is a dreadfully hot time to be in town, and Laura will insist on bringing Wally and the baby."

The newspapers were dusty and disordered, not well-maintained. It seemed simplest just to go through them all systematically, shelf by shelf, sorting them as we went along. Walter had brought a notebook, so that we could record details about Daisy Darnell or Louis – Count Ludovic – Bradamante. Without difficulty I found the issue of 8th January, 1857, with the very account I had read aloud to Mrs. Hartright. Walter insisted upon doing the shifting of newspaper piles and stacks, so that all I had to do was put my feet up on a chair and leaf through them.

We propped the door open for coolness's sake, and occasionally other club members drifted by in the hallway or came in to consult a book. One paused and said, "Hartright, is that you?"

"Moore, I hope I see you well."

"And this? Your mistress?"

"This is Miss Halcombe, my sister-in-law."

Entirely unembarrassed, the rather shabby artist said, "How d'ye do, miss. I thought m'memory was going. Was certain

Hartright's wife was fair."

"Marian, this is Albert Moore, a painter in oils."

"How do you do," I said politely. Mr. Moore clearly meant no offense. He seemed in poor case, a very young man, down at heel and with the lean and hungry look of one who did not get regular meals. He sat down at the end of the long table, pulled out a sketchbook, and began scribbling without further ado.

After some time Walter said, "Would you care to join us for luncheon, Moore? We plan to just step round the corner in perhaps half an hour."

"I would be most charmed, Hartright," the young artist said with gratitude. "And that will just give me time to finish this crayon of the lady."

By some mysterious telegraph system the news that a more well-off member was on hand spread through the club. When we tidied ourselves and descended for refreshment another two or three hungry artists had joined us. Walter, clearly remembering lean years in the past, included them all with grace.

In the noisy and crowded chophouse I was the only female present, and my condition had gone past the point of concealment even with shawls and cloak. But under the protection of the host of the meal I was honored and complimented and plied with shandygaff. Mr. Moore suggested painting my portrait, and when I declined, pleading my condition, offered to immortalise the new one to come for a lesser fee.

It was strange to see Walter in this milieu. Six years ago he had been like this, a working man scrambling to piece together a living between meager illustrating jobs, grateful for a free meal. But since our removal to Limmeridge he has become the complete gentleman, in clothing and speech and manner. He's one of those rare men who can convincingly move in the highest circles. I had never thought before however, of how far he had come. It is family policy, to never look back at the past. Now I wondered if he missed it a little, woodcuts, drawing, the society of his fellow artists. Using his skills. What fills his days, now?

After luncheon we returned to our several labours. Mr. Moore presented me with the crayon sketch, which had been carefully drawn to soften my over-strong features, omit the shadow on my upper lip, and in general make me as handsome as possible. I promised him I would have it framed and hung in a place of honor, and to mention to Theo the idea of a family portrait while the children were still engagingly young.

The library was hotter and stuffier than ever, and to get our hands black with printer's ink yet again was unpleasant. But by teatime we had a schedule of Daisy Darnell's newspaper adventures drawn up. It was not quite congruent with my memory of Margaret Camlet's thick manuscript. "Where is the smuggling trip from Brindisi?" I said, scanning it. "And there's no mention at all of the swordfight with the Wallachian partisans in the dockside warehouses of Odessa."

"The lady's own account is clearly more complete than that of the news reporters," Walter said. "But I think there are no contradictions, simply a greater or lesser amount of detail."

"Do you realise what she must have been doing, returning to London? Walter, she was hiding from the rival anarchists, the Blue Hand band. Remember her heavy veiling – so that she could not be recognised. The way she never went out of doors, and never met male callers."

"That is so! And surely these anarchists are responsible for her death. Mr. Smithee will be pleased... Marian, may I urge you to take the brougham straight home? You must be weary and hot, and these errands do not call for your presence. I can easily make my own way to Lincoln's Inn, and then to Hampstead again."

Remembering my last visit to the lawyers, I agreed that this would be prudent. Mr. Plockton might have recovered from his scalding injuries. My feet and back ached from sitting so long, and my growing bulk was uncomfortable in the summer heat. How much more burdensome is the lot of woman! As the carriage jostled and bumped its way along the crowded streets I thought about Daisy Darnell. Her politics were terrifying, her actions – slaying the duke of Sarajevo! – deplorable. But her qualities were plain to see. For months now my mind had been taken up with Theo's unhappiness in his first union.

But reading her account showed me that two people had been made miserable. She had been co-heir to Covenant, but Theo ran it. Even if she had been inclined to theology, working in a business would have been entirely closed to a female. The other activities open to a woman of our class – calls, housework, sewing the occasional dress – could never have satisfied the most dangerous woman in Europe. Margaret Camlet had known she deserved better, and intrepidly reached out and grasped for happiness when her chance came. I had to salute that. And for a brief few years she had had her joy in full. I would work to uncover her killer, not only to save Theo, but because she was so like me.

Walter Hartright's account

When my beloved Laura was in the family way she never went out, except of course to church. She secluded herself from all male company and vanished from public view. I knew better than to urge such a demure course of behavior upon Marian, but it made me acutely nervous to escort her around the city as time passed. What would I do if she fell ill? Guiding her up the staircase at the Mahlstick it was borne in upon me that if she slipped and fell I would be helpless. And that she could sit placidly eating a meat pie in a teeming chophouse surrounded by my fellow club members – being her sole escort was a trying business. Camlet had to be acquitted, if for no other reason than to take over management of Marian again. His talents were wasted, luring sparrows with birdseed. He should have tamed lions – or lionesses.

When I delivered our summary to Mr. Smithee he promised that the copying of the manuscript should be finished on Monday. He was having not one but two copies made. I undertook to go with him at that time to present our findings to Inspector Radenton. That evening after dinner I wrote my usual twice-weekly letter to my dear wife. Imploring her to come to London before Marian's time was upon her would, I was certain, have a prompt effect, and I yearned to see her and the little ones again.

On Monday I arrived at the offices of Plockton, Smithee & Erbistock and took charge of the original manuscript. We took the copies and the newspaper-derived timeline over to Scotland Yard, where Inspector Radenton had been warned to expect us. In spite of this he did not look pleased when I walked into his office. "Mr. Hartright, you seem to be possessed with the idea that the police cannot do their job without amateur assistance."

"By no means," I said, as peaceably as I could. "But I do

know my friend Camlet is innocent, and I believe that we now have proof. Mr. Smithee, if you would?"

The solicitor hastened to produce our documents, and summarised our case: "This is not a woman who could have been killed by a mild-mannered publisher. She does not seem to have been a woman who could have been slain by an army. Daisy Darnell was the most dangerous woman in Europe. Her death was surely caused by the throng of enemies she acquired abroad, as you will easily believe if you read this."

The inspector stared at the five-inch-high stack of paper, his mouth sour with disgust under the handlebar moustache. "Tchah. You have no concept of the difference between direct proof and circumstantial evidence. That some foreign johnnie could have killed her means nothing. You need to find the actual man."

"Now that we have pointed the way, I am sure the police forces can track the culprit down," I said. "We are, as you can see, most anxious not to intrude upon your sphere of expertise."

The inspector's sharp grey eyes glinted with what I uneasily recognised as glee. "Wait. I do believe I have it. Was the late Margaret Camlet really Daisy Darnell? Or was she just a frustrated woman, probably subject to erotomania and womb disorders, mining the newspaper accounts to write a series of imaginary adventures?"

"Impossible," I exclaimed.

"Oh, I see it now," the inspector went on. "Another Isabella Robinson, creating a jumble of fact and lurid fiction. Only instead of swooning trysts with a handsome doctor, she's journalizing about adventure in the Balkans. A morally loose and already barmy woman, abandoned in some Continental dive by the oily criminal Lothario she gambled all upon. With no other recourse or refuge left to her in the dead of winter, she comes crawling home to husband and hearth. Only to discover that he's a sensible fellow, intends to remarry, and will divorce her for her adultery, leaving her in the gutter. So, at her last prayer, she locks herself in her bedroom and gives free rein to her inflamed and diseased imagination. The creation of a more heroical version of her unhappy self doubtless kept her from complete mental collapse. No wonder Camlet hit her over the head. If I were he, I would plead justifiable homicide. I feel sure the jury would sympathise. Show them this sheaf of guff."

Mr. Smithee and I exchanged glances of dismay. "A ring," I said. "She has a ring, inscribed from her lover to herself."

"Doubtless a gift while they were still on terms, eh? Or before the villain's execution, at any rate. Gentlemen, generating airy theories is easy. Find me proof, Mr. Hartright. Hard, material objects for choice, or witnesses who will swear to their statements under oath. Otherwise, don't waste my time. I'll see you in court in two weeks."

And with that we were out in the hallway, hats in hand. I took a deep breath. "Mr. Smithee, let me invite you to luncheon."

"At Sandett House?"

"Yes."

"You fear to tell her alone."

When had Smithee learned of Marian's mettle? But if she could resort to a feminine stratagem, so could I. "I'm trying to discourage her from going out. Her condition, you know."

"Ah, I quite see." We flagged down a cab and in half an hour arrived in Hampstead. It was a grilling hot day, nearly a hundred degrees, and the only tolerable place was in the deep shade of the garden, where Marian and the children were dining al fresco. Raspberry vinegar, potato salad with dill, cold tongue and cold ham made for a cooling and attractive meal.

"Don't get up, Marian," I called. "I brought Mr. Smithee for luncheon."

The children were barefoot, and Marian herself was cool in a loose linen gown and a broad leghorn hat with a red ribbon in it. She was leaning back in a low chair with her feet up on a hassock. Obediently she did not stir, but she did say, "Welcome, Mr. Smithee. Micah, give our guest your cushion. Ellen, fetch more plates! Drink, sir. You're quite flushed with the heat."

I sat down in the short grass in the shadiest spot and accepted the glass Lottie handed me. Mr. Smithee said, "This is a paradise, Miss Halcombe. To your very good health!" He drank deeply. He had gone bright pink and had to gently blot his forehead with a folded handkerchief. The warmth made his curly fair hair spiral straight out from his scalp, and his round nose was shiny.

I could see Marian gauging our progress, waiting until we were both served and then had taken a first bite. Only then did she cry, "And what did the Inspector say? Will they drop the charges against Theo?"

"Well…"

I gazed at Smithee, who bravely said, "The inspector was skeptical."

"What? How can that be? Did he read it?" She pointed with her fan at the three boxes of manuscript that Smithee had laid in the grass.

"No." I lay back and stared up at the green leaves above me. Birds perched on the twigs high above, seeming to look for their master. "He suggested that Mrs. Camlet has the most energetic imagination since von Münchhausen. That her account was woven from the newspaper reportage, and has no more basis in reality than the amorous diaries of Mrs. Robinson."

"But –" She sat up and then sank back into her chair. "Oh heavens. I can see how that might be."

"I've met her," I said. "And so have you, Marian, while the inspector has not. The woman I met in this very house, she was not a prey to delusion. She had not erected a phantasy castle to hide her broken self in."

"Certainly not," Marian agreed. "She was … strong."

I lay on my back and groped for the words to express it. "Have you ever seen the painting of Joan of Arc, by Ingres? She was like that. She was a crusader clad in steel and holding the banner of France up before the altar. Only Margaret Camlet had that air pistol instead of the sword of Charles Martel."

"The inspector demands solid evidence, Miss Halcombe," Mr. Smithee said, chewing. "A not unreasonable request. Alas, artistic references will not do."

"Well, if she was hiding from rival anarchists, who discovered and slew her, this cannot be impossible of proof," Marian said in tones of reason. "All we need to do is to seek out the Brotherhood of the Blue Hand, cull the guilty man from among them, and have him confess to Inspector Radenton."

"All." Without raising my head I took a slice of ham and crammed it into my mouth.

"In a fortnight," Mr. Smithee added. "Why would a man

confess to murder and suffer the death penalty?"

"Surely I cannot be expected to answer everything." She looked at Mr. Smithee. "Where does one find foreign anarchists?"

"Clerkenwell?"

"Walter, tomorrow let us go to Clerkenwell and search about."

"Marian." I hauled myself up to a sitting position. "May I suggest to you that we have now come to the end of our resources? Physical excursions are increasingly dangerous for you. Randomly wandering around the purlieus of London is folly. The task is impossible. Let us reconcile our wills to that of the Almighty."

"You must not despair, Mr. Hartright," Smithee said in tones of encouragement. "The case against Mr. Camlet is like ours against mysterious anarchists. It relies almost solely upon motive. They have no solid proof, any more than we do. It's entirely possible that the jury will fail to convict. I have the utmost confidence in Mr. Todwarden, who has served Mr. Camlet so well already this year."

Marian folded her hands demurely on the curving dome of her abdomen, and glared at us. Her eyes were like black ice. Though there was not a sword or a bit of armor in evidence, Joan of Arc came to mind for the second time today. "We cannot, we will not fail Theo," she said flatly. "If you will not go, I shall."

❧ *Marian Halcombe's journal* ✧

20 July

Inspector Radenton's unbelief was a frightful blow. In spite of my brave words it took me all last night to rally my courage to go on. Bitter tears did I shed into Theo's pillow. But at first light this morning I was up, drawing up a list of ideas. There were anarchists in England, I knew. Foreign agitators are kept track of. It is not conceivable that they are allowed to run riot through Britain without some minimal official supervision. What do we pay rates and taxes for? My father, who died before my birth, was the great-grandson of an earl, and my late mother had friends of influence. That very morning I wrote letters to the two or three still alive, seeking for a contact in the government.

After writing my letters I proposed this day to go and seek

about in the quarters of the city that foreigners favor. In my heart I know that this is entirely trusting to luck, and that I am only hoping to happen upon a clue. But after breakfast Walter came into the morning room and spoke with the utmost seriousness.

"Marian, this cannot be."

"Walter, we have but a fortnight."

When Walter knows he is in the right he's, alas! not only immovable, but persuasive. "Consider how it will look, Marian. A woman wandering around the most insalubrious areas of the city asking questions of strangers. Even when I accompany you it's insufficient. Recall how Moore assumed you were a mistress. I do not accuse you of indelicacy. But your condition is but a small part of your larger situation, and this situation is cruelly fragile. Above all, a woman in your terrible plight must cling to the most sedate and demure behavior. You must not even distantly appear to be..."

He did not go on, but the words he would not say rang clear in my inner ear: Loose. Good-natured. Of no character. Fornicatress. A notorious and shameless female, three-quarters of the way to whoredom.

Because Walter was not born a gentleman, he knows to a nicety how one must behave to maintain one's place. He went on with the utmost kindness. "I know that in every fibre of your being you are a person of the utmost rectitude. But to be is not enough, not in the eyes of the world. You must appear."

"And at the moment, appearances work against me." Once again I saw with terror the awful abyss before me. Already I was lost. The veneer of respectability was all I had left. Crushed, I put off my hat and gloves again and set about darning socks. The mending basket is overflowing.

❧ Walter Hartright's account ❦

I had hoped that my kindly admonitions of yesterday were enough to keep Marian quietly at home. But today's post brought her a letter which she hastened to share with me over breakfast. "The good Major Donthorne passed away last year," she said, reading.

"Dear me, was it sudden?"

"A series of strokes. Sad, but he was nearly eighty. A good

old age – it cannot have been a surprise to the family. You remember writing to him?"

"Certainly. He was an intimate friend of Laura's father."

"And a boon companion of my own parents as well, for they were all of the same social circle. I wrote to ask him as a family friend for advice. Of course I only mentioned generalities but because he is gone, my letter was forwarded to his son, a Mr. Roderick Donthorne. And he works in the Foreign Office! He begs me to call upon him there whenever it is convenient. I will reply and tell him we'll call tomorrow."

I would have demurred, but no plausible objection came to mind. This was a perfectly unexceptionable call, upon an old family connection in a respectable government position. Instead I resorted to distraction. "I have a wire here from Laura. She arrives tomorrow on the afternoon train."

Marian clapped her hands with joy, crying, "Ellen, do you hear? Let the beds be made up. And call the piano tuner. Mrs. Hartright will wish to play."

"Laura will bring the two boys, their nurse, her own maid, and probably Luna the greyhound. Sandett House will be full to the rafters."

"Sent a note to Mrs. Hartright, asking if she will house little Wally for the duration," Marian suggested. An excellent idea which I quickly put forward, and received an immediate and enthusiastic reply. Mother also invited us all to dinner. Micah and Lottie shouted with excitement at the idea of their cousin coming to play.

But among her household concerns Marian did not lose sight of her plans. The following morning when she ordered the carriage I said, "I yearn to see Laura as much as you do, Marian. But her train cannot possibly arrive yet. You'll be hours too early."

"That gives us ample time," she said, "to call at Newgate in addition to visiting the Foreign Office."

I had a good deal to say about this program, but she paid me little heed. No one can not listen more vigorously than Marian. "It worries me that Theo's recovery might be compromised by his return to the cell. I packed his basket with raspberry vinegar, a cold meat pasty, and pickles. Perhaps in view of the heat of the day we should go to Newgate first. I do not like the idea of this pasty waiting in the hot weather."

"Marian, let me speak plainly," I said. "The horrors of Newgate are unsuitable for a woman."

"I visited him in the infirmary, which was dreadful enough. How much worse can the prison be? Besides, nothing will cheer him so much as learning of the progress we have made."

"We have made so little progress that word of it will be distinctly lowering!"

"Walter, it must be this hot weather pulling you down," she said. "It is not like you, to be so lugubrious. How fortunate that Laura comes. I shall warn her to take you in hand, and perhaps dose you with a tonic." With an effort I kept from tearing my hair.

❧ Marian Halcombe's journal ❦

22 July

At last we went into the city today! The summer heat has made the usual London stink truly appalling, the worst in memory. The close foetid air in the narrow streets near the prison cannot be healthy. With resignation Walter conducted me through the fearful iron-studded gate guarded by the awful gallows and to the proper portal. Only one visitor is allowed at a time, and so he waited in the courtyard for me while I went in.

It was horrible. My darling, separated from me by a double set of bars – it was deliberately cruel, to see but not be able to touch. When they conducted him into the other cell I noticed that he still had a limp, and castigated myself for not drawing the doctor's attention to it while he was in the infirmary. And he was distant, a distance not only of iron bars but of spirit, as if gaol fever had set some permanent mark upon him.

"Please tell me, my love," I begged. "What can I do, what can I bring, to help you?"

"You come in good time, my dear," he said quietly. "I wonder – will you marry me?"

"Why, Theo, of course. But does this even need to be asked? I am your wife in truth, if not in law."

"I was trying to be provident. Trying to think what best should be done. The poor options I can offer you are both dreadful. Think carefully, my love, if you would prefer to be an unwed mother with a child, or the widow of an executed murderer."

When I gripped the rough iron bars their cold struck right through my kid gloves. His mind was no more set upon daily doings, but beyond, on the end. He went on, "I believe it can be done. Reverend Whistler, the chaplain here, has undertaken to look into the possibility of a wedding before my execution. And I draughted a will. All I own shall be yours, Marian. You shall not want. And I know you'll care for Micah and Lottie."

This was a wounded man, withdrawing and hoarding his strength in an attempt to stanch the bleeding and stay alive. "Theo," I cried. "You may not despair, I absolutely forbid it. They have not even brought you to trial, never mind convicted you. There is yet time for you to be saved!"

"It may be so, my dearest. But I dare not wait to say these things to you."

"You are ill. You are despondent."

"No indeed. I'm better. The day they brought me back to my cell, I gave serious thought to hanging myself. But that seems a waste of effort, if the officials will do it for me."

"Hold strong, Theo, please! You shall not be lost. Freedom is near. We're working to save you, and you must wait in hope for that day." I could not leave him like this. "Do you know what Walter had me put into your basket? If only the prison authorities do not take it, there's a twist of newspaper with some birdseed in it."

"Oh, my dear girl." His smile glinted white in his beard for the first time today. "There's no one like you. It does me good merely to look at you."

It was a wonder he had held on so long. Being kept alone in a gloomy cell for weeks on end would depress any man's spirit. "Walter has set us on the track of Margaret Camlet's true killer," I said. "He is extraordinary, and you must trust in him."

That made him smile even more. "I am skeptical, but not for the reason you think… Tell me of your discoveries."

"Did you ever look at Margaret's memoir? No? Oh Theo, you must read it. It isn't in the least highbrow or theological, and there is not a sermon in it. But it's thrilling, far more exciting than *David Copperfield*. Would it overset you as her husband, to hear that I feel that I really know her now, after reading her tale?"

I spoke of our work with the newspapers, and of my appointment with the Foreign Office. It did him good, I felt, to have other things to think of. I wonder if the prison authorities would allow me to bring in Margaret's memoir manuscript? We have two copies of it now, and it would surely divert his weary hours.

It was not until my allotted time was over and I emerged to meet Walter again that I could give way. "Oh Walter, this cannot go on. It will crush him. He spoke of doing himself harm."

"Marian, if you weep like that you will do yourself no good." Walter pressed his handkerchief into my hand. "Camlet would never do that. He shall endure. You must have caught him at a low moment. The trial is but two weeks away." He hesitated, and then added, "There is a reason, why he begged me not to let you visit."

"My presence makes it harder for him to bear." That I had increased his pain even for an instant was agonizing to think on. "When it's my duty to be his joy, his helpmeet."

"Marian, if we can secure his acquittal then all these woes will be but a fleeting memory. You need to rest. Leave it to me to meet Laura at the station. Do you go home, and –"

"No, no." I sat up and dried my eyes. "Mr. Donthorne looks for us to call. And little Wally will expect me to meet him."

The city was very hot, and the power of the sun was cruel. The Foreign Office is in Whitehall, but a block from the Thames. Too near! But Mr. Donthorne had sent directions to the proper courtyard and stair. The offices were lofty and floored with marble, gratefully cooler, and the clerks had blocked some of the eastern windows with sheets soaked in lime against the odor.

Our destination on the building's western side was less oppressive, and Roderick Donthorne himself was a cheerful man – in his middle forties, but a lean athletic figure. His sleek dark hair showed silver threads at the temples and in his neat moustache and goatee, and he wore pince-nez on a long narrow nose like a ferret. Walter introduced himself, offered condolences for the death of Major Donthorne, and presented me.

Mr. Donthorne startled me by saying, "I must begin by rendering you a long-overdue apology, Miss Halcombe. For this is not our first introduction."

I was certain I had never met this man before, and replied with some coldness. "Indeed, sir?" Surely, with Walter standing right here, he would not offer me a vile proposition.

He laughed, very pleasantly. "I recall our first meeting, although I'm sure you do not. I was eight, and you were an infant in arms."

"This must have been in Varneck Hall, then," Walter said.

"Precisely. Your mother was a guest, and she had brought you, Miss Halcombe. And I am sorry to confess that I was a rowdy lad, just home from Eton. When we were first introduced, I threw a ball at the drawing room window. Not only did it shatter the glass, the tremendous noise startled you awake, a social solecism which gave you great offense. You began to cry, and my governess hauled me out by the ear and spanked me with a hairbrush. From that day to this the crime has blotted my copybook, and I knew my only hope of salvation was to implore your forgiveness."

I had to laugh myself, at this innocent tale. "All the apologies must be on my side, Mr. Donthorne. My intemperate tears surely added to the weight of your already overwhelming troubles. A broken window, dear me, how shocking! I am prostrate with shame, and must beg your forbearance for my self-regarding infant nature. However, I trust that you've entirely recovered from the spanking."

"Thank you, I suffer no lasting deleterious effects," he said. The twinkle in his dark eye was entirely charming. "How long this breach has lasted! But now we have laid down arms and signed the peace treaty. It remains only to celebrate the new agreement with refreshments."

Mr. Donthorne sent his secretary for tea. His raillery was just in my style, and to talk of family with someone familiar with the old days was wonderfully pleasurable. Mr. Donthorne remembered my mother clearly. "A bewitching woman, irresistibly full of laughter and life, with hair of the purest black. You resemble her greatly. My late father aspired to her hand, did you know?"

"Why no, I did not know that," I said. "A widow with a tiny infant, truly? Do tell!"

"Is not family gossip delightful? And entirely purified by time, since nobody is left to be offended." Mr. Donthorne passed me the sugar bowl. "She had the county at her feet, your mother. And my own mother had sadly passed away five years previously. But my good father the Major was ever a man of deliberate and slow action, a true John Bull. He was pipped at the post by Philip Fairlie, who swooped in and cut him out in a twinkling. And it's just as well, a very fortunate circumstance. For consider – otherwise we would now be brother and sister,"

This idea struck us both as very droll. "And you know that my half-sister, Laura Fairlie Hartright, is Philip Fairlie and Celeste Halcombe's daughter."

"I had heard, and hope to meet her one day," he said. "Mr. Hartright, you must possess a prized treasure. If she inherited her father's fair face and her mother's fascination, your wife must be the belle of the north."

"She is indeed adored by all," Walter said. "But we should not trespass too much upon your valuable time, Mr. Donthorne."

"You must be a busy man," I agreed. "Left to my own devices I would chat with you for hours. I do not know how much you are aware of my current plight, Mr. Donthorne." He professed complete ignorance, and as briefly as possible I outlined to him my dreadful situation. I was sure he would be too much of a gentleman to express open contempt for my ruin, but after his warmth and friendly reminiscence I scalded at the thought of even the slightest repugnance. Scandal after scandal: desertion, bigamy, murder, a child to be born out of wedlock. No respectable man could hear it without disgust.

But Mr. Donthorne proved his sterling quality. "Your situation is deplorable, Miss Halcombe," he cried. "What a dreadful coil you are ensnared in."

His kind words moved me tremendously. "You have a great heart, sir," I said, the tears coming to my eyes in spite of myself. "I've discovered that your opinion is not common."

"You are not in the least at fault," he said. "None of this was your doing at all, and anyone of sense could see that you are purely an innocent victim. Let me know how I may serve you in this!"

I swallowed my tears. "My goal is to secure Mr. Camlet's

acquittal," I said. "Mr. Hartright and I believe that Margaret Camlet was slain by political enemies acquired abroad, who followed her when she went to ground in London. If we can find these partisans, we should be well on our way to seeking out the actual culprit. Does the Foreign Office keep track of foreign partisans?"

"We do, and we do not, Miss Halcombe." Mr. Donthorne sighed. "The Foreign Office's sources of information vary widely in reliability. It is not unknown for us to resort to the *Times* for the latest intelligence. If a spy, or even a group of them, is discreet, committing no outrage and living quietly and respectably in England, they may jog along for decades without our ever knowing."

Carefully I did not meet Walter's eye. Professor Pesca was one such hidden agent, and Count Fosco had been another. "But what are they doing here?" I asked. "Are they simply in exile, hiding from rivals in their native lands?"

"If that were the case then there would be no difficulty, Miss Halcombe. Think of our civilization as a building – a beautiful house erected by many loving hands over the aeons, in which human beings, a greater number than ever before in history, can live and thrive. Each person has his or her allotted role in the building, and must work cheerfully and happily there. The role of Her Majesty's government is to run that beautiful house." Mr. Donthorne leaned back in his chair and stared up at the elaborate ceiling, his long nose giving an impression of a stork contemplating the sky.

"But even the grandest buildings must be maintained," Walter said, the provident caretaker of Limmeridge House. "The roof, the guttering, the gravel in the drive."

"This is true, sir. You see the value of my analogy. Civilization too must be maintained, for it is eroded from all sides by the forces of chaos and disorder. If foreign visitors come seeking a refuge, it is of no importance. It is when they are pests – the termites, the wood ants, allying themselves with chaos, destroying the building, undermining Britain. It's then that we must act. With the signing of the Treaty of Paris, ending the Crimean War, Russia is barred from the Black Sea. This has had many beneficial effects from our point of view, but southern

Europe in general has become less stable. I foresee another Italian war. There has been a surge of shady and dubious foreign nationals into Britain."

"Mrs. Camlet's memoir was curiously lacking in specifics," Walter said. "But her paramour Count Ludovic Bradamante seemed most exercised about Slovenia and Croatia."

"His name, and Darnell's, are familiar to us. But all our knowledge is derived from reportage in the popular press. I regret to inform you that the number of partisans and groups in that region is exceptionally large. There are a thousand thousand divisions and sub-groups, none of them working together and often, cloaked in their secrecy, in direct opposition to each other. And the most deplorable development is when they shade over into criminal enterprise. To draw the line between political anarchism and villainy plain and simple often cannot be done."

"There may be a thousand groups in the Balkans," I said, "but the number here in London cannot be quite that large."

"You are intelligent, Miss Halcombe," Donthorne remarked. "But the cell system they favor means that penetrating such groups is very nearly impossible. And they are fiercely loyal. These little ethnic groups are almost tribal in their structure;. You are born in the group and you die within it."

"So the Blue Hand organization is unknown to you."

"Alas, yes. But it would help me greatly if I could read that manuscript." Mr. Donthorne thoughtfully stroked his goatee. "My analysts may be able to identify places or events. If the late Mrs. Camlet was really Daisy Darnell, you have hold of an important identification. We might gain an incomparable insight into the workings of the anarchist groups of the eastern Mediterranean."

"Inspector Radenton has cast doubt upon her veracity," I said, "but I'm certain that your experts could quickly determine if she was genuine. We have three copies of the memoir, and I shall see that you get one. I ask only that you keep it within the Foreign Office. You shall see – it's so thrilling, the temptation to share it is severe."

"We're accustomed to discretion in these parts," Mr. Donthorne said, smiling.

We rose to take our leave, and he rose with us. "I feel so

much better," I exclaimed. "This is too large a task to be accomplished alone. Allies are what is called for. If only it's not too late!"

"If Camlet comes to trial, we need not fix the guilt upon another," Walter said. "We need only cast enough doubt upon the police case against him, so that the jury shall acquit."

"Let us conduct some inquiries, Miss Halcombe," our host said. "At the very least we may be able to produce an expert witness for you. With any luck, a jury of bumpkins will be swayed by a suave Foreign Office diplomat in a swallow-tail coat."

"God bless you, Mr. Donthorne." I took his hand in both my own. "Thank you, so much, for all your kindness. You give me hope, and your understanding is a balm to my soul."

"You've had a cruel time of it, Miss Halcombe. Your courage and fortitude astonishes me. Mr. Camlet must be very dear to your heart."

"Oh, he is indeed." The tears rose in my eyes again at the very thought of Theo, and Mr. Donthorne pressed my hand in tender sympathy.

"Your loyalty does you the greatest credit," he said. "You're a woman in ten thousand, Miss Halcombe, and I'm very glad to have renewed our acquaintance. And after such a rocky beginning, too."

I had to laugh at that, and so we parted on a happy note. "What a kind man, Walter," I said when we were down in the hot stinking street. "I have not laughed so much this age. I had feared there were no such men at all, except Theo and yourself. But he redeems my faith in the gender."

"The two of you hit it off with marvelous ease," Walter agreed. "He was notably helpful – I wonder why?" Walter's tone made me look at him. He's right, he has a naturally suspicious mind.

It was high time to go meet Laura. As the brougham struggled through the teeming streets to the station I had time to think about Roderick Donthorne's comment about sleeper agents in Britain. "Walter," I said. "A secret group of partisans in Britain working for political independence. We know of one such partisan."

"Professor Pesca, of course. But he's Italian, and pays no

heed to the politics of any other nation."

"Perhaps he knows somebody who knows of a Balkan faction?"

"We can but ask. I'll invite him to dinner tomorrow. He will like to see Laura."

"Excellent. And, another thought. It would be useful to talk to Father Ercole. He's the only man we know of who ever spoke to anyone associated with Margaret Camlet in her Daisy Darnell identity. Is he still in London, do you think?"

"He may well be. The Italian states are in some turmoil right now, and as Donthorne noted, England is a refuge. But Pesca would know. I'll send him a note immediately we get home."

Impeded by traffic, we arrived at the station just in time. What amazing refreshment, to see Laura waving from the window as the train pulled in! Little Wally dashed out and flung himself yelling into his father's embrace, and Laura and I exchanged kisses and hugs. She was beautiful as ever, her fair hair braided up under a straw hat and her blue linen gown bringing with it an air of country summers.

"Marian," she cried. "I'm so glad to see you, but you should not have come."

"Just what I said to her," Walter said.

"You should be staying within doors, resting." In a lower tone she said, "Marian, have you consulted a medical practitioner? You look very large for the seventh month."

"I had not considered it," I admitted. "But all shall be made right now that you are here."

I had put no thought at all into the progress of my pregnancy, and it was good to have an experienced mother like Laura here. Walter took little Wally and all the baggage in a cab, and we rode in the carriage with baby Fairlie, Luna, and the maids, chattering like magpies. My unborn child consented to do some kicks and wriggles, and Laura, feeling, agreed that this was a very healthy sign.

The entire family had dinner that evening at Mrs. Hartright's cottage. Its parlour was far too small to accommodate us all, but it was more pleasant to sit out in the garden anyway. Little Wally was wildly excited at the idea of having his own room at his grandmama's, and undertook to be the man of the house immediately. With her long residence in the area Mrs. Hartright knew of the best obstetric doctor in the district and at Laura's request immediately sent a note begging him to call at Sandett House the following day. We ate cold chicken and salad, and the occasion was so entirely happy that I missed Theo sorely – the only blot upon my joy.

BOOK 5

❧ Marian Halcombe's journal ✥

23 July
It was not until this morning that the full extent of Walter's cunning was borne in upon me. "Visit Newgate?" Laura exclaimed. "Never, Marian. It is far, far too dangerous for you. And in this summer weather? Heat prostration will overtake you."

"I will visit Camlet for you instead, Marian," Walter said promptly. "And recall that Dr. Lamington is calling in the forenoon, and Pesca is coming to dinner tonight. Surely that's a full enough schedule for a woman in your condition."

"It's already too active," Laura pronounced. "You must take a nap before dinner, and put your feet up."

Against their loving and united opposition I could not prevail. Laura especially, with her maternal experience, had a fond authority that was difficult to argue with. I was obliged to sit with my feet on a hassock in the shadiest angle of the arbor of the garden and cast on for a baby cap, while Walter went into town to carry a copy of the memoir to Mr. Donthorne. "I will of course give Camlet your best love, Marian," he said cheerfully to me.

"You are devious, Walter." Mutinously I scowled up at him from my knitting. "What a lowering reflection. Calling Laura in to reinforce you, when you know I cannot say no to her – I had not thought you capable of such underhandedness."

"The pot calls the kettle black. Should I bring him anything else?"

"Take the other copy as well, and see if the prison authorities will let you give it to Theo." I pointed at the original manuscript, which Mr. Smithee had returned to its own pasteboard box. "I'm certain Theo will enjoy it, and he may have some insight into Margaret's activities."

Without more comment Walter seized the manuscripts and fled. Laura came out, bringing me a cool drink and some fruit. "You must eat many small meals, with enough greenstuff and fruit to keep your systems in order," she said gently. "And does Theo keep a cow? Then I must seek out some clean and honest milkmaid, to get you milk."

"I despise drinking milk," I protested.

"Then we'll make it into pudding or syllabub," Laura said. "You must have it, for the baby. I am sure this Dr. Lamington will agree." I had a feeling that she would feed it to me, spoonful by spoonful, if I resisted. Perhaps I can quietly slip it to Luna? As Laura bustled back and forth, the busy housewife, I envied her slender waist and swift feet. I had gained a good stone and a half in weight, and worse was to come. I have two months yet, and in spite of what Walter thinks, I am no Hercules in either body or will. Perhaps I had better become accustomed to a semi-invalid state for a while. As soon as Theo is free!

I had cast on ninety-three tiny stitches and had knit the crucial first round, counting and recounting to be sure I had set the lace pattern up right. I was paying no attention to what was going on in the house, and was startled when Laura suddenly appeared and dropped into the other chair, fanning herself. "I'm furious," she announced. "Oh!"

"Why Laura, what can it be?"

"Dr. Lamington has just come. And gone."

"Gone?"

"Marian, the brass of that man. He was so polite and pleasant, asking me about my health. And then I realised that he thought that I was the patient."

"Not unreasonable," I said.

"But when I told him that it was you, he refused to see you. He said that he only accepted married ladies as patients."

"Only he did not phrase it so nicely, I surmise," I said. "Both Theo and I are notorious in the neighbourhood, you know. His name has been dragged through the mire twice this year alone. Don't let the old quack vex you. I do not want to see a doctor at all. What can a male doctor know of parturition anyway? All he can do is administer chloroform so that I'm dizzy during the delivery."

"He's not worth fourpence," Laura fumed. "Ellen, I hope you dropped his top hat and stepped on it." Ellen, who was setting a tray of cold luncheon down, giggled.

"I'm grateful I did not so much as lay eyes upon him," I said. "You are very kind, to deal with such unpleasant visitors for me."

"Beg pardon, miss, mum." Ellen poured more lemonade into my glass. "If the fine doctor refuses to wait upon Miss Halcombe, there's a respected midwife only ten minutes away."

"Is there?"

"Mrs. Eliza Pinney, her name is, some sort of cousin to our own Ned Matson. He's one of five, you know, and Mrs. Pinney attended all his sisters and sisters-in-law when they were brought to bed. He has eleven nephews and nieces, all thriving."

"So she must know her business," Laura said, sitting up. "Ellen, I should very much like to meet Mrs. Pinney."

"Davey shall run and fetch her," Ellen said. "And ..."

Her glance at me was full of guilt. "Oh heavens, Ellen," I moaned. "You've been plotting against me."

"It was just that you're in the family way, Miss Halcombe," Ellen pleaded. "And with only Mr. Walter in the house, and the children. What good could they do you, if you were took ill? Mrs. Youngblood had a son, but he's a grown man with his regiment in Madras, and she remembers almost nothing of his birth, so long ago. And Nurse and I have neither chick nor child. So I did just take it on myself at chapel two Sundays ago, to tell Mrs. Pinney that if there were a sudden need we might find ourselves calling for her help."

"You did exactly right, Ellen," Laura said. "And I'm very grateful for your forethought and prudence. If Mrs. Pinney is at liberty to call today, your mistress would be delighted to see her."

"I would not," I muttered, but with resignation.

"Marian, if there is anything that a woman must learn when

she becomes a mother, it is foresight," Laura said. "You must prepare and be ready for the trial to come."

"I have other trials to prepare for," I said. "Laura, what if I cannot be in the courtroom when Theo's turn comes?"

"I do not think you can be there," Laura asserted. "And, Marian. Walter has asked me to say this to you. If the worst comes to the absolute, absolute worst …"

"You do not want me to be at the end," I finished for her, tears in my eyes. "Laura, if my presence will comfort him I must be there at his... at the end. Even if it's unbearable for me."

"Marian, the promise you made to him was until death. At some point, when all hope is lost, it is no betrayal to turn your thoughts to yourself and not to him."

"Could you do that, Laura? If it were Walter, facing the gallows?"

Laura gasped at this awful picture, tears coming to her lovely blue eyes at the very idea. "But you must think of the baby."

"I must have you read Margaret Camlet's memoir. We have a third copy. She was there in Dubrovnik when her man was hanged for murder. She stood at the gallows foot, and did not shed a tear."

"Indeed, Marian, really? I can't conceive of that!"

"She called curses like hot sulphur down upon the heads of his killers. But perhaps – perhaps I might not be a comfort to Theo." My tears brimmed over at the thought. "He's no firebrand like Count Ludovic Bradamante. Perhaps he will not wish to see me."

"Please don't cry, Marian," Laura begged, beginning to weep herself. "Tears are bad for babies."

"The poor mite," I sniffled. "I feel I've spent this whole year weeping. If tribulations truly mar the unborn then it shall be the ugliest little thing, for we have had so many."

In spite of ourselves we both cried heartily. Laura's heart has always beat in the closest sympathy with mine. We might indeed have done ourselves an injury, but all at once Luna gave a volley of warning barks. A hearty brass voice cried out to us. "Ladies, ladies. What is this? Are you giving way to the vapors, or is something wrong?"

A tiny woman swathed in several colourful shawls bustled up to us. "Mrs. Pinney," Ellen announced belatedly, as Laura hushed her greyhound.

"And you must be Miss Halcombe," Mrs. Pinney said, the size of her voice entirely a contrast to her height. "I've heard so much about you. What a sad thing it is, that has befallen Mr. Camlet! But we must trust in the good Lord to bring him out of the Valley. And in the meantime, my my. You are well along, aren't you, my dear? How are you feeling? Do you discern any quickening?"

I liked her immediately. Laura glanced at me. We both marked Mrs. Pinney's snow-white linen and scrupulously clean hands, even though she had had very short notice of our invitation. We adjourned into the house and she examined me, Laura assisting, and then we had tea. She pronounced me to be quite healthy and progressing nicely, and I was fascinated to learn of the possible emotional symptoms of my condition. A tendency to tears, even sudden surges of amativeness, all quite normal. A most comfortable and informative visit, and I was happy to engage her to assist when my time came. "Which will be sooner than September, my dear," Mrs. Pinney said.

"Why, I made sure it was September. Nine months since January."

"Well, you must have miscounted, missy," Mrs. Pinney said. "Measuring your belly, its time will be August. Unless it's twins you have in there."

"Twins? Oh no!"

"They don't run in your family? Then don't fret yourself about it. Far more likely you miscalculated your last flow. The size you are, you don't have long to wait."

"But I have a great deal to do before I'm confined."

"So do we all, my dear," Mrs. Pinney assured me. "Never was a baby that arrived at a convenient moment. Deb Treadle, your Ned's sister, she had a baking of bread just into the oven when her second began, and in the excitement it was burnt quite black. Fit only for the pigs."

When Mrs. Pinney departed, with many assurances on either side, Laura insisted that I rest. All my protests of energy and unsleepiness were for naught, and I was put to bed with the shades drawn down. In the warm crimson dimness of Theo's four-poster I surprised myself by dropping off, only waking when the sound of cab wheels proclaimed Walter's return with our dinner guests.

"Mrs. Marian," Pesca greeted me when I came down to the drawing room. "You bloom like the rose!"

"Oh professor, you are the most shameless flatterer," I said, shaking his hand heartily. "And is this Father Ercole? Will you present me?"

The two Italians still presented the most comic aspect, Pesca being so little and well-dressed, gaiters, umbrella and white hat all complete, and Father Ercole such a beanpole all in shabby black. Pesca introduced me in a flood of energetic Italian, and Father Ercole favored me with an enthusiastic handclasp. Pesca had painted me as the rich patroness of his journey to Britain. The good Father was effusively grateful, Catholics apparently not being nearly so bothered as we about women in my condition.

Walter said to me, "Having come so far, Father Ercole went on to Cambridge to inspect their collection of Italian manuscripts, and is only recently back in town."

"I'm glad you have had profit from your long journey," I said to the priest.

"He is going to write a book," Pesca translated to me. "All about the English. Especially the spiritual significance of their climate!"

"Most edifying," I said, with all the tact I could muster. By the time the meal was over we were able to move on to business. Walter explained to Pesca our desire for detail about the Salerno funeral of the false Margaret Camlet, and labouriously, sentence by translated sentence, Pesca extracted this from Father Ercole as I took notes:

The elderly lady with the long grey braid was already insensible, on the point of death, when Father Ercole was called in. He never exchanged conversation with her and could not administer absolution, but trusted in the mercy of the Lord to save her. Four men had been in the group purchasing her burial in Salerno. They were none of them native speakers of Italian, and only one of them had any pretense to fluency. They had paid the fees with ordinary ten-lira notes, doled out from a thick wad in a leather wallet. The ceremony was middling, neither very opulent nor of the humblest. They had promised a stone marker for the grave later, but nothing had ever come of it. Disappointing, since the St. Donatus church could have used the funds and the town stonecutter was Father Ercole's grand-nephew.

"Can he speak of the four men?" I suggested. "Perhaps he could describe them. Who seemed to be the leader?"

"The one with the money," Pesca translated, after some discussion. "He was tall, with black hair. He wrote the address down on a piece of paper, where to send a letter about the lady's death."

"And a moustache?"

When Pesca translated this the priest beamed at me and nodded. With his fingers he pantomimed the swoop of a waxed moustache. "Excuse me," Walter said. He went out and came back with my own sketchbook, the one with the marbled-paper cover from the desk drawer in the second bedroom. He had also brought down a handful of pencils and crayon, and turning to a fresh page he began to sketch. "Like this?"

"Oh, excellent Walter," I said. "A picture is worth a thousand words." Guided by Father Ercole, Walter delineated four faces that the priest felt were approximately correct. It was a pleasure to watch Walter's skill and speed – he is really an expert artist. And I felt that Walter too enjoyed returning to pencil and crayon. He has not done this in many months. And when I looked at the image of the square-shouldered mustachioed man with waving black hair – "Count Ludovic Bradamante. What do you think, Laura?"

Laura, who had begun reading the memoir while I napped, said, "It can be no other. Margaret Camlet described him so well. But what of these?"

"His fellow conspirators, I assume." Under Walter's clever pencil and crayons the figures sprang into life on the page – a tall, hulking brute of a fellow with a shoulder-length mane of brown hair and deep-sunk eyes, a smaller plumper man, rosy-cheeked and button-nosed like a Father Christmas with a pointed beard, and a tall, bony-featured man with a wild sheaf of curly chestnut hair. "But if Ludovic Bradamante was there, then we must assume that Margaret Camlet knew and approved of this false death."

"This happened in 1852," Laura reflected. "It must have been just after the explosion that murdered Duke Stefan of Sarajevo."

"She was covering her tracks," I mused. "Changing her name the way one would turn one's coat, to put off pursuit. Margaret Camlet died so that Daisy Darnell could be born. And that is why there is no mention of the false funeral in the memoir."

"Marian, she must have been absolutely fearless," Laura said. "More like a tigress than a woman."

"That is how Theo remembers her," I said. "And the letter."

"The letter Theo showed us?" Laura said. "If it was Bradamante who told Father Ercole to write it, then she knew of it."

"She told Bradamante to have it sent," I said, thinking hard. "She wanted Theo to be free. To live his own life, seek his own happiness. Because she did not plan to ever return to him. Margaret Camlet had been Theo Camlet's wife, but Daisy Darnell had her own true mate. Only after Bradamante's execution, when she was fleeing pursuit on all sides, did her thoughts turn towards the safety of England… Have you seen her ring?"

"No, you must show it to me."

"Walter judges it's worth a fortune. I'm afraid its price probably was not come by honestly. It is engraved 'From L. to D. Love.' From Ludovic, or Louis, to Daisy."

"How wonderfully romantic! Marian, she really does not sound suitable for Theo in the least."

"It was a match made in Hades, certainly. But…" I gripped my hands together. "I'm no better for him. If he had not met me, he would have been spared so much."

"He might well still be suspected of murdering her," Laura comforted me. "And without your aid, and Walter's, to help prove his innocence, he would be in terrible peril. You've made him happy, I know you have."

"It's the goal of my life." I looked up and met her smile. It is entirely impossible to speak of such things, but I had to smile back. Yes, we both loved, and knew all the joys of being loved. The knowledge passed between us without a single word, only a shared blush. "How did you become the confident and bold one?" I asked in wonder, fanning my hot cheeks.

"I've been married to Walter for some years now," she reminded me gently. "When you've been Theo's wife for more than a year, you too will be able to repose in his love."

I had to sigh at the thought of that. To repose in Theo's love, what a felicity that would be – we had scarcely been wed for ten months. But the gentlemen were pausing in their discussion of Walter's sketches, giving me the opportunity to ask the foremost question in my mind. "Pesca, my dear fellow," I said, refreshing his teacup. "I would like to find some of the Balkan independence partisans that must be in Britain. How would I go about talking to anarchist conspirators?"

"Mrs. Marian! Are you gone mad? Nobody wants to meet such people, by God! They are like rats, like wolves, not for society of ladies."

"Walter theorises that Margaret Camlet was killed by some such group. They killed her once, after all." I glanced at the sketches.

Poor Pesca's thinning hair seemed to crisp with horror. "When they are found, they are arrested. By police! These people, they throw bombs, they make explosions, for nothing. For some revolution! They live in Ireland, or Greece. God grant that they never come to England. We want no such disorder here. Mrs. Marian, you know what anarchism is?"

"I thought it was the sort of thing odd Nonconformists experiment with in America," I said. "The belief that collective action, rather than a government, is the way to rule a country. Communism, in other words."

"That is one definition." Suddenly the Professor's antic manner was sobered, and he looked years older. "But the other philosophy, that shares the same name, is illegalism. The use of violent acts as retaliation against perceived evils. What they call the propaganda of the deed. Murder, under the guise of fighting oppression. Theft, spoken of as 'individual re-appropriation.' Death, masquerading as life. Politically, Mrs. Marian, it is the road to chaos."

I thought of Roderick Donthorne's termites, undermining the nation. Unwillingly I quoted Thomas Carlyle, whose *The French Revolution: A History* I had so happily and innocently read at Theo's behest at the beginning of our courtship: "'Surely Peace alone is fruitful. Anarchy is destruction: a burning up, say, of Shams and Insupportabilities; but which leaves Vacancy behind.'"

"Ah – very sound! Such people, Mrs. Marian, they understand and use only power. The strong survive, and impose their will upon the weak. And they are dangerous, because they conceal themselves under the mask of good – of helping the worker, of uniting the poor. They are grossly perverting an important force."

Pesca never speaks of political matters. I believe he is involved with the movement to unify the Italian states, though Walter refuses to confirm this. So this was new. "You do not hold that every man in Britain has his proper place, in which he must work and be content?"

"What if content be not possible? For the masses of poor there is no recourse. They do not control their factories, their tools, even their lives. You cannot know, Mrs. Marian, the misery of the very poorest. The ones who lose their jobs every winter when harvest is done. The ones who are dismissed from the factories at whim. They have nothing, no savings, not the least resource. Their only path is starvation. It is cruel, Mrs. Marian. It cannot be just. It is clearly not Christian. Does not our good God command us to love the poor and feed the hungry? And we give them no hope. There is nowhere to go, no chance of improvement, no prospect of change. Those above, they say that this is the way it is supposed to be. We must say no! We must show them that this is not the way, that this cannot stand. And if their blindness must be washed away in blood –"

Pesca's words had been tumbling out faster and yet faster, propelled by his passion, and when he suddenly halted he looked almost ill. "We do not want this to happen in England," he concluded, much more quietly. "You, above all, must avoid these people, Mrs. Marian. Because you will see only their good, being an angel of goodness yourself. And then you will be destroyed by their evil."

He was embarrassed, and I tried to help by speaking more lightly. "Professor, you are too gallant. What will Theo say? I'm so sorry he is not here to make your acquaintance. I long to introduce him to you."

Pesca took a deep breath, relaxing. "To have won you, Mrs. Marian, he must be a saint among men." He mimed the halo above his head. Then old Mrs. Hartright arrived with Sarah and young Wally, who remembered Pesca with joy. He clattered into the drawing room dragging his newest toy, a wooden popgun. Laura opened the piano, and the conversation became general for the rest of the evening.

ஓ Walter Hartright's narrative ௸

It was about this period that I received a letter from Roderick Donthorne. He wrote to tell me that his analysts have concluded that Margaret Camlet was probably in truth Daisy Darnell, and at need one of his experts would testify to this at Camlet's trial.

I was startled, however, by the next paragraph. It was subtle and indirect, written by a master diplomat, so that while it never made a flat statement the meaning could not be mistaken. He intended to address Marian if she was widowed. Perhaps in the New Year, when she was safely delivered and her grief was likely to have abated somewhat. I was certain of his intent, because he concluded with the usual summary of the suitor's position and ability to support a wife. He has never had the opportunity to wed, having been posted in Mexico, Berlin and Peking for years.

Donthorne's assumption that there would be a throng of suitors, and that therefore he must apply to me promptly, made me blink. The son was determined not to be left at the starting gate as his father was. Laura and I always assumed that Marian was too uncomely to ever wed. Camlet was not typical, an outlier scarred by his previous disastrous adventure in matrimony. Despoiled, unwed and the mother of a bastard, Marian would seem to be ineligible for all time.

But now I reflected upon my sister-in-law's family history. The widowed Celeste Halcombe, poor and encumbered with a tiny daughter, had nevertheless had the county at her feet. Major Donthorne had aspired to her hand. She had instead wed the wealthy Philip Fairlie, one of the handsomest men in England, and held his complete devotion her life long. He had never married again after her demise and the grand white marble tomb he erected in the Limmeridge churchyard was a landmark of love in the district. Perhaps simply the perpetual contrast of dark

Marian with Laura's luminous beauty had not served her well. My dear wife had the right of it. Marian needed to move into her own space for her brilliance to properly shine. Certainly in London she had no difficulty in acquiring admirers. If she kept on at this rate she would indeed have the dozens she had once mentioned to Laura. Donthorne was of her class, a member of the gentry, eminently suitable. Neither Camlet nor I myself were of that level.

However, Providence had made me responsible for my sister-in-law. Donthorne wrote so obliquely, I considered myself justified in not showing Marian this letter. It was not an offer, which would be inconceivable at this juncture, but merely the suggestion of the intent to make one. It would be interesting to see how solid the testimony of this Foreign Office expert might be. If Margaret Camlet was shown to be Daisy Darnell, then it immediately became much more credible that she had beenslain by foreigners. But if the testimony was botched or unconvincing, so that the jury believed Radenton's version of events, Camlet might well hang. And Donthorne would then be first in the queue for the hand of a woman heir to both Theophilus Camlet and all that he himself inherited from his late wife. I replied to Donthorne suggesting that he bring the subject up again next year when matters were more settled. And I would listen attentively at the trial, before I rendered him a decision.

Marian Halcombe's journal

2 August

The idea of seeing Theo again haunts me. If I cannot visit him in Newgate, nor attend his trial, nor be at his execution, then I shall never see him again this side of eternity. And this is completely intolerable. The mere thought makes me want to wail aloud. But, against that, there is the fearful idea that he does not want to see me. That my presence actually causes him pain, and that therefore my desire to be with him is purely selfish in nature, not considering his dreadful straits at all. The idea racks me in the stuffy bed at night. I am already too bulky to sleep very well, and after all these weeks the bedding no longer smells of Theo but only of my sweaty self. And furthermore, it is less than ten days until his trial. I should not waste time to no purpose in Newgate.

I should instead find the mysterious Blue Hand anarchists, and winkle out from among them the true killer.

Torn as I am by these doubts, it is all too easy for my darling Laura to swoop in and take complete charge of my days. Instead of taking a hot and jolting carriage ride down into the dirty and odiferous city fruitlessly searching for I know not what, this past week I have been under her loving management. Laura has set me to hulling berries to be made into preserves, or doing the mending, all the housewifely tasks that I had been neglecting. I spent an entire day hemming some sheets! And I cannot tell if she is saving me from hopelessness by diverting me into these small tasks, or strangling me with that same loving busyness. I have never felt these doubts before.

Today her plan was to raise our parasols after breakfast and stroll very slowly down the shady lane half a mile to Mrs. Hartright's cottage, carrying some freshly laundered socks and shirts down for little Wally. With unprecedented cunning Walter did not come down to breakfast, so that I could not task him with errands on my behalf.

Thus by ten in the morning I found myself perambulating down the lane, attended by Lottie and Micah, who as the male in charge was given the honor of carrying the bundle of clean laundry. The nurse carried little Fairlie, Laura carried a further basket of cakes and bread for our luncheon, and Luna the greyhound followed at her heels wearing a smart red leather collar and lead. I had nothing to hold but my umbrella, and even this was deemed to be too large and heavy, being my favorite grey man's umbrella. Instead I had to change with Laura, and carry her white-lace sunshade. A pretty and domesticated picture we made with our wide crinolined skirts, trailing down past the lush undergrowth and the overhanging oak boughs. The blackberries were nearly ripe, and the wild rosehips were scarlet in the hedgerows. And, by encouraging Lottie to pick some daisies to give to our hostesses, Laura ensured that I had a rest on a convenient bench halfway along. No one would know, looking at her delicate face under the brim of her white straw bonnet, that my sister was so conniving and devious.

Nor was my situation improved when we arrived at the cottage. I got the best armchair in the parlour, and Mrs. Hartright pushed her own footstool under my feet. Instead of romping with the children or hulling strawberries or even dandling little Fairlie, I had no choice but to sit with my hands folded over the dome of my enormous belly and listen to Laura catching the fond grandmother and aunt up with all of Fairlie's doings. She recounted the perfidy of Dr. Lamington, and went thoroughly into Mrs. Pinney's qualifications with Mrs. Hartright. By the time I had heard every last detail of half a dozen deliveries she had presided over I had lost all appetite for luncheon.

There had been a time in my life when such small doings were fully sufficient, filling heart and mind completely. Marriage has changed me, enlarged my heart as Laura had wanted for me. And if loving Theo has altered me so much, what will the birth of this new little one do? I stand on the brink of a fearful cliff, looking out over an unknown country of motherhood into which I will soon, will I or nil I, descend. And I had looked to explore this new land with my dear man. Can I bear to do it alone?

But I already am alone. No longer am I united with Laura and Walter, our hearts as one in purpose. I lost my heart to another, and now even if I would, I can never return, never fit back into my safer, smaller self.

As when Theo first came to Limmeridge, I could neither sit nor stand nor walk quietly. The unborn child refused to let me rest, kicking and turning, and the weight of misery in my heart drove me lumbering to my feet. Doubly burdened, I went out behind the cottage, ostensibly to let Luna out, but instead I leaned my hot forehead on the bark of a convenient tree. Laura, ever sensitive to my heart, followed in alarm.

I turned and faced her. "I cannot let him go," I said. "I cannot give up, not now. Not so close to the end. We must make one more attempt. And Laura, if you and Walter do not approve, I am sorry."

"Oh Marian!" She hugged me, and I felt her tears. "We only thought of your own health, your welfare. You must always do as you feel right, always. And I will always support you and be with you. But, please, do not destroy yourself. Because to lose you would break my heart."

"I am not so fragile as all that. Not yet," I had to add. "Will you come with me? To Newgate? Then perhaps you can be easy about my health. I know that my condition is making Walter positively nervous."

"Must you visit Theo, Marian? Will it help him?"

"I don't know," I said. "But I do know that, if Mrs. Pinney is right, I will not be able to be there at – at the very end. It may even be physically impossible for me to attend the trial. How can I never see him again, Laura? This may be my last chance. And he knew this, the last time I was there. And I failed to understand." My tears overflowed, and I groped for my handkerchief.

"But I understand," she said. "Oh Marian, I do! To see him for the last time – I have done this, you remember…" We were both weeping again, a pair of sponges, so weak of us! Luna whined and pawed Laura's skirt, and then Sarah came out and offered to send Milly for Mrs. Pinney on the instant. With difficulty we prevented her from doing this, and to calm our hostesses went indoors and ate salad, cold beef, and lemon tart.

And now, in the cool of the evening, having set all this down, I see that I have, in essence, lured my darling Laura away from Walter to be my partisan. How lowering it is, to reflect that I divided husband from wife not with reason and sense, but with tears! However, her temporary disloyalty can do no harm. We will go into the city tomorrow and come back, sedate and safe, and he shall have no cause for complaint.

3 August

Laura cannot bear the slightest deception or dishonesty, and will never lie. How I wish I were like her. I was therefore not at all surprised at breakfast today to confront Walter looking like a thundercloud. "Marian, Laura has told me all," he began.

"I was certain she would," I said. "Now give me your opinion of this butter. Would you say that it has turned?"

"That you neglect your own health is something I can do nothing about," he went on. "And that you endanger the one yet unborn is beyond my aid."

"Cook has been keeping the milk and eggs in earthenware crocks on the stone floor of the pantry. But in this sweltering weather things simply do not keep as they ought."

"Laura is my responsibility and under my care. I will not allow her to feel pain or trouble."

"Then you must sever her from me, Walter," I said, unoffended. "For pain and sorrow are my lot, at least for a good while yet. I daresay if the butter were made into a cake its dubious qualities would pass unnoticed. I shall mention it to Cook."

"Marian, I have forbidden Laura to go into town with you this day."

"Would you enjoy a walnut cake flavored with coffee? Or perhaps a sponge, to be served with Devon cream and the gooseberries, would be better housekeeping. I shall ask if Cook has some other plan for them." I watched with placid interest as Walter dug the fingers of both hands into his hair and then seemed to wrestle with a powerful impulse to bang his head on the tablecloth. "If you would prefer raspberries you need only say so, Walter."

"The devil take the raspberries!" He leaped to his feet and stormed out.

"Then I shall tell Cook it is to be gooseberries," I called after him, before he slammed the door.

I have ordered the brougham for ten, so that we may perform our errand of mercy before the heat of the day becomes too great. There is time for me after breakfast to catch up with this journal. The windows and doors are all open, to cool the house as much as possible, and Laura paused in my doorway to ask, "Will this white bonnet show the city grime too much in your opinion, Marian?"

"The soot is not so annoying in town at this season, when fires are fewer," I replied, "but it is never nonexistent. You might do better to wear the grey ruffled one, and your lavender gloves. I shall be wearing my straw with the blue lining, and the blue gloves to match."

"Very well. I'll be ready in fifteen minutes."

"I also." Poor Walter! He should know by now, that he cannot stand against us.

4 *August*

So very much has happened that I must take care to record everything in the most precise order. Else I shall lose myself in the confusion of my own thoughts!

It was once again a very hot day, so hot that the speed of our carriage gave no refreshment. The stony streets and walls of the city seemed to hold the heat in like an oven. Laura has never been down to Newgate and the Old Bailey, and she found the walls and gate with its guardian gallows as fearful and intimidating as everyone does. "I read of this in Mr. Dickens' essays," she said. "Oh Marian, how can Theo bear it?"

"If one only has the hope of leaving, I believe it may be borne," I said. "It is the thought of being immured forever, of dying and being buried within these walls, that is so deeply crushing."

"And executed men are buried within," Laura recalled, shivering. "Give him my love, Marian, and tell him we all pray for him." She had to wait for me in the courtyard with its frowning spiked fence. The stone corridors and barred gates were cool, but not refreshing; there was no comfort here. And the hateful barred visitor's box, with its gap to prevent all contact – it was agony to see him and yet be separated like this.

And yet Theo seemed in somewhat better heart, not living on his nerves as he had before, nor sinking into despair. When I looked only at his dear face – not the crumpled suit or the stony cell or the bars, but only into the intelligent hazel eyes behind the steel spectacles – I could pretend. I could speak with the old easy frankness. "Do you wish to see me, or would you rather not? I fear that my visits only make you unhappy."

"If they make me unhappy, it's because seeing you makes me want so much more," he said. "You are the light of my eyes, and I would rather bear that unhappiness than not be in your presence."

My relief was so great I almost laughed. "I've worried that it's my duty to spare you."

"And my dread is that your exposure to these horrors will do you, or the one to come, an injury. And..." In the brown beard his smile was rueful.

"Tell me, my dearest."

"Well. It's but vanity, but I dislike being viewed by the woman I love in the posture of a caged and dangerous animal in a zoo. How dearly I would love to have my hair cut and take a bath before you visit."

This masculine foolishness was utterly adorable, so naturally I flew out at him. "Theo, do you fear to disgust me? Of all the silly things! I nursed you through typhus, and you were extraordinarily ill-groomed during that illness. Consider that I'm an equally repelling sight. I've gained every ounce you've lost and more. There is no disgust, no dread between us, not when we ..." I looked down at my fingers, twisting them together as the heat came up into my face. When I dared to glance up through the bars at him I met his gaze and knew our thoughts were one.

All I could do was listen to his breathing, a little heavier and faster than before. After some time he said, softly, "How I wish I could kiss you. Just that, at this point."

"Soon, my love." If we did not talk of something else I would cry. "What did Rev. Whistler say? Could he perform a Newgate wedding?"

"It has never been done in his time. He doubts the Archbishop will permit it."

I smothered a sharp comment upon the Archbishop's character, and cast quickly around for a less fraught topic. "Did you have a moment to read through Margaret's manuscript?"

"The press of my affairs has been considerable," he said, with smiling irony. "But I did manage to devote my scant leisure to it."

"Theo, isn't it thrilling?"

"She was a goddess, was she not?" He was sitting on the little wooden stool that was the cell's only furniture, and now he leaned back and hooked his clasped hands over one knee, just as he might have done in our own morning room. "I read it through twice from beginning to end. Fortunately the daylight is long at this season. And there are some salient points that may have escaped you in your first swift perusal."

I was both ruffled at his tone, and delighted, that his spirits were so lively. "Such as?"

"The narrative is very scant on motive and the reasons behind what is happening. You read it, my dear. Why did events occur? What was the Blue Hand actually doing?"

"I don't know," I said, struck. "It never occurred to me to ask, in the whirlwind of events."

"Because she simply neglects to tell you. And the excitement of the narrative obscures all its flaws."

"Only you would think of it that way, Theo," I said. "You publisher!"

"But a close reading allows one to infer motive, in spite of authorial failings." Theo stared thoughtfully right through me. "Do you remember in *Wildfell Hall*? Although they at first seemed foolish, all of the mysterious Mrs. Graham's actions were rational. They made complete sense from her perspective and were undertaken by her with a solid end in view."

"And so you're saying you comprehend Margaret's motives, even though she said nothing of them."

"Yes indeed. For instance, it's clear that at the beginning that Louis Bradamante – and therefore Margaret – comprised the entire Blue Hand organization. They were its heart and soul. But by the end of the narrative the organization had fractured into not one, nor two, but at least three factions. Another lens to view the story through is character. These people seem to fly off the handle with great ease, and part brass rags on the slightest impulse. I wonder if they could even articulate the source of their discord. It was possibly rooted in political philosophy, of which the text is entirely free. She probably omitted all abstractions intentionally, for fear of boring her reader."

"She certainly avoided that pitfall," I said. "And it was in the dissension between these factions that Margaret was murdered?"

"A logical surmise. She didn't say so, but the dissension was certainly what the fight on the docks in Odessa was about. The division of the assets of the organization led to violence. And the man, that Vjenceslav ..."

"Is that how you pronounce it?"

"I hope so."

"Their opponent."

"First their lieutenant, and then their opponent, yes. In the text he's clearly the most dangerous of their subordinates. All of them were dangerous, of course, and I'm sorry to say that Margaret was as ferocious as any. But this one seemed the most murderous."

I cast my mind back to the memoir. "Yes, I remember. He was the man who slew their artificer and accomplice."

"Wragsland," Theo recalled. "During the dock battle."

"Yes! Ran him through with a bayonet, and kicked the body

into the harbor. Is Vjenceslav a surname, or a given name? I know nothing of Balkan naming conventions."

"Neither do I. It's not very common in England."

"Theo, I always grasp books better when I read them with you. That is clearly your gift. Margaret, on the other hand, seems to have been amazingly blessed in the more criminal arts."

"Yes, she has used her shooting skills to enormous effect." He smiled, reminiscently. "However vehement and fiery Margaret was, she would never condescend to theft. Whatever those organizational assets – notice we are never told what they are – they were genuinely hers, or Bradamante's. She was always a woman of quality. Stealing would be beneath her. This anarchist tarradiddle of 'individual re-appropriation' would fill her with disgust and contempt. She might slay you in a cause she felt right, but she would not stoop to loot your corpse after."

I had to smile at him. "I'm glad the memoir has diverted you so well."

He grinned back at me. "If she had let me have the editing of this – well! An expository sentence, here and there, would clarify matters considerably."

There was a rattle and a shuffle behind me. My allotted visiting time had flown as if on wings, and the turnkey was come to lead me out. Awkward in my bulk I rose to my feet, the farewells sticking in my throat. Could this indeed be my last sight of him? Theo rose as well. Thank God, he was self-possessed as I was not. Silently I blessed Margaret Camlet's departed soul. To use his powers and do his proper work, that was what had brought him back to himself for a little while, and she had secured this for us. For this last time! I realised now what he had long known, that every meeting might be our last, and every parting a farewell for all eternity. When he spoke his tone was wistful. "We have been happy, have we not?"

"How can you doubt it?" My voice wavered. The iron bars helped. I could not fling myself at him, I had to be strong. "You have been the greatest joy of my life, the joy to which all hearts yearn. And it is not over. We shall be happy again, Theo."

"May it be so, my love. You have given me great happiness. And having had your heart, I am content."

I was able to turn away and get out into the hallway before

breaking down. The turnkey did not regard it, being well used to misery and tears, and I followed him, sobbing, out into the hot sunshine. Laura had been sitting with her parasol in a shady angle of the grim stone wall, and she hurried over to embrace me.

"Oh, Marian," she said softly. Her own tears were falling. "I advised you ill. My dearest sister, I've done you a wrong, urging you to adventure beyond our family fireside. Better that this never should have happened, that you had lived all your life safe at home in Limmeridge. Then you, and I, never would have known this pain."

My sobs were stilled. "No, Laura," I choked. "Just now, I told him he was the greatest joy of my life. Both of us, we would rather bear the unhappiness than not love."

"Pain seems to be the price of love," she agreed. "Then – you do not wish you had never met him."

"No, oh no. To grow, to change – we cannot help it. But it is so hard." I broke down completely, wailing in her arms.

I might have wept for hours, except that a warder came over. "Begging your pardon, ma'am," he said, with repellent cheer. "But would you ladies move along? Your noise is disturbing the prisoners. Some o' their windows face the courtyard, don't you see."

I would have struck out at him, but Laura held my hand. But this interruption diverted the torrent of my grief, and by the time we threaded our way out through the walks and grim courtyards I was more composed.

"We'll go home and have some tea," Laura soothed me. "I'm sure it would be a comfort to take off your gloves, bathe your face and perhaps soak your feet in cool water. This hot weather must be terribly uncomfortable for you."

"The size I am, yes. What a blessing you are, Laura. I would perish without you."

Arm in arm we walked out of the main prison gate, which shut with a clang behind us. I was just scouting the bustling narrow street for Matson and the brougham when suddenly I heard a wild cry. "Miss Halcombe!"

The little figure in the pink bonnet flung herself into my arms. "Joan? Oh, Joan, what's wrong?" But I knew immediately. These sobs, they were so like my own. "Joan, is it Bill?"

"He's dead, Miss Halcombe. Oh God, he died this morning. Oh God, oh God!" She screamed in her grief like a wounded animal.

Laura shrank back. Hastily I said, "Laura, this is Joan Porter. Her Bill came into the infirmary a week before Theo left it. Joan, this is my sister Laura Hartright. Laura, do you have a dry handkerchief?"

"I'm sorry, Marian, but you seem to have used them all." More quietly she said, "Marian, who is this person? Is she respectable? Was she ... married to this Bill?"

"No more than I am married to Theo, I suppose," I said with some impatience. "Perhaps Matson will have a spare handkerchief."

But Joan took a deep shuddering breath. "You. With the ring on your finger! What would you do, to save your man? Would you put yourself to shame? Do vile things with other men, so that his child could be fed? I did! Because he needed it. And, oh God. Now he's dead –"

She wept anew into her bare hands. Shocked, I said, "Laura, she is overcome with grief. Do not take umbrage, I beg you. Joan is not an ill-intentioned woman."

Tears stood in Laura's clear blue eyes. "No, it is for me to apologise, Marian. Joan, I'm sorry. I spoke far too unkindly. The troubles of others do not bring out the best in me, and I constantly battle against the impulse to uncharity. Is it far to your home, Joan? May we take you there? You are not fit to make your way back alone."

"Now that is a kind thought, Laura," I said. "But surely Walter did not fail to extract a solemn promise from you come promptly back?"

"He did," Laura said. "But a brief errand of mercy he cannot object to, I'm certain."

"And, poor Joan. You've worn yourself to nothing, nursing Bill. Feel how thin her hands are, Laura. Come, here is Matson with the carriage. What is your direction, Joan? Will Matson know the way?"

"Near Gull Court," Joan said, gulping. "It's off Bonhill Street in Shoreditch."

When he heard this, Matson glanced at me with dismay.

"That's in the East End, madam."

"There can be no harm in simply taking her home, Matson," I said. "And have you a spare handkerchief?"

He did, a red one with white spots, and having wiped her eyes with it Joan climbed up into the brougham, Laura following. I needed Matson's help to carefully climb up. In the past week or two I seem to have gained not only weight but girth. I felt as ungainly as a ship under full sail. "Madam, you and Mrs. Hartright may not know this, being from the north country," he said. "But Shoreditch is no fit place for ladies."

While we were hiding from Count Fosco we all three of us lived under assumed names in the East End, although not in the worst sections. And so now I was unsympathetic. "How dangerous can it be, in the middle of a summer afternoon? Let us be off, Matson."

The sweltering streets were thronged with traffic, and there was an accident ahead involving an overturned wagon, so it took us some time to make the journey. Laura had thoughtfully brought sandwiches and a flask of cold tea, and I pressed these refreshments on Joan. "It's been weeks since we met," I said. "Tell me of Bill. Did the fever overcome him, or were there complications?"

By the time Joan told us of all her woes – in addition to the decline and death of Bill her daughter Addie had been ill – a considerable time had passed. For the first time I noticed now outside the windows the mean and ill-kept buildings we passed. They were made of ugly cheap brick, with many a broken window mended with paper or stuffed with rags. The streets teemed with people, ill-dressed and visibly ailing, thin as bone. The air was close, laden with fume and stink. I had always thought of London as a grand city. This was nothing of the sort. It was the abyss that they wrote of in the newspapers, the realm of the lost.

By the time we arrived at Gull Court it was far later than I would have liked, nearly five o'clock. The sun was low in the west but its heat had not abated, and the swooning streets baked in misery. The court, merely a wide place between brick tenements, was barely big enough for the brougham to turn in, and Matson hastened to do this. Ragged urchins surged up around the vehicle. He would have driven them off with the whip, but Joan opened the door and jumped out. "Now you stop that, Bob! Herb, Roger, leave off this moment."

Their cries and comments were almost incomprehensible. The Cockney accent and the East End cant were like another language. Joan had Walter's gift, of being able to move up and down the social scale. What enabled her career as a mistress was that she could shift accents at will, sliding her speech up and down in gentility the way an Oxford graduate might shift from Latin to Greek. "If you are near to home, Joan," I began.

"No no, Marian," Laura interposed. "She is going to show me Addie's rash. It may only be chicken pox."

"Oh Laura, are you sure?"

"I can tell, but only by touching the child." I recognised the chatelaine of Limmeridge, indefatigable benefactress of the poor.

After defying Walter so often, I could not now point out to Laura that he would definitely dislike this. "Well then, I must come with you, and we must not be separated. Do you have a purse? Put it into your innermost petticoat pocket. I'm putting mine into my bosom."

Joan selected five of the biggest and most trustworthy boys. After some brisk negotiation I gave them twopence each to defend the horse and carriage, on the understanding that Matson would enforce failures with his whip and that I would further give each of them sixpence if he gave me a good report when we returned. In spite of my caution my sodden handkerchief was spirited out of my pocket with incredible deftness, and I worried about the horse's shoes. Theo's gleaming brougham stuck out here in crowded Gull Court like a gold coin in a bowl of porridge. But Joan shooed away other possible pickpockets, and led the way into a narrow side street, crammed with pedestrians and bannered with greyish laundry hanging from clotheslines to dry in the gritty air. The street ended in a filthy alley, which conducted us into another teeming side alley, and so to a block of crumbling tenements, their bricks black with soot.

Between the two most ramshackle of these buildings was an open sewer, reeking with standing fluids and foetid solids. This channel was covered over with cross timbers wedged between the buildings, and then a miscellany of boards. On this entirely inadequate foundation not one or two but three wobbly wooden stories had been erected. Only because they were braced between two relatively more sturdy buildings did the crazy structure stay up at all. Stepping with care Joan edged down this corridor, which was only wide enough to enter sideways. I followed her, and Laura came last, clinging to my hand. I could feel my wide skirts catching on splinters and nails. When I looked up I could see sunshine trickling through the patchwork roof above. God only knew what the place was like in winter. It must leak rain like a sieve. The wooden boards beneath my shoes were squashy with rot and slick with green mold and the whitish fingers of fungus. In the summer swelter the stench was appalling. There was not a breath of air, only the unmoving miasma that choked breath.

"How can people live like this?" Laura whispered in my ear.

These were the utterly destitute that Pesca had spoken of with such heat. And yet not utterly destitute, for this was shelter of a sort. How much worse could the worst off be? "They do what they must," I replied.

Stepping with care, Joan led us halfway along to a low door on the right. This she unlocked with a key. As the door groaned open there was a squeak and the scuttle of a rat. The windowless room beyond was little wider than the corridor, and not high enough to stand upright in. It would have made a generous coffin but an inadequate kennel. Daylight was visible through the cracks in the wobbly floorboards but otherwise there was no light. "Begging your pardon, Miss Halcombe, but there's not room for all of us," Joan said. "And you being so heavy…"

"I'll stand here in the doorway," I hastily agreed, waving Laura to pass me. "If I should fall through the floorboards you may never get me out."

Laura ducked under my arm into the room. "And is this Addie?" she said with brave cheer. "How are you, little one?"

"Yes," Joan said. "Just fancy! You'll be three come winter, won't you, lovey?"

There was no furniture in the cubbyhole, not so much as a block of wood to sit on. The child's bed was a shakedown, a mere heap of rags. Stepping carefully, Laura removed her gloves and knelt down to see as Joan lifted the girl to display the rash. I moved cautiously back out into the narrow corridor, to let in what light there was through the doorway.

But when another tenant entered the passageway I retreated into the doorway again – there was not room for two. However, he did not pass. He halted two doors up, unlocking the door and then thrusting a match into the short pipe clenched between his teeth. As the match flared I glimpsed his face clearly. And it was familiar. An instant later the match was flung onto the damp boards, the door opened and shut, and the fellow was gone. I leaned on the grimy doorpost, ransacking memory, instinctively knowing that this was important. Only recently I had seen that countenance, but where? Round apple cheeks, a nose like a cherry, a short spike of beard –

"Oh, great heavens," I whispered to myself. "Walter, you are a genius!" For dear Walter had sketched that exact face, in pencils touched up with coloured crayon. This was one of the men who had been at the funeral of Margaret Camlet in Salerno. For the first time I had in my grasp one of Daisy Darnell's accomplices. "Joan," I cried. "Is this place Gull Mews?"

"O'course. Because it's off of Gull Court."

She had written the address inside the pasteboard box! "And who is the man that lives two doors up from you?"

Distracted between grief and worry, Joan replied, "Fellow named Antun Jones. Bill did some papers for him."

And Bill had been jailed for theft – and forgery. A foreign insurgent in Britain illegally would of course need papers. And Antun Jones sounded like a false name anyway. "I believe we have acquaintance in common," I told my companions. "Excuse me."

"Marian?" Laura looked up from feeling the tiny girl's pulse. "How on earth?"

But I was edging as quickly as I dared back along the wobbly and fragile planks, to that door. It was no more stout or well-built than any of the others, but it was locked. I knocked twice, tried the rusty handle, and knocked again. The room within must be like Joan's, less than four feet wide. Where could he be? Just now when he had held the match to the pipe his hand had been steady. Could a sober man drink himself dead drunk in a mere minute?

Suddenly the door opened, just a crack. Peering in the gloom, I recognised the Father Christmas pink cheek. "Sir," I began. "I'm told you are Antun Jones. Is that correct?"

He stared blankly at me, his dark eye dull and unintelligent. "Sir," I persisted, "do you speak English?"

He replied in some foreign tongue. Behind me I heard Joan, who said, "Well o'course he uses English. Bill talked to him perfectly fine."

So he was being cunning? I pushed forward, leaning on the door. "Mr. Jones. I'm making inquiries about a lady you may know as Daisy Darnell. She is –"

Quick as a whip the door swung fully open. Awkward on my feet, I overbalanced, stumbling forward. And there was a cracking sound almost in my face that made my ears ring. A whiff of hot gunpowder smoke right over my head, and a scream. There was a gun in his hand, a tiny pocket pistol, and he was pointing it at me!

There was a click of the mechanism, once and then again. Of all the silly things – if even I knew that these little derringers held only one shot, then this fool surely must. Behind me Laura cried, "Joan! Joan! Marian, she's bleeding!"

The idiot was fumbling in his pocket for another charge. Furious, I snatched the useless gun right out of his hand. The steel barrel was hot, almost burning my hand through my glove, but I was too angry to regard the scorching kid leather. "You are criminally stupid," I cried. "She never did you a morsel's harm! To fire, at nothing but a civil question? And at a female! In my condition! What sort of a man do you call yourself? How dare you men bill yourselves as the nobler and better sex? Rather you're a cur, a worm of the lowest sort!"

All my frustration and rage of the past months boiled up in my veins, and I beat Jones without mercy around the head and shoulders with his own firearm. I'm sorry to report that he was a little smaller than I, though much heavier, and I cut him up somewhat. "And this toy! It's worthless –"

Without warning a door beyond opened. This little room – it was not a cell like the others, but the vestibule outside the door of a room in the tenement beyond. And my victim reeled back against a much bigger man who held a large business-like revolver. He held it rock-steady, aimed at my head.

I fell instantly silent with my mouth open. "Who are you?"

he demanded, in accented English.

He had a bristly black moustache, a big flat face and a cloth cap pulled low over his forehead. I did not recognise him. He was none of the four men that Walter had sketched. But I could not give up now, not when I was so close. How to explain my interest in Daisy Darnell? "My name is Marian Halcombe," I said. "But you may be more familiar with my title. I am the second Mrs. Camlet."

This had a far more powerful effect that I had intended. Anton Jones clutched his bleeding nose and poured out what sounded like very bad language indeed, full of spitting consonants and grating vowels. The big man's mouth dropped open under his moustache. His eyes bulged with horror, and he cocked the gun to kill me. Behind me Laura cried, "Marian!"

"Laura, shut the door and go fetch the police," I said evenly. Any woman sure of her own wits is a match for men unsure of their temper. If she shut the door and he shot me, my fallen body would block the portal. The size I am now, it would take time to push it aside, and there was hardly any room for manoeuvre in this little vestibule space. There would be time for Laura to escape.

But, alas! Laura is not swift of action. She is less nervous these days but still delicately constituted, and in moments of stress especially she tends to fall back into the helplessness of the past. Now she simply stood there, unmoving, as the big man barked a command in the strange language. He held the gun at my head while the smaller man cringed past me and stepped over Joan's motionless form to seize Laura by the arm. "Now," the big man said. "Walk. Follow."

Laura cried out at the strange touch, and I said, "I'll hold her. We will obey." I stepped over Joan's body to take her hand.

Quivering with terror, she quickly wound her arm around my waist, gripping us together. "But what of little Addie? And Joan? Marian, I fear she's dead!"

"Leave her," our captor said. "Follow!" The smaller man went ahead and we perforce followed him, the big man with his gun close behind us. I only got one glimpse of Joan's fallen body. Blood masked her face and soaked her hair, pooling under her head and trickling through the cracks in the boards.

In this procession we went not out, but further down the noisome and rickety corridor. We passed the open door of Joan's room, and on beyond. The way ended in a slightly more open place, a reeking midden surrounded on all sides by the black square eyes of tenement windows. A greasy rainbow sheen glazed the surface of the standing pools. Something large and dead, either a big dog or a small donkey, lay grotesquely swollen in one of them, greenish-white and trembling on the verge of explosion. Doorless privies stood against the walls, some of them tenanted. Laundry lines zig-zagged across, drooping with clothing that surely could not be very clean. But there was a path on around the corner, just slimy bricks set down in the oozy sewage, dangerous footing when our wide skirts did not allow of seeing our feet. We had to go in single file and I had Laura go first, though we continued to hold hands. If the big man fired he would hit me before her. When a rat scuttled right under my lifted foot I almost screamed.

Soon there was another grimy alleyway, dark but at least drier, and into this we turned. In no time I completely lost my bearings, as we turned left and right and then left again. But I kept my eye on my surroundings. The sultry August evening was closing in fast, but it would not be fully night for some time yet.

"Laura," I murmured. "If we pass near Gull Court, where Matson waits with the brougham, I shall turn and fight. I still have the little gun here in my pocket, though it has no ammunition. You run for the carriage and then fetch reinforcements."

"I will not leave you, Marian," she said, trembling. "We live or die together."

There were crowds of people about in this less noisome lane, but there was nobody I dared cry to for help to, no policeman or clergyman. Respectable women do not go out at night into these districts. Shadowed by groveling poverty and the oncoming night, every face looked villainous. These people were more likely to aid our captors than a pair of slumming ladies. Nor did any speak to us. We were far, far too well dressed, and the threatening faces of our captors did not invite comment. At last we came to our destination, yet another teeming brick tenement building, a-whisper with tenants and vermin. The interior stair was in passable repair for once, but I looked up at the flights going up and up into the smothering dimness and groaned in spirit. "How far is it?"

"Soon. Go."

I sighed. I had walked far further than usual this day, and I could feel the lacing of my shoes beginning to cut into my feet as they swelled. Laura said, "Lean on me, dear one. We'll go slowly."

We were both sweating from fear and the oppressive heat, and Laura's light blue dress had a great splotch of blood on it, from where she had knelt beside poor Joan. "Who are these people, Marian?" she whispered as we scaled the first flight. "What do they want with us?"

"That I don't know," I said, breathing hard. "But I think that we may have found some of Daisy Darnell's foreign anarchists."

The second flight. "Oh no." In spite of the swelter Laura shivered. "I would far, far rather read about them than meet them."

I did not dare to voice even to Laura my hope, that somehow I could turn the tables on this entire nest of villains, and pluck the murderer out from among them. Surely if the actual perpetrator were delivered to Inspector Radenton, he would believe. It was getting difficult to talk, even to breathe properly, between the pressure of the child within and the demands of my lungs for air. My voluminous grey and blue skirts and petticoats caught at my legs and weighed like lead, clogged six inches deep at the hem with dirt and damp. When I paused on the third landing to pant the evil little man ahead of us turned, from the advantage of one step up, and raised his hand.

"Shame!" Laura cried, before his slap could land. "She's doing the best she may!"

He turned on Laura instead. That I do not allow! The tiny gun was useless without bullets, but its metal lent weight to my hand. I pulled it from my pocket and before he could strike her rammed it as hard as I could into his soft little stomach. The breath left his body with a whoop, and he nearly plunged down the stairs between us onto his companion. The larger man upbraided him bitterly in their own language before urging us onwards.

At last we were at the very highest landing. Here at the top of the structure the heat was oven-like, and I had to gasp for air. The roof above us, innocent of ceiling, was decrepit wooden shingles, many of them missing. Only one door opened off the narrow landing, and when we passed through we were in an attic. The rafters and shingles sloped down to a gritty wooden floor on the right and the left. Down the middle was just enough space for me to stand upright; our taller captor had to stoop.

The low part of the space was filled with bundles and bags. We went down the middle to the end, where there was a window with no glass. Here it was very slightly cooler. Outside the roofs of endless miserable grey slums stretched away baking in the last light of the day, as far as the eye could see. Under the window was a low rickety table, and beside the table sat a man. Our main captor was big, but this man was bigger yet, a veritable giant. He must have stood nearly seven feet tall, and had to stay sitting for fear of knocking his head on the low roof. A mane of wavy brown hair fell to his shoulders, and in the big meaty face his eyes were deep set but light brown, almost tawny – a wolf's eyes. Walter's drawing had caught him almost exactly.

"Vjenceslav," I guessed. "I hope I pronounce that correctly. Is that your given name, or a surname?"

Before he could reply the other two broke in, babbling in their foreign tongue, overriding and interrupting each other, waving eloquent hands in the Continental style. My feet hurt, there was a stab of pain low in my back, and the long climb seemed to have dragged my burden down in my belly. Everything felt two inches lower than this morning. "Laura," I whispered, "I must sit down."

She spied a cane chair supporting a pile of garments in the low angle of the roof, and swept them off onto the floor before dragging it up. I sank into it with a groan of relief. "Shall I take off your shoes for you?"

"Oh, bless you. That would be heavenly. But just loosen the laces, if you would. We may need to walk or run, and going barefoot in Shoreditch would be unwise." It did not look right for my dearest sister to sit on the floor before me, but there was no hope of reaching my own filthy shoes myself. With swift fingers she untied the constricting cords and rubbed my poor swollen feet before knotting the laces together again more loosely.

I had no doubt that our captors could quarrel for hours, but I was thirsty and tired. And there was certainly not a hope of a chamber pot! It seemed imprudent to draw their attention to us once more, but I did not want to lurk here all night. Walter would dislike it excessively, and poor Matson was patiently waiting for us somewhere below.

When the combatants paused in trading invective I broke in. "Sir," I said loudly. "You seem to be in some difficulty."

"We!"

"Perhaps," I pressed on, "we could be of mutual benefit."

"You are a pair of mewling women," Vjenceslav said in contempt.

"That strikes me as a hasty and overly-emotional assessment," I said. "Antun, perhaps you disagree."

The little man's nose had stopped bleeding by now but he had wiped it on his coat sleeve, where the stains still showed. Also he sported a nasty cut over an eyebrow, and some fine bruises. I smiled at them while he poured out a torrent of complaint to his superior.

"Idiot," Vjenceslav snarled. "And you, you fat ugly cow. You cannot be Mrs. Camlet. She is nothing like you."

"Indeed, we are entirely opposite in every way." This, I realised, was why Theo had been attracted to me. "But, Mrs. Camlet having eloped to the continent, Mr. Camlet replaced her. With me. And, although we are not alike, we do share one trait: a will of steel."

"You are nothing like her," he said. "You are not a true warrior, a soldier of the revolution."

"I care nothing for your revolution. But do not doubt my will."

"What do you want?"

I watched them all with the closest attention as I slowly spoke. "On May 15th of this year Margaret Camlet was struck on the head and set afire in her house in Hampstead. I want the man who killed her." Vjenceslav's countenance was like iron, revealing nothing, but the other two? They were not poker-faced Englishmen. Under his cloth cap the big man's eyes slid to glance at his fellow. And the little elfin man's Adam's apple bobbed as he gulped. Of course! A man of impulsive violence, who would strike out almost at random with deadly force the moment he was startled. If they wanted a poor soldier, here was one. And here was Theo's freedom, almost in my hand. Triumph was so close I could almost smell it. I took a deep hungry breath. The stuffy hot air could have been perfumed with roses.

"What would you do for your vengeance?"

"Anything," I said, and wondered if I looked as wolfish as he.

"Would you –" He made a gesture which I had never seen before, and I knew Laura, behind me, had not either. But it was unmistakable. She gasped, but I was able to betray nothing.

Instead I set my teeth. "You cannot wish to ... consort with a woman in my condition."

His eyes, that flat light brown, glinted. "Women are full of ... possibilities. Prove it. Prove that your will is adamant. Come." He gestured, beckoning.

I realised my hands were gripping each other tightly, too plainly showing my fear. Deliberately I relaxed, letting them fall to my sides as I rose to my feet. Stepping lightly I approached him, closer and yet closer. Laura said something, a choked exclamation, and I heard the click of the big man's cocking pistol. "Laura, please do not move, and say nothing," I said.

"Kneel." He pointed at the bare floorboards between his scarred and worn boots, and awkwardly, balancing my ungainly weight, I knelt. When he looked down into my upturned face I could smell the garlic on his breath, very foreign and un-English. "You will falter," he said. "You will cringe. No? Even if..." I held perfectly still as his thick hard hand brushed my cheek. Suddenly he pushed a hairy finger into my mouth. With a supreme effort I held back a scream. "You know what I can demand?"

The rough fingers probed my lips. "Yes."

"And you will pay this price?"

To be vilely used, in front of these men and Laura too – and it would not stop there. If I let this encounter shift into outrage and assault, all three of them would be upon us. It would end in both our deaths. At all costs I had to hold onto the initiative. I held my voice steady. "For what I want? Yes." The wolflike eyes stared down into mine as he reached, lifting my hands and setting them upon the coarse woolen front of his trousers. When the large hairy hands relaxed I did not let mine fall. Without looking away, without ceasing to hold those fearful eyes, I unbuttoned the top trouser button.

A waft of garlic as he exhaled, moving back. There was a short raucous burst of argument. The small evil one was vehement in his disappointment. But Vjenceslav overrode them with a snarl. "Darnell was a Judith," he grumbled, deep in his chest. "I do not want to be Holofernes."

Suddenly I was kneeling alone beside the table. Weak with tension I sagged down to sit on my heels. My knees and hips protested at the posture. The table was not too rickety to help me to my feet. I had to act as if I had triumphed. Laura pushed the cane chair forward and I positioned it to sit across the table from him – an equal. Remembering what the manuscript had told of Daisy Darnell's desperate attempts to save Count Ludovic from the Croatian gallows, I remarked, "You do not want to be a Baron Neretva."

"She spoke to you of him?" He stared at me. "It took him four days to die from her bullet."

"They say that the teeth of a human being inflict the most dangerous of all carnivore bites," I remarked in my most genteel conversational tone. It was quite satisfactory to see all three men flinch. "Your men murdered Darnell, and yet failed to find what you seek. Tell me."

Vjenceslav fixed me with his tawny eye. "Do you know of the plans?"

I recalled Theo's needle-sharp analysis of Margaret's manuscript. An asset that they could not agree how to divide… "In the sketchbook," I ventured. "It had a red paper cover."

Surely that exclamation was a curse. "You she-devil. You do know."

"The drawings, in the back. They were plans. For what?"

"A ... device. You do not need to know its purpose."

"Oh, do not let us waste time, I beg," I said crossly. "A bomb, was it not? An explosive. Something to be flung. The way Bradamante murdered Stefan of Sarajevo."

He swore again, so viciously that I thought he would seize me and force himself upon me after all. "The plans, they are incomplete. That swine Ludovic, he began to burn them before our eyes. He laughed when we yelled for him to stop, the devil. And Darnell, bitch that she was, she let us have the sketchbook with what was left. But she had a prototype as well. The complete device. We must have it."

I stared at him, my thoughts racing. "And it was small, you say. Perhaps this big?"

"You know? God damn you to hell. You are cut from the same cloth. Where is it?"

Margaret had put all the pieces into my hands, and Theo had shown me the pattern behind them. Slowly I said, "I believe I do know."

The man in the cap twisted his moustache and made a suggestion that sounded extremely unpleasant even though I could not understand it. Antun seconded it, saying in his heavy accent, "We make her speak. Not this one, but that." He pointed at Laura, who had perched herself on a bale at my back, and I felt her hand, icy cold in spite of the heat, creep into mine.

"How many more follies can you afford to commit, sir?" I leaned back, holding my free hand around the roundness of my abdomen. Within, the baby seemed to be attempting a quadrille. I pressed back, hoping to quiet it. "Your device is valuable, yet you stupidly slew your associate Wragsland, who made it. You betrayed Bradamante to the authorities, thus making the most dangerous woman in Europe your mortal enemy and successfully setting the capstone upon your strategy of eliminating all accomplices of greater intellectual attainment than yourself. You secured the plans, yet failed to find the prototype. Now, your only hope being to find the actual device, you allow your monkey to mouth empty threats." I smiled across the table at Vjenceslav. "I have told you what I demand for it. My price is a man. The man who killed Margaret Camlet."

I jumped as he pulled a long knife, almost a sword, out of the top of his boot. "Do you want his head?"

"No," I said casually, as if men offered to decapitate each other before me every day. "I want him to go down to Scotland Yard. To go in, and to tell everyone there, all who will listen, over and over until they hear and believe him. The truth: that he broke into Sandett House. That he surprised Margaret Camlet and struck her down, and fled."

"Impossible. We are sworn, a blood oath, to keep the revolution utterly secret until its glorious dawn. That you know of it – you should die, both of you."

"Recall," I said, "that I do not care in the least about your politics. I know nothing of your revolution and do not propose to learn. Nor does Scotland Yard. He need not have killed for political purposes. Let him be a common or garden housebreaker."

He thought this over. "For what would he be breaking in?"

"He saw her with a ring, a valuable ornament, and wished to steal it. It was a gold ring set with three sapphires."

"Ah. I remember it, on her finger." He frowned at me. "You, the two wives. You knew each other."

"You might say that." To mention the thousand pages of memoir in Margaret Camlet's desk drawer would be imprudent.

"Two of you, in the same house!" He shook his head in what I realised was wonder. "Your shared husband must be a titan. Very well then. A bargain."

He held out an enormous hand, like a young ham. I clasped the thick fingers firmly, knowing that he could snap mine like twigs if he liked. But I was released without injury.

"Antun." He nodded at the little man. "You hear her. Go."

A babble of argument, as they debated and discussed it, but I watched the faces carefully. It did not seem that Antun was hoping to die for the cause. But in the end he seemed to agree. He pulled on his hat and slunk out. "You know that murder is a capital crime in Britain," I said. "Will he confess and face the gallows?"

He shrugged. "It is for the revolution. We are all martyrs to the cause. And," he added, "if you are treacherous, he can easily recant. We will tell your policemen he was drunk, or deluded."

"I do not renege on a bargain. And if you renege on your part, I will immediately reveal your entire conspiracy to Roderick Donthorne at the Foreign Office. So all is safe between us." I stood up and took Laura's hand. "I assume you are willing to return with me to Sandett House."

"Immediately. We have horses." When he rose to his feet his head did indeed scrape the rafters, and he had to stoop like an ape. The other man scooped up riding coats, and Vjenceslav reached for a hat.

"My carriage is in Gull Court."

Even night-shrouded, the teeming slums were unlovely, but our hosts knew the most direct route and we only walked for ten minutes. Out in Gull Court Matson was waiting by the horses. "Madam," he cried, almost weeping with relief. "Great God above! If only a bobby had passed, I would have sent him in search of you."

"You've done well, Matson," I said. As if by magic the slum children appeared, and I dispensed the promised coins. "I do not at all wish to see a bobby. If you will hand me up into the carriage?"

With his help we climbed up, dragging our filthy and sweat-stained skirts, and collapsed onto the leather seat. Laura hugged me and our tears of stress and fright mingled. "Marian, Marian," Laura wept. "I was so frightened for you."

"I was terrified."

"And you terrified me! How did you dare?"

"You did very well, being quiet," I said, gasping. "If you had tried to interfere I don't know what would have happened. But oh! It is such a comfort to have you near."

"And would you have let yourself be put to shame? Marian, what would Theo say?"

"What choice did I have, to save him?"

It was quite dark now, but there was a single gaslight, and in its feeble glow I could see Laura's wide eyes. She had never looked at me that way before. "You've changed, Marian."

"Well, marriage does alter one, there is no denying." I wiped my nose. "All's well that ends well. Perhaps there's no need to lacerate the gentlemen's feelings with the details. Is there any more cold tea? My throat is like a desert."

Matson tapped at the window and I lowered it. "Riders, madam," he said. "Two of them."

"Very good. They're escorting us home, Matson. Let us be off."

Matson climbed onto the box and the brougham jolted into motion. When I peered out the windows I saw Vjenceslav on one side and his moustached associate on the other, riding their job horses with the ease of men born to the saddle. Escorts, or guards?

I decided I did not care. The child within was wildly active, knocking painfully against its fleshly casing. I wished there was a way to tell it to go to sleep. "You're uncomfortable," Laura said.

"It is ever so, late in the term."

"You should be at home in bed, not gallivanting around in the middle of the night with banditti."

"Well, we're hurrying home as fast as we may, and once we are there I'll be happy to go to bed." After the gasping heat and mephitic stenches of Shoreditch it was glorious to be in motion. We lowered the windows and breathed gratefully of the cooler air.

"Marian." Laura took my hand again. "You know I will love you, always." We had come to a more prosperous street now, where the streetlamps were more frequent, and in the intermittent light I could see the worry on her face. "But have you become utterly devious?"

"I?" Astonished, I cast my mind back. "There may be serious questions about my use of female wiles, to be sure. And I do confess to being artfully incomplete in my accounts of certain subjects. But on the whole I think I was quite truthful. Not one actual lie passed my lips."

"You were not telling an elaborate fiction? You are saying there truly is a dangerous explosive in Theo's house?"

"I think there must be, Laura."

"You are not sure!"

"How can I be, until I go and look? But I think I know where Daisy Darnell must have hidden it. I wonder, if only she had had another dozen sheets of foolscap, whether she would have confided its location to her memoir." And what she would have said about me!

"We must evacuate the building! The baby and Walter are sleeping there this very moment!"

"If it's there, Margaret hid it when she arrived," I said soothingly. "It cannot be primed, or lit, or whatever it is one does to a mechanical explosive device to set it going. It's been in the house since winter, doing no harm to anybody."

"I cannot rest with it in the house!"

"We'll give it to Vjenceslav, who will be very glad to take it away."

"And – if you're wrong? If it is not where you think it is?"

"Then I expect that our bargain will collapse to the ground on the instant. They may or may not murder us all this very night, but Theo assuredly will go to trial." I fidgeted, unable to get comfortable. I could feel my fingers getting puffy, and my abdomen visibly bumped with the movement of the unborn child. What on earth was it doing in there, a dance? I had to acknowledge the reality. "I'm done, Laura. This is the end of striving, for me. I can do no more. Thank you, for letting me make this final attempt."

"Put your feet up, here." She shifted her place so I could do this. "And lean your head on my shoulder. And promise me, Marian. Never, ever do anything this frightening again."

"If the people I love will only refrain from deathly peril, I would be happy to." Now that it was cooler it was no hardship to be supported by her. I did not exactly fall asleep, but I dozed comfortably until we came to a halt.

It was very late when we arrived at Sandett House, past eleven o'clock, but all the lamps were still lit. In the portico Walter paced back and forth in a fever of worry, and Luna the greyhound lay patiently on the mat. I sat up and Laura leaped out of the carriage into his arms.

He gripped her like a drowning man clasping a spar. "Marian, I know you're responsible for this," he said, between his teeth. "Laura, are you hurt? This is blood on your garments! And who the devil are these?"

Matson hastened to help me descend. "Yes, I am to blame," I agreed. "Please do not be alarmed, Walter. These gentlemen's visit will be short. This is Vjenceslav the Balkan anarchist, and his associate, whose name I cannot tell you since he has a healthy fear of being known to me. Come through to the drawing room, sirs. And wipe your feet! Were you born in a barn?"

I unpinned my hat and handed my gloves, horribly soiled with gunpowder, to Ellen. "Mrs. Hartright and I are perishing of thirst. No, you need bring no refreshments for our guests, they will not be staying any length of time. But run baths for both Mrs. Hartright and myself."

There is a water closet in the back hallway and I let no one distract me from my beeline towards it. Then, much relieved, I went to the drawing room, detouring only to fetch a spoon from the sideboard and kick off my shoes.

In the big drawing room the air crackled with tension. Luna the greyhound cowered behind the sofa. Walter stood by the fireplace, bristling like a watchdog whose yard has been invaded, and not at all soothed by Laura's arm around his waist. Our visitors, still in their coats and hats, glared back at him.

The moustached man with the cap had not drawn his revolver, but simply leaned on the piano and rested a hand menacingly upon it in his belt. Vjenceslav had taken the knife out of his boot and was whetting it on the vast calloused expanse of his palm without turning his molten gaze away from Walter. "Is this your husband?" he demanded.

"Mr. Camlet is in prison," I said with dignity. "Mr. Hartright here is my brother-in-law." It's becoming second nature, to gracefully evade the truth. If the habit becomes permanent what a sad stain it will be on my character!

The man in the cap suddenly jerked his pistol out. "Look!" He gestured at the fireplace. On the mantelpiece against the big mirror Laura had propped the four sketches that Walter had made when Pesca brought Father Ercole to dinner. "Christ above. It's Ludovic!"

Vjenceslav's tawny eyes flared when he caught sight of his own countenance executed in pencil and crayon. He rounded upon me like a tiger. "How did you get these images of us? Are you some damned witch?"

"May we dedicate our attention to what you came for?" Ignoring these histrionics I moved over to the Wardian case, which stood in the bay window on its marble-topped table. "Laura, Walter – you remember reading my account of meeting Margaret Camlet in this very room. She had arrived in London only hours before. She came to this house, and shed her winter wrappings. And then, what? Instead of going upstairs, having supper, sitting down even? She began to dig the ferns out of this little greenhouse."

"And she knew nothing of ferns and plants," Walter exclaimed. "Camlet said so. Even she herself. She told me she would not know an apple tree from an orange, unless the fruit was on the bough."

I raised the hinged glass lid of the case and with the spoon began to pry out ferns. They were large and healthy, well-rooted. "And of all the growing things in this house, only these thrive. Only these did she water. Why? Surely, so that no one would dig in the earth here." With some effort I tugged the unlucky plants apart and laid them out on the marble tabletop as she had done. Seeing what I was about, Vjenceslav swore like sulphur and brimstone. Eagerly the moustached man in the cap came forward, raising the butt of his pistol to smash the case.

I waved him off. "A Wardian case is expensive," I rebuked him. "Theo would not wish it to be broken."

"And how urgent she was, that you should not be in this room," Walter recalled. "She bustled you out in haste. Camlet she knew she had power over, but she knew nothing of you. Her secret must have been lying on the table there in plain sight."

"Ah, here we are." My spoon clinked on something solid. I pried it out, shaking off the mould. It was long and cornery and yet rounded, like a fat squarish sausage, and closely wrapped in oilcloth. I had to hoist it in both hands because it weighed extraordinarily heavy, dense steel all the way through. When I lifted the edge of the oilcloth the surface within was dark not with corrosion but with a brown metal finish, and my fingers could feel complexity – bits to turn, or pull, or push. I was very, very careful to do none of these things.

I only held it for a moment. Vjenceslav was there, his huge hand held out. I looked up into his fierce face and set the device carefully into his palm. He too took both hands to it, but not because of the weight. He blew out a deep breath. "I should beat you to death with this," he rumbled.

"If it is at all fragile that would be very foolish," I said. "Unless you know how to repair it."

"Our cause still has artificers." He smiled without humor down at me and tucked the loose flap of oilcloth down. "Someday you will read, in your newspaper, of its use. And you will remember when you held death in your hands."

"I will not fail to look for the account," I replied calmly. "And now, good night. I encourage you to visit Mr. Antun in Newgate. The rigors of incarceration can be severe."

Without another word he turned, gesturing for his

companion to follow. He paused for one more moment, shooting me another ferocious glare, and then snatched his own portrait off the mantelpiece, crumpling the sheet and stuffing it into his coat pocket. Then they were gone.

Walter thrust the air pistol back into its usual place behind one of the cloisonné vases – I had not noticed he was holding it ready at his side. "Oh, thank heaven," Laura sighed. "If I had known that device was here, Marian, I would have never been able to rest easy. But now it's loose in London, in the hands of desperate men."

"I think you need not worry, Laura," I said, taking up my spoon again.

"You surely do not propose to replant the case tonight, Marian," Walter said. "Are you aware that both of you reek to high heaven? Laura, your shoes are clotted with muck. You must bathe immediately, or contagion will be carried into the house."

"Do you go wash first, Laura," I said, digging. "And every stitch we have on, both of us, must be laundered and boiled. Theo would dislike it if I left his ferns neglected as Margaret did. And …" On the bowl of the spoon I balanced another piece of metal about the length and thickness of my finger. "What do you think, Walter? Could this be an essential part of the mechanism of an explosive?"

Delicately, with finger and thumb, he picked the piece up out of the spoon and brushed off the earth. "It's certainly the same colour. And cunningly made. See here, where the gear-teeth are precisely machined – more like something from the innards of a watch."

"We must remember that Margaret Camlet resided here for some months before her death," I said. "One does not become the most dangerous woman in Europe without being highly intelligent. She would not have slept at ease above a bomb ready to explode. I think she took it apart, disarming it, before concealing it here. So that it could not accidentally go off."

"And so your ugly friends have galloped off with only three-quarters of a bomb?" For the first time this evening Walter laughed out loud.

"Now how can I know that, Walter? A mere female cannot judge these things. Besides, I find I do not entirely trust anarchists. Let us put this piece in a fresh hiding place so that if there is need for some additional persuasion, it may be found." I took the finger of metal and glanced around the room.

My eye fell upon the Chinese cloisonné vases that stood one on each side of the mantelpiece above the cold fireplace. These were not open-mouthed like flower vases but had long slender necks like bottles, and were enameled with a rainbow menagerie of serpents, birds, and fish romping upon a dark red ground. With some difficulty, because my feet hurt even without the shoes, I went over and reached up on tiptoe to drop the metal bit into the narrow mouth of the one that was not supporting the air pistol. It clattered down the long slender neck and fell with a solid clink into the oval belly.

"Marian," Laura said with firmness. "You must give over and go to bed. If I'm exhausted, you must be on the verge of doing the one to come a serious injury. I shall help you up the stairs to bathe, this instant. Give Walter the spoon, and he will replant Theo's ferns."

"And Laura will give me a complete account of your adventures," Walter said. His tone was such that I took Laura's hand as we walked out. Her slender fingers gripped mine with a speaking pressure. Thank goodness, we need no words to understand each other.

Later

I must just catch up, for I foresee that writing in this journal will become impossible very soon. It was so delicious to take a bath last night that I cannot express it. When I contemplated my frame in the hot water it was scarcely recognizable. My feet were swollen, my fingers podgy, all of me distorted and strange. I am about ready to move from carrying, on to the bigger adventure of motherhood.

This morning I slept luxuriously late in Theo's four-poster, allowing Ellen to bring me breakfast and then dozing off again for some hours. If one does not go downstairs, then confining clothing is unnecessary. With my feet up I lounged in my linen wrap on the chaise in the second bedroom, writing. This journal of course, but my first task was an urgent letter for Walter to carry to Mr. Smithee in town.

"I'm certain you grasp what needs next to be done," I said to him, tucking the folds under. "Mr. Smithee must see this today. Under no circumstance mention to anyone the conspiracy, or the bomb, or our visitors. The rumor is that a burglar has confessed to the Camlet murder, and our wish is that now the real culprit is in custody, Theo be released."

Walter leaned to look into the mirror as he tied his cravat. "Are you removing to this chamber, then?"

"When Theo is released he will want his own bed, and not to be disturbed by the fussing of a newborn." Through the open connecting doorway I could see Ellen making up the four-poster with fresh sheets. She had already moved my dressing case and clothes.

"You're certain that this Antun will be convicted."

"No," I had to admit. "But I do believe his confession casts sufficient doubt that Theo will be released. It shall be the task of Mr. Smithee to use these developments to that end."

"He never actually admitted to killing Mrs. Camlet."

"Not to us," I said. "But it can be proven that he killed Joan Porter. Both Laura and I saw him shoot her. And I have the weapon." I nodded at the writing table between the windows, where the derringer lay on the blotter. "If necessary we can give it and our testimony to the police."

"Great heavens, Marian! You brought it away with you?"

"In my skirt pocket," I said. "If Antun Jones does not hang for murdering Margaret Camlet, he shall swing for shooting Joan Porter. They can only hang him once, and once will satisfy me."

Carefully Walter examined the little firearm, which seemed none the worse for the abuse I had subjected it to. "You do not know how to use this."

"I could learn. But not any time soon. Surely gunpowder fumes are bad for babies."

"I have no doubt of it!"

Laura came in, tying on her bonnet. "It might be useful to bring Davey, Walter," she said. "I know that Matson was greatly worried yesterday, and having assistance will give him peace of mind."

"What, to drive to Lincoln's Inn?"

"No, to Gull Court," she said. "We must go back. Addie

Porter is an orphan now, and we left her in that horrible little room with her mother lying dead in the hall."

"Oh, brave Laura!" I applauded her. "Be sure that you have plenty of small coins, and secure your purse and your handkerchiefs. Walter, do you put your money into your shirt pocket and button your waistcoat tightly. And bring a stout walking stick."

Walter's mouth dropped open. "Laura, what do you propose to do with an ailing slum orphan? You cannot bring her back here. Sandett House is full to the brim, and Camlet will not thank you for bringing disease in among his little ones."

"Then we will take her to the hospital where she may be nursed until she is better," Laura said. "Walter, you cannot conceive of the horror of that place. I cannot leave this child there."

Walter frowned – at me, if you please! "Will you take responsibility for the little creature?"

"Theo shall decide," I said, as a good wife should. I have no idea why Walter raised his hands as if imploring Heaven for mercy as he left the room.

Laura bent to pat the shawl draped over my feet, and obediently Luna hopped up and turned several times to make herself a nest there, her mistress's representative. "Be sure to eat and drink, small amounts often," she said. "Ellen will bring you trays, and be within earshot until I return. And Mrs. Pinney will call in the afternoon. I hope to be back in time to see her. I'm anxious to learn her opinion of your delivery date. If I had to guess, I would say it will be within the fortnight, possibly this week."

"No, I refuse to permit it," I said. "It must be a biddable child and wait until Theo is freed and we are properly married, to be born in wedlock."

Laura laughed at this. "If anyone doubted that this is your first, they would believe it now."

"Oh, and Laura. This is important, if you're going with Walter to Lincolns Inn. If Mr. Smithee is not in, under no circumstance see Mr. Plockton. Insist on Mr. Smithee, or at need Mr. Erbistock, but Mr. Plockton never."

She stared down at me, her blue eyes wide. "Will you tell me why?"

"You have no time now. See Walter in the hall, waiting for you. Be off on your errand, and I shall tell you later." She kissed me in parting, and when they were gone I finished writing this account. Ellen brought in the promised tray: a ripe peach cut up with sugar, some buttered toast, and a glass of milk. I spooned up the peach and then poured the milk into the emptied bowl. When I set it down on the cold hearth Luna happily lapped it up. "Good dog," I told her.

But as I stood there, I felt it – a trickle and a gush. Stunned, I stared down. A warm pool of fluid, forming at my feet? Hastily I blotted it up with the hearthrug, and lay back down again. Mrs. Pinney had warned me of the signs of oncoming labour. My waters have broken! Perhaps putting my feet well up shall delay the delivery? "You cannot be born today, baby," I pleaded, stroking my enormous belly. "Not now, so close! Your papa must be released, so that we might be married. Just another day or two, I beg, there's a good child. You want to be born in wedlock, don't you?" I received a kick in reply. I hope that is an assent.

BOOK 6

≈ Walter Hartright's narrative ≈

As we drove to Lincolns Inn, I brooded upon the two Mrs. Camlets. Marian might claim to be entirely the opposite of Margaret Camlet. Perhaps superficially, in height or colouring or beauty, this was true. But they were sisters under the skin, twins of the same birth. I could easily believe that Marian Camlet had succeeded to the title of the most dangerous woman in Europe. She is, beyond all question, the most redoubtable female in Britain.

Laura, perceiving my low spirits, took my hand. "The end's in sight, Walter. Do you remember? How fearful and exciting it was, just before little Wally was born? I hope that Theo will be back in time to support Marian. A woman needs her husband with her at such a time."

I had to smile at the happier memories. Whatever else one could say about him, Camlet was happy with Marian and so his choice must be, in some sense, right.

Arriving at the lawyers' offices we learned that Mr. Smithee was not in. "He's gone down to the Yard, to confer with Inspector Radenton," the clerk said. "Perhaps you would care to see Mr. Plockton?"

"No," Laura said, before I could get a word out. "We do not stay, thank you." And before I could object we were out the door again. "Marian told me," she explained. "We must only deal with

Mr. Smithee, or perhaps Mr. Erbistock."

"And avoid Mr. Plockton? I wonder why?" For an instant a host of lurid possibilities surged into my mind, but I took firm hold of my imagination.

We made our way to Scotland Yard and were fortunate enough to run into Mr. Smithee just making his farewells to Inspector Radenton in the courtyard. I presented Laura to both men, and she shyly shook hands with the Inspector as I buttonholed Mr. Smithee. "There have been important developments," I said.

"So I heard. A confession from a housebreaker! I'm sure I need not say to you, Mr. Hartright, that this is a most promising turn of events."

I passed him Marian's letter, which was not sealed. "You will read in this that Miss Halcombe is most urgent about exploiting it to the full. Camlet's release cannot come too soon."

"This time I believe I am indeed correct in predicting it by week's end. I shall put all my powers to it." He unfolded Marian's letter and with it, unexpectedly, my own pencil sketch of Antun Jones.

The inspector's sharp grey eye was instantly caught. "What is this? How did you come by this image, Mr. Hartright?"

"I drew it," I admitted reluctantly. Since he had just watched me put the missive into Smithee's hand I could hardly deny ownership. "I used a B pencil and Conte crayon –"

"And were you working from the model? Had the fellow in front of you?"

"Of course not. I have never seen this man in my life." I could see Laura's blue eyes widening in alarm as I skated near to the edge.

"Mr. Hartright. Would you swear to that? On your oath, mind!"

"Certainly," I said uneasily. "Since it's true."

"Great God. Then you do not know? This is the confessed murderer of Margaret Camlet, to the life! How did you draw his portrait without seeing him?"

Reeling, I realised that I could not tell the inspector of Father Ercole's eloquent description, or the menacing mourners at the dubious Italian funeral. As Marian had warned, all we had uncovered of the Blue Hand conspirators, the bomb – the entire reason for Margaret Camlet's murder – had to remain secret, so that Antun Jones could stand a swift trial as no more than an incompetent housebreaker in search of a sapphire ring.

Hastily I ransacked memory for some hook upon which to hang an even distantly plausible tale. "You remember the worries of the ladies of our neighbourhood, about burglars," I said. "Miss Halcombe and my dear wife here, being from the north country, wanted to know what a London burglar might look like. And so I sketched this. It was an impulse merely, a whim. I put no thought into it."

"This is amazing," the inspector said. His grey moustache seemed to quiver with excitement. "You have a gift – a gift of sketching culprits you have not seen. I've heard of such mesmeric talents in America, but never yet in Britain. Have you read of the latest dastardly gang? Footpads in Cheapside waylaying pedestrians, using handkerchiefs dipped in chloroform to render them helpless. The men are robbed and the women assaulted. Supposing I were to lay all the files before you. Do you think you could sketch me a face?"

"No, I do not. I could not do any such thing!"

Radenton didn't seem to hear me. "Or here's a better one. Covent Garden is oppressed by a cutpurse. Not one of your usual deft johnnies with a razor, but a cruder villain. He uses something like an adze or a cleaver, maiming as well as stealing. If you could indicate even some details, his height, his hair colour –"

"Let me remind you of your own wise words, sir, which I have taken to heart now and always. That amateur participation in police work is particularly to be deplored!"

"You've converted me, Mr. Hartright," Radenton declared. "Like St. Paul on the road to Damascus, I see the light. Do you not see how useful it would be, for the police force to know who to look for?"

Trapped, I gazed imploringly at my dear wife, who gently interposed, "Perhaps you could call at Sandett House, Inspector, and discuss this at leisure. We will be resident there for some weeks yet for my sister's confinement. We are on an errand of mercy that cannot wait, to visit a sick child."

"In Shoreditch," I said, seizing upon the change of subject. "I do not suppose you know the district, Inspector?"

"You propose to take Mrs. Hartright to Shoreditch? Are you barking mad? Sir, you endanger the lady. It's the foulest slum in London!"

"I know it," Laura said. "And no place for a child."

I spoke from the heart. "Believe me, inspector, I would deter her if I could."

The upshot of this, when the inspector learned of Laura's unwavering intention, was that he sent two of his men to accompany us. I naturally welcomed this addition to our party, and in due course we arrived at Gull Court. I and a policeman followed Laura as she threaded the horrific rat-infested maze to the decrepit and stinking home of Addie Porter. It was impossible to believe that human beings could live like this. "How can Britain bear this?" I demanded. "How can the nation allow this to stand?"

"We ladies can do nothing, Walter," my wife replied. "But if you stand for Parliament, perhaps you could help."

As a newcomer to the district, and not born to the gentry, I had been reluctant to step forward on this. But now it seemed not only possible, but my duty. Providence cannot have placed me in charge of Limmeridge House, and all that goes with that role, for nothing. I had never thought to say the words that now passed my lips: "If you wish it, I shall."

"And it will be written after your name in the book of life, that you worked to aid the poor," she said.

We neither of us had mentioned Joan Porter to the police. But appallingly her body still lay where it had fallen yesterday evening on the rotten boards. The wide pool of her blood had dried, where it had not dripped through the wide slimy cracks of the floor, and even though in the heat decomposition was advancing, the odor could not be distinguished in the greater reek.

Our accompanying policemen immediately took charge, calling for reinforcements and the mortuary wagon. Beyond, further down the hall, the door to her room was still ajar, but no one had cared to step past the dead woman. Presumably the little child still lay within. But the way was so narrow and precarious that until the authorities finished the removal there was no possibility of passing to get inside. From Laura's account there was a way through the maze of alleys from the other side, but she could not identify the portal they had emerged from last night, or retrace their journey.

Laura wrung her hands at the delay, tears standing in her eyes, but there was nothing to be done but to retreat to the brougham until the wagon arrived and policemen finished their grim work. They passed the time canvassing the buildings to either side for witnesses, but if there were any I could not be surprised that they declined to step forward.

"Walter, this is horrible." Laura's sensitive lips trembled. "That poor child!"

"This is too much for you, my dear," I said. "Your nervous constitution cannot stand it. Let us leave the situation to those who have the authority to deal with it, and go home. Marian will be looking for you."

But I have noted before, how the courage of women may falter at the small things, but rise to the great. "No, Walter," she replied. "It would surprise you, what my constitution can bear. Look, here are my acquaintances of yesterday, the street lads. Matson, would you help me open the boot?"

I had not realised that our vehicle had been loaded before our departure with half the contents of Sandett House's larder. Laura distributed bread and meat cut into sandwiches, apples and oranges, and jars of jam which the urchins simply opened and dipped out with grimy fingers. A bale strapped on the top of the carriage was revealed to be every article of clothing Micah and Lottie had outgrown. She must have stripped the nursery.

All of this largesse vanished in less than three minutes, devoured, donned, or simply spirited away. When everything was gone I suggested, "Perhaps we should go and find a respectable chophouse or coffee room. You too need refreshment, and it's coming on to rain. We can always come back after luncheon and see how they're getting on."

"Wait, Walter – see, could that be the police wagon?"

A grim and authoritative four-wheeler, long, high and enclosed, rumbled over the cobbles into the tiny courtyard, pulled by two dray-horses. Gull Court was now entirely clogged. There was another lengthy delay while policemen went back and forth. At last, as the afternoon was waning and the rain began, two men came to the wagon with a stretcher. Their sad burden was covered with a sheet.

"Come, Walter," my wife cried. "Now's our chance!"

"My dear, surely the authorities are well able to manage?"

But without replying Laura took my hand, leading me once again through the noisome alleyways past ramshackle tenements to Gull Mews. The police were still interviewing every resident of the dreadful makeshift structure. Treading primly, Laura edged sideways along the precarious floor. It was starting to rain, and the sieve-like roof above gave no shelter at all. Somewhere up above a large policeman was knocking on a door, and the entire crazy building juddered and bounced under his massive tread.

I set my feet with the utmost care lest with my greater weight I break right through. The red stains were still plain to see outside the low door on the right. Two doors down Laura pushed the portal open. "Addie?"

I peered over her shoulder. Never, as God is my witness, have I seen a more degrading domicile. Suddenly I was angry, hotly furious that such things could be in this year, in this country, universally acknowledged as the greatest realm on earth. Laura tiptoed in and fell to her knees beside the pile of rags that did duty for a bed. In the dimness the child looked like a wild beast, kenneled and forgotten. In the corners of the rooms I saw the red eyes and naked tails of the rats.

"Oh, she does not stir! Please, Walter, help me take her out into the light!"

"Stand away then, Laura. There's not room for two."

"Here, here is my shawl. Wrap her up well. I am afraid she's poorly clothed."

We edged past each other in the cramped space. I had to bend almost double so that my head would not knock on the beams above. Laura had said the girl was three. My own little Fairlie was half that age and twice her size. Her head, with a frizz of rusty hair, was the largest part of her; the little limbs were bone-thin. Laura's paisley shawl enveloped her completely, and lifting her was like lifting a cat.

I carried the tiny creature out, edging sideways down the wobbly corridor and out into the pouring rain. A police doctor was there, and on the gleaming-wet tailgate of the police wagon, behind the sheeted body of her mother, I laid Addie down. The doctor made a cursory examination. "Probably died this forenoon," he said. "No rigor yet, do you see?"

"Oh, Walter, we were almost in time! If only we had come here first thing."

"There was nothing we could have done, my dear."

"No indeed," the doctor said. "Heed your husband, madam. These slum children have the stamina of mayflies. Would you like your shawl back?"

"No, no," Laura said, the tears falling fast. "Let it be the poor child's shroud." I said nothing, even though I was certain that the shawl would be filched before the day was out. We had but little information to give the doctor, only the child's name. When this was done I helped Laura up into the carriage.

As the horse turned splashing towards home she said, "Oh, Walter. What is the good of it all? I can help poor people up in Cumberland, but they're not like this. There are so many, so miserable, and what can be done for them all? I understand now, what Margaret Camlet was so angry about. She must have seen this. And she knew it should not be this way. The world must change."

Yes, this was the fury that I had felt, the rage that would, unchecked, drive one to fling bombs or assassinate dukes. "Laura, if you leave me to fight for social justice beside some foreign anarchist I shall be quite cross." I tucked her fair head onto my shoulder. "I shall do it, my dear. I'll stand for Parliament when old Sir Cedric's term is up, and I shall argue for better conditions for the poorest among us. It may take time, to turn the ship. But change shall come." As I had changed and grown, but it was not a long step. The new space before me led directly out of my old smaller one.

"I know you can do anything you set your mind to, Walter. You are a great man."

We were home in time for the evening meal, and after washing thoroughly and changing all my clothes I went into the nursery. Little Fairlie toddled over to greet me, yelling to be picked up. He was nearly fifteen months old now, a bouncing and vigorous tot with a halo of his mother's fair hair that refused to lie over. I hoisted him into the air above my head and he squealed,

"Higher, papa! Higher!" My palms actually tingled with pleasure at the sensation of his wriggling and solid torso between them. This is the way children should be, joyful and full of life.

Camlet's hearing was on the docket Friday morning. I arrived at dawn as they unlocked the doors, so early that I sat for some little while alone on the wooden benches. Mr. Todwarden came in down in the well, and beckoned for me to come down. When he leaned his head close to mine his white woolen wig smelled damply of sweat and cologne. "We're in the soup, Hartright."

I tensed. "How can that be?"

"That housebreaker, that Jones foreigner. Made a break for it."

I gasped. "What do you say?"

"Just this minute. Pried loose one of the iron bars in his cell and wormed through the gap – he's not a big fellow, they tell me. Tied his sheets together to lower himself down, and scarpered."

"But they have his confession, do they not? Signed and sealed. That should suffice, to get Camlet out of the dock."

"This development can't help his case. The hearing shall probably be postponed, so that they can hold onto Camlet at least until it's plain that the other rascal's got away clean."

I set my teeth. Foreigners! They were treacherous, no more to be trusted than snakes. How would this new disappointment affect Marian's health? What of the baby? This morning Marian had bulked enormously, bringing images of whales and mountains to the mind's eye. Birth was surely imminent.

And what were the jailers about, not keeping their captive in leg irons? The unlucky Camlet, innocent as a new-shorn lamb, had been kept as closely as the crown jewels, and yet this criminal had slipped between their fingers. My temper was not improved by the bailiffs opening the windows, which let in a fearful stench from the river. I jumped to my feet and stormed out of the courtroom before the judge could rap his gavel to open the first case.

Out in the street the jailors and bailiffs were running this way and that, calling to each other as they searched. Though it was still early the ancient narrow ways were already oppressive.

The sun, blazing down from a cloudless sky, would make the entire district an oven in an hour. Surely there was nothing I could do that these officials could not do better. I had never even seen the man, only sketched his portrait from Father Ercole's vivid description.

But then I recalled our visitors, the two riders escorting Marian and Laura back from the slums of Shoreditch. There had been the nameless man with a cloth cap, his face large and flat, the revolver in his hand. And also Vjenceslav with that freakish height, his long hair and tawny hot eyes. He would be armed with the enormous knife. Radenton had spoken the truth of it: with a face, a description, you were in with a chance! They must be here, probably very close by, helping their compatriot to escape.

I too began to run, rapidly canvassing the nearby streets. A man nearly seven feet tall could not be easily hid. He could hardly be walking on his knees. Around a corner. Down a trash-strewn alley with a sewer running down the centre, that debouched into a narrow and crooked lane. The buildings dated back more than a hundred years, and had been built wider with every story, so that they seemed to lean in above my head. The grim grey walls of the prison could be glimpsed at the end; we were all canvassing an area of no great size.

I turned down the stifling-hot lane, past the open doors of a shop or two, and then – good God! When I looked down a side lane I saw a tremendously tall silhouette!

To run swiftly yet in complete silence is not really possible, and in the narrow cobbled way there was no cover. As I fell in behind them I slowed down to a fast walk and trod as softly as I could, pulling my tall hat well down over my eyes as I got slowly nearer.

Yes, there were two figures. They looked to be women, dressed like many poor females in coarse linsey-woolsey frocks, shawls and cheap bonnets. But how awkwardly they walked. Perhaps as if they had a full suit of men's clothing under the long gowns. One of them stumbled a little, tripping over a hem. Girls are taught early to walk like females, managing the long skirts and petticoats without catching the bulky layers of fabric in their steps. If I got closer, would I see a man's boots underneath the limp ragged hem?

And both figures were tall. Where was the diminutive Antun Jones? Then I glimpsed, between them, the decrepit hand wagon they were pushing. It was like a large flat wheelbarrow, unpainted and almost falling apart, the sort of wagon that street sellers use when a decent barrow was beyond their means. Its two wooden wheels groaned and wobbled under a heavy burden – of what? It appeared to be piled high with grey reeking rags, which could not be very heavy. Could the fugitive be hidden underneath? But only the height of the one figure was a clue, and only to me. If I could get a look at a face and make certain, I might set up a shout for the authorities.

The hand wagon stuck for a moment where the lane turned a corner, and as the women struggled with it I took a chance. I ducked to the right, into a noisome alley. Then I ran, down and across the yard at the back. Keeping a sense of where I was clearly in mind, I vaulted over a rickety fence, shinned up onto the roof of a privy, and jumped down into the alley beyond. If the ways connected as I hoped, I should now be ahead of them. And I was, but alas not quite as far as I hoped. The barrow trundled creaking past the mouth of the alley, and I only just stopped myself from cannoning into it. Instead I pressed my back against the sooty brick wall and slid down into a sitting position. If the women, or men, chanced to look down and see me I might be taken for a drunkard sleeping off his gin.

I leaned my face onto my bent knees, and tipped my hat forward, peering up under shelter of my hand. The preternaturally tall figure was beyond view on the other side of the hand wagon, but I got a good look at the other one. He or she had her woolly black shawl over her head and tied over her face. No one in their senses would do that, not in this sweltering heat. It must be concealing the black moustache of the nameless anarchist. And as she passed I saw the sole of her shoe, under the edge of the skirt. It was no lady's footgear, but a man's boot, thick in the sole, black leather. Good enough!

As soon as they passed I ran, back down the lane and out into the street, to raise the alarm. "There he goes!" I cried, pointing. "Antun Jones. Two men dressed as women are hiding him in a barrow!"

The searchers stared. "Who the deuce are you?" a bobby

demanded. "What can you know about it?"

Desperate, I surveyed the various searchers. For the first time in my experience the sight of Inspector Radenton, with his tweed coat and grey handlebar moustache, made me want to shout with joy. "Inspector! You know my powers. I saw them and recognised them, I tell you!"

Inspector Radenton almost pricked up his ears like a fox. "Good heavens. This is solid, men. Lead the way, Mr. Hartright. Swiftly!" All at once there was a score of us or more pounding as hard as we could down the lane, filling the alleys, blocking the ways. I saw the barrow and pointed, shouting.

Seeing he was betrayed Vjenceslav threw off the trammeling shawl and the ridiculous bonnet. "You!" he shouted, recognizing me. He snatched a rifle out from among the rags on the hand wagon. But I have been hunted before – on an English country road on Laura's matter, and even before, in the jungles of British Honduras. I knew to watch for when he tensed to pull the trigger. And I relied, as I have in the past, on my own fleetness of foot. At the crucial moment, just as Vjenceslav fired, I ducked.

Such was my passion, I knew only that the bullet passed very near. I could feel the sudden coolness as the hat was plucked off my head, and could fancy the missile parting my hair. Before he could fire again a policeman tackled him, and was thrown aside like a doll. Ignoring all this I ran full out and drove straight forward as fast as my legs could carry me, past them all to the one goal – Antun Jones.

I flung myself full length onto the mound of stinking rags in the hand wagon. As I belly-flopped onto it there was a creak and a snap, and suddenly the offside wheel fell off with a crash. The entire flat wagon lurched down sideways, almost flinging me onto the cobbles. But under my knees I felt something solid and alive, writhing, and someone cursed in a language I did not know. I plunged both hands up to the elbows into the mound of dirty rags and gripped something – a limb!

The two anarchists put up a stout fight, with guns and blows. Policemen flung themselves on Vjenceslav and were hammered down by fists the size of a ham. But sheltered by the tipped hand wagon I dragged Antun Jones out by a leg and an arm. "Quickly," I said to Inspector Radenton. "They need him in court, this very instant, for the Camlet case."

"Excellent, Hartright." He slapped a pair of Darby cuffs onto Jones's wrists. We hauled our prey disheveled and malodorous to his feet as he sputtered profanities. "Well done! I see a bright career before you at the Yard!"

"Oh, not this again, inspector," I snapped. "We have no time to waste!"

But by this point I could do no wrong in the Inspector's eyes. "Stout fellow, that's the way of it – the case comes first." He had the authority to wave aside wardens and other policemen. We frog-marched our captive double-quick down the street and around to the gate into the Old Bailey. Was I too late? But no, the bailiffs were just bringing Camlet in.

The judge, stewing grumpily in his long robes and full-bottomed wig, scowled at Jones' bellowed profanity. Mr. Todwarden, suave as only a barrister may be, spoke as smoothly as if our tumultuous entrance had been rehearsed a dozen times. "Ah, and here is the true culprit. I trust, my lord, that you perceive how his attempted escape proves his guilt."

Camlet took his place in the dock, and when he glanced across at me his mouth dropped open in horror. Abruptly I realised that something wet and sticky was clogging my hair and running down the side of my face. When I wiped it with my sleeve I saw blood. "You're bleeding like a stuck pig," Inspector Radenton said with callus cheer. "Here, I have a handkerchief. There's a doctor around, he can tie it up for you."

Surely a wound that I had hardly felt could not be serious. After all my trouble, I refused to leave until Camlet's issue was no longer in doubt. More policemen poured in, to secure Jones and tell of his recapture. I was grimly pleased to see the leg irons brought into play.

The judge rapped his gavel for order in vain. "What is this, eh?" he bellowed over the turmoil. "A damned circus? Case dismissed. See to it you hold fast to the real culprit this time." And Camlet was a free man!

Since I knew of the customary delay at the prison gate, I employed the time usefully by visiting the infirmary. The overly-young doctor wiped the clots from my scalp and pronounced the injury minor. "Not even worthy of a stitch," he said. "You probably shall have no more trouble. But if you perceive any neuro-logical symptoms, don't delay to consult your own medical man."

And that gave me a notion. "What symptoms?"

"Oh, the usual warning sequelae. Double vision, headache, dizziness. Any of those would indicate that the brain beneath has sustained some injury. They're delicate organs, as you're probably aware. Even a quite minor knock to the head can have deleterious consequences."

Inspector Radenton waited for me in the prison yard, and greeted me with enthusiasm. "When can you come down to the Yard, Mr. Hartright? I want to lay those Covent Garden files before you. Bring your drawing materials, eh? How about Monday morning, would that suit your convenience?"

"I'm not certain I shall be well enough, inspector," I said, clasping my brow. "I've lost a lot of blood. And my vision is off."

"Off? What do you mean?"

"There are two of you." I stared dolefully at him. "Overlapping, how very queer. I hope my brains haven't been jingled. All artists are entirely dependent upon their vision, you know. In any case I may have to give up my painting. My wife wants me to stand for Parliament."

"What? But you have a gift, Mr. Hartright. Like none I've ever seen!"

"And now there are three," I declared, gazing past his left shoulder. "I had better go home and lie down."

"Yes, yes, do that. Recover your powers in quiet!"

Having thus laid a firm foundation for the sad and permanent loss of my psychical abilities, I maintained the wan and ailing demeanor as I tottered around the corner to the other gate. Camlet emerged even more gaunt than last time. His trousers hung from their braces, and he still favored one foot. The marks of sickness and incarceration were plain to be seen on his pallid face, and his light-brown beard had grey threads in it that had were new. But his collar was fastened with precision and his cravat faultlessly tied.

And, characteristically, his first words were of my state. "Hartright, your shirt – the blood! You're wounded!"

"But a scratch." I shook his hand once again. "You cannot

keep doing this, Camlet. The repetition of your effects creates a tedium that's insupportable." When I clapped him on the shoulder its thinness under the coat was shocking.

"I shall endeavor to find some fresh material," he said, smiling broadly. "Great heavens, Hartright. It's a delight to see you."

"You're too polite. I can see you peering past me, to see if Marian's in the carriage."

His laugh sounded as if it had gone unused for too long. "I'm glad she is waiting at home, like a sensible creature."

"Sensible?" The word choked me.

He was briefly unable to mount the step of the carriage. "Mr. Camlet, sir, welcome," Matson said. "Let me help you up. Thank God! We've all prayed for this day."

"Thank you, Matson," Camlet replied. "It's merely being out of doors, making me dizzy."

As soon as the door was shut, even before Matson could climb up onto the box, I said, "Camlet, I need to make my feelings completely plain. I cannot accept any credit for securing your release."

"Eh? Why not? You discovered this housebreaker fellow. You recaptured him finely, at a sanguinary cost."

"The proof of your innocence has been entirely the work of Marian, who has dared appalling things to achieve it."

"Hartright." He frowned at me. "You had charge of her. You didn't permit her to endanger herself?"

With difficulty I resisted the impulse to grind my teeth. "Permit? The concept is entirely foreign to her! Perhaps your short married life has not yet required you to try and restrain her in any way. Wild horses are nothing to her, Camlet. She's completely unbridled."

"You simply have not the way of it, Hartright," he said mildly. "Patience and gentle handling is the proper method."

He might have been talking of taming birds. Without heeding any of this nonsense I went on, "I warn in you advance that she has perversely insisted to all that I am responsible for your happy outcome. She's gone so far as to completely pull the wool over the eyes of the police forces, who now labour under the delusion that I have a psychical perceptive power that allows me to depict evildoers."

Behind the round steel spectacles his eyes glinted with outright glee. "That does not sound easy to do."

"If anyone in authority asks about my mesmeric powers of discernment, Camlet, this valuable and convenient head injury seems to have put paid to the gift. I do not intend to recover it."

"Your modesty is becoming, Hartright, but I don't believe it for a moment. You can lay your hands on an escaped culprit in ten minutes. You, the hero of Central American exploration, are surely more powerful than a gentle highly-bred lady like Marian. And in her condition, too! I shall be forever grateful to you. I rely upon Marian to indicate some way for me to express my gratitude to her."

"Are you aware that she has allotted to you yourself some of the credit?"

"I, the prisoner helpless in Newgate? Impossible."

"She says that you explicated Margaret Camlet's memoir to her with such completeness that she was able to face down a cell of Balkan anarchists."

To my intense annoyance Camlet's face held only gentle incredulity. "Surely you have misunderstood her. We shall sit down together and hear the entire story. After luncheon, perhaps. How I long for a decent meal! But tell me of her health, and that of the children."

For once traffic was not severe, and in a short time we arrived at Sandett House. The entire household turned out to welcome the master home. As soon as the carriage halted Micah and Lottie ran up, shouting. Camlet embraced them, lifting Lottie briefly up before his weakness made him set her down again. "I cannot toss you in the air, you have grown so! Micah, you have surely grown taller."

As an artist I have a decided preference for beauty in woman, and in this Laura has no equal. Marian's chief attraction has always been in speech, motion and form. Her figure is entirely admirable, more vigorous than Laura's. But every pretense to good looks was gone now in her ninth month. She moved slowly, leaning on Laura's arm. Her loose linen gown only escaped being a nightdress because it was striped in blue. In it her figure was distorted and hugely bulky, and her face was puffy and blotched.

Camlet stared at her over the heads of his clamouring children with his mouth open. From the way he gazed she might have been the Botticelli Venus rising nude from the ocean foam. "Marian," he said, and with the inexorable motion of a ship under full sail she moved into his embrace.

She leaned awkwardly on him, sobbing until he had to protest. "If you weep into my shirt front I cannot kiss you," he said, in mild and reasonable tones. "And I have dreamed of it for weeks, every night without fail."

"Oh, my dearest!" There was nothing reasonable in their salute. They probably would be kissing yet, but the children became too vociferous. "You must never do this again. No more prison."

"I think I can make that a promise."

Meanwhile Laura flung up her hands at the sight of me. "Walter, you're injured! Oh dear, your shirt, your coat! Does it hurt? We must call the doctor, instantly!"

"It's only a scratch, my dear. How long can your sister stand out in the sun like this? Let us adjourn indoors."

But first Camlet had to accept the felicitations of his staff. From somewhere Matson had procured a gigantic bird's-nest fern which the maids had adorned with two Union Jacks and a flag that said 'Welcome Home.' Knowing her man, Mrs. Youngblood held a steaming cup of fresh-brewed coffee which she pressed into his hand.

"I have not had a cup of coffee in three months," he declared, grinning, but had no chance to drink it as Marian kissed him again.

"You must eat," she declared. "You've grown so thin, Theo, it's shameful. Cook has an enormous luncheon planned, and by the time you have washed –" She stopped. A look of blank dismay descended upon her countenance like a veil.

Camlet halted with the cup halfway to his lips. "Marian?"

"It hurts," she said, in a tone of outrage. He set the cup down on the baluster rail, his smile vanishing. She embraced him again. "Pay me no heed. It's nothing."

But over her head Camlet peered through his spectacles at Laura. "Hartright spoke of a midwife, Laura. What did she say?"

"She said that Marian was due any day," Laura said. "Have you had any symptoms, dear one?"

For a moment Marian's swarthy countenance had all the look of a child caught stealing sugar from the bowl. "Well, there was the water."

All three of us, experienced as she was not, gasped in alarm. Laura cried, "You have broke your waters? Then the birth is imminent! Davey, run for Mrs. Pinney instantly!"

In her most aggravating and bull-headed way Marian insisted, "I cannot have this baby now. It has to wait until after we're married, and so I informed it only yesterday."

Only Marian could possibly believe that the onset of childbirth could be held back by force of will. "Now's your moment," I said to Camlet. "Patience and gentle handling, you may demonstrate your method."

Camlet grinned with cheerful confidence and took her hand. "My love, let us go in. You cannot be comfortable standing."

She swayed, leaning heavily against him. "Oh..."

Only his grip kept her from falling. "My dearest, my love. We must bow to the will of the Almighty in this. If today is to be the birth, then so it must be."

It took her some moments to recover enough to speak. "Theo, I have another and better thought. Let us go and get married."

He blinked. "I do not understand you."

"It's dreadfully unwomanly of me to say it so baldly," she said, "but you know I am frank and forthright, and delicate evasions are not in me. We've waited so long, and come so far. There can be no reason why this last final gap may not be overleaped. Marry me today, my dearest man."

"Great God, Marian, what an awful idea," I exclaimed. "Jauntering around the city in your condition was appalling enough. You're in labour, and cannot go anywhere but to your bed."

Camlet gave a little cough of laughter. "Are you certain, Marian? Not about the marriage, but about yourself. Can you bear to do this, now? Recall that by law weddings may only be held in a church. And no later than noon."

"It's but ten in the morning," she pointed out. "Plenty of time. The church isn't far. And I can promise you that this baby will not arrive in a mere two hours. From all the accounts, the labour is likely to take much longer than that. So we may as well do something useful and practical in the interval."

"Marian, this is not heard of," Laura cried. "You would be more comfortable at home."

"I would be more comfortable married," she said. "No, I've endured worse, I assure you. This is nothing."

"The pangs will get worse, Marian," Laura warned.

But Camlet was as incorrigible as she. "If you say you can bear it, my love, then I cannot doubt you. And it is true, there is time... What do we need? A licence. Alas, I believe that as the bridegroom I may be the only one empowered to secure it. Matson, would you saddle my horse? Your mistress will need the brougham. Hartright, I must entrust you once more with all that I hold dear. Do you make your way slowly to the church, and I'll meet you all there with the licence."

"Is this the method, Camlet?" I demanded. "To just lie down under the wagon wheels and give way to her absolutely, without the smallest cavil?"

"You note it's far the easiest route to harmony," he conceded. "But consider. In law, it makes no difference when the wedding takes place. So long as it occurs before the moment of birth, the child is born in wedlock. I would do anything to relieve our child of the burden of illegitimacy, and so would Marian. And here is our first and last opportunity. We've all heard of six-month, even three-month babies. This shall be a one-day infant, the wonder of the neighbourhood."

I opened my mouth, to decree that no woman under my care should be out and about at such a time, but Marian's dark eye transfixed me with such a glare that the words stuck. "Oh Walter, you do fuss," Marian said. "Drink this, Theo. There is not time for you to dine. Should you wear boots?"

"That would be as well." He took the coffee cup and drained it. "If I ride a distance I will ruin these trousers."

"Run in and change, then. You'll find your room all ready for you. Cook, while he is pulling on his riding boots, could you cut him a sandwich? Walter, where is your hat? You cannot go to church without one. And you should change your shirt, it's in a shocking state. Laura, is there anything we should bring to the church?"

The idea of traveling during the birth process was so unheard-of that Laura had to think. "Well – linens, yes, towels and cloths, that would be wise. A blanket. And water, yes, something to drink, and bathe your forehead with. Perhaps a pillow, for you to rest on?"

Everyone scattered to their tasks, and I was left perforce to manage Micah and Lottie. "I foresee that there will not be room for us in the carriage," I said. Surely it would be inappropriate for children to be in the presence of a woman in labour? "Do you think you can walk so far as the church, Lottie? Or should you both rather stay at home with little Fairlie and your nurse?"

"Is Papa going to marry Miss Marian all over again?" Lottie asked.

"Yes, there was a mistake last time and so they're going to make it right."

"Then we must be there," Micah said. "We were there at Limmeridge, so it would be only decent."

"I could carry flowers in a basket again," Lottie said.

"It may take some while," I warned. "You might bring a book or a toy instead."

They ran off to gather amusements to bring to the church, pausing only to hug Theo again as he appeared in the portico. He had exchanged his rumpled suit for breeches and boots, his long riding coat and a hat. The more tailored garments showed how much weight he had lost, but the support of the stiff leather boot seemed to improve his limp.

"You're a scarecrow," I said. "Camlet, this is too much for you, the first day you're out of prison."

Camlet laughed. "No, Hartright. Today is my day. With your help and hers, I've stepped out of the mouth of my own grave into the light. Nothing is beyond me." Behind the round spectacles his eye had the glint of steel, and I saw that there would be no turning him, any more than I could persuade Marian. The pair of them were clearly made for each other.

Matson came, leading the horse. The sight of his mount, unexercised and far too fresh, filled me with new misgiving. I had only seen Camlet's favorite horse at a distance before, and had not realised its size and spirit. The creature must be seventeen hands high. Luna the greyhound incautiously ran too near and nearly had her empty head kicked in for her pains. I dragged the dog back. "Find a safer mount, Camlet. You're too worn to handle this one."

"What, Boreas? He would never hurt me. Give him his head, Matson." The coachman looped the rein up onto the saddle and let go of the bridle, and sure enough the huge beast trotted up to its master and bowed its head to snuffle his shirt front. Camlet leaned on the glossy black neck. "Give me a leg up if you would, Hartright. This foot is annoying."

I did not like it. In his weakness Camlet might easily be thrown. But there was nothing else for it but to boost him up into the saddle. "Oh, this is good," he said, arranging the reins between his gloved fingers. "I can survive anything, if only it be under the open sky. But, wait. The licence fee. Hartright, have you any money on you?"

I pressed my purse into his hands. "We'll gather every coin in the house, to pay the clergy fee."

"Excellent. Mrs. Youngblood will fetch you the housekeeping funds. Marian?" The beast was restive, fretting for its head, but Camlet reined it in and Marian approached his stirrup, leaning heavily on Laura's arm. "You're quite certain, my dearest?"

"There are hours and hours to pass yet," she said, smiling up him. "All will be well, Theo."

"Yes indeed – we've come too far, to fail now." At the very last instant Cook dashed up with a sandwich knotted in a napkin, and he circled around to scoop it from her upstretched hand. Then he was off at a fast trot, waving at the children as they leaned from the nursery window and shrieked excited farewells.

In spite of her pangs Marian was completely mistress of the situation. "The Rev. Angier must be called in," she said. "Ellen, Mr. Hartright shall write a note for you to carry to him. Laura, we must not forget to bring the ring. Will you fetch it? Mrs. Pinney, you are very welcome. How fortunate that Davey found you at home. I believe we have time for a brief consultation indoors, before we must set out. You will come with me in the carriage?"

"My dear, where can you be gallivanting off to?" Mrs. Pinney cried in tones of brass, her three shawls in three clashing colours fluttering behind her. "You have no business out and about, missy, not now. You should be tucked up in your own bed!" I heard no more, retreating into the safety of the study to write the note to the vicar. Poor Mrs. Pinney had no notion what attending upon Marian was going to entail.

Within the hour we set out. Marian was helped carefully up into the brougham, and Laura and Mrs. Pinney went with her. Matson was abjured to go at a slow walk. The children and I walked behind, easily able to keep up with their gentle pace in spite of the heat of the summer noontide.

From Sandett House it was but a mile and a half to the village, where the church of St. John-at-Hampstead stood on a rise of land, guarded by handsome wrought-iron gates and surrounded by its own burial ground. The sun was sufficiently warm that it was a pleasure to come to the shade of the trees planted there.

The church was a substantial brick building, with an imposing square central tower surmounted by a greenish copper steeple. The big double doors were locked. Until the vicar arrived there was no reason for Marian to stir. While she rested in the carriage I sat in the shade on a convenient flat tombstone, and Lottie wandered through the grass gathering flowers for the wedding.

At last the twitter and complaint of birds above the lane heralded the progress of the vicar's dog-cart. The portly Rev. Angier climbed down, beating the dust of the road from his driving gloves. His big square face was brick red between the bristling grey side whiskers. "How do you do, Mr. Hartright," he greeted me. "What's this you tell me, eh? A wedding by licence? Who are the principals?"

The awkwardness of the explanation was fully borne in on me. I led the vicar to our carriage, hoping for Laura's help. "You're acquainted with them both, sir. You will not have heard, but this very morning the charges against Theophilus Camlet were dismissed. Margaret Camlet's true murderer confessed to the crime, and Camlet is proved innocent. He was released from custody this morning."

"Why this is excellent news indeed, and an answer to prayer! It must be a great joy to all of the family."

"And in consequence of his previous acquittal for bigamy,

Camlet's wish is to make an honest woman of my sister-in-law Miss Marian Halcombe. This very day."

"What, now?"

"He's off to get the licence and should be here any moment."

The vicar's red face was blank with astonishment. "Hartright, this hugger-mugger is highly irregular. An excellent thing, indeed yes, that Camlet wishes to do right by your sister, but surely there's no need for such unseemly haste."

I was flushing myself, with self-consciousness. Why were two men being forced to discuss these matters? There had to be some delicate form of words to indicate to the vicar that Marian's delivery was imminent, but they eluded me. "They both desire the matter to be concluded as quickly as possible," I said feebly.

"It is essential that all of these rites be enacted properly, with due and deliberate dignity," the reverend said. "To have such an important event, the union of two immortal souls before God, scrambled together in a shady way does honor to no one. The appearance of propriety, of decency must be preserved, sir. Perhaps next week would be –"

All the windows of the brougham had been lowered because of the heat. Marian suddenly appeared in the open window, looking extraordinarily hot and cross. "Reverend Angier," she said. "Do you suggest to me that you will not perform a wedding for us this day?"

Hastily he doffed his top hat. "Dear Miss Halcombe, I meant only to suggest that the appearance of haste –"

Her great dark eyes flashed with a truly terrifying light. "Haste is precisely what is called for. Once, reverend, you assured me you would be my protector. I cherish that, sir. After all your wonderfully Christian kindnesses to me, I would be very sorry to learn that you propose to do an irreparable and permanent injury to my child."

"A child? What child?" Suddenly the reverend's ruddy cheek went livid. "Oh, great God in Heaven. Never say you are, are …"

"I expect to give birth very shortly," Marian said. "Very shortly indeed, sir. I've made the journey here in the face of great trouble, in the hope that the child may be born in wedlock."

"Mrs. Pinney," the vicar almost wailed. "Is this safe? How

did you come to allow this? Miss Halcombe should not be abroad at this time!"

"Oh sir, the lady is in no need of my permission," Mrs. Pinney returned tartly. "Miss Halcombe knows her own mind. And I will say the pangs are but six minutes apart, so there's yet time for any morrissing about she may fancy."

Marian said, "I think it would be good for me to come down. The carriage is too hot, and I shall be more comfortable in the open air."

"Oh, merciful Saviour," the vicar moaned, as with majestic slowness Marian climbed down from the brougham, Mrs. Pinney and Laura assisting. "Miss Halcombe, you – this is shocking. No lady in your circumstance should be abroad!"

"No lady should be in my circumstance, I agree," Marian said. "Unwed and yet expecting. The Female Preventative and Reformatory League would deplore it, I know. Would you oblige me by unlocking the church doors, reverend? Else I must dispose myself upon your front step."

"No, no! By all means. Allow me."

The vicar hurried to unlock the tall double doors, and very slowly, with pauses that I could only describe as pregnant, Marian passed down the walk past the ancient gravestones, and through the portal. The church is well-off, and boasts an organ of some renown built by Willis. Its nave was furnished in the latest style, all dark wood columns and heavy pews.

Once through the narthex into the nave Marian lowered herself carefully down into one of the rear pews. "How beautifully cool it is here, reverend. It must be the height of the ceiling. I feel much better. If you permit, I shall wait quietly here until Theo comes." She leaned back, visibly immovable, and Laura fanned her.

The vicar seized me by the arm and dragged me out into the narthex. "Great Heavens, Mr. Hartright," he said in an undertone. "How can you allow this? It's a scandal! What shall the vestry say if they hear of it? Or, oh my stars, the Bishop? The woman's in labour!"

"My advice was not called upon," I said with some bitterness. "Camlet and Marian have fixed upon their course of action without consulting anyone else."

"What if she – what if…" Horrific visions seemed to swim in front of the vicar's eyes, each worse than the next. "What of the aisle carpet? Whatever shall the Altar Guild say, of the pew cushions? And where is the bridegroom? Where is Camlet?"

"He went on horseback to fetch the licence."

"Is he aware that weddings must be celebrated before noon?"

"Yes, he knows he must be back within the hour."

"Before! One cannot conduct a wedding all in a moment." He pulled a gold watch out of a waistcoat pocket. "It's already past eleven. He must arrive before the three-quarter."

"That's quite reasonable." I spoke with more confidence than I felt. Had Camlet taken into account how little time remained? I left the vicar to talk, nervously, to Marian and Laura and went out to consult Matson.

Out in the roadway beyond the ornate iron palisade the coachman had filled nosebags for his team, and there was a horse trough. "You know Camlet's black horse," I said. "How reliable a mount is it?"

"You should have seen it before Mr. Theo gentled him a bit," Matson said. "Our own circus show, right here in Hampstead. He's got Boreas tame as a lamb now, but the beast's so strong he's still a rare handful on occasion. And fast, fast as a racehorse. The master'll be down into town and back again in a twinkling. You wouldn't ever think it with that milk-and-water manner of his. But even from boyhood Mr. Theo had quite the appetite for danger."

At last I understood. I inclined towards fragile fairness and delicate beauty. But Camlet's tastes ran to a wilder ride. What filled me with terror and dismay, he enjoyed! "You're wonderfully perceptive, Matson. I should have talked to you months ago." I shaded my eyes to look down the hot sunny lane in the direction of town. The vista was utterly placid, green and bucolic, a vision of the dozing English countryside. There was no sign of any rider approaching up the long slope, no cloud of dust or disturbed birds flying up. If Camlet failed to return it could only be because he had come to grief along the way. Once the clock struck twelve and it was too late, I resolved to hire a horse at the Bird in Hand, follow his route, and hope to come upon his shattered body by the side of the road. Laura and Mrs. Pinney could take Marian and the children home again in the carriage.

I went back into the church again and sat down in the rear pew next to my wife. "I'll thrash him," I growled, "if he's gone and killed himself on the way. After all the trouble we've been to, to rescue him."

"If he is injured or slain then we must hide it from her," she whispered into my ear. "As long as we can. Until – after."

I nodded in agreement. Although whether even childbirth would stop Marian from seeking out the truth was an open question. She sat with one of Laura's pillows behind her, half-reclining on the hard wooden pew as Mrs. Pinney fanned her. Her long loose striped-linen gown was crumpled and blotched with perspiration, and her coal-black hair was beginning to come down from its usual knot at the back. The pangs were wearing on her.

But her demeanor was entirely calm. "You worry far too much, Walter," she said, breathlessly. "Theo shall not fail. Go and look again, if you will."

Such confidence in a beloved was admirable, but if it was dashed, the calamity would be doubly crushing. Hiding my misgivings I rose and went out again. Not until I was safe in the narthex did I consult my watch. My heart sank – oh God, it was already half past.

Beside me the door to the dark curving stairway up into the gallery and the central bell tower stood invitingly ajar. That gave me a fresh inspiration. I pushed through and climbed up the ladderlike stair, emerging from its dusty darkness into the organ loft. It was a small and cluttered space, stacked high with musty hymnals and lit by a single oval window. When I leaned on the sill and pressed my forehead to the glass I could see a long way, further than from down in the churchyard.

And, thank the Lord! From the billowing green tops of the trees that lined the lane, the blackcaps, sparrows and great tits were fluttering up, first one and then many. The birds must be unsettled by the noisy passage of a swift traveller. I shaded my eyes with my hands and breathed a sigh of relief. Surely that was he. No vehicle could trundle along at such a spanking pace, and uphill too. Still, I did not go to warn the vicar and the bride until

I was sure. But soon horse and rider could be seen through a gap in the foliage, and I recognised my man, his coattails flying. I hurried back down the narrow stair. "He comes – Reverend, perhaps you should prepare."

"I shall warn my clerk," the Rev. Angier said. "I only hope that the licence may be in order. I must just look it over."

"Oh, thank Heaven," Laura said. "Dearest Marian, I'm so happy for you! But perhaps you should stay sitting until the very last moment."

"That would be as well," Marian agreed. "Dear me, birth is an annoying process. And so tedious. This is to go on for hours? I begin to see why Sir Charles Locock received a title for administering chloroform to the Queen."

I went back out into the churchyard again and was in time to see Camlet rein up outside the iron gates in a cloud of dust. Micah and Lottie ran up shouting, and he dismounted and handed the reins over to Matson. "In plenty of time, am I not, Hartright?" he said, breathing hard.

"By a whisker. It's nearly a quarter to. Come in, quickly."

The children scampered up the walk between the gravestones with alacrity, their father following more slowly and favoring the bad foot. When he took off his hat it could be seen where below its covering Camlet's over-long hair was pale with dust. He reeked of horse and sweat, and his spectacles were streaked with grime. "Have I time to wash?"

The Rev. Angier, beholding this grubby sheep of his flock, said, "Come avail yourself of my own basin, here in the vestry."

Camlet thrust the folded licence into the vicar's hand. He took off his glasses but had no clean surface on which to wipe them. Laura snatched them from his grasp and rubbed them on her skirt. Marian beamed up at him. "You look very hot, Theo."

"And you do not look your best either," he returned, grinning. "We are well matched."

The instant Laura put the spectacles back into his hand I gripped his elbow and bustled him down the aisle. "Swiftly, man, or it shall be too late."

He hooked the earpieces over his ears. "Lend me a comb, would you? If you have such a thing."

I handed him a pocket comb. At the front the vicar took him

in charge, leading him through the choir into the rear premises behind the altar. I went back again and helped Laura ease Marian to her feet. "And this is an overly-long aisle," she declared.

"I shall hold your arm on this side," Laura said. "Walter, will you take her other arm?"

"I'm quite steady on my feet," Marian said. "We're told that walking is good for the process, is that not so, Mrs. Pinney?"

"I'm glad to hear that some of what I said has penetrated your hard little head, Miss Halcombe," the midwife returned in tones that echoed up into the roof. "But I wish this were well over, and you safe in your home. There's no need at all for the gentlemen to be present at occasions like this. I will be just behind you."

"And, Miss Marian!" Lottie cried. "You have to have flowers, to get married."

"Oh, thank you, Lottie." Marian accepted the handful of limp wildflowers and daisies. "Now we have everything that is needful."

And so we set off. The entire group of us processed at Marian's slow pace through the patches of colour cast by sunbeams pouring through the stained-glass windows. The children capered on ahead. The only wedding music was their happy clamour echoing up in the arches of the high cool ceiling. Up at the front from their three arched windows the colourful images of our Lord and His friends the two Saints John gazed benevolently down at our disorderly progress. Mrs. Pinney brought up the rear, a grumbling bridal attendant in three shawls that did not match. It was not at all like the more socially correct wedding procession that had taken place at Limmeridge church nearly a year ago, but it was very like the principals.

In his priestly stole the vicar came down the grey marble steps from the choir. Camlet followed. His clothes were still travel-stained but he had combed his hair back and washed his face, so that it shone damply pale in the dimness.

A conscientious parent, he moved swiftly to corral his leaping offspring. "Sit, there in the front pew. Lottie, if you tip the lectern over the step, the brass eagle will assuredly be dented and the vestry will send me the bill for repairs. Micah, cup-and-ball is not to be played in the nave. You must be quiet and devout for the ceremony. I told the vicar here that you both assist at weddings with grace, and you must not make me a liar."

Laura and I sat between them to ensure good behavior. At her beloved's side at last, Marian slipped her hand into his. The joy in their faces was good to see, brighter in this gloomy space than the noonday sun pouring down through the stained glass. It had been worth all our trouble.

The vicar began the familiar rite: "Dearly beloved, we are gathered together here in the sight of God ..."

"I shall cry," Laura whispered, and I took a handkerchief out in preparation. How much more appropriate the ancient words seemed, this time!

The vicar turned over a page in his prayer book. "... and therefore is not by any to be enterprised, nor taken in hand, unadvisedly, lightly, or wantonly, to satisfy men's carnal lusts and appetites, like brute beasts that have no understanding; but reverently, discreetly, advisedly, soberly, and in the fear of God; duly considering the causes for which Matrimony was ordained."

I waited in resigned patience for one more knot or hitch in the proceedings. Because there had to be one, at the wedding of Marian Halcombe. And sure enough, when the reverend called for the ring, Camlet looked blankly at Marian, and Marian glanced over her shoulder at Laura.

"I have it," my wife said. And she took out a red velvet bag.

"Oh good heavens." I recognised it. But before I could stop her Laura slid out of the pew and went forward to shake it out into the Rev. Angier's outstretched hand.

The vicar held the ring up, a heavy gold band elaborately worked and set with three dazzling square-cut sapphires. His mouth was already open to continue, when Theo broke in. "Where did you get this, Laura?"

"It was in the dresser drawer," she replied, stricken. "I thought it was the right one."

But Marian intervened. "It is the right one," she said. "It's a family heirloom, given to one of Theo's relatives, from a man who loved her. And she wanted you to be happy, Theo. I'm certain of it."

He blinked. "Did she, indeed?"

"It was in your greenhouse – I could almost hear her saying it."

Theo smiled at her. "Very well then. Carry on, Reverend." I watched carefully, and when it came time for Camlet to put the ring on her finger it did indeed fit Marian perfectly.

The register had to be signed, and then Mrs. Pinney was there. "And now, *Missus* Camlet, you have more important things to do this day. Back home you go, snip snap!"

"Yes, I beg of you, please go home!" the Rev. Angier said. "You will let me know the outcome, dear lady. The christening, whether you desire a churching ceremony, anything you wish. But please! For all love, Camlet, get your wife to her bed!"

"You're all in league against me," Marian said. Clearly she was in growing pain, and getting fractious.

But her new husband's deft persuasion was a pleasure to see, far more effective than all our chivvying and pestering. "Does not the idea of lying down sound attractive?" Camlet said gently. "I confess to being worn out myself. I yearn to have a bath and a change of clothes, and a meal. That sandwich was not sufficient." He drew her hand through his own dusty arm and began to walk her casually back down the aisle.

"What was your breakfast, my dearest?"

"At Newgate? It has never been a venue renowned for excellent viands. Skilly and a slice of dry black bread."

"Oh, you poor man. Mrs. Youngblood and Cook put together a welcome-home luncheon for you."

"Let us go home, and I will undertake to devour it."

She leaned heavily on his arm, wilting fast. "I never want to be parted from you again."

"Conveniently, we have married, to ensure exactly that. And if you allow, I shall come back in the carriage with you."

"I insist upon it."

"I foresee it'll be the last time we shall have alone together for a good while to come."

"This is unheard of," Mrs. Pinney grumbled as we emerged out into the sunshine. "None of my ladies have gone on expeditions when their time was come. To let a detail like getting married slip until this late moment, it's not in the least prudent or efficient!"

"Matson will assist you to climb up onto the box," Camlet offered. "Since this is our wedding journey, I do intend to be alone with my wife."

We passed through the tall iron gates and Laura went round to the other side to help Marian into the brougham and settle her comfortably on the seat. Matson and Camlet handed Mrs. Pinney up to the box. "This leaves Boreas to you, Hartright," Camlet said. "What a faithful soldier you've been, ever assisting and helpful in crisis. The licence cost nearly three pounds, by the way. Your purse was invaluable. Laura, are you weary? Would you like to ride back?"

"Is it safe?" Laura stared up dubiously at Boreas, who was tied to the fence.

"He's perfectly tame," Camlet assured her. "Lottie will ride, and there is no need for you to walk the distance back to Sandett House."

"You should do it, Laura," Marian said to her from the open window of the carriage. "You'll be footsore otherwise. Your slippers were not made for walking."

I did not much care for it, but it was true that the horse was no longer fresh and dancing about anxious to run. In any case it was plainly my task to lead him home, since Matson had to drive the carriage. Laura climbed onto the mounting block and with Camlet's assistance was able to perch sidesaddle. While he adjusted the stirrup on that side for her I boosted Lottie up behind. "And Micah will walk on this side, so that you need feel not the slightest uneasiness," Camlet said.

"We must be on our way," Mrs. Pinney blared. "Her pangs are five minutes apart. It is just like you men, dallying while women are in trouble."

"Yes, yes, we're off." Camlet climbed up into his brougham and they set off at a walk.

I came along behind, leading Boreas with Micah's assistance. The summer sun was declining in the sky now, and as we went down the hill the trees cast a pleasant shade. From behind Laura Lottie said, "Is Miss Marian truly our mother now?"

"I do believe so," I replied. "She cannot possibly escape any more."

"Good," Micah said. "I want it to be settled."

"You've been very patient with all our adult fuss," Laura said. "I hope now you shall welcome your new brother or sister with joy."

"I'll consider it," Lottie said with dignity. "If it's a girl."

"A girl would be better," Micah agreed. "I already have Wally and little Fairlie to teach. A third lad would be too much, and after all one does have one's schoolwork."

Fascinated, I could not help asking, "What is your program of instruction?"

"Battledore, fishing, how to throw and catch, and of course how to build a kite."

I glanced up to meet Laura's smile. Of course young Wally adored his older cousin. What a quantity of new relations we had acquired through Marian's union! "But our Quest has been worth the trouble," Lottie said. "Pooh, who cares about the Northwest Passage? A mother is much better and more useful."

"In spite of some setbacks," Micah agreed, "we managed Papa's business beautifully. I wonder now," he added thoughtfully, "what new family project we should undertake."

Immediately my duty became plain to me: to advise Camlet to send Micah to the best school he could afford. These were the children of Margaret Camlet. Left unguided the children would be equally dangerous. The lad's powers had to be channeled for the good of the Empire.

Worn out by his swift trip to town and back, Boreas showed no circus tendencies. I did not hurry him, giving the carriage plenty of time to get home before us. With Marian safely retired to her chambers at long last, and all the women in the house gone to attend her, my happy task was that long-postponed luncheon. After the day's incidents I felt a need for sustenance, and Ellen opened a bottle of claret.

As Marian had promised there was a vast deal of food, and I sat with the little ones in the dining room to ensure they ate properly. Camlet came to join us, fresh from his first bath in months, and immediately noticed the new addition of Moore's sketch of Marian, now framed and propped on the sideboard. He was as worn out as I. Although he was plainly starving he almost fell asleep over his plate.

Still my work was still not done. As the head of the family my final task was to draw up a notice to be sent to *The Times*. It was discreet and as short as possible, but I wanted it to appear promptly. Not only would it usher in Marian's return to respectable society, it publicly handed over her supervision to her lawfully-wedded husband. When I sealed the letter and dropped it into the mail bag I had to take a deep breath. Yes, it was a distinct sense of relief. Let the lion-tamer manage his lioness from now on! I append the cutting here:

> Marriage notice in *The Times*, 10 August 1857, p. 1:
> On the 6th inst., at the parish church, Hampstead, by the Rev. Thomas Wilfrid Angier, M.A., Vicar of the parish, THEOPHILUS HENTON WILLIAM, son of the late WILLIAM THEOPHILUS CAMLET, Esq., to MARIAN CELESTE, daughter of the late JONATHAN LOWRY HALCOMBE, Esq.

The following morning there was still no news. To keep the house quiet for Marian I planned to take the two children, and also the dog, little Fairlie and his nurse, to spend the day at the cottage with my mother, Sarah, and Wally. Laura had sat up all night with her sister, and met us at the breakfast table before retiring for a nap. Camlet was there, devouring a hearty meal. He was once more scrupulously dressed in a collar and cravat, albeit in a brown suit that was now a little loose through the waist. "I must visit my bankers, and the Covenant offices," he said. "But I will postpone my business affairs, if – if you recommend it, Laura. I ... would like to say goodbye."

Laura's eyes widened. "No no, Theo, there is no likelihood of that. A day and a night of labour, it is quite usual in first deliveries."

"May I see her?"

"No," Laura said, with decision. "You must possess your soul in patience. Spend your day as you ought, in your man's duties."

"I shall take charge of him, my dear," I promised her. "Go, sleep while you may. Camlet, see a doctor about that limp. After all these weeks a sprain would have healed, so you probably broke one of the small bones. I know your finances are at sixes and sevens. Go set them in order. There's not a penny of money in the house. Every coin went to the fees yesterday. Laura pillaged your larder, and Mrs. Youngblood needs to pay the tradesmen. You are our host, and as your house guest I demand decent dinners. Or, good heavens. You do not need Marian's signature for documents?"

"Not at all. Recall, she married me. By law her husband owns everything she possesses." Involuntarily I twitched at these words, and seeing this he grinned. "Since all her monies were deeded over to her by me in the first place, I feel she will raise no strong objection to my taking them back again."

"I warn you she's drawn your capital down like a drunken sailor. Your solicitors and barristers had to be paid, and it cost over a hundred pounds to make copies of the first Mrs. Camlet's manuscript."

"I am alive and free, so every shilling was well spent."

"Then be off with you. You have your business, and I have mine." Still he hesitated, and I said more gently, "You've trodden this road before, Camlet. When Micah and Lottie were born, did you not wait downstairs while your wife was in travail?"

"I ... it's different now."

"I understand," I said, yet more kindly. "If she's not delivered by the time you return, we shall walk this evening into the village. Three tankards of ale each at the Bird in Hand should be enough to thoroughly powder our hair."

That made him laugh, but I could see he was moved. "I cannot conceive of you in your cups, Hartright. This is true friendship."

"We're brothers now," I replied, affected myself. "My own brothers died in childhood. I have never had a brother before."

"Nor I. Odd, is it not?" We shook hands and then he took himself off, in a hansom so that the brougham could be left for Marian in case of great need.

Our day at my mother's cottage was entirely satisfactory. Little Fairlie of course is ever a welcome caller, and I was pleased to see that young Wally was not yet utterly spoilt by the adoration of his grandmother and aunt Sarah. The ladies cried out with joy when I told of Camlet's release, and clapped their hands at the happy conclusion to Marian's story.

The tumultuous events of the wedding made Sarah cry out time and again, "Good Lord, Walter!"

Meanwhile my mother pressed her hands to her lean cheeks and exclaimed, "This is amazing. How can poor Marian have borne it all? She is a female of whalebone and steel. Amazing!"

My sociable mother could be relied upon to get the entire neighbourhood up to date on every particular. With such an exciting account in hand, the happy prospect of a week's worth of gossipy afternoon calls and twittering over the teacups opened before her and made her beam. My account of the ceremony was judged disappointingly scant on the details dear to the female heart, the trimming of the bride's dress being entirely lost to my male reportage. In vain did I plead that neither Laura nor Marian had the opportunity to dress for the occasion. But it was agreed that the sapphires had to be viewed and admired as soon as possible, and that a fresh round of wedding calls could be combined with the obligatory congratulatory call upon the new mother. All the social wounds were thus in a fair way to healing over without fuss.

Camlet was praised for his fond generosity in taking advantage of this opportunity to give his wife a yet more opulent wedding ring. "But he has always been so gratifyingly enamored of her," my mother said. "Though she is in no way a beauty Marian is wonderfully attractive."

"So romantic," Sarah agreed. "And he could have married anyone, really."

"The union may all be laid to my good offices," my mother declared, happily taking all the credit to herself. "For I presented her to him my own self in this very parlour, do you recall, Sarah? And the baby! Born in wedlock after all – I am so pleased, although they have cut it very fine. For it would not look quite well for your boys, Walter, to have a cousin who's a natural child."

"Better late than never," I agreed.

And when we returned in the evening, everyone tired out by a day of energetic play, Laura waited for us at the door of Sandett House. "It's a girl," she announced. "A fine healthy infant, nearly eight pounds! I am just watching for Theo."

"How relieved he will be," I said. "And the mother?"

"Marian is doing well, and has been asleep all afternoon. She was all for naming the child after me, but I told her that Lottie and

Laura makes one think of music hall performers. So she has agreed to name her Celeste, and keep Laura for a middle name."

"After your mother, very appropriate. I hope Camlet will have no objection."

"I am to ask him when he comes. But it is my opinion that he'll do anything she asks."

"Yes, that is his sole secret of Marian management, I'm afraid."

Camlet arrived not ten minutes later. A doctor had strapped his foot up tightly. He had also found time to visit his barber, Flex Rowland in Haymarket, and was now more spruce than ever, with his hair cut and his beard once more trimmed into the tidy side whiskers that rose up into a moustache.

We went upstairs and Laura brought out the newborn, swaddled in a white shawl. Seldom have I seen my wife so proud and pleased, even after the birth of her own sons. Only as I write this do I recognise that our own desire for a daughter originated here, at the birth of Marian's first.

The newborn had a tiny crumpled pink face and a single sprig of dark hair. Camlet took the newborn in his arms with the confidence of a veteran parent, and the infant fixed him in a solemn and assessing gaze. He smiled all over his honest face. "What a beauty! And how intelligently she looks at me. It puts me in mind of her mother. But one forgets, what a feather a newly born baby is in the arms. May I go in, or is Marian asleep?"

Laura smiled dotingly down at the little one. "She will wish to see you, I know."

Still carrying his daughter Camlet tiptoed in, and when Marian spoke we followed. In the bedroom the blue velvet curtains were half-pulled against the last of the day's light. Marian lay in the high half-tester bed with an air of smug satisfaction. Her black hair hung in its long thick braid down over her shoulder, and she wore an ivory-white bedjacket, made by Laura and adorned with ribbon-work lilies of the valley and deep ruffles of crocheted lace. She was more in looks than I had ever seen her – maternity suited her.

Camlet set the infant in the new mother's arms and, disdaining the chair, sat on the edge of the bed so that he could put his arm around her and look down at the child. "Ah, how I love you," he said, kissing her brow. "Surely you're the most wonderful woman in the world."

"You are never wrong about these things," she replied. "Is she not beautiful? All the chatter about how troubles would mar the unborn child, nothing but old wives' tales. Her eyes are going to be hazel, like yours and Lottie's – my favorite hue. And these tiny wee fingers! She doesn't take after me at all." When she inserted her little finger into the tiny palm the baby gripped it, and she bent to kiss the miniature fist.

"Indeed she does, for you are beautiful above all others. And as you say I am never wrong."

Marian rolled her eyes at Laura, who laughed. "This is what I wanted for you, Marian. Your happy ending."

"Yes, Laura – and see, how wise you are."

"You promised we should be happy again," Camlet said, and indeed he looked as joyful as any man I had ever seen.

Marian leaned back against his breast with a sigh of contentment. "Oh, but we're poor now, are we not, dear man? Laura said you were calling on your bankers."

"This past year has been cruelly expensive, I admit," he replied, stroking her cheek. "I must turn the business around as quickly as may be, and then we shall be on a sound footing. Do you know, I believe Margaret had the right of it all along. Her memoir? Covenant shall publish it."

Marian smiled up into his face. "Oh nonsense, Theo. How? Edit it as you will, you cannot possibly transform it into a theological tome."

Camlet laughed quietly. "Well, it cannot be denied that if we're to make a great deal of money quickly, a sharp change in editorial direction is called for. The simple solution would be to create a separate imprint. And I shall adjust the punctuation. Margaret was always a martyr to comma mismanagement, and even young Micah has a better grasp of semicolons. But my most important contribution shall be title and subtitle. *Daisy Darnell: A Memoir by the Most Dangerous Woman in Europe.* Does it not sound likely to sell?"

"Put in an explanatory foreword," Marian suggested. "The manuscript was left at Covenant's editorial offices by…"

"By a mysterious tall woman, of course," I said. "Who left

no direction."

"Heavily veiled," Marian added. "So that no one could recognise her. And she confided that she is on her way to Stockholm or Boston or Buenos Aires, or some such exotic locale."

"But she clearly intended it for publication," Laura offered.

"You could give out that she chose Covenant because she admired your English edition of Calvin's *Institutes*," I put in.

"Oh brave, Walter," Marian applauded. "Although if that induces people to go and purchase Calvin, its want of incident and dense prose style shall be a sad disappointment. Dear me, our anarchist friend Vjenceslav will have an apoplectic fit. Laura tells me that the newspapers report he escaped the clutches of the police after all. Perhaps it would be wiser to publish it as fiction."

Camlet was laughing so hard that the bed squeaked. "It will make a fortune," I said, unable to keep from laughing myself. "I read the first ten pages aloud to Mother and Sarah this afternoon. When I halted I feared for my life. They wanted to tear the manuscript out of my hands. If you do not get it into print so that she may read the entire tale, Mother will camp in your drive until you do."

And so we come to the end of our story. Marian has set aside her journal, alleging that happiness, and nursing a new baby, takes up so much of her time that it is impossible to write. In any case her blue Morocco journal volume must be full, with nearly two years' worth of incident. But also I rather suspect her of moving her writings to some other, more secret volume, in the manner of a bird abandoning a nest that has been disturbed. Or a nautilus, adding a new and more commodious chamber to its shell. So I conclude this account myself, with one more incident.

Little Celeste Laura Camlet was christened at St. John's in September, the Rev. Angier presiding and Laura and myself standing as godparents. The following week, my family returned north to Cumberland. The four of us, along with the dog, the nursemaid, and Laura's maid, filled an entire train compartment.

As we were passing through the grand staircase hall at Euston Station to our platform I noticed the headlines on the papers the newsboys were selling. "An Heir to Jack Sheppard!" the boys shrilled, waving news sheets with headlines two inches high.

Jack Sheppard was the greatest jail-breaker of his generation. I halted in my tracks and bought copies of all the papers on offer. They were full of the story of a fresh jail break at Newgate Prison. One Antun Jones, a foreigner being held on charges of housebreaking and murder, had made his second daring escape this season. Despite his manacles and leg irons, he had bludgeoned a turnkey with the leg from a wooden stool, and then escaped in a load of linens as it was carried out. Accomplices on the outside were thought to have assisted, but his recapture was declared to be imminent.

Reading in our train compartment, I was skeptical. All the reportage was similar and had clearly sprung from the same prison spokesman, especially noticeable when they were compared with the variety of vociferous commentators deriding the poor prison security and how criminals could stroll out of Newgate the way a cow might stray from her pen.

When I folded up my last newspaper our train had trundled out past the outlying grey districts of London into the green countryside. "So he will not hang for the murder of Mrs. Camlet after all," I said to Laura.

"As I recall, Vjenceslav's bargain was that Jones would be arrested for the crime," she replied. "He said nothing of conviction or execution."

"We must count our blessings. At least this ensures that they'll all scurry out of Britain to avoid recapture, and their bomb with them. If fortune favors us, they shan't learn of the publiccation of *Daisy Darnell* for many years."

"Marian has promised to send me a copy," Laura said. "And, you will scarcely credit this, Walter, she says that if they have another daughter some day, they will name it Margaret."

"What?"

"The middle name, at least," Laura said. "As a gesture of gratitude."

For a second wife to bear such goodwill towards the first? Magnificent. But that has always been a good term for Marian.

ACKNOWLEDGMENTS

Thanks to all the stalwarts here at Book View Café, who've been helping me wrestle with Victorian mores and manners, the niceties of melodrama, and the management of all these volumes. Especially Sherwood, Jen, Marissa and Chaz!

Also by Brenda Clough from Book View Cafe

Novels

Speak to Our Desires

How Like a God

Revise the World

Edge to Centre series

The River Twice

Meet Myself There

The Fog of Time

Short Stories

Grey to Black

ABOUT BOOK VIEW CAFÉ

Book View Café is a professional authors' publishing cooperative offering DRM-free ebooks in multiple formats to readers around the world. With authors in a variety of genres including mystery, romance, fantasy, and science fiction, Book View Café has something for everyone.

Book View Café is good for readers because you can enjoy high-quality DRM-free ebooks from your favorite authors at a reasonable price.

Book View Café is good for writers because 90% of the profit goes directly to the book's author.

Book View Café authors include New York Times and USA Today bestsellers, Nebula, Hugo, Lambda, Chanticleer, National Reader's Choice, and Philip K. Dick Award winners, World Fantasy, Kirkus, and Rita Award nominees, and winners and nominees of many other publishing awards.

Printed in Great Britain
by Amazon